A
Heart *for* Home

Books by
Lauraine Snelling

Golden Filly Collection One *
Golden Filly Collection Two *

High Hurdles Collection One *
High Hurdles Collection Two *

SECRET REFUGE
Daughter of Twin Oaks

DAKOTAH TREASURES
Ruby • *Pearl*
Opal • *Amethyst*

DAUGHTERS OF BLESSING
A Promise for Ellie • *Sophie's Dilemma*
A Touch of Grace • *Rebecca's Reward*

HOME TO BLESSING
A Measure of Mercy • *No Distance Too Far*
A Heart for Home

RED RIVER OF THE NORTH
An Untamed Land • *A New Day Rising*
A Land to Call Home • *The Reaper's Song*
Tender Mercies • *Blessing in Disguise*

RETURN TO RED RIVER
A Dream to Follow • *Believing the Dream*
More Than a Dream

* 5 books in each volume

HOME TO BLESSING • *Book Three*

A
Heart *for* Home

LAURAINE
SNELLING

BETHANYHOUSE
MINNEAPOLIS, MINNESOTA

Cover design by Dan Pitts
Cover photography by Mike Habermann

Scripture quotations are from the King James Version of the Bible.

Published by Bethany House Publishers
11400 Hampshire Avenue South
Bloomington, Minnesota 55438

Bethany House Publishers is a division of
Baker Publishing Group, Grand Rapids, Michigan.

Printed in the United States of America

Library of Congress Cataloging-in-Publication Data

Snelling, Lauraine.
　A heart for home / Lauraine Snelling.
　　p.　cm. — (Home to blessing ; 3)
　　ISBN 978-0-7642-0817-1 (hardcover : alk. paper) — ISBN 978-0-7642-0611-5 (pbk.) — ISBN 978-0-7642-0818-8 (large-print pbk.) 　1. Indian reservations—Fiction. 　2. South Dakota—Fiction. 　I. Title.
　　PS3569.N39H44　　2011
　　813'.54—dc22
　　　　　　　　　　　　　　　　　　　　　　　　　　　　　　　　　　　　　2010041222

To Kelli,
who has a heart as big as Texas and
blesses so many people with
her amazing skills and creative spirit.
You are one of God's gifts to me,
and I am thankful.

LAURAINE SNELLING is an award-winning author of over 60 books, fiction and nonfiction for adults and young adults. Her books have sold over two million copies. Besides writing books and articles, she teaches at writers' conferences across the country. She and her husband, Wayne, have two grown sons and a bassett named Chewy. They make their home in California.

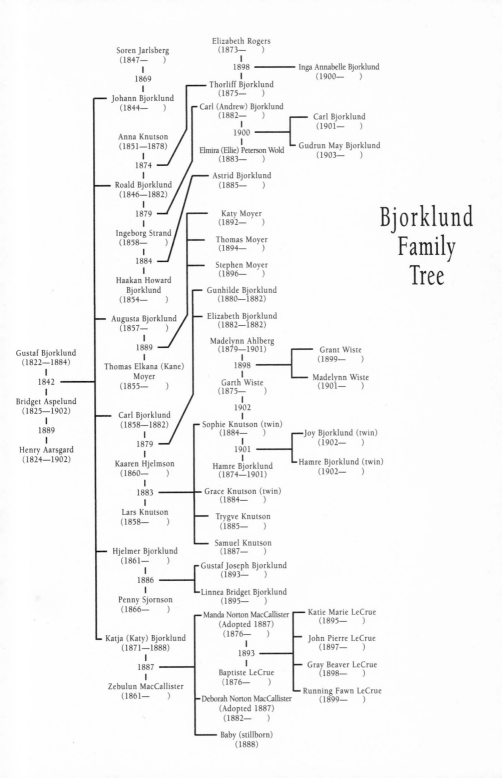

Bjorklund
Family
Tree

1

JULY 1904
ROSEBUD INDIAN RESERVATION
SOUTH DAKOTA

*H*ow can people live like this? Far takes better care of his animals.

"Doctor, we will get someone to clean this tepee." Thomas Moore, the Indian agent, stood beside her. "I will find help."

So why haven't you done so before this? Dr. Astrid Bjorklund clutched the handle of her black leather bag, the universal accoutrement carried by all in her profession. She felt like lancing him with recriminations but knew that would not help. At least he was trying to help now. Better late than never. The stench was the worst she had ever smelled, other than gangrene. "Let's take the two women and the child into the building we've already cleaned. We will bathe them first in the other tepee and leave their clothing to be washed."

"They most likely have nothing else to wear."

"Then we will cover them with the halves of sheets. When they are better, they can have their clothing back all clean." Astrid knelt beside the elder of the women, listened to her lungs, and checked her eyes. She was barely responsive. The younger woman looked to be halfway through her pregnancy. The small child's bones poked up through the blanket. All were hot to the touch.

It was all she could do not to break into tears. Even the tenements of Chicago had not been this terrible.

"How many more do I have yet to see?"

"I'd say you are half done." Mr. Moore had not come into the tepee but spoke from the entrance.

Astrid and her helpers had arrived three days earlier to a warm reception on the young agent's part but a decidedly cool one from the Indians. After the Chief, Dark Cloud, had greeted them, he had ignored her and talked instead, in his very broken English, with her father, Haakan Bjorklund, and Pastor Solberg. It was only because of her acquaintance with Dr. Red Hawk, whom she'd befriended during her training at the hospital in Chicago, that the chief was willing to accept their assistance.

The group had spent the first two days scrubbing the single building that had a stove and windows, a roof and a floor. Or rather the men had cleaned while she had started checking on the ill. They had moved the supplies, which had been donated by the people of Blessing, into the building and were doling those out. Haakan had a huge iron kettle of soup cooking on a tripod over a fire outside so they could feed broth to those too weak to eat solid food. They'd not accosted the Indian agent yet as to why the people were starving. Where were the promised government supplies?

"How many have died?" Astrid asked Mr. Moore.

"I . . . I'm not sure. They don't always tell me."

She swallowed her "Why did you not ask?" and stepped out of

the tepee and into the sunshine, relief at breathing clean air almost making her giddy. *God, these are your children too. Why are they suffering like this? How do we make a difference here? Give me wisdom and guidance.*

Two of the steers they'd brought from home had been slaughtered and the meat passed out to the families, along with flour and beans. They kept a guard on the chickens and hogs that were in side-by-side pens so that no one would steal them. Granted, it would be some time before there were hogs ready to slaughter, but getting breeding stock going was imperative. The eggs were being kept for those too sick to eat meat. Samuel Knutson, along with a young Indian boy, was weaving a roof of willow branches to keep the hawks from claiming the chickens.

Haakan and an Indian brave moved the older woman to a litter and, after settling her in the tepee for washing, came back for the younger woman and the child. An old Indian woman, who had not succumbed to the disease, would then bathe them with soap and warm water.

Astrid looked into the next tepee. Empty. Did that mean everyone had died, or were some people hiding from them? *Red Hawk, you didn't begin to tell me how bad this was. Or didn't you know?* This evening she would be having supper with the Indian agent and his wife. Perhaps some of her raging questions would be answered then.

In the next tepee she found a corpse, along with an old man who was so close to death, she checked him twice to be sure he was breathing. Should she try to help him or go on to someone she could possibly save? She brushed a lock of blond hair, which had escaped from her chignon, out of her eyes with the back of her hand. As far as she could see, all the tepees should be torched or at least taken down and scrubbed to rid them of the germs from secondary infections. She adjusted the man's position to help ease his breathing, but a moment later he breathed his last, and Astrid left for the next place, reminding herself to send Pastor Solberg back here to remove the bodies and maybe say a short prayer.

Haakan found her and took her by the arm. "You are coming to eat now." His gentle but firm voice almost broke the dam she kept in place to keep the tears from flowing.

As she had done as a little girl growing up in Blessing, she followed her father's instructions, knowing that she had to protect her own health too. After she got a plate of food, she sat on a rock in the sunshine, grateful for the cleansing breeze and sun on her back. Who could they get to start a garden and till a field for the wheat? Or, was it too late to do either this year? Would it be better to feed them the seed wheat—either grind it for flour or maybe just boil it to make gruel.

"How is the bathing going?" Astrid asked as she blew on a spoonful of hot rice.

"You now have ten clean patients," Haakan answered. "They are lying on pallets in the building. I should have brought wire for a clothesline. The washed clothing would dry more quickly. A couple of the children are responding already. I think the milk and egg drink with honey helps faster than anything, if they can keep it down. Thank God we brought the milk cow too."

"Have you asked the agent about the government supplies?"

"Not yet. He's been here only a month, and I think he is following that trail, trying to discover what happened to them."

"What about the agent before him? Didn't Hjelmer talk with that man?"

"A scoundrel from the sounds of it. He was selling the beef back to the fort as having been raised by the Indians and ready to sell."

Astrid closed her eyes. "What a scheme."

"The tribe has eaten all their horses, and the game is long gone. If they leave the reservation to hunt, they are thrown in jail—if they make it back to the jail."

"You mean some have been killed?"

Haakan hesitated a moment. "I believe so. Just quoting what I pieced together from the chief's explanation."

"Wish we had brought more of our young men along. They could have gone hunting. Are the Indians running snare lines for rabbits?"

"I think they've eaten everything that moves or can be dug up."

"I was thinking of the seed corn and wheat. Would it be better to feed that to them now, since there is no ground worked up for gardens and fields?"

"No. As soon as we've been through all the tepees, I am going to take a few of the stronger women and show them how to plant the seeds."

"What about the men?"

"Gardening is beneath them. They are hunters and warriors."

Astrid heaved a sigh. "Mor said Metiz had a garden and Baptiste helped her." Metiz was an Indian woman who had befriended the Bjorklunds when they arrived to homestead the land. Baptiste was her grandson, who lived with her.

Haakan nodded. "We'll put the children who aren't sick to work too."

Astrid tipped her head back and from side to side. "Thank you for making me eat. I feel much better."

"Some sleep would help too."

"I know. But please, Far, don't worry about me. I will be sensible." Astrid headed for the building she was now calling the infirmary to check on her patients there. She understood his trying to care for her. After all, she wasn't always entirely sensible as she forced herself to keep going.

Stepping into the shadowed room, she glanced around the rows of pallets full of sick Indians. She had one of the healthy people laying wet cloths on the skin of those with high fevers and changing the cloths as they dried. One person could handle three or four people that way. Another helper was assigned the task of feeding those that could accept nourishment, spooning broth into mouths. Astrid had wanted a clean spoon for each person, but that was beyond reality. So she had the utensils boiled as often as possible.

She knelt beside an older girl and received a shy smile. "You look like you're feeling better."

The girl's fever had broken and she was starting to regain her strength. This would be one of their success stories. In a couple of days she would be up and helping with the others. Astrid moved on when her eyes drifted closed.

The breeze from the open windows helped to cool some of the sufferers. And the two faithful women, who did exactly as Astrid told them, were forcing death to turn around and flee out the door. Had they only had screens on the windows, one more plague, the flies, would be ousted also.

By late afternoon when Astrid entered the last tepee for the day, she found a young brave delirious and burning with fever. The rash of measles that covered his body told the tale. A young woman lay dead beside him, her dead baby at her breast.

Astrid turned and left the tent. This was too much. Why had no one checked on them? It appeared that the woman had not been dead for long, but the baby was only a bundle of bones covered by skin. Astrid closed her eyes and raised her face to the sun. *Lord God, this is too much. I cannot do this any longer.* She paced around the outside of the tepee and fought with herself to open the flap to reenter.

"What is it?" Pastor Solberg asked as he stopped beside her. Astrid gestured to the inside, blinking hard to keep from crying. Dr. Elizabeth had struggled to have children and then, when she finally conceived, nearly died trying to birth one. These babies and children were left to die, to starve to death. *Lord, this is not fair.* She knew that was not the answer, but right now, had God been standing in front of her, she felt like shaking her fist in His face. Did He not care for all of His children? Or, as some believed, were these not His children after all?

"Astrid." After peering inside the tent, Solberg touched her arm. "Astrid, do you want us to take him to the infirmary?"

She shook her head, forcing herself to return to the present. "How do you trust God when you see things like this?" The words burst forth, breaking the dam. "I believe His Word, but when I see this horror, I am furious."

"As rightly you should be. There is no excuse for this. But to blame God?" He shook his head. "Think it through, my dear."

"But He has the power to take care of all of His people. Are these not *His* children too? We have so much, and they are here dying of hunger and disease. When we get sick at home, it is serious, yes, but not to the point of most everyone dying."

"But this is a white man's disease. And our diseases slaughter the Africans and the Indians alike. Someday we will know why and how, but for now, whose fault is it that these people have no food? Who is it that forced them to live on a reservation instead of wandering free, as they did for centuries? Why are they being forced to accept a new way of living, of farming rather than hunting?"

"I've read of other tribes that farm. The Navajo raise sheep and goats and plant gardens. Some other Sioux do too. But you are saying that our government is at fault."

"Yes, and who is our government?"

"The men in Washington."

"Many of whom hate Indians."

Like Joshua does. Astrid's mind flitted back to Blessing, where the man she had thought she was falling in love with had argued with her about her going to help the Indians. "But God is bigger than our government."

"He is that, but He expects us to take care of each other on this earth. He says to love everyone and do good to those who hurt you."

"Always back to that." Astrid heaved a sigh. "Let's get this man moved, and the others can take care of their dead."

"Judging by the symbols on the hides of this tepee, he appears to be an important young man. You would do well to help him recover."

"As if that were in my hands. Where's the litter?"

She assessed the brave again when he was clean and lying on a clean pallet. He reminded her of Red Hawk. The same build, the same nose and wide brow. Could this be a relative? She told the women to keep changing the cloths to bring his fever down and to get some broth into him. Mixing several of her mother's simples, she poured hot water over them to steep them and told the women to give him a few spoonfuls of the tea every hour or so, then pointed out several other patients who needed the same.

"If you mix some honey with it for the children, it will taste better."

One of the older women smiled at her, dark eyes flashing. Astrid nodded. Maybe things were turning around, even a tiny bit. Get women working together and everyone was helped. If only she could talk with them, find out if anyone in the tribe knew of the healing plants. Seeing their dark-skinned faces made her wish for Metiz. Her mother would tell stories about all those years ago when the Norwegians first homesteaded the land, how the old woman had shared her knowledge of things natural with Ingeborg and thusly all the people of Blessing. *Perhaps one of the reasons I am here is because of Metiz. Maybe this is my turn to return the gifts she shared with my family so long ago.* Astrid knew her mother thought that way. It was one reason she was so willing for Haakan to come along.

———

THAT NIGHT AT SUPPER at Thomas Moore's house, Astrid listened more than taking part in the conversation. Pastor Solberg and her father were doing just fine without her. Her mind flitted off to the outside, where she would rather have been. The agent's house was a hundred yards or more from what they were calling the infirmary, where government supplies had been stored at one time. The only supplies in it now were what they had brought from Blessing. The tepees were about the same distance down the creek, and Haakan had insisted they park their wagons upstream from the settlement, establishing the fourth corner of a square, with the fires for cooking and cleaning near the center.

The porches on both the front and the back of the agent's house made it look larger than it was, huddling into the ground as if seeking refuge. An American flag flew from a pole on the northeastern corner of the front porch. With no plants around it, the house looked more military than welcoming.

"Would you care for more dessert?" Mrs. Moore asked Astrid softly.

She brought herself back to the present. "No, thank you. The meal was delicious."

"Then shall we retire to my ladies' parlor and leave the gentlemen to their discussion?"

Astrid almost said, "You go, and I'll stay here, where the discussion is interesting," but she knew her far would not approve. He was as much a stickler for manners as Mor was, and he'd heard the invitation. So she followed the lead of her young hostess, excused herself, and stepped through a curtained doorway into another room.

Glancing around the parlor, she wondered where the money had come from. Walnut furniture, wallpaper, heavy curtains. How many wagon trains had it taken to bring all that finery those last miles? "Your home is lovely," she commented.

"Thank you. So many of these things are my mother's. I couldn't bear to leave them behind, and once we arrived here and saw the desolation, I was even more grateful to have a nice home for Mr. Moore to return to. He works so hard for the Indians, but they don't show much appreciation for what he is doing."

Maybe they don't see this as better. Astrid tried to think of something polite to say. "Have you been trying to set up a school or education for them?"

"No, I don't mingle with the natives. Just with Ann, who comes in to help me. Training her has been difficult beyond belief. Even such simple things as washing her hands."

"And you pay her for working for you?"

"Yes, at least I think so. Thomas takes care of all our financial affairs."

"Have you planted a garden? That was one of the first things my mother did when she arrived in North Dakota. Fresh food is so important."

"Thomas did, but it is not doing well. The lack of rain, you know."

So why don't you carry water to it? "I take it you don't go outside much?"

"Thomas says it is too dangerous out there for me. And besides, this sun is so hot that it beams right through my parasol."

"Where did you come from? Where's home?" Being polite was getting more difficult by the minute.

"I grew up in Philadelphia, and I met Thomas at a cotillion. In his blue uniform with gold trim, he was the most dashing young man there. Land sakes, but he was the delight of every woman who saw him." She spread her fan and fanned her heavily powdered face. "Doesn't this heat bother you?"

I'm sure I don't have all the petticoats and corset and other feminine underthings that you are wearing. "We who live on the prairie learn to dress to fit the climate, so the heat doesn't do us in. Fashion isn't as important here as in the cities."

"That is such a shame. I would hate for my mamma to come clear out here and see what a hovel we are living in. I try to make it as nice as I am able. Also to show the savages that there is indeed a better way to live. Keeping up a stylish appearance is one of the ways I encourage my husband."

Astrid nearly dropped her teacup. She set it back in the saucer and wiped her mouth with the dainty napkin. Casting back through their conversation in an effort to change the subject, she thought of the uniform. "So Mr. Moore was in the army?"

"Yes, but when he learned they wanted civilians as Indian agents, he left the service. He felt he could be more useful this way. My Thomas has always desired to help those less fortunate."

"That is a very good thing." Astrid paused, again trying to think of what to say. "You know, you could read to the children."

Mrs. Moore stared at her. "Why? They wouldn't understand the story."

"You could teach them."

"Mr. Moore is seeking for a teacher to come out here. And while I have not met Dr. Red Hawk, he will be back in the fall."

"I am acquainted with Dr. Red Hawk. I attended school with him for a time. Medical school in Chicago. He cares deeply for his people." *He and I did a lot of sparring over that corpse we dissected.* "His request for help is what brought me and my companions here."

"I do hope he is learning some culture while he is there."

Astrid placed her saucer and cup very carefully on the table and rose. "Thank you, Mrs. Moore, for a lovely dinner, but I need to return to my patients for a last check before bedtime. No, don't bother to see me out. I'll leave the men talking and slip out the back door."

She smiled again and made sure she walked sedately out through the kitchen, where Ann was cleaning up from the dinner. "Good night," she said with a smile to the young woman.

She hoped stomping her feet all the way to the infirmary would release her anger, but it didn't. In the infirmary, she cuddled a baby who was crying, and that did help. The smile that she received when handing him back to Gray Smoke, a woman with silver hair and only two lower front teeth, did the rest. If the price of having a meal with the Moores was making polite conversation in the parlor with Mrs. Moore again, she would simply choose not to attend supper.

2

BLESSING, NORTH DAKOTA

I ngeborg Bjorklund brushed the back of her hand across her sweaty forehead. July was surely trying to make up for the cooler June. A rain shower had blown through, and while that had cooled the air for a bit, now everything dripped moisture. Including her. She flipped her sunbonnet back off her head so the slight breeze could fan her face and hair. If Astrid were there, she would laugh and say, "I told you so." They had always been in contention about sunbonnets and sunburned skin. So much for the dictates of proper etiquette. Not that she'd been much of an adherer to the rules of society this far west, since keeping food on the table was far more important than milk-white skin.

She pulled her leather gloves back on and continued hoeing the potatoes, hilling the dirt up around the plants to keep the sun from burning the potatoes that grew too close to the surface. Emmy, the little Sioux Indian girl who had been found in their haymow last November, came behind her with the kerosene can, picking off the potato bugs and dropping them into the kerosene to die.

"Gramma, this can stinky." She held up her can.

Ingeborg had failed in keeping sunbonnets on Emmy and Inga, her oldest granddaughter, too. One day she'd found the one she'd sewn for Inga hanging from its strings on one of the apple trees. Whatever Inga did, Emmy copied.

"I know it is stinky, but the bugs will eat our potato plants. Then what will we eat?"

"The bugs?"

Ingeborg smiled at the joke but wondered if perhaps the little girl's tribe had been forced to eat bugs or starve to death. The thought made her shudder. While she felt Emmy was a gift to her from God so that she could have another child in the house, she knew that the old man they'd assumed was the girl's uncle could come back for her at any time. He'd come to visit one day, but after he and Emmy had talked, he'd left her there, and the little girl had seemed relieved.

"When is Inga coming?"

"After dinner."

Thorliff had promised to bring his daughter out to visit that afternoon and to spend the night so the three of them could go picking wild strawberries early the next morning. The plants in the garden were not ripe yet, but the secret patch of wild berries was, since it was always ready first.

"All done."

"You looked under all the leaves?"

Emmy sent her a disgusted look. Once shown how to do something, Emmy always did her best.

"Good. I am almost finished here. Why don't you go pick some lettuce for dinner?"

"How much?"

"An apronful."

Emmy looked down at her apron, then at Ingeborg's.

"Your apron." She'd shown Emmy how to pick the biggest lettuce leaves so new ones would grow back. Once the plants went to seed, she would sow new seeds to keep the lettuce growing all summer. She smiled to herself. The first time she'd put salad on Emmy's plate, the little girl had stared at the torn green leaves and shaken her head. But when she tasted the salad, the dressing sent her back for more. Ingeborg mixed milk, sugar, and vinegar together and shook them well before pouring it on the salad. As soon as the green onions were large enough, she'd chopped and added them too. She'd also introduced the girls to the delicacy of just-washed lettuce dipped in sugar and rolled lengthwise like a cigar. Emmy had not needed further instructions.

After hoeing the potatoes, Ingeborg searched through the peas and picked a good handful. She'd seen baby potatoes, so creamed peas and new potatoes would soon be an option.

She picked lettuce leaves along with Emmy until they had enough for dinner and strolled toward the house. Dinner would be ready right on time since the sun was at about eleven o'clock high now. How she wished Astrid were there to enjoy the garden. While she'd agreed that someone needed to go help the Rosebud Indians, she'd been so looking forward to Astrid being home, at least for a while.

A letter would help. "Let's wash the lettuce at the pump, and our feet too."

"I pump."

"If you want." Since they now had running water in the house, she'd not had to pump water at the well that spring. The hand pump on the side of the kitchen sink saved them all plenty of hours. Emmy loved to pump. The first time she'd seen water come out of the spout on the pump, she'd been mesmerized. She'd looked under the sink and kept shaking her head. Did the Indians have wells, or were they still getting water from the creeks? Another question to add to her list. Getting wells dug would cut down on the diseases. She and Emmy laughed together as they took turns pumping cold water over their feet, then filling the bucket for washing the lettuce.

"Men coming."

Ingeborg glanced up at the sun. Sure enough, they'd managed to fritter away nearly an hour. "Come, let's get dinner on the table." At least they'd set the table before they went out to cultivate the garden. While Emmy cut the lettuce, Ingeborg mixed the dressing. She would pour it over the salad just before setting it on the table.

The pot of rice sat on the back of the stove, kept warm from cooking earlier. The roasting pan full of rabbit pieces that had been baking smelled delicious when she pulled it from the oven. Adding sour cream to the gravy was her own special touch and always brought raves from the diners.

"You want to slice the bread?"

Emmy nodded and brought a loaf of the bread they'd baked the day before from the pantry. She set it on the cutting board and pulled a knife from the drawer. Holding thumb and forefinger about half an inch apart, she raised her hand. Emmy never wasted words when an action could speak for her.

"Yes, about that thick."

"Men here."

"Oh, I forgot to set out the basins. Uff da. Where has my mind gone lately?"

Ingeborg filled two basins with hot water from the stove reservoir and then each carried one outside, getting to the bench just as the men did. Had she been thinking ahead, she'd have set the basins out and let the sun warm the wash water.

"You heard from them yet?" Lars Knutson asked. He and

Haakan farmed the homesteads together, along with the Bjorklunds' younger son, Andrew, who'd never wanted to do anything else but farming.

"No, it's too soon for a letter to get back from clear out there." Spoiled as they were by the telephone system they'd installed in Blessing a couple of years earlier, waiting for letters to arrive seemed like forever.

"Did Far say how long they would be there?" Andrew splashed water on his face and dried it with a towel.

"He figured at least two weeks, but Pastor Solberg seemed to think that was optimistic." Ingeborg returned to the kitchen to place the roasting pan on potholders at the head of the table, where she could dish up plates rather than transferring the meat to a platter.

Andrew said the grace, which was usually his father's job, and held a plate for Ingeborg. Serving bowls went round the table as the meat was passed out.

"Thanks to Solem, we have fresh meat today." She nodded at her cousin's son, whose snare lines kept three houses in meat. While she was feeding the men, Solem's mother, Freda, was over helping Kaaren refurbish the boys' dormitory at the school for the deaf. They'd done the girls' the year before. What they really needed was another building altogether, because the school was bursting at the seams. Then the classrooms in the main house could be converted into bedrooms. As more deaf students arrived in Blessing, the community was already talking about needing another public school building or adding on to the one they had. Once the students at Kaaren's school learned how to communicate, they would attend the Blessing school, as well as continue to learn life skills at the Knutson farm.

There was so much building to be done. The hospital was under construction, and the new company that manufactured the improved seeder attachments, designed by the deceased Daniel Jeffers, had already outgrown the old grain storage building, where Onkel Olaf once had his furniture factory. As people often said, Blessing was growing faster than they had laborers to build it. And thanks to the Jeffers-styled seed attachments, the wheat fields were growing without bald spots and the yields had greatly increased.

Jonathan Gould, who had been staying with the family since late June, shook his head when she offered more of the baked rabbit. "I cannot. I am full already." He returned to work on the Bjorklund farm every summer, both to see his beloved Grace Knutson, Ingeborg's deaf niece, and to learn more about farming. He spent the school year at the state college in Fargo, studying in the agricultural program.

"I had a letter from Grace yesterday," Ingeborg told them. "She said she'd be home soon."

"Well, not soon enough for the rest of us," Jonathan commented. "I think they don't want to let her go."

"You are right. That is making it hard for her to leave, but she knows there is so much to do here." Grace had tried to resign from her post at the deaf school on the East Coast but still hadn't made the break. If she didn't arrive in Blessing soon, she would have little time with Jonathan before he left with the harvest crew and then went back to school.

Lars pushed back his chair. "Well, better get at it. Takk for maten."

"You are welcome," Ingeborg replied as she and Emmy began clearing the table.

"Carl was begging to come and see Grandma," Andrew told his mother. "Is that all right?"

"Of course. Inga is coming out later too. Tell Ellie to send him on over. I'll stand on the porch to watch for him."

LATER THAT AFTERNOON Ingeborg sat on the back porch with her three little ones and told them stories of Norway while they drank their strawberry swizzles and nibbled on sour cream cookies.

"What are mountains?" four-year-old Inga asked.

Ingeborg shook her head. To think her grandchildren had never seen a mountain, or hills covered with pine trees, or streams leaping and cavorting down a rock face and meandering across a meadow. "I'm trying to think how to describe this, Inga. Mountains are part of the earth, very tall, and covered with rocks and snow and pine trees."

"Bigger than the barn?"

"Oh yes. Taller than ten barns stacked on top of one another. They go on as far as you can see, and when you stand on a mountain, you can see across the land to the sea, which is water like the river but goes on farther than you can see, and the sea is salty. You have to ride in a boat to get across the sea." She could tell they did not understand what she was talking about. Did she have any pictures?

"I rode in a boat on the river." Inga propped her elbows on her knees.

"I ride in a canoe," Emmy said.

"I wanna ride a boat," two-and-a-half-year-old Carl said as he reached for another cookie. "Pa me fishing."

"Can we go fishing, Grandma?" Emmy set her glass on the table and went back to sit with the others.

"We'll go fishing if we can find some worms." While she had cooked dinner for the men at noon, they would all eat supper at their own homes. There were now plenty of leftovers for supper that evening. She stood and headed for the kitchen. "You bring your glasses and the cookies in here. I'll get the fishing rods from the porch." Together they carried the willow poles with lines and hooks stuck in the cork bobbers.

"Worms in 'nure pile?" Carl was carrying the lard pail Ingeborg had handed him.

"That's the easiest place to find them." Ingeborg swung by the east side of the barn, where she had planted the comfrey, once she learned that smearing the broad comfrey leaves on one's skin kept away the mosquitoes. She handed a leaf to each of the children. "Now, rub this over any skin that's not covered."

"So the 'squitoes don't bite us." Emmy had learned the lesson earlier.

It didn't take them long, digging around the edge of the pile where the manure had already deteriorated into rich dirt, to get enough fat worms for fishing. Carl held one up, giggling as the worm wriggled from both ends, then plopped it into the pail. Ingeborg rammed the manure fork back into the pile, and they headed across the pasture to the tree and brush line that once again bordered the river. In the early days all the trees had been cut for lumber and firewood.

Carl trudged along beside his grandmother as the two girls ran ahead. They found a butterfly and beckoned Ingeborg to come see it. A yellow and black swallowtail lifted on the breeze as she arrived by the thistle bush. Bending over, she wrapped her skirt around her arm and dug under the prickly leaves to the stalk and, with a grunt, pulled it out.

"Always pull out the thistles before they go to seed, so they don't take over the pasture and the fields."

"But the butterfly?"

"Will find another flower to feed from."

Amazing how fast the thistles grew. Andrew had hoed all the fence lines and sprouting thistles not a month earlier. Keeping them down took constant vigilance.

As they took the path down to the Red River, which bordered their property on the east, Ingeborg automatically searched out the game trails for any signs of deer. A young buck would taste mighty good about now, as their hogs and steers were not yet large enough for butchering. When she saw deer pellets in an area of crushed grass and leaves, she showed the children and wished she'd brought along a rifle.

If she allowed herself to think about it, she missed the early times when she'd gone hunting, not as a sport but as a necessity, to keep her family from starving. She'd learned to shoot a rifle when they'd first homesteaded. Carl Bjorklund, brother to her first husband, Roald, had taught her to shoot deer and geese. Nowadays, it wasn't considered proper for a woman to hunt; it wasn't proper to wear britches either, as she'd done in the early days. She'd hung both rifle and britches up after marrying Haakan, because she knew it would please him.

She and the children clambered over a tree that had fallen and approached the slow moving river. Through the seasons the river dug deeper pools in some places and dropped sediment to fill in others. Samuel had told her about this pool.

"Can we go wading?" Inga asked.

"Not if you want to catch some fish."

"You go in water, scare fish away." Carl set his lard bucket down beside the log and parked himself at the same time. "Pa said so."

Ingeborg rolled her smile back inside. According to Carl, if his pa said so, it was gospel. Inga, however, questioned everything and everyone.

Each of the children took a pole and carefully unwound the line from the willow bark. Like seasoned fishermen, they threaded a worm onto the hook and tossed their line in the water, where the cork bobbed on the surface. Carl's bobber went under first, and he jerked back on the line to send a fish flying over their heads. Together all of them looked up to see the line caught in a willow bush. Giggles broke out like popping corn.

"You really jerked that fish out." Ingeborg reached over and hugged her little grandson. "I didn't know you were so strong."

Her grinned up at her. "Me big," he said and went to fetch his flipping fish.

Ingeborg got up to help him.

"Grandma, your fishing pole." Emmy leaped up to grab Ingeborg's pole as the fish on the line started heading downriver. Her pole banged into Inga's. Inga's cork went under, and with a pole in each hand, she hollered for help.

Emmy caught the end of Ingeborg's pole and saved her from having to wade out to save it. Ingeborg retrieved Carl's fish and, handing him his pole to bait again, ran the stringer through the mouth and gills. She then took care of the fish on her own hook and put the stringer in the water in a shady place, hammering a stick through the end of the chain and into the soft duff.

With all of them laughing and giggling at the fiasco, they settled back down with two fish on the trot line, one that got away, and Carl shushing them with a grubby finger to his mouth. "Pa say quiet or scare fishes."

By the time they quit, they had ten fish on one line and seven more on the other. Ingeborg carried one line, and the two girls stretched the other between them.

"Enough for supper?" Emmy asked, looking up to Ingeborg.

"Ja, we will call Ellie and tell her we'll have a fish fry at Grandma's house." She held up her string. "We really got some big ones."

"Dry fish?" Inga asked.

"Maybe later, when there are more." All those years earlier, Metiz, a woman with both French-Canadian and Sioux ancestors, had taught them the Indian ways of living off the land. They combined her knowledge with the Norwegian customs of preserving fish by both smoking and drying, and the resulting bounty helped them make it through the long winters.

The thought of Metiz made Ingeborg blink. She'd been such a good friend and was still so missed.

THAT EVENING, after the fish were fried and eaten and Carl had gone home with his parents, Ingeborg took her knitting out to the back porch, where the breeze would help keep the mosquitoes at bay. She'd rubbed some more comfrey onto her skin just in case. At moments like these she missed Haakan with almost a real pain in her heart. Many a long evening they'd sit out on the porch—she would knit and he would mend or clean a harness or tend to any one of the myriad small chores that always needed doing, the smoke from his pipe keeping away the mosquitoes.

After Jonathan had gone up to his room to write letters and read, Emmy and Inga brought out jars and sat waiting for the first firefly to light up and dance in the dimming light. Ingeborg had agreed to let them stay up much later than usual in order to catch the elusive insects. Bars of the fast-approaching orange and vermillion sunset tinged the few clouds, turning the sky a soft pink.

Lord, keep them safe. Ingeborg released her prayers to float up through the cottonwood leaves overhead, bypassing the sleepy twittering of the birds and rising toward heaven like a wisp of smoke. A "sacrifice of praise," the verse had called it in her early morning devotions. Right now, praising God didn't take a sacrifice, but at other times it had indeed. Having Haakan gone this long, now that was the sacrifice.

When dark descended and the girls loosed their fireflies from the jars, the three of them washed their hands and feet and made their way back into the darkened house and up the stairs, where Ingeborg put the girls to bed and heard their prayers. Jonathan had already gone to bed and blown his lamp out. Back in her own room, Ingeborg undressed and slipped her lightweight sleeveless summer nightdress over her head. "Please, Lord, keep them safe. Help the Indians receive the help in the spirit in which it is given. For all those years Metiz helped us, this is small recompense. Without her, there might not have been a town of Blessing, had she not helped us stay alive. Without her, we might have returned to Norway, as others did." She trapped that idea. No, they might have gone somewhere else, but not back to Norway.

She lay with her hands locked behind her head. Who else could they bring over from Norway? Laborers were so needed in the booming town of Blessing. Tomorrow being Sunday, Thorliff would preach the sermon, and Lars would lead the service with the help of the musicians. Elizabeth was well enough to play the piano again—Jonathan had been filling in for her since he returned from Fargo—and Joshua Landsverk would play his guitar. Worship just wouldn't seem right without Pastor Solberg.

3

How could the Bjorklunds take in that little Indian girl like they did?

Joshua felt like shaking his head, but since he and Dr. Elizabeth were playing the music before the Sunday church service, he needed to keep a smile on his face, or at least not a frown. If he frowned, people would either make assumptions or plain out ask him if something was wrong. He'd never lived in a place where people were so concerned about each other as in Blessing. Especially Mrs. Bjorklund. Astrid's mother. And his future mother-in-law if his dreams came true.

His fingers stumbled on a chord, causing Elizabeth to glance up at him. He had to be careful. But his mind refused to obey. After they'd played the final chords and Lars stood to begin the service,

Joshua exhaled a sigh of relief. He still wondered how they could have
a real worship service without Pastor Solberg.

Everyone rose to sing "Holy, Holy, Holy." As he lost himself in
the beauty of the hymn, he could let his spirit fly.

"Holy, holy, holy, Lord God almighty!
Early in the morning our song shall rise to thee.
Holy, holy, holy! Merciful and mighty.
God in three persons, blessed Trinity!"

His voice soared, leading the others to put heart and soul into the
singing. After the fourth verse everyone sat and Lars Knutson stood
with his Bible in hand.

"Dearly beloved, we are gathered together to worship our Lord
and Savior."

Joshua felt each word settle into his heart, first the hymn and
now the lessons. " 'Beloved, let us love one another,' " Lars started,
reading from First John, " 'for love is of God. . . . He that loveth
not knoweth not God; for God is love.' " The words were no longer
settling gently but rather were stabbing into the dark spot he kept
trying to ignore.

The argument going on inside him started right up again. The
contention: his hatred of the Indians. *But I have a right to feel so,* he
argued back. *What if they take Astrid away like they did my aunt and keep
her captive until she no longer wants to live as a white person? My father
spent the rest of his life hating the Indians for destroying his sister.*

*Right, and look what good it did him. He became mean and bitter.
Do you want to do that?*

Clapping his hands over his ears would not be good in public,
and if he left the service . . . That did not bear thinking about. Think
about something else. *Lord, please protect Astrid and those with her.*

The nasty voice snuck in. *You think you have a right to ask God to do something for you when you hate some of His children?*

Lord, I thought I was beyond this. I even gave Pastor Solberg some money for the first shipment of assistance to this Indian tribe. I thought I knew how to forgive. Why am I back in this situation? I know . . . it's Astrid. Before it was just giving money, but now part of my heart is down there. Only in the quiet of the church service could his mind sort through his feelings like this.

He heard the first chords of the next hymn coming from Dr. Elizabeth on the piano. He'd done it after all—made a complete fool of himself. He picked up his guitar and joined the music, feeling what he knew to be red heat flaming up his neck.

By the end of the service he just wanted to stalk off across the prairie and keep on going. They played the closing hymn, and after Lars gave the benediction, they segued into the medley of songs they'd chosen and practiced.

"Are you all right?" Elizabeth asked as she closed the lid on the piano.

He nodded, not daring to meet her gaze, which he could feel clear through his skin.

"You know, if you ever need to talk to someone, a doctor is a pretty safe listener."

He could see the question marks in her eyes, so he didn't give her a direct answer, responding with a question instead. "How is Linnea coming with her piano lessons? Will she be able to play with us one of these days?"

"She's doing well, but learning a guitar is far easier. She is amazing, though. While she is learning to read music, she picks up most of her songs by ear. I play the song once, and she figures out the chording. What a gift she has."

Linnea was Penny Bjorklund's daughter and now nine years old. Joshua had taught her some chords on the piano while Dr. Elizabeth was recovering from the loss of her baby. He too had been amazed at the speed with which she caught on. Since she didn't have a piano at home, she spent hours at the church, practicing on the one there.

"Maybe we ought to add playing a banjo to the ad in the papers for workers."

"That would be great. Someday we'll have an organ here in church, and I dream of playing that. Once Jonathan Gould is out of school, he can take over the piano. Who would have dreamed we'd ever have so much musical talent here in Blessing?"

When they left the church, he found Mrs. Bjorklund waiting for him. "Won't you join us for dinner today, Mr. Landsverk?" she asked.

"I really need to spend the afternoon working on my house," he told her, hoping his excuse would be accepted. He knew Thorliff and his family would be there as usual, and he didn't have a chance between those two perceptive women. He'd end up confessing his feelings and feel like an even worse fool.

"I'm sorry to hear that. Perhaps another Sunday, then?"

"Thank you for the invitation. I would much rather go with you, but I've been so busy, I've not had time to finish the cellar so I can order the house kit."

"Well, when you do and it arrives, you know we'll all take a Saturday or two and see how far we can go in getting it up."

"Thank you." *I don't deserve such help.* But he kept his smile in place and guitar in hand as he headed back to the boardinghouse to change clothes. Miss Christopherson would be keeping a plate hot for him, since he'd missed the noon seating.

A breeze kept the prairie from becoming too hot, rippling the growing fields like waves on water. He never tired of seeing the growing crops, even though he'd chosen not to be a farmer. He loved building things: First he'd built windmills, then houses and barns, and now he was lead man on the crew adding on to the former grain storage building, where the new attachments for improving the seeders would be manufactured. He wished his father had used one of the early seeders pulled by a team of horses. The seeding by hand took far too long, and even though his father was adept at it, the crops were spotty. This new addition would make both old and new seeders far more dependable and efficient. Hjelmer and Mr. Sam had made several prototypes and welded them on to the Bjorklund seeders. The grain sprouted evenly down the rows, row after row. Not one row extra thick and the next one bare.

Knowing he was part of making this idea become a reality kept him going to work with a light step and a smile. With construction, one could see the daily progress, and it wouldn't have to be done all over again the next year, as in farming. Building didn't depend on the weather for success either.

But today he would work on his own house. He needed to finish up framing the final cellar wall so they could mix and pour the cement. He never knew who would show up to help him, but someone always did. Life on his father's farm in Iowa had not worked that way. Thoughts of his father made him grateful he'd gone back home when he did. He never would have believed his father could age so fast had he not seen it with his own eyes.

If only Astrid were here.

That thought led him back to the Indians of the Rosebud Reservation. Not a good thing. He mounted the steps to the boardinghouse and took the inside stairs two at a time, hoping to outrun the devilish thoughts that plagued him. He washed up and then headed back down the stairs.

"How was church this morning?" Miss Christopherson, assistant manager of the boardinghouse, asked when he took his place in the dining room.

"Fine." He glanced up to see a shadow cross her face. *Great, now I've offended her. What's the matter with me?* "We missed Pastor

Solberg, though Lars did a fine job with the Scripture reading, and Thorliff can speak his piece right well."

"I could hear the singing clear back here. One of these days I will get to attend church on Sunday." She nodded and half smiled, a pensive look still shadowing her eyes.

Why someone didn't marry her was beyond Joshua's understanding. But then, there weren't many single men in Blessing. "It sure smells good in here."

"Thank you. I kept your dinner warm. I'll bring it right out."

"Have you already eaten?" His own question caught him by surprise.

"No, we all eat when the guests are finished."

Joshua glanced around the room. "Looks like I'm the last. If you all will be eating now, why can't I eat with you, or you come out here and eat with me?" For a man who grew up in a house where not a word was spoken during a meal, he had learned he enjoyed mealtime conversation.

"Well, I . . . ah . . . I mean . . ." She glanced over her shoulder to the kitchen.

"Please."

"I'll be right back."

He watched her hustle back to the kitchen. If he weren't so pie-eyed over Astrid, this young woman would have made a fine wife. He thought of his younger brother, Aaron. Aaron wasn't married and wasn't courting anyone either, as far as he knew. Joshua smiled to himself. He'd write to Aaron and invite him to come work in Blessing, where the lack of help was slowing the building down. Aaron had never complained about working on the home farm or hiring out to others when the work slacked off. If only both of his brothers would come to Blessing, and his sister too. He'd have a real family again. He nearly snorted on that thought. Thanks to his father, they'd never been what one would call a close family. But they'd sure welcomed him home last Christmas when he went back to Iowa. Good memories to replace the bad.

Verses from Thorliff's talk that morning slipped through his mind. *Whatever is true, whatever is honest, whatever is just, whatever is pure, whatever is worthy of praise, think on these things.* He knew that wasn't a direct quote, but he couldn't remember all of it. And besides, too many of his memories didn't fit the criteria.

"Here you go." Miss Christopherson set down a tray and placed one plate in front of him and the other across the table. She added a plate with warm rolls in a napkin and then set the empty tray on another table before sitting down. "The others are already eating in the kitchen. They said to go ahead."

"I could have come back there."

"I know, but you know Mrs. Sam. Right is right and there is no swaying her." She placed her napkin in her lap and glanced up to find him watching her. "Can I get you something else?"

"No, no." He bowed his head. Saying grace was another growing habit. He silently thanked the Lord for his meal and looked up to see her dropping her gaze. Had she been watching him or praying? Should he have asked if he could say the blessing? What was proper? Ignoring his thoughts, he smiled. "This looks mighty good, as always." Roasted chicken had become the standard Sunday meal at the boardinghouse, unless it was a holiday, along with mashed potatoes and gravy. Today, the vegetable was canned green beans combined with bacon and chopped onions.

"This week we'll start serving fresh vegetables from the garden," Miss Christopherson said with a smile. "The peas are coming in nicely."

"Do you work in the garden too?" He usually saw Lemuel and Lily Mae, Mr. and Mrs. Sam's grown children, out working in the half-acre patch that supplied the boardinghouse.

"Not unless there is a rush. Trying to fit the canning and drying in along with the usual duties takes long hours. And since Mrs. Sam isn't as young or as well as she used to be, we all have to help out."

"You need more help here, like every other business in town?" Joshua asked.

"We do. Especially as more people are staying here longer. That nice Mr. Jeffers has reserved a room for his mother when she comes. They should be here any day. Whoever thought we would have a housing shortage in Blessing?" She passed him the rolls. "Mrs. Wiste said we might have to ask the men to double up in the rooms, the way we are going. Some places build bunk beds and sleep four to a room."

"If my brother comes, he can bunk with me."

"Your brother?"

"Aaron, he's the youngest. My sister Avis is the eldest, then my brother Frank, then me and then Aaron. I'd like them all to come out here, but Frank will probably stay on the home farm. He doesn't mind being a farmer."

"But you did?"

He nodded. "Pa expected us to stay there and farm, maybe eventually build a house when we got married. When I homesteaded the first time I was here, I realized I just didn't want to farm any longer. I went back home and worked in town. Pa wasn't happy with that, and he really gave up on me when I came back here."

"What brought you back to Blessing?"

He couldn't tell her it was Astrid. He had memories of a girl with golden hair down her back and eyes that captured bits of sky and sparkled when she laughed. Joshua mopped up the remainder of his gravy with a roll. Looked like that dream needed to do some dying. After the way he'd acted, she'd probably never speak to him again. Maybe it was time he moved on.

4

ROSEBUD INDIAN RESERVATION
SOUTH DAKOTA

The baby died."

Astrid stared at her father, the words barely registering. One more gone. Even though she'd not had much hope for the little one, the thought of another dead baby lay heavy on her heart. The youngest and the oldest were usually the first to die. Right now she was fighting to keep the young brave alive. While the old woman, called Shy Fawn, was changing the wet cloths, his fever was so high that they dried almost instantly. If only they had some ice to nest him in or at least a tub large enough to hold him.

"We have to find something to hold enough cold water so he can be immersed. Ice would be best, but—"

"But we have no icehouse here, like we do at home." He thought a moment. "I wonder if they have boats around here. We could put the water in a boat."

"Or lay him in the creek."

Haakan nodded. "I'll get some help to carry him there. Perhaps there is a deeper pool nearby."

Astrid studied those in the sickroom. Who else would benefit from such a radical procedure? The real question: Why had she not thought of it earlier? *Thank you, Father, for the idea now.* She checked her packets of simples. Willow bark was running low—that could easily be remedied—as was echinacea. But that would not be available until the roots had matured enough to dig up, usually in the fall.

Taking a cup of broth mixed with willow bark tea, and a spoon, she knelt by the brave's pallet and, nodding to one of her helpers to raise his head, spooned broth into his mouth. It ran out the side and down his cheek. She motioned for the woman to raise him a little higher and tried again. This time his throat moved as he swallowed. Smiling at her helper, she tried to give him more. Success. The first nourishment they'd been able to get into him.

Her father and Mr. Moore hustled into the room.

"Dr. Bjorklund, are you sure this is what you should do? If he dies under your care, the men will accuse you of killing him."

"If you can think of a better solution, I'm ready to listen, but we have to break his fever. Ice would be better, but the creek is what we have, so it will have to do."

Mr. Moore swallowed and blinked before inhaling a breath of courage and nodding. The second time he nodded more firmly. "There is a spot where the women used to wash their clothes. I will show you. But how will you keep him from drowning?"

"Someone will sit with him and hold his head above the water."

"Er, someone?" her father asked.

"I will do it if I have to, but it would be better if someone in the tribe would do it. Let me talk to the women." If only she could actually talk with them, instead of using the rough signing and hand signals, which took far too long.

"I will talk with them," Mr. Moore said. "I know a few words."

As Mr. Moore and Astrid communicated their idea, Shy Fawn nodded her understanding. She held up a hand as if to say *Wait* and hurried out the door. She returned in a few minutes with an elderly man who had already had a light case of measles and was regaining his health by the time Astrid's team had arrived at the encampment.

Mr. Moore and Far moved the younger man to a litter and then carried him to the creek. Shy Fawn waded into the water and beckoned the elderly man to sit, legs crossed, in the water. They lowered the litter until the sick man's head was cushioned by the old man's legs.

"Let's remove some of the rocks so he can be in deeper water," Astrid instructed.

Shy Fawn shook her head and instead backed into the stream, gently pulling the spotted man's legs. The old man inched forward until the water was over his legs and the brave was floating.

Astrid dipped a cloth in the water and laid it over the brave's hot forehead and eyes. Glancing at Pastor Solberg, she mouthed, *Are you praying?* His emphatic nod told her he understood.

How long do I leave him there? Astrid wondered. *Till the fever breaks?*

The patient's body twitched, and he mumbled something.

She glanced around to see a circle of Indians of all ages watching and muttering, exchanging apprehensive glances.

"Please, God, let this work," Solberg whispered, leaning close to her.

"Amen to that." She soaked the cloth again.

The old man shivered.

At least someone was cooling off. "Mr. Moore, if you could suggest that the people go about their business . . ."

After a good soak in the stream, Astrid had the men lift the brave from the water, but instead of taking him back to the infirmary, they moved the litter to the shade of a tree and had them brace the poles of the litter on rocks so air could flow under it. With one of the children set to fan the flies away, she returned to inspecting the remaining tepees, with Mr. Moore in tow.

She found an elderly couple who were both comatose and burning with fever, the telltale spots all the evidence she needed. This time she had them taken directly to the creek and set to soaking while still in their filthy garments, soiled not only with grease and dirt but the effluvia of illness. As the creek washed the filth away, caring for the ill took more able bodies.

"I think you are on the right track," Pastor Solberg said, leaning close so others would not hear. He nodded toward the first brave. "Check on him. He seems better."

Sure enough, the heat emanating from his body was greatly reduced. As she watched, his eyelids flickered. A deep sigh relaxed his body, and he settled into sleep.

Astrid swallowed the lump named fear that had strangled her for a moment. "Far, see if you can get some more broth into him, please, while I check another tepee. Mr. Moore, can you find us some more help? Those tepees need to be cleaned out."

"Usually the tribe moves on rather than cleaning."

"I see. Well, these people are too weak to move unless they choose an area nearby, like that meadow over there, and just move one tepee at a time. Is that a possibility?"

"I'll see what I can do, but it is the work of the women to move the tribe." Doubt rode his shoulders and dogged his steps. "Mrs. Moore said to tell you that supper would be served at six."

And the tribe? Astrid kept the question inside. "Mr. Moore, what has happened to the supplies promised these people?"

"I am looking into that. Part of the problem is that these people did not want to move nearer the main station. The supplies are shipped there and then sorted out and distributed. After the fighting this group hid and then settled here on the southeast corner of the reservation, far away from the settlement."

"Can they not go to the station and bring food back?"

"They no longer have their horses, and as I understand it, their old chief refused to become slaves to the white man, as he put it, by living over there."

"And where is he?"

"He died early on. That is when Dark Cloud became the temporary chief."

"I see. So if we took our wagons to the station, we could bring back supplies?" Astrid asked.

"I believe so, but I have not been here long enough to rectify all the situations I have been slowly discovering." He drew himself up, as if ashamed at having disclosed this information. "I will see if I can find more help."

Astrid watched him stalk off. She heard her mother's voice saying, *"You can always catch more flies with honey than with vinegar."* Men did not respond well to accusations from a woman, especially a young woman with such a forthright manner. "Sometimes I wonder if stubbornness isn't more of a sin than all the others combined," she muttered, then hoped no one had heard her.

Shy Fawn beckoned her over to the stream, where they were washing the two new patients. Both appeared to be resting and relaxed, floating in the water.

Astrid nodded and smiled her appreciation. She then made her way back to the tepees yet to be inspected, observing that Mr. Moore was attempting to talk with a small group of men sitting around a fire pit of ashes.

———

LATE IN THE AFTERNOON, Astrid found a family of four alive but too weak to walk. She also found three young children hiding in another tepee, not wanting to leave their dead mother—two of them recovering but one very sick that needed the creek. How many of these people had died from the measles and how many had starved to death? The question, like so many others, had no answer.

When Pastor Solberg came to escort her to supper at the Moores' house, guilt that she could eat while others starved almost made her refuse. But she knew she didn't want to antagonize the Moores. She was there to help, not cause more problems. Yet when Mrs. Moore served canned peaches for dessert, Astrid nearly choked on them. Instead, she reminded herself that canned food was probably all they had too, because there was no game left to hunt. Since Mr. Moore had been in the military, surely he knew about living off the land.

"Are there any rivers close enough to fish?" she asked. "Or lakes?"

"The Missouri and the creeks. The tribe used to spend time at the river on their travels and smoke or dry fish, but their primary staple for all their needs was the buffalo. Once they were all killed off, the people had nowhere to turn."

"But why were the buffalo killed?"

Mr. Moore shrugged. "It never made sense to me either, but the government ordered it, and some people made a lot of money doing so. The hides were taken and the rest left to rot."

Back to the government. Astrid caught a glance from her father, a reminder to be gentle. She gave a slight nod to show she understood and pasted a smile on her face. "Thank you for the meal. I need to return to my patients now." She pushed back her chair and fled the room.

Finding Johnny and Samuel tending the fires, she said, "You boys go eat now. Thanks for keeping the fires going." How could she ever thank these two from Blessing? Johnny Solberg had come with his father, and Samuel Knutson was her cousin. They both worked from dawn to dark like the rest of them. If they'd thought they were coming on an adventure, she was afraid they must be disappointed.

She first checked on those in the infirmary and then headed to the creek. Shy Fawn and Gray Smoke were bringing the children out of the creek. The old man and woman were asleep on pallets in the shade of a cottonwood tree next to the brave and a younger woman, who was holding a young child. Astrid checked each of the patients, instructed her helpers to give them as much broth as they would tolerate, and thanked them. Even if the women didn't understand her words, they responded to smiles and nods, a universal language.

When her father and Pastor Solberg returned from supper, they took the brave back into the creek because his fever was climbing again. He blinked at the shock of the cool water and looked wildly around before Shy Fawn said something to calm him. The elderly man took up his seated position in the creek again, and the brave settled back down.

"What is his name?" Astrid asked Mr. Moore when he returned.

"I cannot pronounce his Sioux name, but it translates into He Who Walks Tall. He will not have anything to do with me—he always sits outside the circle when I meet with the elders."

"When did you last meet with them?"

"Two or three weeks ago. While I've had the measles, my wife has not, and I have been keeping my distance for that reason."

And here we ate with them. At least we all had scrubbed up well.
Astrid scolded herself for not asking about that. One more assumption
she'd made without having all the information. But then, they were
white, and the whites didn't have as bad a reaction to the measles as
did the Indians. Besides which, they were not starving to death at the
same time. The two went hand in hand.

By the end of the day she had gone through all the tepees. They
had put the last of the beef bones into the kettles to boil for broth,
and those families that were able were cooking beans with bits of
smoked beef. Racks were tented over the fires to smoke the remainder
of the beef. One more steer could be butchered when this was gone.
At home they would have canned part of it.

Astrid sent her two helper women off to bed and took the early
watch while most of the group from Blessing slept. Johnny was outside, keeping the fires stoked and making sure nothing was stolen.
Tomorrow was Sunday, the Lord's Day, a day of rest. But like taking
care of animals, taking care of the human patients would leave little
time for rest.

She made her rounds, laying the back of her hand against cheeks
to check for fever, listening to hearts and lungs of those who coughed.
She was quickly running out of honey, which helped soothe coughs
and made the other medicines go down more easily.

When she stopped at He Who Walks Tall's pallet, he opened his
eyes and tried to raise his head.

"Easy. All is well." She used the same gentle tone she used to
comfort children and animals, hoping the tone communicated more
than the words. When she saw his fist clench, she started to back away
but then straightened her spine and held her ground.

"Do you speak English at all?"

Did the tip of his chin indicate he did? *Please, Lord, let it be so.*

"Did you mean yes?"

The same motion again. He cleared his throat with a guttural sound.

"I'll be right back with some water for you to drink." Her steps seemed to barely touch the floor. Someone could speak her language! Perhaps there would be answers for the myriad questions she had stewing inside. By the time she returned, he had drifted off to sleep. Perhaps she should give him some broth the next time he awoke. He wasn't as emaciated as some of the others, but a fever like he'd had left one weaker than a newborn.

One of the children started to cry. But when she tried to hold him to comfort him, he drew back, fear clouding his eyes. His piercing scream jerked all the others awake, and Shy Fawn came running through the door from the room where the women and healthier children slept.

Shy Fawn took the boy, her eyes apologizing for the child's behavior. Gray Smoke went down the rows, talking softly to the others, and they lay back down. Surveying the room, Astrid saw that He Who Walks Tall was half sitting and looked like he was about to collapse. She picked up a cup of broth, now cold but still sustenance, and returned to the man's pallet.

"I'm sorry. I frightened the child."

"Yes."

"I brought some beef broth for you. Would you drink it or use a spoon?"

"Drink." But when he reached for the cup, he collapsed back against his bedding.

"I'll help you." She knelt beside him and spooned the liquid into his mouth. When his eyelids refused to stay open, she stood. "Very good. You've had the measles, but you will recover." *Please, Lord, let it be so.*

She shared her good news when Pastor Solberg came to relieve her, then made her way back to the wagon and crawled into the empty bed.

"Is everything all right?" Haakan asked.

"Yes. I'll tell you in the morning."

CAMP NOISES WOKE HER in the morning sometime after the sun had risen. "Why didn't you wake me?" she asked her father as she tied on her medical apron.

Haakan was sitting on a rock beside the fire, drinking his morning coffee and watching the kettles. "He Who Walks Tall has eaten breakfast, and two of the children are up and have been fed, so now they are helping our nurses. I'm afraid the old woman is not going to make it, but the man is responding."

"Our nurses," Astrid repeated. She nodded at his news but kept thinking on his comment. What if those two women were indeed given medical training, a short course probably, so they could be available to help Dr. Red Hawk when he returned? If only the chief would talk with her and become amenable to their help. Was Red Hawk planning on returning to this tribe, or would his offices be at Rosebud's main settlement? Why was it she always had more questions than answers?

She took the coffee offered and helped herself to a slice of cheese. Pastor Solberg handed her a bowl of oatmeal with a bit of milk and brown sugar.

"I gave most of it to the children and the sick ones."

"That is what we are supposed to do. We get to go home to good food, clean houses, clean clothing, and gardens growing so fast you can measure the progress daily." She sat down on one of the rocks. "Shoot me if you ever hear me grumbling again, all right?"

"That might be a bit extreme." Pastor Solberg sat down beside her. "I've planned a worship service for noon, right here around the fire. I'm hoping curiosity will bring in some of our Indian friends. The Moores are planning to come."

"And we'll serve a meal afterward?"

"That is the plan. I've added beans and onions to the kettle and will empty the jars of vegetables and tomatoes too. Do you think I could get Mrs. Moore to bake some biscuits?"

"It's worth a try," Astrid said. "Perhaps her helper knows how to make biscuits by now."

"I thought you might like to be the one to ask her," the pastor said.

"Wouldn't she find it harder to turn down a preacher?"

He rolled his eyes. "You are too sharp for your own good."

"How much milk did the cow give this morning?"

"Near to a gallon, and we have ten eggs to beat into it," her father answered. "Though the honey is running low, we have some brown sugar and strawberry jam. I thought to mix some of the jam into it too."

"Good idea. How long do you think the cow will last?"

"Since she's been bred, several years if they treat her right."

"I mean without being stolen and butchered for her meat."

"I've been thinking on that," Haakan said, scratching his jaw. "Shy Fawn has learned to milk her. We could send a bull along in the fall and maybe another cow. Got to get them farming, but you need hay for feed in the winter and a barn."

Astrid washed her bowl in the dishpan, rinsed and dried it, then put it back in the box mounted on the side of the wagon. Where would they find enough bowls to feed all these people?

Greeting Shy Fawn, she entered the infirmary to begin checking on her patients. What she needed most was an interpreter. He Who Walks Tall was sound asleep, the spots on his body more a fading rash. Two of the children followed her on her rounds, the little girl scratching her head. The older man's temperature had abated and he was now drinking some broth. His wife was no worse. Maybe there was hope for her after all. Of the fifteen in the infirmary, only three were comatose. She asked her two helpers to carry one of the three back out to the creek and then set them to continue feeding any who could accept it.

Glancing up when the doorway darkened, Astrid saw the chief observing their work. Without a word he turned and left. While he had not been frowning, he'd not shown any pleasure either. Didn't he care if his people lived or died?

5

BLESSING, NORTH DAKOTA

G randma!"
Ingeborg turned from the screen door at the insistent voice.
"What is it, Emmy?"

"Can I go to Inga's house?"

"Let me telephone Dr. Elizabeth and see if it is all right." Grateful
for the distraction, Ingeborg picked up the receiver to hear Gerald's
familiar voice.

"What can I do for you, Mrs. Bjorklund?"

"Thorliff's, please. How's Benny doing?"

"Our Benny is so excited about that baby coming that he hates
to leave Rebecca by herself, afraid he might miss the big event."

Ingeborg chuckled. Benny had come to Blessing last winter, after
he'd become a patient of Astrid's in Chicago due to an accident

that cost him his legs above the knees. Gerald Valders and his wife, Rebecca, had gone to Chicago to get the little boy and bring him to a forever home. Everybody loved Benny, and he reciprocated with absolute joy.

"I'll ring for you. Have you heard anything from Haakan and the rest?"

"No, and the time is stretching worse than during harvest."

"You want Benny to come cheer you up?"

"If Emmy goes to Thorliff's, Benny could maybe go too."

"Why don't you come too and bring them all over for sodas? My wife has some new syrups she's experimenting with."

Ingeborg loved the way Gerald said *My wife*. "This is sounding better all the time. Thank you."

"I'll tell Rebecca you are coming. Make it a party. I'll ring for you."

Ingeborg hummed to herself while waiting for someone to pick up the phone. When the housekeeper, Thelma, answered, they chatted for a bit before she asked to talk with Elizabeth.

"I'll get her for you."

"Is she far from the telephone?"

"No. She and Inga are reading on the back porch."

Hmm, must not have any patients, Ingeborg thought. *That is wonderful. Elizabeth needs the rest.* "Good morning. Am I to understand things are slow at the surgery?" she asked her daughter-in-law.

"They are, so I put up a sign that says *Emergencies Only*. You would be proud of me. I have a cushion behind my back and my feet up, and Inga is fetching for me."

"Would you like some company?"

"If you mean Emmy, yes. If you mean both of you, I will force myself and my darling daughter to not dance around the porch but wait patiently for your arrival. Oh, Ingeborg, I am thrilled."

"Well, that certainly settles that matter. I think we will walk rather than hitching up the buggy, so we should be there soon. Can I bring anything?"

"Just yourselves. Bye."

I forgot to tell her we are invited for sodas. She turned to Emmy. "Are you ready?"

"Both you and me?"

"Ja, both."

Emmy spun in a circle and clapped her hands. "Get sunbonnets?"

"Ja. But we will wear the straw hats. We shall dress up today. Do you need a clean pinafore?"

Emmy looked down the front of her white ruffled pinafore, flew to the sink for the dishcloth, and scrubbed at a spot. "No, all better now."

Ingeborg hung her apron on the hook by the door, placed a wide-brimmed straw hat on her head, and handed a smaller version to Emmy. She leaned down to tie the bow under the little girl's chin, then kissed the tip of her finger and planted the kiss on Emmy's button nose. After banking the stove, she shut the door behind them, and they walked down the lane. Crossing the fields would be quicker, but then they'd have to go through the barbed wire fences of the pasture for the dairy cows. With a happy smile, Emmy took her hand. This little one had changed so much in the months since they'd found her nearly frozen to death in the barn. For months she'd not spoken a word or smiled, but she had watched every move they made and copied what she could. Ingeborg felt like scooping her up and twirling around, covering her cheeks with kisses. *Thank you, Father, thank you.* Had she been remiss these last few days in sending up her bursts of gratitude? Perhaps that was why she was feeling Haakan's absence so acutely.

"Grandma." Emmy stopped and pointed at a perfect spider web, still dew bedecked in the shaded portion. The sun reflected through one perfect droplet, a dazzling rainbow. "Ooh." Emmy squatted, her pinafore touching the dust, and reached one finger to almost touch the droplet before pulling back.

Ingeborg felt doubly blessed, first by the beauty for her own eyes and also for the delight of her little sort-of-adopted daughter. A bumblebee buzzed by, bounced off the spider web, setting it aquiver, and continued on its bumbling way.

Emmy giggled and watched his flight, then stood and took Ingeborg's hand again. "Go see Inga." She added a little skip to their strides.

When they got to town, they saw Inga swinging on the garden gate, and as soon as she saw them, she jumped off and pelted down the street, her little dog yipping beside her. The two little girls hugged and danced, chattering like the house finches in the cottonwood tree at home. They each took one of her hands and pulled her faster toward the grand two-story house ahead. Other than the boardinghouse, the Bjorklund home was the largest in town to accommodate the needed room for the surgery.

"Grandma, we have kittens," Inga told her, dancing in place. "Out in the horse barn. Scooter chased her off the porch."

"She tried to have her kittens on the porch?"

"Uh-huh. In a basket by the swing, where Ma kept her papers to read."

"I see. How many kittens?"

Inga held up her hand with a scratch on the back. "I don't know. She wouldn't let me see. My scratch bleeded."

"When was this?"

"Two days ago. Did you know kittens can't see?"

"Dog babies either," Emmy put in.

Ingeborg was constantly surprised at the things Emmy knew and then disgusted at her surprise. Thanks to Metiz, she knew that the Sioux tribes had great funds of knowledge of the natural world. Her old half-blood friend had shared so much with them, thus making their early years on the prairie far more comfortable than many other settlements.

"Ingeborg, I am so glad to see you," Dr. Elizabeth called from the porch. "What a treat."

"And no patients?"

"Not a one. Only three yesterday. It's like God is giving me time to recuperate, yet be here for those in need. We have Sophie's baby due in September. She says she's already as big as a house, then laughs and compares herself to carrying the twins." While the two girls darted off to the barn to try to catch sight of the kittens, Ingeborg climbed the three steps and hugged her daughter-in-law.

"You look the healthiest I've seen in too long a time."

"I know." Elizabeth locked her arm through Ingeborg's and led the way to the padded chairs set around a glass-topped table. "Thelma has been cooking up a storm since you called, and if I know her, she will bring out the coffee as soon as it is ready."

Ingeborg sat down and inhaled deeply. "Cinnamon, for sure."

"Inga showed you her badge of honor?"

"She did, and if the girls are not careful, they will probably sport more. Whose cat is it?"

"I think she belongs to the boardinghouse. There's probably too much coming and going for her over there. I'll let Mrs. Sam know one of these days."

"You know Inga is going to want to keep all the kittens."

"Too bad. She has her dog, Scooter, and Mr. Tom, who lives here outside. He is probably the father of half the kittens in town."

"That Scooter follows her everywhere."

"I know. He hears me call sooner than she does. She was over playing at Sophie's, and when I called, he yipped at her and headed for the gate. She got the idea."

"A child watchdog. Paws used to watch out for the children too.

Andrew needs to find a dog like that for Carl. If you hear of one, let me know."

Ingeborg glanced up at the ceiling, following the flight of a sparrow. A nest up in the corner housed three open beaks. Bits of dried grass and white splotches decorated the porch floor. She smiled and glanced at Elizabeth, who was shaking her head. "Inga is enthralled with all creatures young. Thorliff put the board across there just for this purpose. They are above the level of the feline hunters this way. The birdbath is out in the center of the yard so the birds can see the cats coming. You should have heard the scolding Mr. Tom received when he brought a dead bird in and left it for me."

"He likes you."

"I know. It's really thrilling when a cat brings you gifts. One of the mice was still alive one time. Mice have never been my favorite creatures. Since we got Tom, though, we've never had mice in the house. Thelma used to use the broom on them, along with traps."

"You are talking about me?" Thelma set a tray down on the low round table and handed each of them a cup of coffee. "Dinner will be ready at noon. Out here?"

"Please. This is too perfect to waste." Elizabeth motioned around the porch. "We need to enjoy it as much as possible before the flies get bad."

The girls came running across the yard and pounded up the steps. "There are three kittens!" Inga held up three fingers. "We saw them drinking."

"Nursing." Elizabeth always tried to make sure her daughter used the proper words.

Inga stopped and Emmy plowed into her. "Nursing? They're not sick."

Ingeborg rolled her lips together to trap her laughter. Leave it to Inga to question and put her mother on the spot.

Elizabeth rolled her eyes. "That's what they call it when babies of all kinds suck milk from the mother. Babies nurse. And yes, we call women who assist doctors nurses too. And no, I do not know why."

"Can we have a cookie?"

"May we?"

"You already have one." Now it was Inga's turn to roll her eyes. "Oh, all right. May we have cookies?"

"You *may* have one each."

Inga looked at Emmy, and they giggled, chose a cookie, and ran to sit on the steps to eat.

"Mr. Jeffers is bringing his mother here on today's train. Sophie is already planning to have a tea to introduce her to the women of the town. I hope he is doing the best thing for her, since she is still mourning the death of her husband. Daniel was so concerned about her and yet wanting and needing to stay here to oversee the building of the factory to produce the new part for the seeders."

"But since Mrs. Jeffers is in mourning, if she is really proper, a tea might not be a good idea."

"You know Sophie. She'll figure out a way around that." Elizabeth thought a moment. "I am glad we here in Blessing aren't as dogmatic over some of the traditions as other places."

"Me too."

By the time they finished dinner, Elizabeth chose to take a nap, and Inga accompanied Emmy and Ingeborg to the Blessing Soda Shoppe. Benny was waiting for them on the boardwalk that Gerald had made wider so tables could be set outside in the summer. He had built a high counter along the window with stools for people who wanted to sit there and had painted all the tables red and white.

"You came, you came," Benny shouted, waving his arms. "Ma, Inga's here and Emmy and Dr. B's ma."

"You mean Mrs. Bjorklund," Rebecca remonstrated as she met them at the door.

"That's what I said. She's Dr. B's ma." He grinned up at Ingeborg. "Okay?"

"We call her Grandma, and you can too," Inga told him. "She's a good grandma."

Benny cocked his head to the side, curls bouncing as he did so. "I never had a grandma before I came here. Now I can have two?"

Ingeborg bent down and kissed the top of his head. "What kind of soda should we order?"

"Strawberry is best. Pa says chocolate is real good too."

"I say you should try some of my experimental flavors." Rebecca stepped back for them to enter. The inside was bright with red and white, like the tables.

"This is such a cheery place," Ingeborg said with a smile. "I need to come here more often."

"Me too," added Emmy, which made them all giggle.

Rebecca prepared a number of samples for her guests.

"I think I like raspberry-chocolate best," Ingeborg said after tasting several syrups. "Although that caramel is delicious too."

Rebecca stretched and patted the small mound under her apron. "At least I feel good again. Makes me think about Ma having babies."

"I remember when you were born—your mother thought you would never come."

"I wish she were here. Guess I've been missing her more than ever lately, all because of this little one."

"We all miss Agnes," Ingeborg said, reaching across the counter to squeeze Rebecca's hand.

Setting the glasses on the work top, Rebecca got each of their requests and made their sodas, the girls' eyes growing rounder as they watched the sodas fizz. Each of them carried a glass outside and sat at a table. Benny followed on his scooter. Rebecca shook her head when Ingeborg got out her money but gave in at her insistence.

When they were all seated outside, they heard the whistle of the westbound train. Mrs. Valders left the post office with the mailbag for the train and waved at them.

As they heard the train pull into the station, Benny bounced in his scooter. "I came on the train. I came on the train." His little chant made the women smile.

"I should go greet Mrs. Jeffers," Ingeborg said. "You all stay right here, and I'll be back." She got up, then looked at Inga. "And don't you go drinking Grandma's soda," she warned, setting both girls to giggling again.

Mr. Jeffers and the conductor were just helping a black-clad woman down the steps of the train. With her veil in place, she looked the picture of a mourner, and the way she clung to her son's arm expressed how weary she was.

Or weak, was Ingeborg's first thought. She crossed the wide-planked platform and smiled back at young Mr. Jeffers.

"Good afternoon, Mrs. Bjorklund. Thank you for coming. Mother, this is the woman I've told you about. Thorliff's mother."

Ingeborg gave a little bow of her head. "I am pleased to meet you, Mrs. Jeffers, and to welcome you to Blessing."

Mrs. Jeffers bowed also. "I am glad to meet you and to thank you for the welcome you have given my son. He speaks so highly of all of you and of this town."

While the voice sounded tired, it was firm. "We are all looking forward to welcoming you here. I hope you find the boardinghouse to be comfortable. I can assure you the food is very good and the people caring."

"She is so right in that, Mother. Our luggage will be delivered later. Can you walk that far or . . . ?"

"Yes, I can walk. Thank you for coming to meet me, Mrs. Bjorklund. Such a friendly thing to do." She gave a small nod and turned with her son to walk slowly across the platform.

For a moment Ingeborg watched them go and then returned the

way she had come. Perhaps a tonic would help Mrs. Jeffers feel better. That and plenty of sleep. Back at the soda shop, she visited with Rebecca for a while after she finished drinking her soda and then called the girls to return to Elizabeth's. "Would you two like to go ask Mrs. Valders for our mail? Get Andrew's and Tante Kaaren's too."

Hand in hand the two bounced up the steps, blond braids and black ones slapping their backs. A thought of Joshua Landsverk slid through her mind. *If only he could accept the Indians like these two little ones, who'd become such fast friends. One of these days maybe he will tell me his story. Please, Lord, help him heal. Especially if he still dreams of marrying Astrid, like he said.* She shook her head. Somehow she felt that might no longer even be a possibility, knowing her daughter.

"You could stay for supper," Elizabeth said a bit later.

"No, I think we'll head on home, thank you. And yes, Inga, you can come tomorrow. I'll make sure and invite Carl too."

"Can we go fishing again?"

"I don't know why not. Invite your pa to come fishing with us. He hasn't been for a long time."

"I'll suggest that to him," Elizabeth said. "He's printing the paper now, so tomorrow will be his day to take some time away."

"Or to sleep."

Emmy skipped beside her, stopping to sniff some blue bachelor's buttons and pick two clover heads, handing one to Ingeborg so they could suck the honey out of the tiny florets. She commented on some of the things she and Inga had done. "I liked the kittens."

After stopping to pick another flower, Emmy said, "Can we have one?"

Ingeborg was not surprised. She'd been expecting Inga to offer one. "We'll see." As they neared the house, they could see someone sitting on the steps. Emmy recognized him first, sent Ingeborg an unreadable glance, and ran ahead to greet the older man who

Ingeborg assumed was her uncle. He stood as Ingeborg came up to him and nodded.

"Welcome," Ingeborg said around the lump in her throat. *Please don't take Emmy. Lord, please. You know how I love her.*

"She come." He tapped his chest. "Me."

"Emmy, can you tell me this man's name?"

Emmy said two Indian words and then translated. "He my mother's brother. . . ." She squinted. "Wolf Runs."

"Wolf Runs, I thank you for leaving Emmy with us." Ingeborg spoke slowly in the hopes that he understood more than he spoke.

"Em-my?"

"I don't know her Lakota name."

He spoke again, in Lakota.

"Little Sky," Emmy said, staring at the ground. "I go with him."

"Please, please . . ." Ingeborg stopped and straightened. "Will you please bring her back to go to school again?"

Emmy translated and watched the man's face. She shook her head when he asked her a question.

He stood silently for a long moment and then nodded to Ingeborg.

Emmy went into the house and returned a few minutes later, clad in her soft leather garments. She threw her arms around Ingeborg, hugged her tight, and without another word followed the man out of the yard.

"You could stay for supper," Ingeborg called.

But they kept walking, neither of them turning to look back.

Ingeborg collapsed on the steps and let the tears flow. Emmy was gone, but soon she would return. *Or did I only imagine Wolf Run's nod?*

6

Dear Aaron,

I know this letter must be a surprise to you, but I need help out here. I am now foreman of a crew building an addition onto an old building, and we are short on men with building experience. There is a hospital going up too, and housing is in short supply. If we can get my house roughed in, we can live there. I am working from dawn to dark, and the progress seems far too slow. You would like this little town. People are friendly and work is plentiful. The farmers around here grow mainly wheat and feed crops for the milk cows for the local cheese house.

If you can get to a telephone, you can call and leave a message at the Blessing Boardinghouse. They'll get it to me. Just bring your tools and clothing. And hurry.

Your brother,

Joshua

He reread the letter and added a postscript.

Greet the others for me. Wish they would come too. J

He'd drop the letter in the mailbox downstairs on his way to the dining room in the morning. Normally he would be asleep almost before his head hit the pillow, but he couldn't get Astrid off his mind. There she was, a state away, taking care of the Indians. Always putting her doctoring ahead of everything else, especially him.

Had he burned his bridges this time? He heaved a sigh and rolled over. The breeze billowed the curtains and smelled like rain. At least his crew now could find plenty of work inside if it were pouring outdoors. He knew the crops needed a good rain, but no hail, please. He knew he needed to be praying for Astrid, but somehow he struggled with that. And when he prayed that all would work out, his prayers seemed to settle on his shoulders rather than wing their way to heaven.

Joshua flopped over again and locked his hands behind his head. Staring at the ceiling did no good. A puff of breeze brought in a spatter of rain, so he got up to close the window. His mother had trained him well. There was no need to soak the floor. He could hear her voice. *"Pay attention to small details, and the big ones will be taken care of too."* A good word for his mother was *practical*. Strange how it seemed he thought of her more now that she was gone, than when he knew she was in her house taking care of his father. And now his father was gone too, not long after he had seen the rapidly declining man at Christmas. When he went home to ask for forgiveness. So sad.

Staring out, he could see the raindrops splat against the window and join forces to run down the glass pane. He'd hoped to be joining forces with a certain blond-haired woman who felt like a bit of heaven dancing in his arms. He crossed his arms on the window frame and, resting his chin on them leaned his forehead against the coolness of the window. Lightning jabbed the sky, followed a couple of seconds later by a roll of thunder that kept on rolling, like a belly grumbling when hungry.

Wind sent the rain waving in sheets, with puddles forming to hold the wet until the earth could suck it up. He opened the window on the east side of the room, since he had a corner room, and inhaled the wondrous fragrance of trees and plants delighting in the cleansing rain. Lightning lit the sky again, showing the trees dancing along the river banks. When he flopped back in bed, he fell asleep instantly, the cooling breeze making him draw up the sheet.

———

"WASN'T THAT a glorious rain?" Miss Christopherson asked as she poured his first cup of coffee the next morning.

"That it was. Not sure how long it lasted. Sleeping in that cool breeze felt mighty good." Joshua smiled up at her. She was always so cheerful. It made eating in the boardinghouse dining room a real pleasure—her attitude and the good food.

"I know. Blew away the heat for sure. Mrs. Jeffers arrived with her son yesterday. She's such a nice lady. You want oatmeal with your plate this morning?"

"Yes, please."

"I'll be right back." She stopped and looked over her shoulder. "You want fried corn meal, biscuits, or both?"

"Both."

"I thought so."

Her smile made him return one. He held his coffee cup in both hands, elbows propped on the table. If Daniel Jeffers was back in town, there would most likely be a meeting this morning. With Hjelmer out of town selling windmills, it would be Thorliff, Daniel Jeffers, and possibly Toby, who was running the hospital job. Joshua wished he had the blueprints with him to refresh his mind on the questions he had. The main one concerned flooding. Since that happened often on the Red River, did they need to build the first floor higher to avoid water damage? Pour more concrete? While flooding had not been a problem that year, a year ago it had.

He was writing notes to himself when Miss Christopherson set his plate in front of him. Actually it could probably be called a platter, because it was oval shaped and held what looked to be enough for two men—three eggs, two pieces of ham, fried potatoes, fried slices of cornmeal mush, and two biscuits. He wished he'd not asked for the oatmeal when she set the bowl down.

"Looks mighty good."

"Thank you. I'll tell Mrs. Sam. She said to tell you she's making dried-apple pie for supper."

He smiled up at her. "Hope there will be a piece left for my dinner pail tomorrow."

"Never fear." She turned to answer a question from the men seated at one of the other tables.

Joshua dug into his meal. This promised to be a busy day, but then, when weren't they busy? He stopped with a fork halfway to his mouth. He'd forgotten to say grace again. At least he could remember to do that. He'd not read his morning devotions like he had promised Pastor Solberg either. He would have to do so after supper and after he'd finished up at his house. The house he was building for Astrid. Somehow the shine had gone out of working there, and now he just needed to get it finished. If she really had turned him down, he could sell it easily enough. The thought wrinkled his forehead.

A short time later Joshua walked into the building that housed the *Blessing Gazette* and noticed Thorliff was already in the small area set apart as an office.

"How can you be here so early when I heard the presses running last night until the rain drowned them out?"

"I'll sleep later. Daniel will be here at eight for a meeting. You'll need to be here too, but I thought we could get the ball rolling right away. I'm assigning Jonathan Gould to your crew for a week or so. He's been working on the hospital, as you know, but now he can help you with the forms. I hope to pour the concrete day after tomorrow. The sand and gravel should be on the train today. Good thing we finished that railroad spur when we did."

Joshua nodded. He had to admire young Gould. Instead of staying in New York and living a life of ease, he'd chosen to learn farming and now construction too. He'd be accompanying the threshing crew as soon as harvest started in August. The haying was nearly done, but that storm during the night would mean a setback for the hay crop. They'd have to turn it again to dry.

"Will Lars be bringing the steam engine over today?" Joshua asked. They used the steam engine that ran the threshing machines to mix the concrete.

"Tomorrow. He'll stay to run it too. I wish Far would get back," Thorliff said. "This not having any contact makes me uneasy."

Joshua narrowed his eyes. "You think there could be danger with the Indians?"

"I pray not. But remember Hjelmer said these weren't the friendliest Indians he'd ever worked with."

Something else for Joshua to worry about. "I'll go get the men started, so let me know when you want me. I'm wondering if we have enough concrete planned. That rain last night made me think on the spring floods. I'd hate for this machinery to get rusty from a flood."

"Good point. We've talked about that. Maybe it is time to start thinking about a dike along the river to protect the town."

"Right. One more thing to build." Joshua took out his pocket watch as he walked back to the old granary, as they all still called the building that was now twice as big as it once was. Five to seven. He should have been to this point ten minutes ago. His four regulars, now five including Jonathan, had their tool boxes open and were waiting for him. After the "good mornings," he partnered Jonathan with the senior Geddick to work on the forms and set one of the Geddick sons at the sawhorses to cut the boards for the forms. The other two men returned to work on the exterior siding of the north wall. He needed twice as many men. As soon as the meeting was over, he would work on the siding too. If they could get the heaviest work done in the next few weeks, having some of the men leave for the harvest crew wouldn't be quite so bad. Maybe Aaron would be there by then too, or Hjelmer might find some more construction men.

At the meeting Daniel Jeffers laid out more schematics, this time various views of the machinery to be installed in the plant where his deceased father's invention would be produced. "In accordance with my father's dream, I have hired a man away from John Deere, and he will be arriving sometime in September. If the shipments are on time, the first of the drill presses will arrive by the middle of September. Some of the equipment is coming from Germany and some from Pennsylvania."

"How about operators? Were you able to locate men for those positions too?"

"Well, we won't be operational until later in the fall. The sooner the better if we want farmers buying for spring work. I'm aiming for shipping the first of the seeder additions the middle of January, and we have orders for the new seeders for March. So the answer to your question is no—for now."

Joshua and Thorliff exchanged astonished looks. "You really think we can do this by then?"

"We have to, or someone else will take the market. I plan to start running ads in farming magazines in January and in newspapers by March."

"And we haven't finished the building yet." Thorliff shook his head. "We have to have more men. That's all there is to it. I'll run ads in some papers for skilled labor. We can house the new men in tents for the summer if we have to. Sophie said she will rent rooms at the boardinghouse with four bunks in each, but even so . . ." He scrubbed a hand across his face. "Maybe we need to do like the railroads did and advertise in Europe."

"There are plenty of immigrants coming in. We just have to find them. How about running ads in Duluth?"

"You speak Norwegian, Thorliff. Why don't you go on over there."

Thorliff rolled his eyes.

Jeffers looked to Joshua, who shook his head. "I only speak English. Sorry, can't help you there."

"I'll run the ads in the Norwegian and German papers, then. Mr. Geddick can help with the German."

When they broke up the meeting, Joshua returned to his crew. "Do you men know of any skilled construction workers? We need more men to work here. Write 'em, call 'em, just get them here."

"How many do you need?" Jonathan asked.

"I imagine twenty or thirty. They need to bring their tools and be ready to work long hours."

"I'll place a telephone call to my father tonight," Jonathan said. "Surely there are men in New York needing work." He thought a moment. "Will you pay their fares? Many of the immigrants might not have the money. And do they have to speak English?"

"I'll look into that," Joshua said and then they all got to work.

AFTER THE NOON BREAK Joshua put all his men and himself to work on the forms. Quitting time arrived and passed, and they kept sawing and pounding. It was dusk before they pounded the final nail and put their tools away.

"Thank you," Joshua called. "We'll be working the concrete tomorrow. The railcars are parked on the siding, so all the supplies are here."

"Are you going to work on your place?" Thorliff asked.

"Not tonight. Wasn't planning to." Joshua stretched his neck from side to side.

"Did you order your house yet?"

"Wanted to finish the cellar first." He bent over and closed the hasp on his toolbox. "Why?"

"Just thinking maybe we could order several at a time and see if we can get a reduced rate. Jeffers wants one and you do; and we could order a couple of spec houses. The way things are growing here, housing is critical. You're doing the floor-and-a-half model with the dormers, right?"

Joshua nodded.

"I'm thinking if we ordered three or four of the two-bedroom one-story models, they would go up fast."

"You could probably rent them right away, if not sell them."

"True." Thorliff paused and then shook his head. "Whoever would have thought we'd have a housing shortage in Blessing? Elizabeth keeps reminding me we need more schoolhouse space too. If some of our new workers are family men, that will really stretch the space. We'll have to add another classroom, and we'll need another teacher, who will need a house."

Thorliff clapped Joshua on the shoulder. "Thanks for taking over a crew like you have. We appreciate it. See you in the morning. Oh, and let me know what you decide. I'll probably send the order in a day or two."

Joshua looked after him and headed for the boardinghouse. More decisions to make. Sometimes he wished he were back on the traveling crew that dug wells and erected windmills. Less pressure and less people. He had run the first crew with Trygve and Gilbert. Built the wagon too. Life on the road like that had been good. But when Thorliff asked him to leave that and head the construction crew, he'd agreed. The pay was better, but mostly, he'd be near Astrid. Until he blew up at her over the Indian question. But still, his greatest wish was for Astrid to overlook his failings and agree to become his wife. Maybe he should just walk away from all this and go down to South Dakota and talk with her. If he had an address he would write a letter, but as far as he knew, they might be back before a letter could reach them—if he even could find an address. Sometimes the mountain called despair pitched too steeply to continue to climb. Why, oh why, had he allowed his temper to take over?

7

ROSEBUD INDIAN RESERVATION
SOUTH DAKOTA

W hy did two weeks feel like an eternity?

Astrid gazed around the infirmary, where three children sat listening to Shy Fawn tell a story while Gray Smoke kept changing the wet cloths on the latest measles victim. Along with her measles patients, she had two people with eye problems and one with an ear infection, along with the brave, who was improving, but they still struggled to keep his coughing under control.

She'd asked her father to build a slanted board so He Who Walks Tall could sit up a bit and breathe more easily. When that helped, he built two more and padded them with hides. An older woman was using one, and the other was shared among several of the others. If only she could hold the adults over a steaming kettle as she did the children. Once they were strong enough to stand, she demonstrated what to do, and they did it.

Her attention kept returning to He Who Walks Tall, whose pallet was separated from the others. Haakan had taken over caring for him to free up the two women who'd worked so tirelessly. What good nurses they would make for Dr. Red Hawk when he returned. If only she could take them with her to Blessing and give them some real training in medical procedures, like dressing wounds, listening to hearts and lungs, and assisting in surgeries. She also wished she could learn what they knew. If only they had an interpreter. If only she had learned the language from Metiz. She turned at the hacking cough that had awakened the brave.

Going out to the kettle simmering on the edge of the fire pit, she dipped out some soup and carried the gourd back to him. "Drink this. It seems to help."

He reached for the gourd.

"I'm grateful you understand me."

Dark eyes studied her over the rim of the drinking gourd. Red Hawk all over again. When the man gave an abrupt nod, she smiled and nodded back. "Good. I am hoping you can help me."

His eyes changed, as if shutters had slammed down over windows.

So much for that idea. "Do you know Red Hawk?"

A nod and more drinking. He cleared his throat and drank again.

"Are you related to him?"

Another nod.

"I wondered, because you so strongly remind me of him." *Please, Lord, let him be willing to help us.* "A brother?" She'd have missed the shake of his head had she not been watching him, albeit as unobtrusively as possible. "Cousin?"

"Yes."

Why would hearing just one spoken word feel like she'd received

76

a medal? "Red Hawk will be a good doctor to his people. He is the one who asked us to come. He wrote a letter, saying that measles, the spotted sickness, was killing his people and asked if we could come. So we did."

"White man's disease."

"I know. So many have died. I am so sorry." She took the empty gourd he handed her. "Would you like more?"

A nod.

She rose to her feet and returned to the kettle, near where her father was splitting wood. "He can speak English, as I suspected. He is a cousin of Red Hawk."

"Good. That should be a help."

"It makes me wonder if more of them speak English too but are refusing to do so. And if that's the case, why?"

"This is one of the bands that hid out in the Black Hills after the massacre at Wounded Knee. They were without supplies for a long time, and when they finally came to Rosebud . . . well, it has taken a long time to catch up. Then the troubles they had with the first Indian agent who was assigned to this area. They don't have much respect for the white man."

Astrid heaved a sigh. "And now this epidemic. Trust that is lost is hard to regain."

Haakan refilled her gourd. "Our government has a lot to be ashamed of. I am glad we can bring the Indians some help now. They need to get back to school. There used to be local schools wherever there were enough families to warrant one. This band is so small. . . ." He shook his head. "Mr. Moore has a lot to overcome."

"When will supplies arrive again?"

"He's hoping next week."

"The land here is so barren, how will they plant gardens? Will wheat grow here?"

"I don't think so. There's not enough rain. Cattle and sheep are about all that can survive here."

"Do you think this creek flows year-round?"

He shrugged and turned to answer a question from Johnny Solberg.

Astrid took the gourd back to He Who Walks Tall. But when she found him asleep, she didn't wake him. They could talk later. Instead, she dumped the soup back in the kettle and scrubbed the gourd. Metal cups were far easier to sterilize, but they had so few. Where did the Indians buy things and what did they use for money? She had so many questions and most had no answers.

When Mr. Moore hailed her, she turned with a smile. "Good morning."

"Dr. Bjorklund, I've been meaning to talk with you." He joined her at the fire. "How is He Who Walks Tall faring? He has been silent, not forthcoming with me. After Chief Night Hawk died at the beginning of this epidemic, the tribe chose Dark Cloud as temporary chief. He Who Walks Tall is to become their permanent chief. He can speak English but would rather not."

"Do you have any idea how many of the tribe are still alive?"

"Depending on how those still in your care will fare, I'd say thirty-five, forty. This is not a large enough group to have a station here, but . . ." A faraway look came into his eyes. He brought himself back. "We will do what we can."

"What about a school here?"

"I asked for that too." He studied the fire and then turned back to her. "My list of requisitions was long. I'm not sure how much of it I will receive. I am writing a letter to go along with my next request for supplies. Are there items you would like to request?"

Astrid swallowed her surprise. "You mean besides sufficient food so the people are no longer starving?" At his slight backward step, she bit off the remainder of her diatribe. "I'm sorry. That wasn't fair to you. I do understand that you are doing all you are able."

When his shoulders relaxed, she continued. "Red Hawk will be returning soon, and it would be good to have things like bandages, carbolic acid, sutures, needles, surgical supplies, sheets, blankets, and perhaps an examining table."

"I am not certain he will be returning to this portion of the reservation. The government will most likely assign him to the Rosebud station. I don't know if there is a doctor there now or not."

She had a feeling that Red Hawk would make sure these people were cared for. "Would they do better to move closer to the station themselves?"

"I suggested that."

"I see." From his frown she realized the elders did not take well to Mr. Moore's opinion. "Would you like me to write up a list of medical supplies?"

He almost smiled. "Yes, thank you. I will put it in the mailbag that goes back with the lead driver." He started to leave and then turned back. "Mrs. Moore would be delighted if you could join her for tea this afternoon. I know she is wishing for female companionship."

Thinking before she spoke was a trait her mother had long sought to instill in Astrid. "Ah . . . um . . . Tell her thank you, and I'll see her about three, if that would be all right." Since none of her patients was critical, she had no excuse. After all, she'd turned down two invitations to dinner, pleading her patients' care came before socializing. Her far was talking about leaving in a few days, so she'd better make an appearance again.

When He Who Walks Tall awoke, she thought the better of serving him herself and asked Pastor Solberg if he would see if he could get the brave talking. Solberg had spent much of his time with the elders, seeking to build the kind of relationship that could allow continued assistance. He and Haakan and Mr. Moore had spent hours in discussion also.

"Of course," Solberg answered. "You know that keeping this young man from dying is a real feather in your hat."

"As if I want a feather in my hat?" She motioned to the flat straw hat she wore because the sunbonnet was far too hot.

He chuckled at her sally. "You have done well, my dear doctor."

"We have all worked around the clock to return these poor blighted people to some kind of health. I'm sure the epidemic would not have been so severe were they not starving too."

"They have no resistance to the white man's diseases, as you and I have discussed. Smallpox wiped out hundreds of thousands of native people."

"It wasn't too good for the whites either."

"True." He filled the gourd with the soup and headed for the infirmary.

Astrid washed herself, redid her hair, and donned a clean apron to go visit Mrs. Moore. At the last moment she removed the apron and shook the dust off her skirt. To be proper, she pinned a brooch at her neck, wishing for a mirror. She would have to make do with what she had.

When she knocked at the door, Ann, the young Indian woman, answered. "Mrs. Moore expecting you. This way."

Astrid followed her. Ann must have learned some English at school before the massacre. Everything seemed to be tagged to before or after the massacre. At least in her opinion. Interesting the difference in her attitude now and her attitude when she'd read of it in the newspaper. It was even different from when Red Hawk had told her about it.

"Good afternoon, Dr. Bjorklund." Mrs. Moore greeted her from a chair in the shaded room, fanning herself all the while. With the drapes drawn and the windows closed, the room felt like a steamer.

Why didn't the woman sit out on the back porch in the shade, where a breeze would feel cooler?

"Good afternoon."

"I hope you brought a fan along. This heat is dreadful."

"What if we were to move the chairs outside on the back porch in the shade? At home that is the favorite gathering place in the summer."

"Oh no. The flies are dreadful. And the dust blows something awful. Why, my face would wrinkle up like an old prune." She fanned harder.

"If I might make a suggestion, from a medical point of view of course?"

Mrs. Moore shrugged.

Astrid sat in a chair and leaned forward. "Life on the prairie is a far cry from life in the cities." She almost smiled at the rolled-eye response. "Please, put away the corset and the petticoats. You should be wearing lightweight dresses, with one petticoat at the most. You might get heatstroke otherwise." She stopped before saying anything about the woman's powdered face. She had read that the white powder could be poisonous.

"But Mr. Moore needs a wife who represents the finer things of life. Fashion and art, music and dancing. As my mother's letters constantly remind me, it is important for me to keep up appearances, to provide him a home that is a respite from the terrible conditions he is working under." She shook her head, perhaps to disguise the quiver of her chin. "No matter how difficult it is for me."

"I see." But she didn't. "How old are you?" The question popped out.

Mrs. Moore raised her chin. "Why, I am twenty years old, if it is of any matter to you."

She is trying too hard. Surely there is a soft spot inside her, if I could only find it. Astrid smiled. "Why, you and I are much the same age."

"How did you become a doctor so quickly?"

"I studied with our local doctor and then in Chicago." She leaned forward. "I am fully accredited."

"And you came here to treat these Indians. Why?"

"Because a friend of mine from medical school, Dr. Red Hawk, asked me to."

"I don't see how anyone, a woman especially, would choose to come here." Mrs. Moore leaned back in her chair. "I just don't."

Astrid was forced again to not say what she was thinking. "It is a shame that you cannot enjoy the people your husband is working so hard to help."

"Enjoy?" The fan picked up speed. "What is there to enjoy out here in this desolate place?"

"Have you ridden out over the hills, watched a sunrise or sunset, heard the meadowlarks singing, planted some flower seeds and watered them carefully so that you could have fresh flowers, especially ones that smell good?" She ignored the shaking head and continued. "In the spring the daisies bloom to cover the hills with robes of white and green. There might be wild strawberries. They are so sweet and so tiny that it takes a lot to make strawberry shortcake, but it is so worth the time and effort. The women of the tribe would know where the wild things grow."

She paused and heaved a sigh. The look on Mrs. Moore's face would be funny if it weren't so sad. *Aghast* would fit. *Horrified* too.

"Your tea is ready," Ann said, stopping in the doorway with the tray in her hands, waiting for acknowledgment.

"Set it here." Mrs. Moore indicated the round table in front of them.

Astrid watched as Ann crossed the rug-covered floor and set the silver tray carefully on the table. The tray bumped a porcelain figurine that might have toppled to the floor were it not for Astrid's quick catch.

"I told you I don't know how many times to be more careful," Mrs. Moore hissed. "Clumsy." She glared at her maid.

"Sorry." Ann's face went blank, as if she'd just stepped out of her skin and left the room.

"Where is the sugar bowl?" Mrs. Moore asked, a whine joining her anger. "I cannot have tea without sugar."

"I will get it." Ann straightened and left the room, her moccasin-clad feet making nary a sound.

"What am I to do? Mr. Moore tells me to be patient, but this woman is impossible." She inhaled as much of a breath as her corset would allow and straightened her spine. "I swear I will have my mother send a woman from her own staff out here to help me. There is no sense in trying to bring civilization to these . . . these savages."

Were those tears in the young woman's eyes? Could fear be causing all of this? Astrid clamped her teeth, her jaw aching with the effort to be polite. If there was any hope for Mr. Moore to become a successful Indian agent, his wife would have to make some changes in her attitude. Perhaps it would be better when Red Hawk arrived and she saw that the Indians could learn as well as any white person. If the Moores lasted that long.

She accepted the cup of tea offered in a porcelain cup so thin the light shone through it, with a matching saucer. "I believe you wanted to ask me something?"

Mrs. Moore finished fixing her own tea and took a swallow before answering. "I know you are most likely the only doctor between here and Omaha."

Astrid nodded. "There might be a physician at the Rosebud station or maybe Pine Ridge. But how can I help you now?"

The woman, only a girl really, dropped her gaze. "I . . . I believe I have missed two of my monthlies."

"Ah, I see." *Lord God, send your grace and mercy here please. How can this woman possibly have a healthy baby under these circumstances? Wisdom, please. I need wisdom.*

"Have you ever delivered a baby?"

"Mrs. Moore, in spite of how young I appear, I assure you that I am qualified to assist you. I have delivered many babies and look forward to many more."

"Pardon me, I didn't mean to . . . to cast aspersions on your training." Her hand shook as she set the cup and saucer on the table.

"Perhaps not, but the advice I will give you could mean the difference between life and death, for both you and your baby."

The woman across from her tried to hide the fear in her eyes, but Astrid caught it. *Be gentle,* she reminded herself. "I have several questions for you." At the nod, she continued. "Have you felt tenderness in your breasts?" A nod. "Are you usually regular in your monthlies?" A shrug this time. "Does that mean yes or no?"

Mrs. Moore stared down at her fingers gripping the cup as if to a lifeline. "Not always, but I've never missed two before." Two bright red spots graced her cheekbones.

"Mrs. Moore, if you find it so distasteful talking with me, a woman, how would you be able to discuss this with a male doctor?"

"I . . . I don't know."

"Have you told your husband yet?"

"No. I wanted to be sure."

"Is this your first pregnancy?"

A nod. "I think Ann knows. She has seen me rather . . . indisposed in the mornings."

"Indian women understand that having babies is part of a woman's life and usually make nothing of it."

"I . . ." Mrs. Moore stopped and started again. "I think I shall ask Mr. Moore to take me back home while I can still travel comfortably. Not that coming here is in any way comfortable. My mother will be delighted to take care of me and her grandchild. We can return when the child is old enough to travel." She stared into her teacup, as if seeking wisdom or perhaps permission.

"That is between you and Mr. Moore, but I recommend that you stop wearing corsets immediately and wear light dresses that will allow you to move freely. And walking is good exercise for a mother-to-be. You will be stronger that way and ready to deliver your baby when the time comes."

Mrs. Moore looked away. "Thank you for coming. I will take your suggestions under advisement."

"If you have any questions, I will be glad to answer what I can. But we will most likely be leaving in the next few days." Astrid stood. "Thank you for the tea. I'll see myself out."

"Yes, Doctor."

Does the woman not know how to say thank you? Astrid smiled at the young Indian woman stoking the stove, most likely to begin cooking supper. The kitchen was hot enough to send a trickle of perspiration down her spine just walking through it. "Thank you for making the tea."

Ann nodded, a smile almost reaching her mouth. "Thank you."

Astrid paused midstride. "For what?"

"For my sister's life."

"She had the measles?" A nod was her only answer. "I am glad I was able to help."

The young woman nodded again, the smile catching in her eyes. "For my family."

"Good. That is why we came." Astrid felt lighter than when she'd entered the house. It was such a shame that Mrs. Moore held the Indians in such disregard. They could teach her a thing or two about manners—and life in general. *Lord, I should have been more gentle with her. What would my mother say about this?* She was fairly sure she knew, and it did not make her feel any better.

8

BLESSING, NORTH DAKOTA

The days plodded by. Ingeborg went about her chores and gardening by rote, missing Emmy more than she'd thought possible. When Inga came out to visit, she was subdued too.

"Grandma, when is Emmy coming home?"

"Hopefully in time for school."

"In September, right?" When Ingeborg nodded, her granddaughter continued. "August is next and then September?"

Another nod. "How do you know so much?"

"I ask questions."

Ingeborg picked up the pan of cookies. "Did you put raisins on all of them?"

"Uh-huh. School is a long time away." She popped a raisin into her mouth. "Emmy wants a kitten. Can she have one?"

"We'll have to see." *If Emmy does indeed come home.* Surely that had been a nod from the old man when she asked him to bring the little girl back for school? Emmy didn't even turn around to wave good-bye to her. Ingeborg sniffed. Such interminable tears. Where had her backbone gone? She knew better than to allow herself to stumble toward the black pit of despair that had trapped her in the past. But sometimes knowing better and doing better were two different things.

Inga stood looking up at her. "Grandma, you sad."

"I know." Ingeborg forced a smile to her mouth and hoped Inga wasn't paying enough attention to read her eyes. Her granddaughter's shaking head quickly dispelled that hope.

"You want to read me a story?"

"Let's finish the cookies, and then we'll do that."

Inga went to the oven door and sniffed. "These are done."

To go along with the comment, Ingeborg took up a potholder and, using her apron to protect her left hand, opened the oven door. "Well, look at that. You are right." She pulled the pan out, the round cookies all wearing a collar of tan, and set it on the table. "You be careful, and you can lift the cookies over to the rack."

"Who made the rack for you?" Inga asked, holding the tray with the potholder in one hand while moving the cookies with a pancake turner with the other.

Ingeborg smiled, a real smile this time, at her helper. "You know this story."

Inga nodded and grinned over her shoulder.

"Thorliff made the rack for me when Onkel Olaf was teaching the boys about woodworking in school. He gave it to me for Christmas."

"How old was he?"

Ingeborg squinted her eyes to help remember better. "Maybe ten? Nine? Somewhere in there."

Inga took the pancake turner and slid it under one of the waiting rolled-out cookies. "I didn't put faces on these 'cause Grandpa don't like raisins so much." She slid the cookies onto the cookie sheet.

"How do you know that?"

" 'Cause he always gives his to Carl."

Ingeborg dropped a kiss on the part in Inga's hair. "Maybe Grandpa knows how much Carl loves raisins."

"Can I put this in the oven?"

"I'll help you." Ingeborg pulled open the heavy oven door and closed it after the cookie sheet slid onto the middle shelf. "There, now we clean up and then—"

"Then you read me a story?"

"How about I tell you a story while we go pick some peas?"

While Ingeborg scraped the flour off the cutting board, Inga put the mixing bowl and wooden spoon into the pan of soapy water on the stove. She put the top on the tin that held the raisins and carried it back to the pantry while Ingeborg washed their utensils and set them to drain on the top of the reservoir for Inga to dry.

Inga sniffed the oven door. "They're done."

Shaking her head, Ingeborg checked. "Sure enough."

A bit later, with the cookies cooling on the rack and the cookie sheet draining, they took two baskets from the hooks by the back door and headed for the garden.

"Do they have garden peas where Emmy is?"

"I don't know."

"She liked to eat the pea pods before there were peas in them. I like the peas even better."

"I know." *Please, Lord, bring her back to me. I don't mind sharing her so much if she can come back. How do I get in touch with her? We don't even know for sure which tribe she belongs to. If I could write her a letter, it might help.* She shook her head. *Do they ever pick up mail at the tribal agency?*

She felt a small hand slide into hers and looked down to see Inga studying her. "I'll be all right, little one. Let's pick the peas. Do you have a favorite story?"

Inga nodded, a frown wrinkling her forehead until a grin chased it away. "I know. *Three Billy Goats Gruff.*"

"Which one do you want to be?"

"The troll."

Ingeborg blinked. "Are you sure?"

"Uh-huh. Then I can sound mean and growly." She fit actions to words, and then smiled up at her grandmother. "Pretty good, huh?"

Ingeborg handed her a fat pea pod before slitting one of her own and using her tongue to release the peas into her mouth, a trick she'd taught all of her children. Inga did the same, and they munched their first ones together.

"Once upon a time a mean nasty troll lived under a bridge that crossed a river between the barn and the pasture. Every day the three billy goats had to cross the bridge to get to the field to graze. One day the youngest billy goat tiptoed onto the bridge."

"Who goes there?" Inga growled her most fierce.

"It is I, the littlest billy goat." Ingeborg spoke as a little billy goat would speak, if a little billy goat could really speak.

"I am coming up to eat you," snarled the troll.

Ingeborg tossed a handful of pea pods into her basket. "Oh, please don't eat me. My brother will soon be coming, and he would be far tastier than me. I'm too little, barely a mouthful."

Inga giggled. "You put in extra." She deepened her voice. "You go ahead, you worthless little mouthful."

Ingeborg grinned through the pea vines to Inga on the other side of the row. "And then the sound of hoofbeats hit the bridge again as the middle brother crossed to the pasture." She caught Inga popping peas into her mouth. "Hey, I thought you were putting the peas in your basket."

"I am. See." Inga held up her basket to show the pea pods. "But that one asked to be eaten. After all, this troll gets hungry."

"I see." Ingeborg's mind flitted back to telling this story to Andrew and then Astrid. Of them all, Inga was the most creative. When she knew the story, she loved to act it out. What if they were to do a drama at the school? While they did a Christmas play every year, they'd not done a real play at any other time. They could use the church, and . . .

"Grandma, where did you go?"

"I just had a marvelous idea."

"What?"

"A play."

"Play what?"

"Like the Christmas story."

"Linnea almost dropped baby Jesus one year."

"I know. But Johnny caught him."

The audience's collective "Ooh" had turned into "Oh good" and applause at the boy's quick action. The incident would live among the Christmas tales of Blessing for a long time.

"I hope I can be in the play again this year."

"You will be. Everyone who wants to will have a part."

"I could be the troll and hide under the manger."

Ingeborg swallowed a chuckle. "That would most surely be a different kind of character in the pageant. Maybe you ought to think on a different person to play."

"Is a troll a human or an animal?"

"Ah, I'm not sure. A sort of human, I think."

"But with a big nose—and ugly."

"Right."

"And mean."

"True."

"Did you ever eat a goat?"

"No, we used to eat mutton, which is sheep, but we never had goats." She thought a minute. "Maybe I did back in Norway. A neighbor had goats. I'll have to think on that." Just the mention of Norway carried in a pang of sadness. She'd never seen her mother again after they left. Anji Moen had gone by the farm and visited with Ingeborg's mor and far one year, but they were both gone now, and her brother had the farm there. That was why he had never come to America. None of her immediate family had immigrated. She should write to her brother and find out how things were there. Perhaps there was indeed someone else who wanted to come, especially if offered a job. Like Freda had come at Ingeborg's request for help and brought several members of her family with her.

"Grandma, do we have enough peas?"

"Not enough to can but enough for dinner tomorrow." It was her turn to cook dinner again. "I'll make creamed peas and new potatoes with ham steaks. And biscuits." Haakan loved creamed peas and potatoes poured over his biscuits. Would he be back before the peas were done? Hot as it was, the peas wouldn't last long.

"I didn't get to butt heads with the big billy goat gruff."

"He would knock you in the river."

"I know. Can we go fishing? Or wading?"

"We don't have Carl here to catch the big fish."

"You can call him on the telephone and invite him to come. I'll go dig up the worms."

"I thought we were going to shell the peas."

"Oh. We can shell fast and then go fishing."

"Fish for supper would be good, all right." Ingeborg tipped back her head to gauge the sun's position. "Let's go make that telephone call."

Ingeborg poured them each a glass of cold lemonade from the pitcher she kept in the icebox, and while Inga arranged cookies on the plate, Ingeborg went to the telephone to ring for Ellie. As she approached it, the phone jangled once, then again, her ring.

"Hello."

"Mor, May's choking."

"Turn her upside down and slap her on the back."

"I did!" Ellie screamed. "Nothing came out. She's turning blue!"

"Push on her chest. I'm coming." She turned to Inga. "You stay here. Do you know how to use the telephone?" At Inga's nod, Ingeborg pulled a chair over to the phone mounted on the wall and motioned for Inga to climb up. "Tell Mr. Gerald to call for your mor to come to Carl's house right away. Then ring the dinner bell."

Ingeborg grabbed her black bag and ran out the door. Catching a horse would take too long. She headed out across the field to Andrew's house, which seemed miles away. *Dear God, dear God.* She let her brain scream her prayers as her feet pounded the pathway. Halfway there she had to slow down to catch her breath. The internal litany continued. Running again, she ignored the stitch that ripped her side and kept one foot pounding in front of the other.

Ellie, the baby in her arms, came flying down the steps to meet her.

"Push on her chest."

"I did. Oh, God, please!"

Ellie laid the little one down on the bench on the porch so Ingeborg could listen with her stethoscope. She probed the child's neck with shaking fingers. She could barely hear the little heart above the trip hammer of her own.

"She's alive. Keep pushing on her chest. Like this: push, one two, push. Right on the sternum." While she talked, Ingeborg dug in her bag for a tongue depressor. One in hand, she tipped the little head back over the edge of the bench and depressed the tongue to see if she could see anything caught in the throat.

Did she dare do a tracheotomy? *What if I kill her? What if I don't* and she dies? The questions pounded through her brain, matching the pounding of her heart. *Dear God, dear God.* She dug in her kit again and withdrew a scalpel. Selecting the spot where she knew she needed to cut, she dug a piece of tubing from her bag. "Hold her still."

"Ja." Ellie, tears pouring down her cheeks, laid both arms over her seventeen-month-old daughter.

With one more prayer for wisdom, Ingeborg set the scalpel against the blue skin and pushed. Air whistled from the hole she held open with the blade while fighting to insert the tube. Tube in place, she ordered Ellie to hold it steady.

With a sigh, Ingeborg collapsed on the porch.

Get up, her mind demanded. *I can't. Get up now!* She sucked in a breath, and the scene flooded her mind. May, the baby, the blue baby. Ingeborg forced her eyes open, hearing something pounding, someone screaming.

Someone was saying something about Andrew. The words went on forever.

The pounding was no longer her heart. A horse's hooves.

"Ellie!" Andrew threw himself off the horse and leaped the porch stairs. "What happened?"

"May choke!" Carl grabbed his father's leg. "Pa!"

"She's breathing again, thanks to your mother." Ellie tilted her head toward her prostrate mother-in-law.

Ingeborg could hear all the commotion, and most of it even made sense, but for some reason, moving, as in sitting up, seemed impossible. She carefully moved her hands and feet. Yes, they responded. Did she hit her head on something? More pounding.

"Mor, Mor, answer me!" Andrew patted her cheek. "Can you hear me?"

She thought sure she nodded.

"Good. May is breathing again. Thank you, heavenly Father." Ellie spoke around her sobs.

"I'm going to help you sit up." Andrew laid a hand on her shoulder.

She shook her head.

"All right. Carl, get Grandma a pillow." He leaned closer. "If you can hear me, blink once."

Ingeborg ordered her eyes to blink. What strange thing was going on with her body?

"She ran all the way over here. Could it be her heart?"

Sometimes the words seemed to come from a distance. But she knew Ellie was speaking. The whistle must be the baby breathing. She'd done the right thing. *Thank you, Lord, for your great mercy. Whatever is happening here, is this my time to come home to you?*

A light smiled around her. Gentle words impressing her mind. *No, my dear daughter, not yet. But right now, you rest.*

And May will be all right?

Yes. Now rest.

Ingeborg felt a tear slide out of her eye and down the side of her face. Floating on peace, as tangible as a feather bed, she let all her cares slide away. Floating on water felt wonderful, but this was far, far better. She was sure that if she could open her eyes, she would see her heavenly Father's eyes smiling into her own. Since the voice said *Rest,* she decided to follow the instructions.

"You are smiling, Mor. Are you going to be all right?"

A slight nod answered the tear-and-fear-filled voice of her younger son.

———

WHEN SHE AWAKENED, she lay in her own bed, darkness all around, a gentle breeze dancing with the curtains at the open window. Had it all been a dream?

"Can I get you anything, Mor?"

Elizabeth's voice. Ingeborg shook her head. This time it worked. She felt loving fingers check her pulse at the wrist. The scent of rose water drifted across her awareness, making her smile again.

"I am all right." The words sounded hoarse, as if she'd not spoken in a long time. She'd almost said "I'll be" but changed to "I am."

"For that we are all exceedingly thankful."

"He said I should rest for a while."

"Rest is always good. Now, who is the he?"

"God."

"Ah, I see." Tears almost shrouded the words.

"I asked Him if I was to come home now and He said no, not yet. But that all would be well, and that I should rest for a while. How long have I been resting?"

"Dawn is nearly here."

"And May is all right?"

"Yes," Elizabeth said, "thanks to your quick action. We almost lost her."

"I know. Her heart was so weak. The scalpel was clean but not sterile."

"I swabbed the incision with alcohol. If God said she would be all right, who are we to worry about something like germs?"

"I agree." Ingeborg heaved a sigh and then stretched her arms above her head. "I feel like I've had the most wonderful sleep, and yet—" she covered her yawn with a hand— "I think I will rest some more. You go lie down now and get some sleep too."

"I will. Thorliff and Inga are upstairs, and I will join them. But first, what do you think happened to you?"

"I either fainted or my heart did not respond well to the run across the field. I was fine, and then suddenly I was on the floor and my body would not respond. Then I heard God. That's all I know."

"We'll go with that, then."

"Good." Ingeborg glanced at the window. The sky had not begun to lighten.

———

SHE WOKE SOME TIME later to the smell of coffee, the birds gossiping in the cottonwood tree at the corner of the house, and Inga trying to whisper. The last made her smile, or widened her smile further. Her stomach reminded her that eating might be a very good idea. When she sat up, she felt fine. In fact, she felt better than she had for a long time. No lightness in her head, her whole body seeming to work fine. She stood and stretched, took a dressing gown off the hook by the head of the bed, and sliding her feet into slippers and her arms into the sleeves, she tied the sash and strolled into the kitchen.

"Grandma, you slept forever." Inga darted across the room before anyone could grab her and threw herself into her grandmother's loving arms.

Thorliff threw up his hands. "I tried to keep her quiet."

Inga looked over her shoulder. "I was quiet."

"Yes, you were." Ingeborg kissed the top of her head. "I think the smell of coffee woke me."

Freda turned from the stove. "You sit and I'll pour." Freda Brunderson was a cousin of Ingeborg's and had proved to be a huge help, especially in the cheese house.

"I'm not an invalid, you know."

"Thank God for that." Thorliff lifted Inga onto his lap. "You gave us a nasty scare."

"I told Andrew I was to be all right."

"Yes, well, you might have heard a heavenly voice, but he didn't and you weren't responding. Well, at least not waking up completely."

Ingeborg smiled her thanks to Freda and held the cup so she could sniff the fragrance of coffee. One of her delights in life was that first sniff of coffee in the morning. This morning it smelled better than it ever had. A thirst for cold water hit her as if she'd not had a drink for weeks. "Inga, could you get Grandma a glass of water right from the pump?"

Thorliff stood and carried his daughter to the sink, handed her a glass, and pumped the handle until the water flowed. He set Inga down, and she scampered over to the table to hand Ingeborg the glass.

"You want more?" She watched carefully as if to make sure her grandma could really drink.

Ingeborg drained the glass and set it down. "My, that was the best water I've ever tasted. Mange takk."

"Do you want your eggs fried or scrambled?"

"Scrambled. Inga likes them best that way."

Elizabeth joined them as the food was set on the table.

"You're all ready for the office?" Ingeborg was surprised. Was it really that late?

"I'll eat first, then check on May. Inga, you are going to play over at Grant's house today, so eat quickly."

"Want to stay with Grandma." Her lower lip came out, but she kept eating.

"I think Grandma needs to rest today. Freda will be here to take care of her."

"No one needs to take care of me. I think I'll shell the peas we picked yesterday." She smiled at her granddaughter. "I can sit out on the porch and shell peas."

"I can shell peas too. I helped pick them." Inga glared at her mother.

Ingeborg thought a moment. "You come back and help me tomorrow. You will have a good time with Grant and the other children."

"Promise?"

"Oh, I do." Ingeborg held out her arms, and Inga slid off her pa's lap and ran to Ingeborg.

"I rang the bell hard. And Andrew galloped up on the horse and yelled to me to stop. But you said ring the bell, and I thought my arm was going to fall right off."

Ingeborg kissed the little girl's shoulder. "I'm glad it didn't."

After the little family left, Freda sat down at the table to dish up her own plate. "That was some scare. Gerald called us at Kaaren's, and when I came over here, Inga was still ringing the bell, and Thorliff drove Elizabeth out here. Andrew said when he got there, May was breathing, both Carl and Ellie were crying, and you were out cold on the porch floor. He thought you'd had a heart attack."

"I wonder what closed off May's throat like that."

"Was she sick?" Freda asked. "Coughing, like?"

"I don't know. I think Ellie said she woke up from her nap and couldn't breathe. I'm sure we'll get it all straight. Praise God for His mercy and grace."

"We all been doing that." Freda paused, cleared her throat, and looked up. "Did you really hear God speak to you?"

"I did. I've never felt such peace in my entire life. I floated on it or in it. He said to rest, and so I did."

"Well, I never." She shook her head. "I sure am glad He didn't take you home now."

"Me too. I guess. But I think being with Him must be some kind of wonderful. When the time comes, I know one thing."

"What?"

"I won't be the least afraid."

9

Surely they would be coming home soon. Joshua pulled a kerchief from his back pocket and wiped the sweat from his forehead. Going over to the lidded barrel that held the drinking water, he turned on the spigot and soaked his kerchief before tying it around his neck. Filling the tin cup that hung on a hook, he downed that and hung the cup back up. Good thing he was so busy he really didn't have time to think about Astrid during the day, and at night he fell into bed like he'd been poleaxed.

Good thing tomorrow was Sunday. They all needed a day of rest.

The train whistled off in the distance. Maybe Astrid would be on it.

"Joshua!"

He turned back to the job. They were pouring concrete now and would finish the floor before quitting. They'd gone ahead with the plans made, and discussion had started on building a dike before spring. Which really meant before winter and the dirt froze too solid to be moved.

"Yeah?"

"Jeffers wants you over at the office."

"Okay, thanks." He crossed the street and headed for the printing shop, where a construction office had taken over the front room. How Thorliff was managing to put out his newspaper every week in spite of all this was beyond him. He should have brought his dinner pail. He could hear the screech of the iron wheels on the rails as the train ground to a halt. The bell tinkled over the door when he pushed it open.

Thorliff waved him over. "I need to get this order in today, or we won't get anything until September. I am ordering six house-building kits, and you will get a fifteen percent savings if you go in with us to make it seven. What do you say?"

Joshua pushed out a deep breath. "I can't turn down an offer like that. When do you want payment?" While he spoke, he tried to figure how much he had in the bank.

"When you can. I'm writing a check for the entire amount, so you will pay the company."

Since he had already paid off the note on the land, he didn't think he had enough for the entire cost of the house. Going into debt again. He could hear the disappointment in his father's voice. At least it was no longer a sneer. Gratitude for the time with his father before he died was a good thing.

Joshua ignored the voice. His father had kept his farm from growing by not being willing to work with the bank. He lost one son and almost a second. If Aaron came to work in Blessing . . . Surely he had gotten the letter by now.

"Write me up a note so I can sign it, then."

Thorliff shook his head. "We'll deal with that later."

The noon whistle blew, another newfangled invention, as Mr.

Valders had been heard to say, especially since the official clock hung on the bank wall.

"Bring your dinner pail over here so we can talk while we eat. I think you might as well make that a habit. Oh, and please stop by the house and tell Thelma we are ready to eat." He stood to clear rolls of blueprints off the table. "On second thought, we'll eat on my back porch. It's cooler there than here."

When Joshua returned to the old granary, he saw Pastor Solberg walking up the street.

"Welcome home," Joshua called.

"Thank you. It's good to be back. Do you know where Thorliff is?"

"Setting up for dinner on the back porch of the surgery. I'm sure Thelma would set another place. I'm getting my dinner pail and going there myself."

"Good. I'll wait for you." Solberg set down his carpetbag and mopped his head. "Here I thought it might be cooler in Blessing."

He's all alone. What about the rest of the group that went south? Mostly, what about Astrid? Joshua grabbed his dinner pail, and after taking a minute to assign duties to his workers for the afternoon, he returned to the street, where Solberg was now talking with Hildegunn Valders.

Solberg smiled, nodded, and motioned to Joshua. "I have to go now, Mrs. Valders. I'll talk with you after church tomorrow."

"So good to have you back," she said with a wave and started toward the post office. She turned. "Oh, and Mrs. Jeffers has arrived. We are going to plan something so she can meet the ladies of the town."

"Good. Good." He waved again and picked up his pace to meet with Joshua, exhaling a *whew* when he arrived.

Joshua grinned. "Have you had dinner?"

"No, but let me tell you, I am extremely grateful to be sitting down at a table with Thelma as the cook."

"You look like you've not been getting enough to eat."

"That's true. None of us had enough to eat. It is very hard to eat when people around you are starving to death. Combined with the measles, the reservation was indeed a pit of despair."

"Where are the rest of them?" Joshua asked, trying to keep his voice neutral.

"Dr. Bjorklund felt several of her patients needed a few more days of medical care. They should be here later this week."

Leave it to Dr. Bjorklund. . . . Joshua felt his jaw tighten. He'd heard of the near tragedy at Andrew's house a couple days before. News got around Blessing even faster now that the telephones connected everyone. Would it have been different if Astrid had been there? What if her mother had indeed been struck dead? Instead of staying home, Astrid had to go off helping a bunch of Indians who didn't much appreciate the help, as far as he'd heard from Hjelmer.

"What is it, son?" Pastor Solberg asked, laying a hand on Joshua's arm.

"What? Ah, nothing. Nothing at all." Joshua stared at his boots. "We'd better get a move on. I know the others will be glad to see you're home."

"Joshua, you do know that any time you need to talk something over, I have a good listening ear."

"Thank you, sir, I know that. I guess this is just something I need to work out for myself." He held the gate open, and they took the sidewalk around the house to the back porch, well shaded by a cottonwood and a maple tree, both trees now as tall as the two-story house.

"Pastor Solberg, welcome home," Thorliff said as he and Daniel Jeffers stood and came across the porch to meet the two new arrivals. "Come sit down and make yourself comfortable. Thelma will set another plate."

"Good to see you, Mr. Jeffers," the pastor said as they shook hands.

"It feels good to be here. Wait until you see how much we've accomplished in the short time you've been gone."

"You don't know how good this feels," Solberg said.

"Being home again?" Thorliff asked.

"Ja. Blessing and friends and family. We worked so hard, and yet the heart always finds time to miss home."

"Where are Far and Astrid?"

"They all stayed a few more days. I wanted to be here for church tomorrow, to let everyone know what their contributions have done."

John Solberg took the chair he was offered. "I understand your mother came with you, Mr. Jeffers."

"She did. We are living at the boardinghouse for now. She must be feeling better already. She's beginning to get restless, says she has nothing to do."

Solberg turned to Thorliff. "Have you taken her out to meet your mother?"

"I thought tomorrow would accomplish that, but now that Mor has been ordered to rest, she might not invite everyone over for dinner like usual."

"You better catch me up. What happened?" He glanced at the men gathered. "No, you go ahead. I can see this is a business meeting. Just tell me she will be all right."

"Oh, she is and will be. Wait until you hear the story." The smile Thorliff wore made Solberg settle into his chair and set his black fedora on the bench beside him.

Thelma greeted him with a smile and a glass of lemonade. "I'll set you a place too. Welcome home."

"Thank you." He drew a letter from his chest pocket. "Could you please see that Dr. Elizabeth gets this letter from Astrid and also ask her to telephone me when she has time?"

"Of course."

Solberg turned back to the others. "Sorry for the interruption."

"We're talking about housing and how to provide some quickly, since we are in desperate need of more construction workers." Thorliff nodded as Thelma set the plates in front of the men. "Thank you. Is Elizabeth back yet?"

"No. She telephoned to say she and Inga are at your mother's."

"Thank you." Thorliff laid the various pictures of the Sears and Roebuck house kits on the table. "That's the one Joshua is ordering. Jeffers, you decided on this one. Right?"

"Yes, for now. I need to get my mother into a home of her own. We can build a larger one later, if we need to."

"Good. Then this is what I'm planning. We'll build three two-bedroom single-story houses on speculation, and two that are a story and a half. All will have indoor plumbing and be wired for electricity. We'll have electric lights here in the not too distant future, so we might as well be prepared."

Now that he was committed to finishing his house, Joshua let his mind roam, only half listening to the discussion. Surely if Astrid cared for him, she would have included a letter for him. After all, she sent one to Dr. Elizabeth. The slow burn ignited in his belly again. Why was it that every time he thought he had his feelings about the Indians under control, something else blindsided him? He'd not realized how much he was counting on talking with Astrid again. When was she going to return, anyway?

"What do you think, Joshua?"

His mind snapped back. "Sorry, I was thinking on something else. Could you repeat that, please?" He could feel the heat climbing his neck. After all, this was a business meeting, not a social call.

"How do you think young Gould is doing?"

"He's a hard worker, and he listens to Mr. Geddick, who is teaching him how to use the tools. Willing to help any way he can."

"Good. He said he called his father in New York and asked him to try to find us more workers. Today Mr. Gould telephoned to say that he has ten men ready to get on the train tomorrow. All have experience in construction. Some have a few tools of their own. He asked how many more we need."

"Ten men?"

"I know. I was as shocked as you. Can you manage with five more? We'll send the other five over to work on the hospital until the house kits arrive. The man I talked with at Sears and Roebuck said we should have the houses in less than two weeks."

"I see." Joshua's mind kicked into high gear. "What languages do the men speak? Any English?"

Thorliff looked down at his list. "Three Norwegians, four Germans, two Swedes, and a Russian."

"Russian? Does anyone around here know any Russian?" When they all shook their heads, Joshua leaned back in his chair. "How will we communicate?"

"When will their families come?" Pastor Solberg asked.

"He didn't say anything about families."

"Can we get more information?"

"I told him I would telephone him back later this afternoon."

"What if we took all but the Russian?" Joshua drank half the glass of water sitting beside his plate. "We've got the other languages covered." *Aaron, get out here. I need you.* He paused. "What about tools?"

"I'll have Penny order what we need. The supplies should be here by the time the men arrive."

"When will Hjelmer be back?"

"Not till late August or early September."

Feeling he needed to catch his breath, Joshua nodded. "Is there anything else for now?"

"No, that's about it. We'll keep you up-to-date."

Standing, Joshua picked up his dinner pail and headed back to the site. How would he manage five more men? No, that wasn't the problem. He had plenty of work. How would he manage five more men who did not speak his language?

They finished troweling off the floor just before the whistle blew. Joshua laid the three-foot level at different corners. "Now if those clouds will blow over without dumping rain on this concrete, we should be able to remove the forms in three, four days." He debated. Should they just cover what they could with the tarps they had? Were there any extras over at the hospital? They'd not poured any more concrete for weeks now over there. He could hardly believe what he was thinking, but having a telephone on each construction site would sure make life a lot easier.

"I'm going over to the hospital to check on more tarps. Spread out those that we have in case it rains, and then you can go on home. Thanks for getting this done so quickly."

"I'll go with you," Jonathan Gould said.

They brought back two wheelbarrows loaded with tarps and spread them as far as they went.

"Better safe than sorry. That's one thing my father always says." Jonathan stuffed his leather gloves into his back pocket.

"Mine too. Guess that's what prompted me to do it." Joshua picked up his dinner pail. "See you in the morning. Hey, and thanks for asking your father to find us more construction workers. With all these new people coming in, things are going to be different here in Blessing. That's for sure."

"You know, I was thinking of something else," Jonathan said after a nod. "What if someone asked Mrs. Knutson if she'd like to rent out some of her dormitory space for the rest of the summer? After all, there might be more than these ten men that come in."

"Good idea."

"You going to work on your cellar tonight?"

"For a while. I'm about done."

"Want some help?" Jonathan asked.

Joshua started to say no thanks but surprised himself by accepting the offer.

"I thought you'd be helping finish up the haying."

"Lars knew I wanted to learn more about construction, so he said coming to work on this building was the best training. They'll be done haying in the next couple of days. Barring any more rain, that is."

The two stopped at the hole in the ground that would soon become his house. Sooner than he had dreamed possible. And for less money. "You spent these last couple of days putting up forms over on the work site, and now we need to take these down. The concrete has cured long enough," Joshua said as he knocked on the concrete. "We'll use these boards over again for the next house."

By the end of two hours they'd stripped off most of the forms and stacked the boards on some two-by-fours he'd laid for a base to keep the air circulating.

"Don't you ever quit?" Toby Valders asked as he stopped by on his way home.

Joshua looked up at Toby, who was leaning over the cellar. "Thanks to Gould here and all the rest of the help I've had, I'm nearly ready to set the beams in place."

"Guess we are working on your house first, least that's what Thorliff said."

That caught Joshua by surprise. But then, none of the other houses had cellars dug or foundations already built. "Shame we don't have anyone to dig out the cellars. If we did we could get all the houses dried in and then finish them during the winter." The two walked up the ramp built for the wheelbarrows when digging.

"You sound like a real construction man. Do you like it better than farming?" Toby asked.

"I do. Thanks for the tarps." Joshua caught a flash of lightning off to the north. "We all better pray this blows over. It'd be a shame to waste any of the hay left on the ground."

"Oh, they won't waste it. These folks, they don't ever waste anything."

Jonathan chuckled. "That's for sure."

Joshua clapped him on the shoulder. "Thanks for your help. Mr. Geddick says you learn quickly, and it shows."

"When my father sent me out here that first summer to find out what manual labor was like, he sure had no idea I'd want to stay." Jonathan swept his arm in an arc. "All this, the town, the land, farming, the people—beats New York any day. Talk about two different lives."

Toby snorted. "When my brother and I snuck off that westbound train to get something to eat, two snot-nosed kids running from the police in New York City, we never knew what hit us. All of a sudden we had a man and woman who wanted to adopt us, a real home, a school, and soon friends. We'd probably be dead by now back there, and look what we have here."

Joshua just listened. What was there about Blessing that provided for so many? He too felt at home there. If only Dr. Bjorklund could be the woman for him, life would be perfect. Lightning flashed again, but this time the thunder rolled farther away. If only.

10

H as running away helped solve things in the past?"

Joshua stared at the pastor who had become his friend and confidant but never asked easy questions. "It's easier." He threw the final board onto the stack of concrete-crusted form material, staring at the woodpile so as not to face his friend. Sunday evening and he'd gone to work on his house, and Pastor Solberg had stopped by to help.

Turning, Joshua continued. "I've not needed to solve anything. It's something that happened in our family. You can't change history. I remember as a little boy seeing my aunt when they brought her back after being an Indian captive for ten or fifteen years. She was wild. Never could adapt to her home again." He paused. "And then she killed herself." The words fell as bleak as he felt. "My father hated the Indians. That never changed."

"Joshua, that was a terrible thing to have happen. But when you let him, God can change your heart, to let the hatred and bitterness go, so you can live as one forgiving and forgiven."

"I thought it was taken care of before, and then Astrid goes off to doctor the Indians, and it all blew up again. If she had just stayed here . . ."

"So this is Astrid's fault?"

"No. I mean, yes." He shook his head. "I don't know. But I am sure she hates me now, and all I want is another chance."

"Another chance?"

"To convince her that I love her." Joshua swung his arm around. "I'm building this house for her, for us. Doesn't that say that I love her?" He stared up at the darkening sky. "And I thought she loved me, but . . ." He shrugged.

"Let me get this straight. You are saying that if she truly loved you, she would have stayed here in Blessing rather than obeying the call to help keep other people alive?"

"That sounds terrible. If only it hadn't been Indians."

"You want the Indians to die, then?"

"Well, no. What kind of man do you think I am?"

"I think you are a man who is carrying on a family tradition of hate, and God is calling you to let it go, to bury the hatred, to forgive those who have wronged your family so that God in His infinite mercy can forgive you and guide your life."

Joshua stood, head bowed, shoulders curved around his heart. "I thought I did."

"But God peeled back more layers and is showing you that you truly haven't."

A pause lengthened. "Do you ever think that God asks too much?"

"That seems to be a fairly universal cry of mankind." Solberg brushed a pesky mosquito away from his face. "That's also why He sent His son to live and die here on this earth so that we can live in His grace."

"So you are saying that if I don't forgive, I will not be forgiven?"

"What does the Lord's Prayer say?"

Joshua mentally ran the prayer through his mind. "To forgive us our trespasses as we forgive those who trespass against us."

"*As* is a mighty big word."

"But what if I do as you say, and she still won't have me?"

"Then maybe God is showing you that Astrid is not the woman He has in mind for you."

"You believe He chooses who we will marry?" Joshua hoped he was keeping the shock off his face. Since when did God actually do the things Solberg talked about?

"If we let Him. He cares about every aspect of your life, everything that you care about. He says, 'Trust me.'" The words lifted on the evening breeze.

Joshua stared at the line of light on the western horizon. "Sometimes I wish I had never come back here."

"I know that I, for one, am certainly glad that you did. I know many others who feel the same way. You have become part of the town of Blessing, and we care deeply for those who live here."

"So what do I have to do?"

"Remember the verse from First John? 'If we confess our sins, he is faithful and just to forgive us our sins, and to cleanse us from all unrighteousness.'"

"I just say I'm sorry, and it will be all better. Only I did, and it isn't all better. The anger came back worse than ever."

"Satan delights in nothing more than catching Christians in their old habits and fighting to keep them there. Sometimes when we try to follow God's instructions, that riles the old devil up, and he attacks with all he is worth. Remember, he attacked Jesus too. Three times."

"Would that this were only three times."

"Well, Jesus kept in close contact with His father, so He got through the lessons more quickly than we do."

Guilt added to the affront. He'd not been living up to his word to read the Bible daily and pray, not only daily but whenever the need arose. When had he last said thank you for good things that had happened? Like getting a big discount on his house kit or Pastor Solberg returning home safely and showing up to help with the house. Joshua shook his head. "I just can't manage to do it all."

"None of us can. That's what grace is all about. God's free grace and mercy. Joshua, God loves you, right now, just the way you are. You can't be good enough so that He will love you more."

"But what if Astrid—"

"Can you trust God to take care of that too?"

"I don't know."

"Now, that is indeed an honest answer. Choosing to trust God is not a one-time thing, but an over and over thing. Just like love is a choice, not necessarily a feeling."

I can't do it. The words echoed and re-echoed through his mind. *I can't forgive. I can't love enough. I can't trust God for everything.*

"You can only do this through the grace of God, one tiny step at a time." Solberg stood silent. A nighthawk called out on its forage for flying insects. The buzz of a determined mosquito sounded loud in the silence.

"You always say the beginning is with the Word." Joshua blew out a breath and tipped his head back to stare up at the stars, pinning the heavens in place. "Thank you." *I guess.*

"Anytime you need to continue this discussion, just let me know.

And in the meantime, God's grace is sufficient for anything. Amen. Enough of my sermon. Johnny said he is really missing his guitar lessons and playing with you. You've taught him a lot."

"He is so anxious to learn that he makes a great student. I've missed him too." He extended his hand. "Thank you, sir."

Pastor Solberg took the hand and shook it, using his other hand to bind the two together. "You and Gould were great this morning. The congregation sings so much better than it did before we had strong musicians."

"Everyone is so glad you are home."

"And I am glad to be here. 'Night." The two men parted ways, and Joshua heaved another sigh. "Just let go" seemed to be the song of the cottonwood trees. "Just let go" fluttered on the curtains, whispered in the sheets when he crawled into bed.

Even the birds sang it with their morning arias. "How?" he wanted to scream at them all. Instead, he shaved and dressed and was the first one to arrive in the dining room. He could hear Mrs. Sam's laughter from the kitchen.

"Let go of that, boy." Her admonishment to her son stabbed right in Joshua's heart. She could be saying it to Joshua himself.

"Good morning, Mr. Landsverk." Miss Christopherson wore a bright smile. "I'll have your breakfast out shortly. You want to start with a cinnamon roll? I'm sorry they aren't fresh today. They were baked yesterday. I'll warm it for you."

"That would be just fine. I need to leave early this morning, so could you please fix my dinner pail right away too?"

"Right away." She paused. "Are you feeling all right?"

"Yes. Just a lot to think about."

"All the responsibility of your job would cause me to lose sleep too."

"Right." *If only it was the job and not my life that's hanging in the balance.*

Let go. That's all he had to do. *Let go.*

He set the men to building forms for the next pour, an addition to the rear of the last one and half as large. By the time they finished this, they would be ready to strip off the former and begin framing the walls. When the new men came . . . That was another of his concerns—how to handle a crew that didn't all speak the same language. How would he know what they could do? Toby would be having the same problem over at the hospital. Life used to be so much easier. Digging wells and erecting windmills. A couple of days and the job was done, and they were on to the next. Almost like Gypsies.

He heard the westbound train whistle off in the distance. Now, that would be an idea—gather up his tools and get on that train. But, as Pastor Solberg reminded him, running hadn't solved his problems before. He'd sold his land and gone home, only to return to Blessing, mostly because of his memories of a certain yellow-haired girl. And now he might have lost her.

"Joshua, there's a man here to see you about a job," Mr. Geddick called to the front of the building.

"All right." He strode around the corner of the original building, hearing a familiar whistle. "Aaron, is that really you?"

His brother turned and raised his hand. "Guess it is. You said come, and I came as soon as I could." The two met and started to shake hands, but Joshua grabbed his baby brother in a back-thumping bear hug.

"Talk about a sight for sore eyes. You are it." He stepped back, hands clasping his brother's shoulders. "Thank you for coming. How's the rest of the family?"

"Doing well. I think Frank wanted to come too, but he can't

seem to leave that poor piece of dirt. I'm glad to be away, just like I know you are." He looked down the main street. "Looks to be a thriving place."

"Blessing is that. Come along, and I'll introduce you to the big bosses, finer men you couldn't find anywhere. We got some other men coming in on the train from New York—immigrants. Good thing you worked on a building crew for a while. You'll like it here." He named all the buildings as they strode the block to the newspaper office, now also the main construction office. Pushing open the door, he stepped inside.

"I got us a new man come to work here," Joshua said as he stepped to the side and indicated the man behind him. "My younger brother, Aaron, ready, willing, and able to work."

"Glad to meet you, Aaron. I am Thorliff Bjorklund, and you are hired on your brother's recommendation. When do you want to start?"

"Now is fine with me. Don't have any other plans for right now."

Thorliff turned to Joshua. "I take it you'd like him on your crew?"

"If that is all right."

"Suits me. If you need to buy any tools, you can get them at Blessing Mercantile. Penny will expect payment on payday. We pay the first and third Fridays. Each of our foremen keeps track of his crew's hours. Do you have a place to stay?" While Aaron shook his head, Joshua nodded his.

"He'll room with me until my house is roofed in. Then we'll sleep there. Still take our meals at the boardinghouse." Joshua nodded to Thorliff. "Thanks."

"Thank you for finding us some more hands. Any more brothers we can entice to Blessing?"

"I wish. I've been working on my brother-in-law, though. Since our dad died, I think my sister needs some new faces in her life. Her husband is a good worker. We'll see."

He ushered his brother out the door. "Well, how about that?"

"Good. Pay's more than once a month too."

"And Pa isn't here to claim half your paycheck."

"That's for true. I always figured that was one reason you moved on."

Joshua nodded, the remembrance of his father huddled in his chair blocking out the earlier memories. "Do you have a trunk or anything at the station?"

"Nope. Just my bag of tools and a carpetbag of clothes. And my banjo, of course."

"Good. You'll find a fine bunch of musicians here. We play for church every Sunday morning."

"A banjo in church?"

"We don't have an organ, so we make do with what we have. We play for dances and parties too." He pointed to where his tool-box stood against a wall. "Put your stuff over there." He chuckled when his brother flinched at a whistle blowing. "That's the noon whistle. You can share my dinner pail, and then I'll show you what to do."

The day seemed to glow with a bright sheen after that. He paired Aaron with Mr. Geddick and set Jonathan to measuring and sawing. By the time the evening whistle blew, he'd nearly forgotten his discussion with Pastor Solberg. Until he showed Aaron the cellar for his house and after supper the plans for the kit he'd ordered.

"I own the land free and clear but will still have some to pay on the house."

"Are you buying that house on credit? You know what Pa always said."

"I know. I thought long and hard on it, but I have a good job, and I'll have it paid off in six months. Other than my rent at the boardinghouse, all my money goes into that house." He almost said he was building it so he could marry Astrid but cut himself off before having to think on that *Letting go* idea again. Maybe tonight he'd sleep decently. He needed all the energy he could find to keep up with all the changes.

11

M other, there is no reason for you to get up so early to have breakfast with me." Daniel Jeffers met his mother coming out of her room at the boardinghouse.

"But I have always made your breakfast, and at least I can pretend, can't I?"

Daniel shook his head and held out his bent arm to escort her to the dining room. "After breakfast, what do you have planned for today?"

"I have been invited to a tea being held in my honor. Mrs. Wiste says this is the best way for me to meet some of the women of the town. During the winter they meet monthly for quilting but take a hiatus in the summer, thus the tea."

Daniel tucked a smile behind his mustache. Now she sounded

more like the woman he'd known all his life, rather than the ghost who'd inhabited that body since his father disappeared. "I'm glad to hear that. Where is the tea to be held?"

"At Mrs. Wiste's house. Two o'clock this afternoon. She said someone would come to walk me over there. Isn't that dear of her?"

"Yes, it is. It is indeed." He patted his mother's hand on his arm. "I know that Mrs. Knutson is interested in starting a lending library here in town. I thought that might be of interest to you too. You will surely meet her there today." *And getting you out of this boardinghouse is the best thing imaginable.*

"How many years did I serve on the library board at home, I wonder?"

"Sometimes I thought you lived there or at the church. I hope Mrs. Bjorklund is feeling well enough to attend."

"What happened?"

"She collapsed after a run across a field to save her little granddaughter, who was choking. Mrs. Bjorklund was the first this town had in the way of medical help. Someone told me she is a natural-born healer, but I've also heard that she gives God all the glory for helping His people."

"There is only one church in this town, isn't there?"

"One very dynamic church." He pulled out her chair at the table. Glancing around the room, he realized it must be later than he thought. He knew Joshua Landsverk would already be on the job, and if the man's brother was anywhere near the kind of worker Joshua was, they had a real team with the Landsverk men. How he wished his father were there to see the enthusiasm the people of Blessing had for the product he had dreamed up. Knowing the inventiveness his father had possessed, he was sure there were other things he'd created but had just not quite perfected. He'd have to bring out all the drawings and diagrams and papers of half-done ideas the next time he went home.

"Miss Christopherson asked what you wanted for breakfast."

"Oh, sorry. Sometimes my mind just runs away from me or with me, as the case may be."

"His father, God rest his soul, used to do that all the time. Why, he'd be talking, then go silent, then jump up and run to his workshop before he lost the idea."

Daniel smiled up at the young woman. "Whatever Mrs. Sam has made for breakfast is fine with me."

"I saved you some ham steak."

"You are such a jewel, Miss Christopherson. Two eggs over easy and toast, then?"

"Would you rather have biscuits?"

"Fine. I know Mother raves about the biscuits here."

"One day, when I have a house again, I'd like that biscuit recipe," his mother said. "They would float off the plate if one didn't grab them quickly."

"I'll tell Mrs. Sam. We have fresh raspberries—with cream and sugar?"

"Oh yes, please. At home I would have been out early picking ours. Surely we can bring some starts here." She glanced at her son, who nodded. "Do you think Mrs. Sam would be offended if I went out in the garden and picked some of the berries?"

"Not at all. I'll be right back."

Daniel leaned back in his chair. How happy his father would be to see his wife coming back to life. He swallowed hard. What would people think to see a man crying in the dining room over raspberries? Some days he missed his father so much it was like a brick of lead sitting on his heart. This seemed to be one of those days.

His mother took her napkin from the ring and laid the white square in her lap. "So what are your plans for the day?"

The same thing she'd asked his father every morning. Daniel leaned forward and propped his elbows on the table, then removed them at the slight frown that drew her eyebrows together. "I'll be in the office all day today. We definitely need more office space, but that will have to wait until we have more carpenters. Which may be soon. I don't think I told you that Mr. Gould from New York has located some immigrant builders for us to use on the project. They are on the train heading here as we speak."

"Where will they live?"

"Here at the boardinghouse until we figure something else out. We could set up tents for them to use until the fall, if need be. Our biggest concern is the language barrier. I do hope some of them have learned at least rudimentary English."

"I used to teach English to immigrants. Do you remember?"

Daniel stared at his mother and then smiled at Miss Christopherson as she set their raspberries before them. "Thank you."

"You're welcome. I'll bring the rest of your meal when it is ready." The woman smiled and turned back toward the kitchen.

He returned to his mother. "I was much younger then. But now that you mention it, you taught a group at the church. Do you remember what you used for supplies?"

"A blackboard, paper and pencils, or slates if need be, and *McGuffey's First Reader*." Her answer came so quickly that he wondered if she'd been pondering what she would do there as well.

"What languages did the people speak?"

"Makes no difference. I spoke and wrote English, and they learned. Quickly too, I might add." She folded her hands and bowed her head. "Would you like to say the grace this morning?"

Daniel did and dug into the brilliant red berries floating in rich cream. "Oh my, I had forgotten how good fresh raspberries taste."

As they finished their breakfast, he asked, "Do you mind if I suggest to Thorliff that you would be willing to teach an English class to the new workers? Maybe two or three nights a week?"

"Not at all. Perhaps I can borrow supplies from the school here."

She sipped her coffee. "Now you just go on to work and leave me here to drink my coffee. I know the way back to my room." Her eyes twinkled, another thing he'd been missing.

"Thank you, Mother." He wiped his mouth and tucked his napkin back into the ring. Rising, he dropped a kiss on the top of her head and, waving at Miss Christopherson, headed for the office.

The rasp of saws and the ring of hammers announced that the carpenters were hard at work on both projects. The grinding stones of the flour mill were strangely silent, as they were being cleaned and readied for the upcoming wheat harvest. The local harvest would start in two to three weeks he had heard, barring unforeseen catastrophes. A grasshopper invasion had taken out wheat fields, gardens, and anything growing farther south last year, thus cutting back on flour production. At least his father's invention was one more asset for the farmers to help them improve the grain production. It seemed that with so many possible strikes against them, a good year was almost more of a miracle than something to take for granted.

Thorliff was setting type when Daniel arrived.

"Do you never sleep, man?"

"I just came in early," Thorliff said. "I sure wish Astrid were here. She could set type faster than anyone I ever saw."

"I'd say setting type might be a bit beneath her skills now that she's a doctor."

"Of course, but if I said I needed help, she would be here if she could."

"I take it she takes after her mother?"

"Come to think of it, I'll bet Mor would be good at this job too."

"Maybe you should ask Inga, or does she not know all her letters yet?"

"Give her a couple of days and she probably would." Both men chuckled at the thought of the little girl standing on a stool to set the type in the tray.

"Her arms probably aren't long enough." Thorliff studied the layout before him. "She'd have to grow some first. I hear there is a big to-do today."

"Mother is so excited. It's the first time I've seen her this interested in anything since Father disappeared. I knew coming here would be good for her. I know for certain it has been for me."

Thorliff paused and smiled at his friend. "For all of us."

By the time Daniel had finished telling Thorliff about the teaching job for his mother, both men were talking so fast it was amazing either understood anything the other said.

"I ordered one of those typewriter machines the other day," Daniel told him. "You know, the one we saw advertised in the Grand Forks paper. Wish we could find someone here who wanted to learn to use it besides me. They say women learn to use it even faster than men. Fast as your fingers go setting type, you would be a natural. Anyone who plays the piano is good too."

"What about Gould?"

"Maybe he's already learned to use one. Lots of eastern companies have been using them for some time."

"Maybe I should expand the help-wanted ad to include this qualification." Thorliff raised one eyebrow.

"Did you send it out yet?"

Thorliff nodded. "To the *Minneapolis Star*, the *Grand Forks Herald*, and the *Chicago Tribune*."

"What about Bismarck and Fargo?"

"I'll add those to the list. I need to send it to Duluth too. Uff da!"

"What happened?"

"I messed up this line."

"I'll leave you alone." Daniel went into his office, which was not much larger than the desk and the file cabinet in the corner. Where would he set up the new machine when it arrived? More space was going from a good idea to a critical one. Thorliff's mention of his sister brought her to Daniel's mind. He wished he'd had a chance to talk with her more, but they were rarely in Blessing at the same time. He'd sure heard a lot about her, however. It was amazing how much she had accomplished already for someone so young. It almost seemed miraculous. What a mind she must have. Besides the fact that she was a lovely young woman.

He pushed thoughts of the younger Dr. Bjorklund out of his mind and sat down to begin writing letters, which seemed to be his primary job lately. Setting up appointments for his next sales trip took an inordinate amount of time. By dinnertime he had a stack of mail ready to take to the post office, so he stopped there on his way back to the boardinghouse to eat.

"Why hello, Mr. Jeffers." Mrs. Valders leaned forward. "We are so delighted to be honoring your mother today. Thank you for bringing her here to us. And, of course, for bringing your business here. I've been putting your mail in the newspaper box, but any time you would like to take out a separate one, you just let me know."

"Thank you, Mrs. Valders." He handed her the packet rather than sliding the letters through the slot. "I'll let you know." He turned to leave and nearly bumped into a young woman he'd not met before. "Pardon me."

"My fault. I wasn't paying attention." She stepped to the side, as did he, both at the same side. First to one side and then the other. He stopped and smiled. "If there were music, we could dance." He lifted his brown felt hat. "I am Daniel Jeffers, and I know this is not a proper introduction, but—"

"I am Deborah MacCallister."

"Haven't I heard your voice before?"

She smiled. "You might have. I have a part-time shift on the telephone exchange board. I am glad to meet you."

"And I you. Have a pleasant day." He touched the brim of his hat and continued on out the door. She was probably married, like all the other young women in Blessing. He shoved his hands into his pockets and whistled his way toward the boardinghouse. Other than the lack of marriageable young women, Blessing was still the town of his dreams. And his dreams were growing bigger by the day. At least they would be if enough trained men could be found to build his father's machinery.

12

Are you sure you feel up to attending the tea?" Freda asked, standing arms akimbo, a frown adding wrinkles to her forehead.

"Of course. What do I have to do but sit there and be polite?" Ingeborg smiled gently. "I have told you and told you that I am fine. In fact, I feel better than I have in a long while." She took a basket off the kitchen counter. "The peace of God is mighty restorative, you know. Now, you go change so you will be ready too."

"I am not going."

"Freda, why is it you refuse to attend the few social events we have in Blessing?"

"I guess I am just not a sociable person. I'd rather hoe the garden or wash the cheese molds than sit there and make polite talk. Besides, I never know what to say. Please don't make me go."

Ingeborg shook her head at the piteous tone. "I won't make you go. Short of wrestling you to the ground and tying you up to drag you . . ." She blew out a disgusted breath. "But you can't work all the time."

"Look who's talking."

Ingeborg heard the grumble, although she had the feeling she was not supposed to. Freda had gotten up before dawn in order to be at Ellie's to start the bread and pies for the haying crew—the final day, according to Andrew. They would have only a couple of weeks before harvest started. With everything late this year, the beans would be ready to can about the same time they were cooking for the threshing crew. While the threshing crew was working the wheat fields around Blessing, the women all brought food to the kitchen wherever the big steam engine was set up to separate the wheat kernels from the straw. Farmers from the smaller farms hauled their sheaves of wheat to the steam engine and threshing machine and hauled home the straw, which was blown into that same wagon. The burlap sacks of wheat went directly to the flour mill and the storage granaries. None of the local farmers sent their wheat to the Twin Cities flour mills any longer, and so were not forced to pay the outrageous shipping costs. The farmers in the Dickinson area, in the southwestern part of the state, had done the same thing. Their flour mill was even older than the one at Blessing.

"I thought you weren't supposed to take anything." Freda nodded toward the basket.

"I just tucked in a jar of raspberry juice and some of the cookies you baked yesterday. I know there will be a lot of children there, and you know how they love cookies and swizzle."

"Meaning Inga and Carl. You'd take the moon along for those two."

"Anna is staying with little May. I am delighted that Ellie is getting to go. She misses out on so many things during the winter because

Carl catches so many colds. I keep thinking there must be some kind of remedy to help that. Maybe I need to do more research again."

"Ellie is picking you up?"

"Yes." Ingeborg checked the mirror to see that her Sunday-best straw hat was on straight. "I hear them now. You can telephone me, you know, if something happens."

"Like what would happen? I'll be out in the garden or out at the cheese house."

"I do wish you would come."

"Have a nice time. And don't let Mrs. Valders irritate you."

Ingeborg rolled her eyes. "Heaven forbid."

"Grandma, Grandma!" Carl bounced on the seat of the buggy. "Sit with me."

"Where else would I sit?" Ingeborg set her basket on the floor and stepped up into the swaying buggy. "There now. Thank you for driving today, Ellie. Andrew said he'd hitch up the horse, but I'd rather ride with you. How is May today?"

"Just fine. You'd never know there had been anything wrong."

"Good. Elizabeth said I did the right thing. A child not breathing like that is so terribly frightening."

"Seeing you fall to the floor was just about as bad."

"Grandma sick?"

"No, Grandma is not sick." She kissed the little boy's nose and then his cheeks, making him giggle. "Grandma feels better than she has for a long time."

"Grandma sick on floor."

"That scared him pretty bad too. He plunked himself down beside you and kept crying and patting your hand. Talk about having the whole family involved."

"That's just the way it should be. I asked God if it was time for me to go home, and He must have been smiling, because there was such a radiant light around me. He said, 'Not yet,' but that I must rest for a while. I guess I did just that."

"I guess so." Ellie covered Ingeborg's hand with one of her own. "I am so grateful He left you here with us. I never would have forgiven myself."

"Oh, Ellie, please don't think that way. You would do anything to save your child, as would I, and that's the way it is supposed to be. If we don't forgive ourselves, it's like saying the crucifixion didn't count. That Christ died for nothing."

"I hadn't thought of it that way before. No, I believe that Jesus died for us and forgave our sins." She puffed a sigh. "We sure do have the most enlightening discussions."

"Me too," Carl said.

Trying not to laugh out loud, Ellie and Ingeborg stared straight ahead.

"I received a letter from Ma yesterday, to say she cannot come next week."

"Oh no, I was so looking forward to seeing her. What is wrong?"

"She says she cannot leave Pa alone."

"Oh, Goody . . ."

Ellie handed Ingeborg the letter.

Ingeborg looked up when she finished reading. "Ellie, I am so sorry. Maybe you should take the children after harvest and go see her."

Ellie nodded. "I'll talk to Andrew. Maybe you could come too."

"We'll see."

Ellie tied up their horse in the shade of a cottonwood tree at Sophie's house, and the three of them walked through the gate of the picket fence and up to the door.

Ellie picked up Carl. "Do you want to knock?"

"Yes." He leaned forward and banged the heel of his hand on the wooden door, more like a thud than a rap. "Use your knuckles, like this." Ellie showed him how, and a nice rap sounded.

Carl grinned at his mother. "You good." At her nod he copied her actions.

"How about we do this together?" Mother and son rapped on the door, and it flew open, with Inga and five-year-old Grant as greeters. Carl flailed his arms until Ellie put him down, and he ran to the other two cousins.

"Play now?"

"Come with us." Grant took his hand, and the three dashed off.

"I think the welcoming committee is headed to the backyard to play. We'll just go on in." Ellie and Ingeborg followed the sound of female voices to the parlor, where all their friends were gathered.

"Oh, Ingeborg, Ellie, I didn't hear the doorbell." Wearing a dress designed to disguise her expanding middle, Sophie crossed the room and took their hands. "Let me introduce you to Mrs. Jeffers. She is such a delight."

Ellie and Ingeborg allowed themselves to be led across the room and waited while Hildegunn Valders chatted with the newcomer. Finally Sophie interrupted. "Mrs. Jeffers, I'd like you to meet Ingeborg Bjorklund and her daughter-in-law, Ellie. Ingeborg is one of the original settlers who founded Blessing. Ellie is married to Ingeborg's younger son, Andrew."

Ellie nodded and smiled. "I am glad to meet you. Welcome to Blessing."

"Thank you, Mrs. Bjorklund." Mrs. Jeffers turned to Ingeborg. "My son has spoken of you and your husband so often that I feel like I know you already."

"Thank you. We did meet the day you arrived on the train, but you were so weary, you probably don't remember."

"I remember being greeted by a gentle-voiced woman. Thank you for making me welcome that day too. My time here has been greatly recuperative, and now I am glad to meet so many delightful people."

"You have a fine son, Mrs. Jeffers. I know he will be a great asset to our community."

"He most certainly is," Hildegunn said. "Why, think how much we've needed a real business to come to Blessing. Producing machinery that will be available to farmers across the country," she said, waving her arm in a wide circle. "Isn't that just marvelous?"

Ingeborg and Kaaren exchanged glances across the room. Farming was not a *real* business? Inside Ingeborg could feel her fume heating up. Her cheese house was not a real business either? Leave it to Hildegunn Valders to sidle up to the new woman in town and at the same time set those who already lived there on edge. She relaxed her jaw and saw Penny standing behind Mrs. Geddick, who was whispering with Mrs. Magron.

"Shame that Mrs. Garrison could not be here," Sophie whispered as she walked by, the set of her shoulders giving away her disgust. "I know she and her husband are too busy working at their business to relax for an afternoon tea, but I was hoping."

"What about Maydell?"

"She says that morning sickness is a lie. Even a gentle ride to town was not possible. You think Dr. Elizabeth should go to see her?"

"Perhaps I'll go see her. She might need a mother more than a doctor. Thanks for telling me."

The doorbell rang, and Ingeborg went to answer it this time—a good way to get out of the room and back in control of her tongue before she said something unwise.

"Sorry I'm late," Mary Martha Solberg said as she entered. After one look at Ingeborg's face, she paused. "Oh-oh. Trouble already. Let me guess, Hildegunn's mouth is—"

"Is running away with her, as usual. I'm glad you could come, and I hope you stay nearby to pinch me if I start to respond." They strolled to the parlor. "Let me introduce you."

"Will we get a word in edgewise?" Mary Martha, who was

excellent at pouring sweet oil on troubled waters, gave Ingeborg a bit of a nudge.

"Pardon me, Hildegunn. Sophie has asked that I introduce Mrs. Solberg to our new guest."

"Oh, of course." Hildegunn was all smiles and sweetness again. "Mrs. Jeffers, this is our dear pastor's wife, Mary Martha Solberg. If you ever need anything, she is a good one to call."

"Why, thank you, Mrs. Valders," Mary Martha said. "I am delighted to meet you and so grateful that Sophie, er, Mrs. Wiste, thought to invite us all like this." Mary Martha leaned forward the slightest bit. "I do hope you will love it here in Blessing like the rest of us do."

"I'm sure I shall," Mrs. Jeffers answered, leaning forward herself. "Could you possibly show me the way to the ladies' room, please?"

"Of course. Right this way." Mary Martha stepped back, managing to bump Mrs. Valders as she sat next to the guest's chair. "Pardon me, Mrs. Valders, we'll be right back."

As the two walked down the walnut-paneled hall, Mary Martha said, "First doorway on the right."

"Thank you. This is indeed a lovely house, isn't it?"

"Yes, and Sophie loves to welcome people both here and at the boardinghouse."

Mrs. Jeffers continued down the hallway to the bathroom, and Ingeborg joined Mary Martha.

"Are you all right?" she asked.

"I am. Just taking a breather." Mary Martha gave a little snort and straightened, shaking out her skirt in the action. "John keeps reminding me that God loves everyone equally, but I sometimes think some people must try His patience more than others."

"Of course we are not mentioning names."

"Right. Nor are we letting a plethora of nonsense— *Plethora*, isn't that a nice word?"

"It is."

"We won't let a plethora of nonsense disturb our serenity and joy in being together for a change."

"Amen to that."

"I will go brave the lion's den, and you will escort our guest to the dining room, where the tea will be served."

"Yes, my friend, I will do that. I suppose that escaping outside to enjoy the children would be considered a faux pas?"

"Indeed it would." The two women smiled at each other. "We need to do this more often." Mary Martha sailed back down the hallway and into the fray.

"Oh, Mrs. Bjorklund . . ." Mrs. Jeffers said as she emerged from the bathroom.

"Yes. Mrs. Solberg had something to attend to. We didn't want you to get lost here."

"I see." Mrs. Jeffers tucked her lawn handkerchief into her waist-band and paused. "Isn't the laughter of children one of God's greatest gifts?"

"It is. Do you have grandchildren?"

"One for sure and one on the way. My daughter's children. I am hoping they will decide to come here to Blessing too, as I know Daniel has his heart set on building the business his father dreamed of."

"You must miss your husband terribly. After all the not knowing what happened."

"I know my Daniel is in a far better place. The Lord said He has prepared a home for us. For a time all I wanted to do was follow him there, but my son brought me here for a reason, and now I am looking forward to learning my place here."

Ingeborg nodded. "You have come a long distance, both in miles and in faith, I would say. And health too."

"I have. Thank you for recognizing that." She sighed. "I would appreciate it if you called me Amelia."

"And I am Ingeborg. Your son is named after his father, then?"

"Yes, they even have the same initials, but their middle names are different. My son is Daniel Jacob and his father Daniel John. That is why he is not titled *Junior* or *the second*. I don't know why we did that. It is confusing."

"Thank you for the information. Sometimes we did things when younger that we wonder about as we get older."

"So true. I have a favor to ask. I would like to talk with Mrs. Knutson if you could arrange that."

"I'll make sure she sits next to you." When they entered the dining room, Ingeborg caught Kaaren's eye. "There, she has a place available beside her." The two women made their way down the table length. "Kaaren, Mrs. Jeffers—Amelia—has something she'd like to discuss with you. May she sit here?"

"Of course. How fortunate I am."

Mrs. Jeffers sat down and Ingeborg went to help Sophie and her sister-in-law serve the platters of tiny sandwiches, bars, cookies, even filled tarts and fancy cookies cut across a two-toned roll.

"How absolutely lovely."

"I found a book on serving teas, and we used those receipts. We need to do things like this more often."

Knowing she would opt for more simple fare, Ingeborg agreed on principle. Quilting had been left until fall because, with all the gardening and putting food by for the winter, the women felt there just wasn't time. And there wasn't, but everyone had commented on how much they missed their get-togethers.

"Have you heard anything more from Astrid?" Mrs. Geddick asked when Ingeborg held the platter for her to choose from.

"No. Nor from Haakan either. But they should be home this week, according to Pastor Solberg."

"I am so relieved and grateful that our supplies were able to save lives like that. God has given us great opportunities to share the abundance we have been given."

"He has indeed blessed us mightily," Ingeborg said.

"Well, it isn't as if we haven't worked ourselves nearly to death for what we have," Hildegunn chimed in.

"That is true," Mary Martha said. "But the Bible never says we would have a life of ease. Just the opposite. God commends the hard worker in many places and castigates the slothful."

"Jesus said we are to sow our seeds in good ground, and we have that here," Dorothy Baard said as she helped herself to the delicate offerings. "My brother settled in northern Minnesota, and he often says he would like to take a wagonload of our good dirt home with him." Dorothy smiled at Ingeborg. "Your Roald and Carl did a fine job choosing this location with its good soil."

"Ja, they were careful and strong men of God. Roald often said that this was our promised land, that God led us here and said to stay here."

"Even now we have things so much easier than you did in the beginning." Mary Martha shuddered. "I remember living in the soddy. I've never been so cold in my life as that winter. Four feet from the stove, and the water bucket had ice on it." She smiled at those around the table. "Remember how we had to make hay twists to have something to burn in the stove? The clinkers along the railroad tracks were pure gold."

"I remember when we bought the buggy. Riding in that made me feel like the queen of the land," Kaaren added. "So when God sends us someone in need, as He has the Indians, I think he is asking for our coat. But Jesus said to give the cloak too. I feel guilty that I have not gone that far."

"Because we give of our abundance, not like the widow who gave a mite, and Jesus knew it was all she had."

"What do you think Astrid will find for us to do next?" A chuckle made its way around the table at Penny's sally.

"So what year did you come here?" Mrs. Jeffers asked Kaaren.

"We came in 1880. Twenty-four years ago. When I think of all that has happened in these twenty-four years . . ." She paused and shook her head. "More than anyone could have dreamed of, I think. Ingeborg kept us alive and saved our land after our husbands died."

"And you refused to allow me to live in the black pit of despair that I fell into. God kept us together for a reason. Two women proving up a homestead. But we had friends. The Baards came first. I will never have a dearer friend than Agnes Baard."

"And one winter, we were near to dying in a little shack. My father had died, and we were sick when the Bjorklunds found us and took us in." Ellie smiled at Ingeborg. "I was such a little girl, but Andrew said right from the first that one day he was going to marry up with me. He was my champion all through school."

Mrs. Jeffers leaned forward and looked around the table. "Is there someone here who is writing these wonderful stories down? Surely this is an important part of the history of this region. I know things were difficult for early settlers, no matter where they went, but this is fascinating."

"I know Thorliff has written some things down. He's turned other events into stories. Some he's published in his own newspaper, some in others."

"Someone needs to write a book."

"Well, it surely won't be me," Sophie said. "Would anyone like more to drink? There's still plenty of food left."

As everyone declined, Mrs. Jeffers smiled and continued. "Didn't my son tell me that many of the women here have businesses of their own?"

"We'll go around the table on this one. I own a cheese house, and we ship cheese all across the country." Ingeborg smiled.

Penny spoke next. "And I own the general store. I sold it for a while but then took it back."

"That imposter who almost destroyed the business?"

"Yes. That was a hard time." Penny looked to Rebecca Valders.

"I own the ice cream and soda shop, but I close it up for the winter."

Mrs. Valders chimed in. "Well, I don't exactly own a business of my own, but I am the postmistress, and my husband runs the bank."

"I see," Mrs. Jeffers said with a smile. "Important positions."

"Sophie owns the boardinghouse. Her grandmother willed it to her," Ellie said.

"And my mother owns a school for the deaf because her daughter Grace, my twin sister, was born without hearing," Sophie said when it came her turn. "Mor learned sign language to teach us all how to talk with Grace."

"I own the surgery, or rather Thorliff and I do," Elizabeth said, continuing the introductions. "He built the house. In medicine it is called a practice rather than owning, but I'm the doctor here. Along with Astrid, when she comes home again."

"Mr. and Mrs. Garrison own the grocery store."

"Such industry going on here," Mrs. Jeffers declared. "I am certainly glad that my son came here and decided to build the business here. I think we will fit right in." She smiled at Sophie. "You are such a dear for welcoming me this way. Thank you."

As the women stood and the conversation increased, Ingeborg stood by Kaaren. "A most interesting afternoon."

"I agree. Kind of the lull before the storm, with harvest so close upon us. I think we need a party once all our children get home and before others leave. Why don't you suggest it?"

"Why don't you?"

"Because you are the party instigator, along with Sophie, of course."

"However, if I suggest it, you know Hildegunn will argue about it, and I've gotten by without an argument today. I don't want to break my record."

Kaaren grinned and shook her head. "Maybe I can get Penny to bring it up." She moved to Penny's side and waited while she said good-bye to Mrs. Jeffers. As Penny turned to leave, Kaaren touched her arm.

"Yes, Kaaren?"

"Didn't I hear you mention we needed a party before harvest begins?"

"No, but I think it is a marvelous idea. Harvest is still two weeks out?"

"I think so."

"Good." Penny raised her voice. "What do you all think of having a pre-harvest party?"

"Where?"

"Our barns are full of hay."

"What about the schoolhouse? The play yard is packed hard enough for dancing. We can have a fire there and serve the food inside. If it rains we could move the party inside like we have in the past."

"Good, I'll tell Thorliff to put an announcement in the paper." Ingeborg smiled at Mrs. Valders. "So good to see you, Hildegunn. You are usually behind the counter. I'm glad you could take time off to join us for the tea."

"Why, thank you. It's good to see you too."

Ingeborg could tell by the puzzled look on her nemesis's face that she'd caught her off guard. Maybe that was the best way to handle the woman, so there would be no more confrontations. Maybe.

13

ROSEBUD INDIAN RESERVATION
SOUTH DAKOTA

D ear Lord, do I take them with me or hope they come on their own?"

Astrid paced the width of the infirmary building again. Not that pacing helped her to think any better or to pray with more attention, but she couldn't seem to sit or stand still. While she'd written of her idea in the letter to Elizabeth, there had not been a way to get an answer back before they left. Her far and the boys had the wagon packed with their things, including some gifts from her grateful Sioux friends.

If only Red Hawk were there. If only she knew for certain he was coming to this forsaken tribe rather than going to the main Rosebud station. If only. She knew better than to think that way. God said

He would provide, and He would. When and how being the only questions.

This particular question involved the two older women who had been so faithful in caring for the sick members of their tribe. While she could tell they didn't always agree with her methods, they were willing to learn and to follow her instructions. Wouldn't that be a remarkable gift to give to Red Hawk—two nurses, minimally trained, for sure, but ready and eager to learn more? When they returned they would be able to bring medical supplies back with them, if the people of Blessing would continue with their generosity.

So now what to do?

"Dr. Bjorklund, are you all right?"

"Yes, of course." She turned to greet Mr. Moore, the Indian agent. "How may I help you?"

"Mrs. Moore said she talked with you, and you told her that all her symptoms indicate she is . . ." He heaved a sigh and stared at his dusty shoes, then looked up at her again, red heat creeping up his neck. "Uh . . ." Another deep breath.

Astrid took pity on him and said gently, "In the family way?"

His nod and flash of a smile thanked her. "She wants me to take her back home to her mother, so she will be closer to a doctor."

"I know." She schooled her face so as to conceal her opinion of his wife's idea.

"Do you think that is necessary?"

Oh, I wish you'd not asked me that. Astrid swallowed a sigh. "That is between the two of you. I know she is not happy here." *But she is making no effort to make friends or show any caring for the Indians.* "Cooping herself up in the house is not good for her health or the baby's. She needs to walk or garden or do something to build the muscles for childbearing." *Even scrubbing the floors would help, or cooking. She needs to get moving.* If only she dared say these things aloud.

"I wish you could stay here or come back when she is close to her time."

Heaven forbid. She would be up in arms if I told her what I believe is necessary for a successful pregnancy. Sitting around in corsets and all those clothes can only cause problems. Astrid knew that nearly fifty percent of babies didn't make it to their first birthday, if they even lived through delivery. And so many women died in childbirth, mostly, she was convinced, because of the corset and lack of exercise. Farm women did far better than city women. Why couldn't women listen to common sense?

He heaved another sigh and slowly shook his head. "I was just beginning to get things in order here, and to leave it now means that by the time I can return, I will have to start all over again." He sounded so sad, Astrid felt even worse for him.

"You could get her to the train and let her return to her home that way. That wouldn't take as long."

He half snorted. "Perhaps. If I had any sense of certainty that she would return." He looked out across the hills. "I am just beginning to see the beauty in this place, to value these people that I am serving, to see them responding. Thanks to you and your folks here, there is still enough of the tribe alive that they can grow again and return to being the proud people I recognize them to be."

"Mr. Moore, I wish there were some way I could help you, but I don't see how."

"Yes, well, thank you for trying. Thank you for keeping these people alive. I do hope that when Dr. Red Hawk comes, he will continue your good work."

"Thank you." She paused, trying to decide whether to confide in him or not. "I have an idea that I would like to discuss with you."

"Of course, I am at your service."

"You know the two women, Gray Smoke and Shy Fawn?" At his nod, she continued. "I would like to invite them to come with

145

me back to Blessing and give them some training in medical things so that when Red Hawk comes, these two women will be able to assist him."

"And you are leaving? When?"

"Tomorrow morning. But I could delay one more day, if they would come."

"Have you mentioned this to He Who Walks Tall?"

"No. Nor to the women." *Nor to any of the people in Blessing, other than in my letter to Elizabeth.*

"What does Mr. Bjorklund say about this?"

"He is ambivalent. My father has a gift of seeing both sides of a situation. The good and the bad."

"The bad being they would leave their own people and their way of life and stay with white strangers who do not know the Indian way of life," he said. "Some of whom may be anti-Indian."

"Yes, but the good side is that they will return with skills to help their people and Dr. Red Hawk. They could learn some of the white man's language. Red Hawk, by the way, speaks excellent English and could be a fine doctor anywhere. He has a deep appreciation for the needs of his people. Hopefully, these women will see Christian love in action and be drawn to faith."

"You wish you could help me, and I wish I could help you." He stuffed his hands into his back pockets and studied the ground, shaking his head. "You could talk to He Who Walks Tall. He could help you the most."

"Thank you for your time, Mr. Moore. I shall continue to pray about this. And I will pray for you and Mrs. Moore too."

"Thank you."

"Go with God."

She turned and walked back to the wagon, where Haakan was greasing the axles. Samuel and Johnny were brushing the horses and checking the harnesses.

"What did he say?" Haakan asked, looking up from his task.

"His wife wants to go home to her mother to have their baby, and while he didn't say so exactly, he wants to stay here."

"Ah, quite a quandary."

"He asked if I would come back near her time, but Red Hawk will be here by then, and he knows how to birth babies."

"You can't be everywhere at the same time."

"I know. But I am back to my ongoing question. What is it God wants me to do in this particular instance? Take the two women back with me for training or leave them here? Offer to return for Mrs. Moore's lying in? I have a feeling she will not listen to my advice and will have a hard time carrying the baby and birthing it too, let alone recovering from the ordeal. I feel sorry for Mr. Moore."

"Ja, me too." Haakan straightened and twisted his body from side to side. "I am ready for my bed at home. I know your mor is praying and watching for us every day. I believe our job is finished here—at least for now. And I am glad Red Hawk will be here before the fall sets in. Perhaps he can be more instrumental in the tribe receiving all they have been promised."

"One thing I know for certain: Red Hawk believes in the value of education and learning to live and thrive in the white man's world. Yet he is very proud of his heritage as a Lakota Sioux Indian."

She found He Who Walks Tall sitting under a tree, his back board braced by the trunk so he could breathe more easily. After they exchanged greetings, she sucked in a breath and began. "I have a favor to ask of you, involving something that will be of benefit to your people." He nodded for her to continue. "I would like to take Gray Smoke and Shy Fawn with me to Blessing to be trained as nurses. I could ask Dr. Red Hawk to stop in Blessing when he is done in Chicago and bring them back here with him. They have been a great help to me, and if they could learn more skills, you would have better health care here."

He studied her, his face so impassive that at first she wasn't even sure he understood what she was asking. Except she knew he spoke English but disliked using it.

"What if they do not want to go?"

"That would be their choice." *But I know that if you as the future chief ordered them to go, they would do so.*

"And your people are inviting them?"

That was the sore point. "Some are . . . Well, most would be."

"And Dr. Red Hawk approves?"

She shrugged. "I don't know. But I can't imagine why he wouldn't. I will contact him as soon as I am able."

"And send them back if he says no?"

"I know he wishes for all his people to be educated, and this would be an education for the two women. I have a feeling they were beyond school age when the tribes lived closer."

"You are correct."

"But they learned quickly as they helped me."

"My people are not stupid."

"No, of course not. I meant . . ." Astrid heaved a sigh of frustration. Why was he twisting her words?

"I will think on it."

"Thank you. We are leaving early tomorrow morning." She waited a moment for him to respond, then turned to return to the infirmary, which would now be used for storage for food and supplies. At least until Red Hawk returned.

Gray Smoke was working over the fire, stirring a kettle of bedding in boiling water with soap.

Astrid wanted to stop and lay out her plan, but something warned her to keep her mouth closed. So she smiled instead and went to pack the remaining bandages, utensils, and supplies in the wooden boxes that had brought other supplies on the wagons. The boxes were strong enough to resist the mice and rats that could and would chew through about anything, even though there was no food packed away.

Her mind leaped ahead. They were going home to Blessing. No matter the distance, thanks to the trains, they would be home in three days. *I will take a bath in a deep bathtub and wash my hair and clothes and all we are returning with.* Which wasn't much, as the blankets and sheets were needed here, along with the cast-iron pots, the tripods for the fires, and sharp axes. While Haakan had showed the tribe how to plant wheat, the season was so far gone that if they had an early freeze, the wheat would not be harvested.

———

AS THE EASTERN HORIZON lightened the next morning, the two older women stood waiting at the door of the infirmary, two small blanket-wrapped bundles at their feet. Astrid greeted them, knowing that her face revealed her delight and not caring if they knew how relieved she felt. She had seen these two women laugh and tell jokes that made others laugh, she had seen them cry when children had died, and she had seen them go without sleep and food so that others might live. She knew they would make good nurses.

"Thank you for coming."

They nodded and picked up their bundles.

"This takes great courage, my friends." Since she still wasn't sure how much English they understood, she decided to start teaching that on the wagon and train rides back to Blessing.

Dear God, please make this all work out, both for these women and for the people of Blessing. I prayed and I am going on the premise that this is your answer. After they all said good-bye to Mr. Moore and the gathered Indians, they stepped into the wagon and Haakan clucked the horses forward.

The sting of tears behind her eyes made Astrid blink rapidly and sniff. While they had saved lives, too many people had been lost. Should she write a report and send it to the Bureau of Indian Affairs? Would it do any good? Surely someone in the governing body cared about the people she was leaving behind. At least they needed to know about the failure to keep the word given to them.

Her father leaned over and patted her shoulder. "You did your best. Now let God worry about the rest. He has broader shoulders than you do."

"That's a good reminder. Thank you." She lifted her face to the sun already floating on the horizon. Would she be back? Only God knew, and He seemed to be operating in His one-step-at-a-time mode.

They arrived at the train station after dark, but the full moon had well lit their way. Rather than finding lodging, they wrapped themselves in their blankets and slept either under the wagons or in them. While the two Indian women had talked to each other, they'd not responded much to Astrid's efforts to engage them in what little conversation they could have. How she looked forward to help from Emmy, who might be able to talk with them. It was a shame she'd not explored more of the Sioux language with Red Hawk, but whoever would have thought she'd need to speak Sioux? Metiz had spoken a mixture of Sioux, French, and English, so that wasn't much help either, and besides, she'd only picked up a few words, like *merci* and *bonjour*.

When they loaded the wagons and the horses into the cattle car, the Indian women walked on and sat in a corner by themselves. Haakan had watered the horses well and filled the water barrel on the side of one of the wagons while Astrid bought bread and cheese and cans of peaches at the local grocery store for them to eat on the trip north. When she handed each of the women a peppermint stick, they smiled and nodded. Candy, like smiles, was the universal language of good will.

"So how will we teach them both the language and the needed medical skills at the same time?" Astrid asked her father.

"Like your mor would say—"

" *'Pray first and know that God is taking care of this.'* Yes, that is drummed into my head too."

Haakan chuckled. He'd purchased a newspaper at the station and returned to his reading. Johnny Solberg leaned back against the quilt he'd propped in a corner of the wagon and, after tuning his guitar, practiced chords and strumming and then picked out some songs. Samuel took out his knife and a piece of wood he'd found and resumed carving on it.

The train started with a whistle and a jerk, and Astrid breathed a sigh of relief. They were heading home to Blessing. A verse floated through her mind. *For the Lord will go before you.* He'd led them to the reservation, and now He was bringing them safely home. Would they all be welcomed, or was she taking her two new friends into captivity?

14

"At least we didn't get shunted off to wait on a siding."

"Was that a possibility?" Astrid stared at her father. She'd not slept well; the noise and rocking of the train had awakened her several times. One time she woke because a baby was screaming, only to realize that was a dream. Her two future nurses woke her early with their humming. Were they singing to comfort themselves or to ward off evil spirits? Of course that would be comforting too. At least it was cooler during the night. Riding in the Pullman coaches would have certainly been more comfortable than riding in the cattle car, but sometimes one had to take what one was given and be grateful for it. And riding on the train was definitely faster than going by wagon.

She brushed the cinders from her hair and coiled it into a bun at the base of her skull. Even though she washed, the vision of soaking in a real bathtub like the one at Thorliff's made her sigh. At least there would be one available when she settled in at home.

While they waited in Fargo for a northbound train, Haakan sent a telegram, telling Thorliff when they would be arriving, so he could tell the others. Meanwhile, Astrid wrote a letter to Red Hawk and sent it with her father to be mailed. The boys found a place to buy doughnuts and brought a sackful back to the others. The two Indian women each took one and nodded, but it was not until after their first bite that their smiles appeared. Like candy, sweet baked goods were good ambassadors of friendship.

Soon they were on their way again, and Astrid dozed until they reached Grand Forks, where they left off several passengers and picked up more. It seemed to be a busy travel day.

As the train left Grand Forks behind, Astrid went to stand at the rear of the cattle car and looked out between the slats that comprised the walls. Ahead of her lay the flat Red River Valley with fields of near-to-harvest golden wheat rippling before the wind and an occasional farmhouse with barns and outbuildings. It looked so much like home. Haakan joined her and began identifying the farms.

"Do you know them all?"

"No, but most. Many bring their wheat to our flour mill, and others I know through the Farmers Union meetings."

"I know you'd like to be more active than you are."

"That's right. Since we don't have a chapter in Blessing, going to Grafton for meetings is just too far to go very often. But I get their newsletters and am grateful for the impact they're already starting to have on our government. Now, if someone could convince those who own the railroads to charge less for shipping, life would be better for all the farmers. They convinced us to farm this land, and now they try to strangle those of us who work the fields and need a way to get our products to market."

"Is it terribly costly to ship Mor's cheese?"

"Ja, but we can set our price for the cheese to include the shipping. The mills in Minneapolis and St. Paul and the railroads dictate the price we get for wheat. Like the stockyards of Chicago do for our livestock."

"I read about strikes happening in other parts of the country, people being killed or maimed."

"And losing their jobs. It's a terrible thing for a man to lose his job and way of taking care of his family. Take the coal mines." Haakan stared up at the blue bowl with white puff clouds that arched above them. "I cannot begin to imagine what it would be like to work in the dark far below the ground." He shuddered. "We are so blessed out here with fresh air, sun, and the wind dancing with the wheat."

Astrid smiled at her far. Every once in a while he'd say something poetic like that. Her mor often wrote those phrases down, called them Haakan's bits of wisdom.

"We're almost there."

The whistle blew, announcing the train approaching the depot. Astrid checked to make sure her belongings were collected and in the wagon, and then approached the Indian women. "We are almost there. Do you want to come see?" She beckoned them with one hand and returned to stand at the slats. They joined her, all of them clutching the slats as the train slowed. "See? This is my home, a town called Blessing." She spoke slowly and distinctly.

"You home?" Gray Smoke asked.

"Ja, my home. We all live here." She indicated the menfolk with a sweep of her hand. Now she wished she'd asked He Who Walks Tall more about the women and their backgrounds. While she knew they'd not been to school, had they ever lived in a house with four walls and a roof? Had they ever spent any time in one, other than the infirmary? She remembered her months of homesickness both in Chicago and at missionary school. Would these women suffer the same way she had? Or possibly more, since they had no idea what they were there for. Or maybe the brave had explained what they would be doing. Clinging to that hope eased the guilt a little.

A crowd of people had congregated at the station to welcome them home. As they walked down the ramp from the cattle car, Astrid heard Benny yelling, "My Doc is home again. My Doc is home again." She looked for his scooter but instead found him on his pa's shoulders. Gerald held on tightly to the boy's thighs, because he was waving his arms and shouting.

"Hi, Benny," Astrid called as she waved back, her whole insides laughing along with her little friend. "We are home."

Her mother greeted her on the platform with open arms. "Uff da, it feels like you've been gone for months, not just weeks." She dropped her voice. "I see you brought company?"

"For nurses training. They helped me so much. I want them trained to help Red Hawk even more so." She reached up to shake Benny's hands and turned to hug Rebecca. "I see the little one has grown some." She patted the little bulge under her friend's loose dress. If only she'd been able to convince Mrs. Moore to dress like this rather than in style.

Astrid turned back to lock arms with her mother. "So you don't get away from me." She blinked and sniffed. "I have missed you so much."

"And I you."

"I need you to tell me all that has gone on while I was gone."

"Not here. There are too many people who want to see you. Come home after you settle your things at Thorliff's."

Astrid hugged her mother's arm, enjoying the way Ingeborg kept on talking with her and yet kept checking on Haakan. "He's fine, Mor. Thinner, like we all are, but he was the rock we needed. I have some funny stories to tell you too."

"Good."

The men backed the wagon out of the train car and down the

ramp, then hitched the team back in place. Thorliff left them and came to greet her. "Do you have any idea where your two guests can stay while they are here?"

"I figured someone would invite them." She followed her mother's indication and saw Kaaren talking with the women. "See, all taken care of."

"What about their training?" Ingeborg asked.

"Elizabeth and I will have to work that out. I'm hoping you and Tante Kaaren will help too. Deborah agreed to do nurses training too, so maybe we should ask if there is anyone else who would like to take part."

Thorliff nodded. "Good idea. I know we've heard from Chicago regarding staffing for the hospital. They too plan to use this as a training facility."

"I know. Isn't it exciting?" Astrid glanced up to see Mrs. Valders glaring at her. *Ah, the trouble has begun.* Why did that woman think she should have the final say on what any of them did? What did it matter to her if they were training Indians?

Thorliff patted her arm. "Don't worry about some of the people. This will all work out."

"I can't understand how you can keep ignoring that glare, Mor. It stabs like an icicle."

"Our mother is a saint. That's how," Thorliff said.

At Ingeborg's chuckle, Astrid continued. "Well, her daughter isn't one by any stretch of the imagination." She sucked in a deep breath. "Pray for me." She strode toward Benny's grandmother.

"Good day, Mrs. Valders. You must be so proud to see Benny become a part of Blessing. Look at him up there, so happy and making other people laugh. If you had seen that boy the first time I saw him, it would have broken your heart."

The frown softened, and a smile fought for her mouth. "Ja, Benny is the delight of our lives. I can never thank you enough for thinking of bringing him here to us."

"Spoken like a true grandmother. I do hope you can welcome these other strangers into our midst like you did Benny. These women worked beside me night and day to try to save the lives of their people. If we can train them to help Dr. Red Hawk, think how blessed they will all be. Another blessing going out from Blessing." *Thank you, Lord, for giving me words for my mouth.*

"That is true. I guess it was just the shock of seeing them. Can they speak English?"

"Not very well. I'm hoping someone here will help teach them."

"You know, Astrid, God does indeed begin the answers before we can even ask them. Mrs. Jeffers was saying at the tea we gave in her honor that she would be glad to teach English to the immigrants Mr. Gould is sending out here to help with all the construction. Can you believe that?"

Astrid chuckled. "I can believe it, even though I feel I am so far behind on what is going on here that I might be a stranger myself."

Mrs. Valders patted her arm. "Oh, never you, dear Astrid. You are one of the first daughters of Blessing, and just see all that you girls are accomplishing."

If Astrid hadn't felt her mother standing behind her, she might have fainted at Mrs. Valders' response. She smiled again. This time it came easily. "Thank you for your information. How would we ever get along without you?" Astrid couldn't believe she was saying such a thing, and the miracle was, she meant every word.

"Astrid?"

She thanked Mrs. Valders again and made her way among the now dissipating group to her tante Kaaren's side.

"If it is all right with you, I will take these two home with me," Kaaren said. "We can put them up in one of the girls' dormitories. We could use one of our classrooms for a training room too. I know your mother and I can do much of the basic training. Then you and Elizabeth can set up more complicated sessions."

Astrid hugged her aunt and whispered in her ear, "You and Mor listen to the Spirit so well. I know I should just expect that God has it all worked out, but I am amazed to see His hand so definitely in action."

"You prayed for help, right?"

"Of course. I try not to run ahead of Him anymore." She shook her head. "But in bringing them, I was afraid I might have. There just wasn't enough time to send letters back and forth. I'm sure He blesses the telephone lines too."

"All good and perfect gifts come from Him. . . ."

"I know, and now I know even more so." She pointed to each of her two nurses and said their names. Then she pointed to Kaaren and said her name. The Indians nodded and repeated *Mrs. Knutson* together. "You go with her." She took their hands and then Kaaren's. "Friends." They grinned.

"I'm thinking that Emmy might help as translator if their languages are close enough."

"Oh, Astrid, the uncle came for Emmy, and she left with him. Your mother is heartbroken. When she asked him to bring Emmy back for school, he appeared to nod, but your mor told me she's not sure if she only imagined his response."

So much for that idea. "Poor Mor."

"It was a blow, and having Haakan gone so long was hard too, since they happened at about the same time."

"I should have sent him home with Pastor Solberg."

Kaaren cocked an eyebrow and turned her head. "You, send him home? You are joking, right?"

Astrid chuckled. "Sometimes I let the title of doctor overtake me and forget I am a daughter first."

Kaaren leaned closer. "You know the main reason he went was to make sure you, his youngest child, were safe."

"You coming with us, Astrid?" Ingeborg called from the wagon seat. In spite of their normal injunction against showing affection in public, she had her arm locked through Haakan's.

"No, but I think these two are." She smiled to her charges. "Go with Mr. Bjorklund in the wagon, please. I will talk with you tomorrow."

They nodded, but she was sure it was fear she saw in their dark eyes.

She looked each one directly in the eyes. "It is safe here. Good place to be." She tried to use other words they knew. "I will come soon."

Both women nodded, but their usually ready smiles were not visible. *Lord, please make them feel at home here. Feel safe and comfortable. Give us wisdom in caring for them and training them.* Could they speak with Red Hawk on the telephone, or would that frighten them even more?

After they waved good-bye to those in the wagon, Thorliff carried her bags over to his house, where Astrid had taken up residence before she left for Rosebud Reservation. "It sounds like your dream was answered—to make a difference?"

"Yes, it was. But all those deaths were so unnecessary. I don't know how to prevent the measles, but those people were nearly starving to death in addition to suffering from the disease. There is no excuse for our government not keeping its word and getting them the necessary supplies. I know there can be mix-ups and the previous Indian agent was a crook, but is there no one to oversee these things?"

"I have a feeling it will be a long time until this is all sorted out. Too many people hate the Indians, and the Indians hate the whites. We are so fortunate to have had Metiz as a friend. Other places have both nations living in peace, but too many are not. And too many in the government are Indian haters. They hate the Negroes too. You know the term *white supremacy*. They are wrong, both according to God's Word and according to the laws of our land."

"Maybe you should run for a government office."

His snort made her smile. "If anyone runs for a public office again, it should be Hjelmer. He likes that kind of thing. I have enough to do here to keep three men busy."

"Couldn't Hjelmer help you out here?"

"Ja, if he didn't want to keep his own businesses going."

"Isn't it interesting that instead of farming, you and your partners are building business companies and houses, and you run a newspaper? You are out of time and out of enough men to do the work. Do you ever think about how God is blessing us here in Blessing? Pastor Solberg and I had some good talks about this. He's right in that we need to keep deep in God's Word and listen closely to His guidance."

"Now you sound just like your mother."

"And that is a bad thing?"

"No, not at all. Mother is one of the wisest people I know, and Far is close beside. They have trained us well." He carried her bags into the house and, dropping the black bag in the office, carried the other one up the stairs and into the spare bedroom she always slept in when she was there.

"I could do that, you know."

"I know, but give me a chance to do something for you for a change."

"Where is Inga?"

"Playing over at Sophie's. And Elizabeth is sleeping, or she would have met us at the door."

"Is she worse?"

"No. Much better, but she has learned to take her rest when she can. I put that one up on the list of miracles."

His chuckle as he left made her smile. Should she take that bath now or wait until that night?

"Astrid, is that you?"

Tonight would be bath time. "It is," she called. She dumped her bag out on the floor. Everything in it needed to be washed. Picking up her hairbrush, hairpins, and toiletries, she set them on the top of the chest of drawers and bundled the clothing to carry back downstairs to the wash.

"Give me a couple of minutes, and I'll come see you." When Elizabeth agreed, Astrid carried the clothing down the stairs, dumped it all in the laundry baskets, and greeted Thelma as she came in from the garden with her apron full of just picked vegetables.

"You don't know how hungry I am for fresh food. It was too late to start gardens down there for this year, but Far plans on going back to help in the spring."

"We will keep extra seeds this year, then." Thelma emptied her apron onto the counter by the sink and looked Astrid up and down. "You've lost weight."

"I know, but it is hard to eat one's fill when others need the meal more. Far made sure I took time to eat more often than I'd remember."

Astrid picked up a carrot and twisted off the feathery top. Scrubbing it under the faucet, she waved it at Thelma. "This is good for both body and soul." Back up the stairs she went, munching as she climbed. She stopped in the doorway and watched Elizabeth sitting on the bench seat in front of her dressing table, brushing her hair. With color returned to her face, along with some of the weight that had melted off her during her illness, Elizabeth looked better than she had for months. *Thank you, Lord.* She caught Elizabeth looking at her in the mirror. "You have improved greatly."

"I know. My skirts no longer fall off me." She smiled, the wide smile of the Elizabeth she used to know. "Welcome home. It feels like you've been gone for months."

"That's what Mor said. I wasn't home much after medical school and missionary school. But we did what we needed to do on the reservation, and I know lives were saved because we went."

"That is the right answer. Did you bring the Indian women with you as you mentioned in your letter?"

"I did. Kaaren has taken them under her wing. I heard that Mrs. Jeffers said she'd like to teach English to the immigrants, so I hope she will work with Gray Smoke and Shy Fawn too. Remember the brave who almost died from fever? It so happens he is not only the tribe's future chief, by the name of He Who Walks Tall, but is also a cousin to Dr. Red Hawk. Their resemblance is truly amazing. I do hope Red Hawk will be able to work with this small band. They need so much, from food to farming to sanitary conditions."

"You didn't sound too pleased with the wife of the Indian agent."

"Not at all. Mrs. Moore is pregnant but insists on wearing corsets and the tightly fitted styles. She hates living on the reservation and wants to return to her mother's house to have the baby. It was all I could do not to scream at her and walk out. She also wears the white powder on her face that I have read is poisonous." Astrid shook her head. "She is also young and afraid."

"I can tell you are still upset with her."

"She refuses to sit out on the front porch in the breeze. Instead she sits in the stifling house. I pity the poor Indian woman whom she is teaching, if you can call it that, how to be a household servant." Astrid shuddered. "Enough of that. It just makes me angry, and there is nothing I can do about it. We did what we could there. Both Johnny and Samuel did men's work. I was really proud of them."

"So now you are back. And besides ordering the supplies and readying the hospital when it is completed and tending our own patients, you want to start a nurses training program, not only for Deborah but for the Indian women too. Anything else?"

"Yes. I want a bath and clean clothes."

"That is the easiest wish of all to manage." Elizabeth's smile dimmed. "Thorliff said Joshua made a comment about building his house for you."

"Oh. I thought we dealt with all that."

"You don't care for him, then?"

"I thought I could care for him if there was any chance we could make a marriage work, but he cannot accept that I am a doctor first and would be a wife and mother second and third. I won't be yoked that way. So no. I do not love him, and I will not marry him." Astrid heaved a heavy sigh. "I thought I had made that clear." Why, then, did she feel a rip in the vicinity of her heart? "What is it you are thinking?"

"I'm just trying to see how much this is common sense talking and how much is Astrid, my beautiful sister-in-law, who felt so strongly that she had found the man of her dreams."

"Some dreams die hard."

15

As soon as Grace gets home, we are going to have a girl party at my house." Sophie spoke in a way that left no room for arguing. Some things never changed.

"I think that is a grand idea. Will we stay all night?" The telephone call from Sophie caught Astrid just after her discussion with Elizabeth. And before her bath.

"I doubt it. Too many are mothers now that want to go home to take care of their babies. I said we have plenty of room, they should bring them along, but I doubt they will."

"Do you know when Grace is coming?"

"We're not sure. She was supposed to be here in June when Jonathan came home, but they offered her a nice bonus if she stayed at the school for the summer."

"What about Maydell?"

"I'll see. I think she is feeling better. Your mor gave her something that helped."

"Oh good."

Astrid looked down at a tug on her arm. "Just a minute." She bent over to hug Inga and scooped her up in her arms. "Uff da. You are getting so big."

Inga kissed her tante on the cheek before announcing, "Ma said to tell you we are going out to Grandma's house for supper."

"We are?"

"Uh-huh, but you can't stay there. You live here now."

"I do, eh?"

Inga nodded and slid back to the floor. "Ma is out on the porch with cookies." She grabbed Astrid's hand. "Come on."

"Let me finish my telephone call first."

"All right."

Astrid smiled and returned to the call. "I'm sure you heard all that?"

"I did," Sophie said. "When she heard you were home, she dashed out of here like hornets were chasing her. We never get to be together anymore. Someone is always leaving, it seems."

"All except you?"

"Strange, isn't it? I was the one who wanted to leave Blessing behind and go on adventures, and now I find plenty of adventures right here in our own, used to be little, town."

"It isn't so big now either."

"No, but it is growing and will be growing even faster. Oops, gotta go." The telephone clicked off. Astrid hung up the earpiece and turned to see Inga watching her. "What is it, little one?"

Inga flew into her arms. "I missed you so. You were gone forever. And Emmy's gone too. What if her uncle won't bring her back and I never ever see her again?" She buried her face in Astrid's shoulder.

Astrid rose from the floor and, taking Inga's hand, crossed the room to a chair, where she sat down and pulled the sobbing little girl into her lap.

"All the Indians I know always keep their word. I am sure he will bring Emmy back if he said he would."

"But Grandma is so sad. Her eyes never laugh anymore."

"Oh, I think her eyes will laugh again. So we are going out to the farm for supper?"

"Ma said so." Inga mopped her eyes with the back of her hands. She looked up to Astrid. "Emmy didn't even get her kitten, but I kept it for her. Benny got one too. His kitten rides in his cart with him. Sure wish I had a cart, but Pa said I have two good legs and don't need a cart." She slid to the floor and pulled on Astrid's hand. "You want to come see me and Emmy's kittens? They are growing up fast."

"Is she talking your ear off?" Elizabeth asked when they stepped out onto the porch.

Inga looked up at Astrid and shook her head. "She has two ears."

"That's a figure of speech about someone who talks a lot." Elizabeth patted the cushioned bench beside her. "Come sit here by me and let Tante Astrid catch her breath." When Inga's mouth opened, her mother shook her head. "That's enough now."

"And the kittens are where?" Astrid asked, taking pity on her niece.

"Sleeping in their basket over there." Inga pointed to a basket in the shady corner. She started to slide off the bench, but her mother touched her arm and shook her head.

Astrid smiled to herself. Elizabeth was obviously trying to settle Inga down, but that would take more than a couple of weeks. "It feels like I was gone for the longest time."

"Or forever," a little voice chimed in.

"We were so busy, the days flew by. Then when Pastor Solberg left and there were not so many critically sick to take care of, I had bits of time to think on our nursing program."

"Lying around here, I've had plenty of time to think too. When I could stay awake, that is."

"Has Mor been in to help you?"

"Yes, but people in Blessing have been wonderfully healthy this summer. No accidents, no babies being born, all the winter croup and coughs gone—you'd think our dream of a hospital was a waste of money, time, and effort."

"Well, I saw many people die because they didn't have any medical care. I cannot begin to describe how bad it was."

"Pastor Solberg came by one afternoon and left me with nightmares. What if we had an epidemic of smallpox or something here?" She sighed and sipped her dripping glass of lemonade. "I know we vaccinate against smallpox now, but there will be other diseases."

Astrid sipped her lemonade. This didn't sound like the Elizabeth she knew. Had the trauma of losing another baby and nearly dying herself changed something in Elizabeth's mind? It wouldn't be surprising. Astrid realized she'd better keep an eye on things here at home and not be wandering off around the countryside in the near future.

"What do you think of our establishing a nursing school right now and not waiting for students to come from Chicago?"

"It looks to me like you went ahead and did just that." Elizabeth's smile belied any sting from her words. "I think it will be good for Deborah. And Kaaren and your mother will love doing this. If Mrs. Jeffers is serious about teaching English to the construction workers, two more students should be no problem."

Astrid bit her lip. "I just thought of something. From what Thorliff said, the students will all be men. Will my two friends be able to sit in the same class? I'm not sure that Indian women are allowed to intermingle with men like that."

Elizabeth stared back at her. "I think we need to be making a list of questions for Dr. Red Hawk and set up a time to telephone him."

"Maybe there could be two classes. What if Mrs. Jeffers spent time out at the deaf school at the same time as Mor and Tante Kaaren taught nursing techniques?" Astrid cocked her head. "Where is she going to teach the immigrant laborers?"

"I think you and I need to go to the boardinghouse and talk with her. Maybe this is more than she wants to do." Elizabeth glanced over to where Inga was sitting by the kitten basket, singing softly to them, trailing one finger over a furry body. "She so loves the kittens. She's calling hers Emmy."

"Emmy being taken away is so sad."

"It's been hard on both your mother and my daughter. The other children miss Emmy too." She shook her head slowly. "But not like those two."

"This continuous sadness isn't like Mor."

"I know Tante Kaaren is concerned. She said that years ago Ingeborg fell into the pit of despair, and it took a long time for her to be free of it."

"Mor has often spoken of the pit. She says that only the Word of God can free one. I wonder if she has been lax in her Bible reading." *Like I have? How does one put God and His Word first and still have time for all the things that need to be done? Like caring for His so very ill children?*

"What is it?" Elizabeth asked, her voice soft in the still afternoon air.

Astrid released a sigh that sounded as heavy as the humid air they breathed. "I think I am beginning to understand my mother more. Down on the reservation I had no time to read God's Word, or feed upon it, as the Scripture says. I learned the value of that at Bible school, and I thought I would always put Him first, but I failed. And the thought of that can be very destructive."

"That is a harsh word."

"Destructive?" She nodded. "True. But which is worse? The failing or the self flagellation? Are they equal sins? While I know that Jesus died to forgive my sins, I didn't want to commit these particular ones again."

Elizabeth smiled and nibbled on her lower lip. "We are so impossibly human. That's the problem."

"And confession is good for the soul?"

"True, but so is accepting forgiveness."

Astrid leaned her head against the back of the chair. "How can it really be so simple?"

"Simple maybe, but not easy. I think you need to spend some time with your mor. The two of you can help each other."

Astrid stared at Elizabeth. "When did you get to be so wise?"

"Nearly dying and spending all that time in bed, much of it contemplating, would change anyone, I imagine. Astrid, I am so grateful to be alive and growing stronger that I feel like shouting it to the world. God healed me. He let me live on this earth longer. Rejoice and be glad!"

The words fell with such intensity that Astrid sniffed back tears, blinking several times before sighing again. "Rejoice, indeed." The two clasped hands across the narrow space between chairs.

"Are we going to Grandma's now?"

"Soon, little one. Soon." Astrid turned her attention to the little girl. "Do you need to change your pinafore?"

Inga looked down and scrubbed at a dirty spot, then looked at her mother, who nodded. "I guess. But if I go out in Grandma's garden, I will just get more spots."

"She's right, you know."

"I know. But one must try."

Astrid stood. "I'm going upstairs to freshen up. I guess that bath will have to wait until later."

"Or you can take a bath now, and we'll wait until you are finished."

"No. I want a long soak, and Inga will drive you nuts with waiting."

"I will take her out now, and you can come with Thorliff when you are ready. And no arguing. I get enough of that from you know who."

Astrid started to say something contrary, but the call of a bath grew siren loud. "Thank you, I will."

Later, with the water cooling for the second time, Astrid stirred herself to let the water down the drain, then rinsed off. Her hair would never dry in time, but she toweled it vigorously and resolved to go brush it in the sunshine until it started to dry. Being clean again had been far more important than going home with dry hair. She dressed in clean clothes from the skin out and, brush in hand, headed to the back porch. The house was so still, she felt like tiptoeing, until she found Thelma ironing in the kitchen.

"Shame you can't just go up and sleep on through the night," the older woman said. "You looked done in."

"But better now?"

"True. There's cold juice in the icebox."

"Thanks, but later." The sun slanted under the porch roof, making one of the chairs the perfect place to sit, back to the sun, and finger-fluff her long hair. She should just comb it out and wrap it in a bun but instead sat listening to the hammering and sawing from the buildings going up. A slight breeze played with her hair as she tipped her head back.

"Sorry. I came looking for Thorliff."

The male voice made her jerk upright. "Oh, Mr. Jeffers, I . . . I don't know where he is. Did you look in his office?" Her fingers wanted to fix her hair. This was mortifying. The heat of her cheeks

171

nearly burned her fingertips. She should have known better than to sit outside like this, her hair down and uncombed. Ladies did not do such things. What must he think of her?

"I did, and he's not there."

"I think I am supposed to ride with him out to the farm." *Should I ask him to sit down? What to do?*

"Maybe he already left."

"Thelma's in the kitchen. I'll go ask." Astrid rose, trying to act as if she left her hair down all the time. "Be right back."

When she returned, she had twisted her hair into a rope and tucked it into a bun. "Thelma said he is already gone but to tell you that he plans to be in the office early tomorrow."

"Thank you." He smiled at her and tipped his head slightly. "I liked it better down." He turned and went down the steps, whistling a tune as he reached the street.

Astrid knew she should be indignant, but somehow all she could do was chuckle. She went upstairs, hung her towel up, and redid her hair into a snood before heading for the farm. The walk would do her good.

16

"Look who is here!"

"Grandma!" Inga darted across the room and threw her arms around her quickly kneeling grandmother. "Tante Astrid is taking a bath." The way she said the last word made her opinion of bathing quite clear.

Ingeborg kissed the rosy cheek and got to her feet. "How are you, my dear?" She held out her arms for Elizabeth to join them. "I don't see either of you enough."

"I saw you yesterday." Inga looked up at her mother, a slight frown between her eyes. "Wasn't it?"

"Two days ago."

"Oh. How come you didn't come to my house this day, after the train?"

"I needed to welcome Grandpa home and help our guests feel comfortable at Tante Kaaren's." She gave Inga a slight shove. "Maybe you could find a couple of cookies in the pantry."

"For just me or for us all?"

"Just you."

Inga gave a happy little skip as she crossed to the pantry.

Ingeborg turned to Elizabeth. "I have missed her."

"She has missed you. She said your eyes don't laugh anymore."

Ingeborg shook her head. "And here I tried to be the same as ever around her. How can one that young be not only so astute but also verbal enough to come up with that?" She blinked as if to remind herself where she was. "Please, sit down. Would you like coffee or something cold?"

"So she is right?" Elizabeth took the chair indicated. "You know, I think we would be more comfortable out on the porch. Unless there is something here that I can help you with."

"No, supper is in the oven. The lettuce is all washed and the beans snapped, ready to cook. I made beet pickles. I know how Thorliff loves them."

"Especially when made by his mor. What do you do that is different?"

"Some allspice and cloves—not much, just a hint."

"I will tell Thelma that. So we can go outside?"

"Certainly. Inga, why don't you put some on a plate for us as well?"

"Okay. One kind or two?"

"Some of each. With her everything must be precise. Sometimes I wonder how children get to be the way they are. And how they grow up."

"What was Thorliff like as a little boy?"

Inga returned with a plate of cookies, one kind to each side as if a line were drawn down the middle. "Outside?"

Ingeborg fetched a chunk of ice from the icebox and chipped it into the glasses, then poured in water and a red syrup. "Leftover strawberries. I sugared them earlier." Setting the glasses on a tray, she led the way to the back porch, where a late afternoon breeze had already risen.

"Thorliff worked so hard from the time his far died and hasn't stopped. I never could have done all I did had he not taken care of the animals and Andrew. Although Kaaren did most of the inside work, I worked like a man. It was thanks to her that I finally climbed out of the pit of despair. Her prayers and her oh-so-gentle love. I have so much to be thankful for."

"But now?"

"But now I have to throw this off, and through the grace of God my eyes will laugh again." She leaned over and touched the tip of Inga's nose with a gentle finger. "Thank you, little one, for the reminder. Grandma must not be sad any longer."

"Tante Astrid is coming soon."

"I know. And that alone makes me want to dance and sing."

Inga rose from the footstool she had chosen to sit on. "I can dance and sing with you. Ma, you sing too." She took Ingeborg's hand. "Come dance."

Ingeborg rose and took both of the little girl's hands. Humming "When Johnny Comes Marching Home Again," the two spun around and tipped from side to side. They danced forward and back, and Elizabeth tapped the time with her foot and sang along.

"Bravo!" called a voice from the gate.

"Pa!" Inga dashed down the steps and around to the gate. "Did you bring Tante Astrid?"

"No. I thought she came with you." Thorliff swung his daughter up in his arms and whirled her around again.

"She took a bath and said she would come with you." Inga wrinkled her nose on the bath word.

Thorliff carried her up the steps and set her down.

"How did you come?"

"I walked, since you had the buggy."

"So what happened to Astrid, then?" Elizabeth rose. "I'll go call her and let her know we are all here."

"I have a feeling she fell fast asleep after her bath." Ingeborg smiled at Inga. "But not *in* the bathtub." She pinched Inga's pink cheek gently. "Grandpa will be up from the barn shortly. Or do you want to go see him there?"

"He's milking the cows?"

"Yes. Along with Onkel Andrew and the others."

"You be careful and do not step in the manure." Elizabeth sipped from her glass. "Maybe we should just let Astrid sleep."

"She'll be upset with us. You know she hates to miss out on anything."

"Come on, Inga, you can ride on my shoulders and not get your pretty shoes dirty."

"I could take them off."

"I know." Thorliff swung her up on his shoulders. "You want any cream or anything, Mor?"

"No. I have plenty." The ringing telephone caught their attention. Two short rings.

"Your ring, Grandma." Inga waved as she and her father bounced down the steps, making her giggle and grab his hair, sending his hat flying.

Ingeborg returned to the kitchen to answer the telephone. "Hello?"

"Mor, is Thorliff there?"

"Yes, Astrid, he is. He is giving Inga a ride to the barn on his shoulders just now. Do you need him for something?"

"I had a long bath, and then I couldn't find him. Thelma said he left but didn't know where he went."

"We thought you might have taken a nap."

"No, not today. I'll walk on out."

"You want us to come get you with the buggy?"

"No, thank you. You want anything from town?"

"Just you. The men should be done with the chores by the time you get here."

"Bye."

Ingeborg hooked the earpiece on the prong, smiling as she did so. For a change she would have all her family around her again. Ellie and the children would arrive any minute. Sometimes the blessings got to be so much she could hardly keep from crying for joy. Using the hem of her apron, she dabbed her eyes and sniffed. *First, sit down with Elizabeth and enjoy my drink and then get supper on the table.* Tears of joy most assuredly felt different than tears of sadness. She much preferred the former.

She heard little feet running up the porch steps.

"Grandma, go to barn!" Inga had taught Carl to shout, and shout he did.

"Watch for Onkel Thorliff. He has Inga." *Or at least I hope he has her.* She knew how quickly that little sprite could disappear but reminded herself that Thorliff was, after all, her father. And he should know.

"Sorry we are late." Ellie carried May up the porch steps and sank down in a chair. "Andrew said he would build me a wagon, but the path is too rough for that, so maybe a wheelbarrow would be better. Ja, to carry May and Carl and the basket."

"I told you not to bring anything."

"I know, but we were out of cookies, and you know Andrew hates that. So I baked some and brought them along. And I made raspberry-rhubarb jelly today. It's the first time I tried this combination, and it is so lovely, I couldn't resist bringing that too."

Ingeborg took the jar of jelly and held it up to see the ruby red glow in the westering sun. "You are right. It is beautiful and will taste the best. I don't think I've made jelly out of that combination either. I'm thinking this year I shall make mint jelly, using some of the apple juice before I can it. The green food coloring makes it look so pretty."

"You are drying mint again for the medicine chest?"

"The first batch is hanging upstairs. Now that Astrid is staying at the surgery, I had Haakan hang me some bars from the ceiling in Astrid's room to tie the herbs to. It is plenty warm up there to dry them quickly. I need to go foraging one day soon."

"I want to learn more about the herbs and things you call simples," Ellie said, dabbing at her forehead and neck with her apron. "I will never know how you managed those years after Roald died. Two children, the house, and the garden and I am done in."

"There will be time for that. Right now you are as busy as can be. And that is as it should be." Ingeborg reached for May and snuggled her in her arms. She kissed the little forehead, one more time grateful that the Lord had guided her hand the day the little one was choking. Before long the scar would be nearly gone.

At the sound of male laughter, she handed May back to her mother. "You two sit here and visit, and I'll have supper on the table by the time they wash up." She smiled at her two daughters-in-law.

"Grandma, the barn cat had kittens," Inga said as she whirled onto the porch. "Four kittens. She brought them out to drink out of the flat pan. Did you see them?"

"Not yet. Do you want to wash your hands and help me in the kitchen?"

"Ja. I will." She took her grandmother's hand. "The mama cat caught them a mouse. It was dead, but they didn't want it. They had milk on their whiskers."

"Wash your hands and bring the salad from the icebox. The dressing is there too."

While Inga did as she was asked, Ingeborg took the smoked venison roast from the oven and set it on a board to slice. Setting the pan back on the stove, she sprinkled flour in a bowl and added hot water to stir the two together into a smooth paste, then stirred that slowly into the meat juices. She drained the new potatoes and added the water to the gravy until it was just the right thickness.

"I'll slice the meat. If you don't mind, that is." Standing at the kitchen counter, Elizabeth picked up the knife.

"Good. Inga, you shake this bottle of dressing, and we'll pour it on the salad." She turned to look at the table. "Oh, and the plate of pickles is in the icebox too."

When female laughter joined the male chuckles outside, she knew Astrid had arrived. And all was ready. She took the dressing jar and poured it around the bowl, tossing the lettuce and other vegetables with a fork at the same time. If only the tomatoes were ready, it would be so pretty.

"Grandma, where's the bread?" Inga picked up the salad bowl and set it on the table.

"Oh, I knew I forgot something. Bring the new loaf out of the box, and I'll slice it."

Haakan came through the door first, the joy of his return catching her again. On one hand it seemed he'd never been gone, and on the other he'd been gone forever.

"Something sure smells good." He paused and sniffed. "There is nowhere like home at suppertime."

"You didn't have to go do the milking tonight, you know," Andrew said, following behind him. "We've been doing just fine."

"Without me, you mean?" Haakan gave his son a raised-eyebrow look.

"We're glad to have you home, so don't go putting words in my mouth."

"Or thoughts in his head." Thorliff ushered Astrid before him.

"I noticed you arrived when we were about done."

"Of course. I've milked enough cows in my time. I'd rather build buildings and run a newspaper."

Ingeborg held out her arms and hugged her daughter, the bread slicing knife still in one hand. "Astrid, you are indeed home. I was beginning to think I'd only dreamed about hugging you at the station."

"She came to my house." Inga carried a plate to put the bread on.

"She probably doesn't even remember how to milk a cow." Andrew unwrapped Carl's arms from around his knee and set his son on the bench that Onkel Olaf had built to set on a kitchen chair so many years before. Sitting in the high chair, May banged a spoon on the tray.

"I think that is something one never forgets." Astrid took the bread knife from her mother's hand and started slicing the loaf, letting Inga arrange the slices on the plate.

Elizabeth set the platter of sliced meat on the table and fetched the bowl of potatoes while Ingeborg poured the gravy into a crockery pitcher. When they were all seated, Ingeborg at the end opposite her husband, Haakan bowed his head and waited for all to settle. "I Jesu navn, går vi til bords . . ." They all joined in, even Carl, who recited many of the Norwegian words correctly, especially the amen.

When Haakan finished the blessing, he sat for a moment, just looking around the table at those he loved. "This has to be the best way to welcome home travelers. I cannot begin to tell you how wonderful it is to see you all healthy and happy and working hard, living the lives God has given us, being together." His voice broke. He cleared his throat. "Thank you for coming tonight."

Ingeborg blinked back the ready tears. One day he would tell her what they went through with helping the Indians, but his speech showed it affected him deeply. Love for this fine man welled up so strongly she couldn't speak. Astrid glanced at her mother and then leaned forward to say, "Help yourselves to the food in front of you and pass it on," an admonition that usually belonged to Ingeborg.

The conversation picked up as the bowls and platter went around the table. Ingeborg watched Haakan nod and answer a question from Carl. He had been gone too long, and harvest would most likely start in about a week. Why did the thought of that bother her less than his trek south had? She caught a stare from Inga. Oh my, her eyes must have been looking sad again. That thought widened her smile, which brought back an answering one from her perceptive little grand-daughter, who then took a bite of her potatoes and gravy. Why had she not invited them all out when Haakan was gone? Because she'd let the pit draw her to the rim—that's why. She mentally shook her head. That was far too dangerous a game to play. *Lord God, thank you for saving me yet again.*

As the bowls emptied and her family refused any more food, she rose to begin clearing away the dishes, but Elizabeth and Astrid both shook their heads at her and took over. Sitting back down, ignoring the guilt that tried to ruin her treat, she turned to Thorliff.

"So catch me up on the latest news."

"Didn't you read the paper?"

"Of course, but that was last week, and I know something has to have happened since then."

"Our immigrant workers arrive tomorrow. Mrs. Jeffers has agreed to teach English to them. They will meet at the school in the eve-nings unless Sophie decides we should use the dining room at the boardinghouse. Her concern is for Mrs. Jeffers walking across town by herself."

Ingeborg's eyebrows rose in spite of her. "Is she frail?"

"I don't think so, but the move out here and losing her husband like she did have taken a toll. We'll get their house up as soon as we can."

"Uff da. Whoever would have dreamed we would have a housing

shortage in Blessing? Sometimes I think God is delighting in pouring His blessings down upon us."

"Leave it to you, Mor. That is exactly right," Thorliff said. "We built bunk beds for several of the larger rooms at the boardinghouse. That should serve for a time. Joshua's brother Aaron arrived."

Ingeborg glanced up to see her daughter watching Thorliff. Had she made up her mind about the young man in question?

With the plates cleared away, Astrid set a stack of dessert plates on the table and began cutting the pies. "Both rhubarb?"

"Yes."

"Rube pie. Grandma made rube pie." Inga clapped her hands.

Thorliff shook his head, and Inga turned to look at him. "Don't you like rube pie, Pa?"

"I love rhubarb pie."

"That's what I said." When all the others laughed, she giggled too. "Grandma makes the best pies."

"Me pie too." Carl banged his spoon on the table until Andrew laid his hand over his son's.

"You definitely are pie," Ingeborg said with a grin.

A knock at the door caught their attention. "Come on in," Haakan called. "You are just in time for dessert."

Joshua Landsverk pushed open the screen door and entered the kitchen. "Sorry to interrupt."

Ingeborg glanced at her daughter to see her smooth away the conflict that had tightened her eyes. "Not at all. Here, you take my chair and join us. I'll get the coffee."

"Thank you, but—are you sure?"

"Just sit down, Mr. Landsverk. My mother never says something she doesn't mean. Would you care for rhubarb pie?" Astrid did not smile as she spoke.

"Yes, please."

Astrid slid the slices of pie onto the plates and passed them around the table. Ingeborg poured the coffee, and the conversation picked up again.

When the table was cleared and Astrid and Ingeborg were washing the dishes, the others trooped outside to take up the chairs on the porch, some sitting on the flat railing board and the children on the floor.

"You didn't look happy," Ingeborg said as she set a washed plate in the rinse water.

"I'm not. I don't really want to see him, but I know we live in the same town, and it would be bad manners to ignore him."

"I think he still—"

"Has feelings for me? Then he should have been kinder, or rather, more understanding when we last spoke. I don't believe he would be happy married to a doctor. At least not this doctor."

"That happens to many female doctors. It takes a special man to have his wife gone hither and yon to care for her patients."

"Like Far?"

"Ja, he is indeed a special man. Roald would not have been able to adjust, I don't think."

"But people will be able to come to the hospital for care, and that should make it easier."

"You are saying you would not go out on a call?"

"Not at all, but . . ." Astrid looked at her mother. "Change, even good change, is not necessarily easy, is it?"

"No, it is not. But nothing is impossible with God."

Astrid heaved a sigh. "That sure was evident down on the Rosebud Reservation."

Ellie and Andrew came in from the porch. "We need to get these little ones home to bed. Thank you for supper."

Carl raised his sleepy head from his father's shoulder. "'Night, Grandma."

"'Night." She reached up to kiss his cheek.

Joshua stepped through the door. "Will you be going back to town, Dr. Bjorklund?"

Astrid nodded.

"May I walk with you?"

Ingeborg took the pan of dishwater to empty outside on her rosebush. *Lord, give her wisdom and the right words for this man.*

17

Thorliff helped his family into the buggy and turned to Astrid. "You want to ride?"

"No. I'll walk with Mr. Landsverk."

"You are sure?"

Astrid leaned closer to lower her voice. "I think this is necessary."

"No blood, now."

"Thorliff!" She whispered his name, but the rebuke was obvious. Turning to the man waiting a few feet away, she nodded. "Let's wait and let the dust settle a bit first."

They paused with neither one saying a word, the silence not one of comfort, at least not on her part. *It's a good thing one can pray in silence,* she thought as she pleaded for God to give her the right words.

"I thought maybe you were going to stay in South Dakota for the whole summer," Joshua said.

Astrid let that comment pass. "Our trip was longer than I'd anticipated." She started off down the lane.

"But you were able to save lives."

"As Mor would say, 'Thanks be to God.' " She fought to find something to say. "I hear your brother has arrived."

"He has. I'd bring all my family here if I could, but my older brother and my sister have decided to stay in Iowa. He has the family farm to run."

Astrid tried to think of something else to say, but everything she thought of would bring up their past.

"Miss Bjorklund, er, Dr. Bjorklund . . ."

She could feel her hackles rising, so she took a deep breath and kept on walking.

Joshua cleared his throat. "I know I have an apology to make."

Surprise caught her and stopped her in her tracks. She turned to watch him.

"I know I was out of line concerning your trip to the Rosebud Reservation. I . . . I'm sorry for getting so angry."

She watched his face, recognizing the strength it took for him to say that. "Mr. Landsverk, I accept your apology."

"Then we can go back to where we were and talk of . . . of ma—of courting?"

Astrid heaved a sigh. "I'm afraid not." She paused. Never had she intentionally wounded a man, but at the look on his face, she'd done it now. "I'm sorry, but I do not believe we are meant for each other. You need a woman who will give you her whole heart, who will think . . ." She stumbled. "I . . . I am just not that woman. My first calling is to be a doctor. Many female doctors never marry for this very reason. Others regret it and the marriage dissolves. Mr. Landsverk, I know there is the perfect woman for you somewhere, but it is not me."

When Joshua stared into her eyes, she could see both fury and sorrow.

He gave a brief nod. "I think you are wrong, but I will not mention this ever again. Good evening, *Doctor* Bjorklund," he said, emphasizing the word *doctor*, turned, and strode off toward town, his feet pounding the dirt, raising dust.

Astrid swallowed the tears and turned to stare at the setting sun, shimmering instead of clear. Why was life so hard at times? She thought of calling him back. Perhaps she was wrong. Was she throwing away the marriage she'd dreamed of? The only person she wanted to talk with was her mother. But she had looked so tired.

Lord, what do I do? This hurts. Why does doing what seems best have to cost so much? She gazed out across the land, watching the changing cloud and color patterns. North Dakota had a gift for sunsets. She'd seen nothing like this while in Georgia. The sky was slashed with vermillion, yellow, and orange, and then shaded to pinks on the clouds with just enough gray to make the colors flare. As the golden disc slipped below the horizon, a breeze waved the grass and kissed her cheeks, drying the tears and bringing her a peace that breathed all around her. Even the dirt under her feet seemed to hold her suspended, as if the entire earth waited with her.

Verses swam through her mind. *I know the thoughts that I think toward you . . . thoughts of peace . . . to give you an expected end. . . . Trust in the Lord with all thine heart, and lean not unto thine own understanding. In all thy ways acknowledge him, and he shall direct thy paths. . . .* The words poured through her mind and into her soul, bringing a comfort she had not believed possible. Until that moment. She blew a kiss toward her mother's house and turned to walk toward town. When she needed Him, Jesus indeed lived up to His Word to send a Comforter, to guide her step-by-step.

"Are you all right?" Thorliff asked when she entered the kitchen.

"I am."

"I saw Joshua come home alone."

"I know. I told him that I am not the right woman for him and that somewhere God has that woman waiting. He was not happy with my response."

"I'm sure he wasn't. He was building that house for you."

"I know. And I am sorry. But better to make the break now than down the road, when he cannot abide one more medical emergency." She poured herself a glass of water and joined her brother at the table. "I still do not understand his antipathy toward the Indians, but I hope he can let that go. Bitterness is a dangerous thing."

"It is indeed." Thorliff leaned back in his chair. "I hope he does not decide to leave Blessing. He has family here now, whether he can believe that or not."

"He has his house."

"Well, he has the basement dug out and the house on order. It should arrive tomorrow. He could sell that easily right now. But I hope he stays. Will that be difficult for you?"

"Not at all. I really want the best for him. We don't have to be good friends, you know. Although I think I can be a friend to him." *Maybe not immediately, but time does make some things easier.* She reached over and patted her brother's hand. "I think my time on the reservation gave me a better perspective on some things. He hated my going down there. That pretty much made up my mind."

Thorliff nodded. "I think that all those years Mor and Far prayed for us are producing the wisdom they asked for."

"They are the best examples."

"I know."

"I've prayed for wisdom so often. In Proverbs it says to seek wisdom with all your heart. To run after her. It is interesting to me that it speaks of wisdom as a woman, not just once, but over and over."

"I'd not thought on that." He smothered a yawn. "Right now wisdom says I need to get some sleep, to catch up with all that I've missed." He pushed his chair back. "Turn out the light when you come up."

She stood. "I am coming now. Tomorrow will be a busy day."

"Are there any that are not?"

"Not that I've noticed."

A bit later, lying in bed, she wondered again at the peace she still felt. She picked up her Bible and turned to Proverbs. She'd not memorized as much in the Old Testament as in the New, other than the Psalms. Maybe it was time to continue—starting with more in Proverbs.

18

"When will you be leaving, then?" Thorliff asked.

"Probably the day after tomorrow. I need to be in Minneapolis on Monday for the first appointments." Daniel Jeffers studied the calendar in front of him. "I should be gone about two weeks, and if I accomplish what I see as possible, we will have enough work to keep us going through the winter." Selling the idea had been his father's job, but *his* job was to sell the machinery they'd be building right there in their new plant. If only his father could be there to see the reality of his dreams.

"Well, if you meet any capable and trained machinists, hire them. And tell them to bring tents to live in. Also, I know the doctors are looking for staff for the hospital, including an administrator. And Elizabeth said she received a letter from a dentist who is interested in leasing space in the hospital for his practice." He glanced at the clock and noticed it was starting time for the construction crew.

"The house packages will really be here today," Daniel said. He was having a hard time believing this would really happen.

"They said they were shipped to arrive today. They'd better, because I've commandeered every able body I can to help and every wagon available to move the supplies to the appropriate lots. Our new workers should be on the train too."

A knock on the office door caught their attention.

"Come in," Thorliff called.

Joshua Landsverk pushed open the door, looking like he hadn't slept for days. "Good morning."

"Good morning. Is something wrong?"

"I've come to turn in my resignation."

"Good grief, man. Why?" Jeffers blurted out. But when he looked at Thorliff's face, he knew this was no surprise to him. Joshua was one of their two best men. He and Toby both ran their crews as if they'd been managing men for years.

"Sit down, Joshua." Thorliff motioned to the chair by his desk. "Do you want to tell us why?"

Joshua sat on the edge of the chair. "It's a personal matter."

"Regarding my sister?"

"I don't want to discuss that. I think it's better that I leave Blessing is all."

"But your brother is here now too."

"He can stay or come with me, no matter."

Questions bubbled in Daniel's mind like a pot of stew on full boil. He sat still in his chair, not even making notes.

"Joshua, there really is no need to leave Blessing. You have created a place for yourself here, and to be right up front, your leaving now would put us in a real bind." Thorliff scratched the back of his head. "We don't have anyone else to step into your job. You know how much construction is going on."

"I just don't know how I can stay here."

Daniel had heard that Landsverk was sweet on Thorliff's sister, even building a house for her, thinking she would become his wife. She must have turned his courtship down for him to want to leave like this. On one hand he felt sorry for the man, but on the other . . .

Thorliff leaned forward. "I have a favor to ask. How about tabling your resignation for a month? See how things go. My pa always says, 'Never make a decision in a hurry, especially one that could make a big difference in your life.' Let it rest and pray about it. In a month we can talk again. As much work as we've got to do, a month will go by so fast we won't keep up."

Joshua heaved a sigh through gritted teeth. "Okay. I hope you are right, Thorliff."

"Trust me. I've been in a very similar situation, and hard work is the best antidote."

Joshua nodded and settled his hat back on his head. "We'll get done what we can, then, before the train comes in, right?"

"Right. Then we'll all move housing materials. Right now I'm wishing we had a yard to store things like this in, but then we'd have to move it all twice."

"A yard by the tracks is not a bad idea. With some roofed sheds and an enclosed warehouse . . ." Joshua headed out the door.

"Right. Another major project to add to those we are already working on." Thorliff shook his head. "We all need to be ten men."

And I'm leaving town, Jeffers thought. He had struggled with this for the last two weeks. They all knew he needed to be out selling their machinery and searching for men to work in the plant. And like the coming hospital, they needed office people, preferably trained on the typewriter and in accounting. As far as they knew, no one in Blessing had that kind of training. He'd thought of the possibility of offering office training to Gerald Valders. Anner Valders had the skills to run the bank, but that was a full-time job. He brought his thoughts back to the needs at hand.

"Mrs. Wiste said the rooms are ready for the immigrant workers. She will bill us twice a month for their room and board. After that she will collect money from the men themselves. I sure hope they understand all that." Jeffers shook his head. "I feel like we are shooting rabbits in the dark."

"All will be well. I am quoting my mor. And I know one thing for certain, she is praying for all of this to work out, as is Pastor Solberg."

"I know they have prayed miracles into existence, and if this does all work out, we will put more up to their credit."

"They would say to give God the glory. Astrid and I were talking about wisdom last night. She said she has prayed for wisdom for a long time, even before she went into medicine. I tell you, I started reading Proverbs again. She lit a fire under me, but if you ever tell her this, I shall deny it to the death." The two men smiled at each other.

As if he would ever have a chance at such a conversation with the younger Dr. Bjorklund.

When the westbound train whistle blew, the entire town and countryside were gathered at the station. Wagons were lined up for half a mile, with the drivers shouting to one other with general joviality, more like that found at a party rather than at the start of a backbreaking job.

Haakan and Ingeborg greeted the immigrant laborers as they got off the train. The number had grown to fourteen, and by speaking slowly in Norwegian, they'd been able to communicate with the Norwegians, of course, as well as the Swedish and German men, telling them to put their belongings on a couple of handcarts, which would be used to deliver them to the boardinghouse. The one Russian man followed the examples of the others. With that accomplished, they herded the men to the siding, where the railroad workers were uncoupling the three flat cars to be unloaded.

Once the railcars were left behind, the train continued on westward, and the real work began. Thorliff and Jeffers, along with Anner Valders, inspected the contents of the cars and made sure that the components for each building were kept together. Then the materials were hauled off the train, loaded onto the wagons, and transported to the homesites that had already been stepped off and marked.

"You take charge of your house, Joshua. Far, you take the Jeffers house; Toby, you oversee the spec houses." Jeffers and Mr. Valders held the sheaves of paper work, checking things off as they were unloaded.

Two hours later the women showed up with sandwiches, cookies, and plenty of coffee, and the work halted while everyone ate. Mr. Geddick sat down with the Germans and further explained the building plans while Haakan did the same with the others. The man from Russia sat alone and watched, following the others carefully. Everyone worked until dark. By that time Joshua's building materials were piled by his completed cellar, and portions of the spec houses and the Jeffers house were in place. The men who had cows to milk left when they needed to and returned when their chores were finished. The women helped Sophie and her staff at the boardinghouse, and at dark all the men trooped in there to eat. The weary men were still able to laugh, and their conversations rocked the walls of the dining room.

"Once we are all unloaded, we will start building your house and digging out the cellars on the others," Thorliff said to Joshua and his brother Aaron, and then he went from table to table, thanking the men for all their work. He ended each message with "We'll start again at daylight."

BY FIVE O'CLOCK the next evening, the railroad cars were empty, ready to be picked up again the following day by the eastbound train. The men unloaded the last of the wagons and slowly trooped back to the boardinghouse, where once again a community supper was served.

"Mor, you could let the younger women do more of the work," Thorliff said.

"You think I am too old for this?" Ingeborg answered with a frown.

"No, but . . ."

Jeffers stood back and watched the exchange, enjoying the conversation. His own mother beckoned him from where she sat with the doctors Bjorklund, who were removing slivers, bandaging cuts, and treating blisters.

"Now, Mr. Valders, you make sure to soak this so it doesn't become infected," Astrid instructed as she finished wrapping Toby's hand.

Toby grinned at her. "*Mr. Valders?* After all these years? Do doctors have to be socially perfect or something?"

Jeffers could see red creeping up Astrid's neck, but she ignored the remark and said, "Next." She glanced up and saw Daniel watching her.

Daniel looked away, embarrassed at being caught out. Dr. Astrid Bjorklund was indeed a pleasure to look at, surrounded by her cloak of caring and her easy smile. But then, she'd known these people all her life. Think of all the stories hidden away under that golden hair, one strand of which insisted on falling onto her cheek, no matter how much she brushed it back. He turned when Thorliff called his name, grateful for the reprieve.

"Did you see our Russian worker leave?"

"No, but then, I wasn't paying attention."

"All the others have gone to their rooms," Thorliff said, "but we can't find him."

"What is his name?"

"Boris Sidorov." Thorliff stumbled over the unfamiliar name. "Sure wish they had simplified this one at Ellis Island like they did so many others."

"Perhaps we better go look for him?"

"I'll gather some of the others. Maybe if he hears us calling his name, he will respond."

Daniel grabbed Toby and told him the situation. Then they headed out to the front porch of the boardinghouse, where Joshua was sitting in a rocking chair. The half moon floated up from the eastern horizon. "Did you see Boris at supper?"

"Sorry, no." Joshua spoke in a hush. "He was on my crew, and I remember him working right until we finished. Then I don't know. I assumed he headed for the dining room like everyone else."

"Do you have any idea who his roommates are?"

"We can check with Mrs. Wiste," Daniel offered.

"No, she's gone home. I'll ask Miss Christopherson." Joshua returned to the dining room.

The three parted and took different sections of the town, calling the man's name. Echoes of "Boris" floated about the town, setting dogs to barking and lights returning to darkened houses.

Daniel found the man, sound asleep and wrapped in a blanket, on the back porch of the boardinghouse. Rather than waking the man, he returned to the front porch and, putting two fingers in his mouth, blasted a whistle that could be heard clear to the river. The others returned, and he gave his report. "But what do we do about this? He didn't run away. Perhaps he was uncomfortable with sharing a room."

"Maybe he's used to sleeping outside," Toby said.

"There was no sleeping outside when confined in the hold of a ship, that's for sure." Daniel shook his head, then added, "He's safe out there. Surely he will come in for breakfast."

"If only we could talk with him." Thorliff rubbed his chin. "I've asked, and no one knows any Russian."

"He sure pulled his share of the work today," Joshua said. "I was glad to have him on my crew."

Thorliff headed toward home, and the others returned to the dining room, said their good-nights and thank-yous, and headed for their own beds. Daniel made his way down the hall past his mother's room and opened his own door. How long would it be before he could open the door to a house again, rather than only to a room? He'd been thinking of his mother. Who could he find to help her so that she didn't have all the work of keeping a house? Maybe they should put out a call for female immigrants too. Someone would be needed here at the boardinghouse to help with the laundry, the garden, and all the extra meals being prepared.

He hung his hat on the coatrack and pulled his tie out from around his neck. His hands felt raw in spite of the leather gloves he'd worn. He'd not done physical labor like this for years, something his muscles were reminding him of quite vociferously. A bath would feel good, but dropping onto the bed felt better. Perhaps one of the miracles Thorliff had mentioned had already happened in Blessing. The way all the people worked together, incorporating the new men as if they'd grown up there too, and getting the job done. He'd not heard a cross word, except when a board had fallen on one man's toes and another had jabbed a long sliver into his palm. The minor wounds had kept the doctors busy. But the amount of work accomplished was amazing.

Might this be one of the reasons Blessing was growing so? Were Thorliff's words indeed true? That all would be well? Ever since his father disappeared, Daniel had had trouble with comments like that. He still wanted to find the man who had appropriated his father's name and spent the money as his own. Who was that man and where was he now? Maybe he'd be able to find out some information on this next sales trip. Would it do any good to pray about it? As Pastor Solberg so often said, one should pray for everything and praise God at the same time, no matter what happened. This didn't make sense to him, but it was probably good advice. Life had taught him that when things were going really well, something terrible was about to happen.

In the morning as he was dressing, he heard a shout from the back porch. Had something happened to Boris?

19

Astrid awakened to banging on her bedroom door and Thorliff's voice calling, "Astrid, come quickly. One of the men is terribly ill."

"Be right there." Please, Lord, now what? Astrid exchanged her nightdress for work clothes and bundled her hair into a snood. Snatching an ankle-length apron from the hook by the door, she ran down the stairs as quickly as possible. Thorliff was waiting for her.

"They found Boris on the back porch of the boardinghouse, burning with fever. They are bringing him here any minute now."

"Is Elizabeth up?"

"Awake, yes, but since she was called out late last night, and since you are here, I asked her to stay in her room and rest. Inga is with her. I telephoned Mor to come."

Astrid heard the men outside and ran to open the door. "Bring him in here." She motioned to the examining room, which Thelma had all ready for an emergency. They laid the man on the table and backed out of the room. The stench made her blink.

"Tell those men to scrub their hands and arms and change their clothes. This might be contagious. Make sure they do so. And scrub, not just wash. They can use the back porch. Thelma will know what to use."

Thorliff did as she told him while she turned to the man lying comatose, filthy from the effluvia of some intestinal malady. Before she could turn around, her mother strode through the doorway.

"Thank God you are here." Astrid indicated the man. "What do you think?"

"Let's get him cleaned up first."

"I'll help," Pastor Solberg said from the doorway. "I was in the garden when I heard the commotion. Do we know who he is?"

"His name is Boris Sidorov. He's Russian, one of the new immigrants." They stripped off his clothing and dropped each item into a tub to be washed.

"What could have hit him so suddenly?"

"Look at his belly. Those spots—like measles." Ingeborg pointed. "He has typhoid. Perhaps he's been carrying it for some time. It can hit hard in that case. He was probably already ill but hiding the symptoms."

"Typhoid. This could rip through the entire town." Astrid blinked, her mind churning as she tried to assimilate the news. "Pastor Solberg, you wash him down. I'll go tell Thorliff what must be done."

"Scrub thoroughly before you touch anything." Ingeborg handed Pastor Solberg the basin filled with soap, water, and carbolic acid. "Be careful of yourself. Don't splash any water on your skin or put your hands to your face. I wish we had kept him out on the porch until he was cleaned up."

Astrid finished scrubbing up to her elbows, dropped her apron in the dirty clothes tub, and headed for the kitchen and the telephone. As soon as she had Miss Christopherson on the line, she gave terse instructions to scrub down the porch and to have anyone who had touched the man to scrub thoroughly. "This is really bad. You need to carefully wash his room with disinfectant and boil the bedding. While he didn't appear sick, he might have been carrying the contagion for some time."

"What about the rest of the men he came with?"

"Tell them all to bathe and to wash everything they touched."

"I can't speak their languages."

"Thorliff will be right over. Don't let anyone leave the dining room." How could they quarantine the men? Would it do any good now that everyone who worked with them for the last two days was already exposed? She set the earpiece back in the prongs and strode to the back porch. "Thelma, we need more hot water in the surgery. Is Thorliff still here?"

"He heard you and has already left."

"Boil all the clothes and cloths we've used on the patient. We'll scrub everything down with carbolic acid as soon as we get him into a room. No one may see him. This is highly contagious."

The bell from upstairs in Elizabeth's room rang.

Astrid stopped at the bottom of the stairs and called, "I can't come up. We have a case of typhoid here. What is it?"

"Telephone Dr. Morganstein. A vaccine has been developed, and we need it here to protect the town. She always has it at the hospital, because there are often typhoid cases in Chicago. Didn't they vaccinate you when you arrived for school?"

"I'd forgotten that. Of course. Well, that's excellent news. So you've been vaccinated too?"

"Yes."

"I'll ask if anyone else has been."

"Good. I'm keeping Inga up here too. The men who traveled with him should be quarantined also, especially those sharing his room at the boardinghouse."

"What's the incubation period?"

"I should know that. Check the contagious diseases section in the reference book in the office."

"I will."

"Are your mother and Pastor Solberg wearing masks?"

"No."

"Mask them up and tell them to strip and scrub down as soon as you get him settled. Only you or I will take care of him."

Astrid agreed and returned to the examining room, stopping in the doorway. She passed on Elizabeth's instructions and went to the kitchen to telephone Chicago. After getting the assurance that the vials would be on the next train, she took in a deep breath and let it out on a prayer for help. This could be worse than the measles epidemic on the reservation.

At a knock on the door she opened it to find Daniel Jeffers standing there. "Good morning. You can't—"

"I know. Thorliff told me, and I came to tell you that I have been vaccinated, as has my mother. We had a situation like this in our former town. Tell us what to do, and we will help as much as we can."

Astrid heaved a sigh and kept herself from slumping by a strong effort. She invited him in. "Would you like a cup of coffee?"

"No, thank you. I thought perhaps we could quarantine the men at the schoolhouse. We can spread pallets for them and bring food from the boardinghouse. I'll start canvassing people to see who came in contact with the man who is ill. Thorliff will talk with the other immigrants to see if they are feeling ill. Ah, and Mr. Geddick will talk with the Germans. I'm thinking the others in the town can go about their business, as long as they have no contact with the men."

"Thank you, Mr. Jeffers. You have no idea what a relief it is to know others are safe here."

"I've canceled my trip, so Mother and I will do what we can."

"Tell your mother thank you in advance for me, please."

"I will. She could sit here and watch over the man who is so ill."

"This changes things. I thought only Elizabeth and I had been vaccinated. Let me get things set up, and I will let her know."

He smiled at her, emanating such calm that she felt herself relax a bit more. No wonder her brother had such trust in the man. As he turned toward the door, his parting words reminded her of her mother. "All will be well."

"I pray so." She returned to the sickroom to find Boris all bathed and dressed in one of the calico gowns made especially for the medical practice. Each one was open down the middle and had ties at the neck, at the middle, and near the hem. "Is he ready to be moved?"

"Ja, but he is not very responsive."

"Let's put him in the first room and try to get some nourishment into him. Thelma is heating up some of the chicken broth she canned. What about adding comfrey to calm his stomach?"

Her mother nodded. "That and ground willow bark. We'll get turnip tops and spinach from the garden and boil those to help with the diarrhea. I'll check to see if Thelma has any mustard in her pantry. I'll look at my reference books when I get home."

"All right. Thanks, Mor." Astrid looked toward Ingeborg and Pastor Solberg. "We can move him together, and then you two take turns at the bath. All clothing must be boiled."

After everyone had been informed as to the procedures, the immigrant workers moved their things to the schoolhouse and set to work digging cellars for the rest of the houses to be built. That way they had no contact with the folks of Blessing. The boardinghouse went back to normal operations after the bedrooms and back porch had been scrubbed down. Even so, for the next few days, everyone in town was extremely careful, and folks pretty much stayed home.

With the wheat fully ripened, harvest began in the southern fields that Lars and Haakan had acquired over the years, including the acres Joshua had formerly farmed. The two Landsverk brothers, along with the crews from both the hospital and the manufacturing plant, framed and roofed Joshua's house in two days. Then the crews returned to their respective jobs.

———

MRS. JEFFERS SPENT HOURS at the bedside of the sick man, changing wet cloths to bring his fever down and spooning liquids into his mouth whenever he would cooperate. One night when Daniel Jeffers was on watch, Boris opened his eyes and, with a sigh, gazed around the room. Jeffers greeted him with a smile and a gentle hello.

"Ja, hello," Boris squeaked with a nod. He nodded again when Jeffers held up the glass of water and drank some before slipping into a quiet sleep, no longer hallucinating and thrashing as he had in the midst of his delirium.

When Astrid came to spell him, Daniel Jeffers smiled. "Look at him. He's turned the corner. He drank some water and spoke."

"How wonderful." Astrid listened to the man's chest and checked his pulse. "Thanks be to God."

"I seriously doubted this time."

"Waiting is always the hardest, especially the longer it lasts. But when he didn't get worse . . ."

"I thought he might just get weaker and weaker and slip away."

"He needs to thank your mother for her care. I think she warned him that he better make the effort to get well because people here had invested so much in him."

"When my mother gives instructions like that, you'd better listen," Daniel said.

"Even if you don't understand the words?"

"Even so."

Astrid chuckled in the gentle glow emanating from the gaslight, turned down as low as it would go. "You are the voice of experience."

"Me and my sister. She moved into our house when Mother left."

"You have nieces and nephews?"

"Just one, but my sister is expecting another. Mother is hoping they will all come to visit when we have a house again."

"Your mother is a remarkable woman. I heard her reading to Boris in English. She said she wanted him to get acquainted with the language as soon as possible. No sense in waiting for formal classes."

"She has always wished she could have taught school."

"And here she will. Good things happen to those who come to Blessing."

"How much longer is the quarantine going to last?"

"If the others are going to catch it, they'll begin symptoms any day now. For the rest, the vaccinations have already taken effect."

They had vaccinated all the construction workers, all those who worked at the boardinghouse, and anyone else who had come in contact with the immigrants. They also had notified the railroad but were not sure if there was much they could do. If the immigrants in Blessing already carried the contagion, she and Elizabeth would soon know, and they hoped any cases would not be so severe. Besides, most of them were in better health already, after eating decent food again and being off the ships for several weeks now.

"Did Mr. Gould know of anyone else in New York who had the typhoid?" Daniel asked.

"He contacted everyone he could. I've not heard of any more cases." Astrid leaned against the doorjamb. "You need to get your rest."

"I know, but I never get to visit with you. All I know is what Thorliff has told me."

"And you better not trust all of that. He was nine when I was born, and from some things Mor has said, he wasn't too excited about a squalling baby. Andrew was much more fun."

"His tales of those years after his father died would tear anybody's heart out."

"I know. Mor and Tante Kaaren worked harder than anyone will ever really know. Mor did all the work the men usually do, and they managed to not lose the land. The day they proved it up was a celebration indeed. My far and Lars worked hard too when they joined the family, and others came to Blessing. As someone suggested at the tea the other day, we need to get the history of our town written down before people start forgetting how it all happened."

"That's a very good idea." He motioned to the chair he had vacated. "Why don't you sit down and be comfortable?"

"Oh, I will. Thank you again."

"Good morning it is, then." He removed his hat from the peg on the wall by the door. "If you need anything more, please let me know."

"I will." Astrid returned his smile and heard him walk lightly to the door and go out onto the front porch. From there he would see the lightening of the eastern horizon. She went to the window and listened. The frogs and insects had halted their chorus, and the birds had yet to begin their morning chatter. His footsteps sounded loud in the predawn silence as he made his way back to the boardinghouse. The sheer white curtains lifted in the breeze and danced around her. One of the kittens, now nearly grown, entered the room and wound around her skirt, looking up with slitted green eyes and chirping to be picked up.

Astrid leaned over and picked her up, then turned back to the window, the kitten purring under her chin. Was there anything more comforting than a purring cat and a man getting well in the lightening of the day? *Thank you, Father, for performing your loving miracles in this house again. This could have been so horrible. Thank you for the vaccines, for Dr. Morganstein, who knew just what to do, for those here who had already been vaccinated and could help. For bringing Mr. Jeffers and his mother to Blessing. For your great mercy on us all.*

She sat down in the rocking chair and leaned her head back, the cat settling into her lap. Closing her eyes, she continued her prayers of thanksgiving as she rocked gently, the song of the chair now joined by the tentative notes of a song sparrow welcoming the dawn. Thoughts of Mr. Jeffers made her smile. She was going to ask him about his own family, but surely had there been a wife or a fiancée in his past he would have mentioned it. To Thorliff, if not to her. But what did it matter? After the fiasco with Mr. Landsverk, she wasn't about to consider another man. Even one as nice as Mr. Jeffers.

20

"I'm starting to think we should go ahead and have a girl party, and then have another one after Grace gets home," Sophie said, clamping her hands on her widening hips.

"Sophie, not right now," Astrid pleaded.

"Yes, right now. The whole town has been so subdued with the typhoid quarantine. I just feel like we need to have a little fun."

"I don't think community events are a good idea right now. It could be asking for trouble." Astrid studied her cousin over her stepson's head. "And besides, three stitches in one's forehead makes for a headache and a cranky child. You don't need everyone at your house right now." She placed a bandage over Grant's stitches and tipped up his chin to check his eyes again.

"It still hurts, huh?"

He nodded, then flinched. "Sorry."

"Me too. You go home and lie down for a while. When you wake up again, you should feel better." She transferred her attention to Sophie. "When you change the bandage, spread some honey on the wound. Honey promotes faster healing."

"I like honey." Grant almost smiled.

"Then maybe your mother should give you a honeyed spoon to suck on too, don't you think?"

He nodded again and touched the white bandage on his head. "It was Nathan's fault. He tripped me."

"He didn't mean to."

"I know, but you said—"

"Forget what I said. No more running in the house. How many times have we talked about that?"

"Can't count that high?"

Sophie rolled her eyes. "No. I probably can't either, but now you know why I say such things." She stood and took Grant's hand. "Thank you, Dr. Bjorklund. Stop over at the boardinghouse for coffee sometime."

"I'll do that. Bye."

Sophie sailed out of the room, as only Sophie could sail in spite of her pregnancy, poor Grant dragging along behind.

Rather than bringing the second ill man over to the surgery, they were taking care of him at the schoolhouse to help contain the spread of typhoid. The first man was still recovering but now living at the schoolhouse too. All the men had been vaccinated at the same time as those of the town who had been exposed to the disease.

Since there were no further patients, Astrid shut the door and turned the *Open* sign over to *Closed*. If someone needed her, they would know what to do. A knock at the door was all it took to summon the doctor. She put away the supplies she'd used, placed the things that needed sterilizing in the tray, and closed the door behind her. The two bedrooms were all cleaned and made up again, and she knew Thelma had finished the laundry earlier in the morning. Strolling into the kitchen and withdrawing the pitcher from the icebox, she poured herself a drink of something pink. Pitcher back and cooling glass in hand, Astrid made her way out to the back porch, fully expecting to see Elizabeth working on the supply lists for the hospital.

No Elizabeth and no Thelma either.

Hmm. Astrid sat down in the well-cushioned wicker chair and put her feet up on the hassock she pulled over. The sound of children laughing and squealing carried over the empty lots. Hammers pounding, wood being sawed, a man shouting instructions were all the normal sounds of the building going on in town. She knew the immigrant workers were digging cellars. Joshua's house stood a story and a half high, with men on ladders hammering on the siding. She checked to see if thoughts of Joshua bothered her, but all she could sense was a feeling of peace and gratitude that he was getting at least part of his dream—a house.

When she looked over her shoulder, she could see Thelma out picking beans in the garden. Where was Elizabeth? Inga was out at her grandma's house, another reason why the house was so quiet. The sound of boots on the sidewalk preceded Thorliff's strolling around the corner of the house. He had papers in his hand and glanced over them when he saw Astrid.

"So where is everyone?"

"I was wondering the same." She held up her glass. "You want some?"

"I'll get it. Thelma is picking beans and weeding at the same time." The door slammed behind him.

Astrid tipped back her head to watch two sparrows arguing on the branch of the box elder tree growing at the corner of the porch. It sounded like the female was scolding the male. Perhaps he'd neglected to feed the children. The thought made her smile. One of the kittens jumped up in her lap. They looked so alike with their dense gray fur that she couldn't tell them apart. Inga could. One was for Emmy when she returned from her summer with her tribe.

"Watch it!" The shout echoed through the sudden silence. A board clattered to the ground.

"That was close."

Feeling like she was eavesdropping, Astrid stroked the cat's back. "Don't get too comfortable. I won't be here long."

"You're never anywhere very long." Thorliff let the door slam behind him and sat down in the chair next to her.

"I should be working on the hospital planning."

"I saw Grant sporting a white bandage on his forehead, and he had blood on his shirt."

"Head wounds bleed a lot. He split the skin tripping over Nathan. I stitched it up."

"He'll be the envy of the younger set."

"What are you working on?"

"Articles for the paper. I interviewed Pastor Solberg about his time with the Indian tribe. Do you have any comments to make?"

"Other than to thank the people of Blessing for sending supplies, no."

"What about the two Indian women who are in nurses training?"

"Along with Deborah. You ought to interview Mor and Tante Kaaren for that. They're the ones doing the training, along with Mrs. Jeffers."

"You know, you should have put a notice of the class in the newspaper. There might be others from the outlying areas who would be interested."

"True. I never thought of that. We weren't really prepared to start an official class. I just thought these two women could be more help to Dr. Red Hawk if they had some training."

Thorliff scratched some notes with his pencil, then tucked it behind his ear again. "Think I'll go on out there. Tell Elizabeth where I went, will you?"

"Of course." Astrid watched him stride off, thinking she should be up and doing something else. Finishing her drink, she set the glass in the kitchen sink, trod softly on the stairs in case Elizabeth was indeed sleeping, which she was, and decided to go get the mail. The train had been through some time earlier.

She stopped in front of the mirror in the hall and pinned on the wide-brimmed straw hat she kept there. Going without a hat would indeed not be proper. If she were really proper, she would carry a parasol too, but even the thought of it made her frown. The thought brought back memories of Mrs. Moore down on the Rosebud Reservation. Was there any chance she had taken her advice so she could have a healthy baby?

Since the men were now digging cellars in the blocks between the surgery and the post office, she didn't cut across but instead walked up to Main and stepped up onto the boardwalk, which was so valuable when the rain caused puddles and mud. Right now they needed a good rain, but rain would be bad for the wheat harvest. There were no easy answers, if ever there had been.

"Hey there, Dr. Bjorklund!"

She looked up to wave at Toby, who was one of the carpenters on Joshua's, or rather Mr. Landsverk's, roof. "That sure went up in a hurry."

"I know. Wonderful, isn't it? At the rate we're going, we'll have them all weatherproofed by fall."

"What about the hospital?"

"That's on hold for another week." He waved again and went back to hammering.

Astrid continued past the boardinghouse on the other side of the street and crossed the side street to climb the stairs to the post office. She could see Gerald at the switchboard in the office across the hall.

Pushing open the screen door, she stepped inside, where a bit of a breeze entered at one door and crossed the floor to the other.

"Well, well, if it isn't Dr. Bjorklund." Mrs. Valders smiled from behind the counter. "We never seem to see your face much."

"No. That typhoid scare kept us pretty busy."

Mrs. Valders rubbed her arm. "That vaccination must have took real good on me. Still a bit tender." She reached down and fetched a couple of magazines and a package and set them on the counter. "Your regular mail is in the box."

Astrid unlatched the door and pulled several letters out, flipping through to see if any were for her. "Is the newspaper mail still here too?"

"Sure enough. Let me put all this in a satchel for you. I think those ads Thorliff has run are paying off." She bundled a bunch into a cloth bag. "Bring the bag back the next time you come in."

Astrid nodded. "You want me to look at that vaccination?"

Mrs. Valders rolled up her sleeve. "If you don't mind, but it looks to be healing."

Astrid inspected the still slightly red and crusty spot. "Do you have any menthol cream?"

"I think so."

"Rub that in. It will soften up the scab."

"Thank you. You doctors sure took good care of this town. We mighta lost lots of our people had you not gotten the vaccine. Benny was so brave about it. The way he calls you "My Doc" just tickles me pink."

"He is one special little boy. I fell in love with him when he came out of the anesthetic after the surgery and realized he'd lost his legs. He glared at me as if I were responsible, and just one tear rolled down his cheek. He's a brave one, all right."

"He's looking forward to school. His pa is putting better wheels on his scooter so he can navigate the path when it gets bumpy. He doesn't want anyone pulling him in the wagon anymore."

"Maybe we should find him a big dog to pull the wagon. Then he'd be the most popular one around. Everyone would want to ride in it."

"My Benny—all the children love him."

Astrid patted Mrs. Valders' hand where it lay on the counter. The woman could hardly talk about her grandson without tearing up. "Amazing how God works, isn't it? Here was a little boy who needed a decent home when he had legs, but when we brought him here, he charmed the town and gave us all a good example of courage."

"I thank God for him every day. Now with the baby coming and all, Rebecca is going to be mighty busy."

"You know, I was thinking that maybe we ought to put out the word that we, as a town, would be willing to have some female immigrants come here to work too. What do you think?"

"They'd have to be God-fearing proper women or girls," Mrs. Valders said, nodding her head while she spoke. "It would be good if they were Norwegian or Swede, but German would be fine." She looked at Astrid. "We are going to be needing more help, that's for sure. I'll ask Mr. Valders what he thinks."

Astrid knew that was a total agreement. Sometimes she wondered if the two really did discuss the news of the town. Those were always Hildegunn's last words. "I'll talk with Mr. Valders about it."

"I better get back and go through this mail. Thank you." Instead of going out the west door and over to Rebecca's for a soda, which sounded like a wonderful way to finish her day, she returned the way she came. Back at the surgery, as everyone called Thorliff's house, Astrid set the mail for the newspaper on the kitchen table and that for the doctors on the dining room table.

"That you, Astrid?" Elizabeth called from above.

"I got the mail. I have a letter from Red Hawk."

"Anything else?"

"One from Dr. Morganstein. You want me to bring it up?"

"No. I'll come down in a while."

Astrid slit open the letter from Red Hawk. She would recognize his handwriting anywhere. Bold, half printing, half cursive. He must have driven his teachers mad when they tried to force him to write correctly.

Dear Dr. Bjorklund,

I have received news from the reservation, and all of the reports are singing your praises to the sky. I am not sure if you realized the precariousness of your visit there. I know that there could have been trouble, but you won their gratitude for keeping so many of my people alive. Especially He Who Walks Tall. He is young to take over as chief, but with the death of Dark Cloud, he was a good choice. I know that had I been there, I would have been forced into the role of chief. Had I lived through the epidemic, of course.

I was surprised that you brought the two women back to Blessing with you. I hope that did not cause dissension in your town. Training them will do exactly as you said—give me assistance when I get there.

Dr. Morganstein has said that if your hospital is dedicated about the time I am finished here, she wants me to stop there with them for the ceremony. Please keep us advised as to how the building is progressing.

I heard that you had typhoid there with the immigrant laborers. We borrowed vaccine from all the hospitals around in order to send you the amount you requested. Since you did not ask for more, we assumed this was sufficient. If only there had been a vaccine for the measles for my people.

Again, I thank you for your help, and I look forward to going back to my people so we can bring them the health care they deserve.

Your servant,

Dr. Red Hawk

Astrid read the letter a second time and then laid it out for Elizabeth to read, opening the one from Dr. Morganstein. Mrs. Izzy Josephson had died. Astrid paused a moment. Such a fiery little lady and one who was helping fund the hospital. Sad she'd not lived to see the project through. *Do not be concerned regarding money for the hospital. She stipulated in her will that funding would continue.* With a sigh of relief Astrid laid the letter on the table. "I left the letters here for you," she called up the stairs.

"Thank you."

"I'm going over to the schoolhouse now, so if someone comes, you will take care of it, or Thelma can just tell them to wait."

"That's fine." Elizabeth appeared at the top of the stairs. "I didn't realize I was so tired." She started down the stairs. "I should be back to normal by now."

"Not necessarily. You went through a lot. Are you limping?"

"My right leg hurts some is all. I banged my knee on the stool in the kitchen. Don't be such a worrywart."

Astrid shrugged. She had to admit she watched Elizabeth very carefully, but she was taking a long time to regain her strength. Maybe Mor could suggest a tonic for the other Dr. Bjorklund.

Astrid took her black bag with her and went around the building lots the other way to head for the church and the schoolhouse. How she would love to stop and see Pastor Solberg for a good long chat.

"Come by for coffee after you visit the sick men," Mary Martha called from her garden. "I'll put the pot on."

"All right." She found Boris sitting on the steps and carving on a piece of wood with his pocketknife. "How are you feeling, Mr. Boris?" she asked, speaking slowly.

He smiled. He had shaved his face and wore clean clothes, so she could tell there was improvement.

She laid the back of her hand against his forehead. "No fever."

"Ja, goot."

"Ja, good is right."

He said something, then screwed up his face. "Ah . . . work?"

How could she say *part time*? "Stop at noon?"

His frown told her he didn't comprehend.

"Work, ja. Till noon." She pointed toward where the sun would be straight up.

He nodded, but she had no idea if he understood what she'd said. She'd tell Thorliff to get it across somehow.

She motioned to the inside, so he stood back to let her pass, then followed her in.

The man on the pallet was sound asleep. When she patted his shoulder, his eyes fluttered open. "Ja, Doctor?"

"I came to check on you." This was easy since he spoke Norwegian. Speaking so often to these patients, she felt more at home in the language again. It had been a long time since they'd spoken Norwegian around town.

"Better." His voice was weak, but he no longer looked ashen.

"Have you been eating?"

"Ja. Boris, he feeds me and helps me."

"Good." She listened to his lungs. "Any coughing?"

"Not much. Just so weak."

"I left some syrup here for your cough."

"I know. I took it."

"You look better than you did this morning. Are you eating well?"

"Better than I have for years."

Astrid smiled. She knew Mrs. Sam would make sure the men had plenty to eat.

"I will see you again in the morning, then. I told Boris he could work for half a day, so he will return at noon. If you need anything, ring the bell." She pointed to the teacher's bell she had set near him.

"I will. Thank you, Dr. Bjorklund."

"Keep scrubbing your hands when you—"

His face turned bright red. "Ja, ja."

Astrid nodded and looked around to make sure things were being kept clean. Someone had come and picked up the used dishes, and the basket of dirty clothes was empty. Clean things were folded and piled on one of the school benches.

"Just rest, then."

"Ja. I can't seem to do much more." He paused. "Dr. Bjorklund, how will I pay for all this?"

"You are not to worry. We brought you here. We will take care of you. When you are strong enough to work, you will have work and a place to stay at the boardinghouse. You will pay for that from your wages."

"Ja, good." He fought to keep his eyes open.

Astrid smiled again at Boris as she left the schoolhouse and headed for Mary Martha's and that coffee she'd promised.

21

He wasn't home nearly long enough."

"What's that you said?" Freda asked from inside the kitchen.

"Oh, sorry. I didn't realize I had spoken aloud." Ingeborg was sitting on the porch step with Inga. She set aside the bowl into which she was snapping beans and stared out across the garden.

"Why you sad, Grandma?" Inga peered up into her grandma's face from the step below, her bowl for snapped beans tipping precariously in her lap.

"Your beans," Ingeborg whispered.

"Oh." Inga set her bowl on the step and stood to wrap her arms around her grandmother's neck. "Don't be sad."

"I am sad because Grandpa is gone again. I really miss him."

"Me too. Maybe we need to have coffee and cookies."

Ingeborg burst out laughing. After kissing Inga's cheek, she raised her voice. "Inga thinks we need coffee and cookies."

"I think Inga is a very smart little girl."

"See, now you're not so sad." Inga sat back down, this time on the same step as Ingeborg, and leaned against her. "You could tell me a story while we snap beans."

"Coffee and cookies *and* a story?"

"About when you were little in Norway."

"Oh my. That was sooo long ago."

"You lived in a house on a hill, and the animals lived underneath the house. How come they did not have a barn like we do?"

Ingeborg picked up her bowl and a handful of beans. "It was like this. In Norway there are lots of mountains and hills—"

"We have flat land."

"We do. The only hill we have here is the riverbank."

"Where we slide down onto the river after it freezes."

"Right. You know we used to make a pond out by the barn for ice skating in the winter. We must do that again this year. You are big enough to learn to ice skate."

"Ice is water all frozen hard."

"Right. Now, in Norway, the animals lived under the house so they could keep warm, and the warmth from the animals helped keep the house warm."

"How?"

"Well, heat rises. That's why the upstairs gets warm in the winter—the heat goes up there."

"All by itself?"

"Up the stairs and through the big square vent over the stove."

"Emmy and me got dressed by the vent last winter."

"That you did. The rising heat warmed your legs under your nightgown."

"And made our nightgowns go big." Inga demonstrated the billowing cloth, and her beans tipped.

Ingeborg grabbed the bowl just in time.

"Coffee and cookies coming right up." Freda pushed open the door with a tray she held in both hands. Setting the tray on the low table between the chairs, she poured two cups of black and one cup of half cream and half coffee along with a bit of sugar.

Inga pulled her grandmother up, and they climbed the stairs to sit in the chairs. Ingeborg passed the plate of cookies.

"What kind are these?" Inga pointed to some lightly browned rectangles.

"They are called icebox cookies." Freda took a bite out of hers. "I found a new recipe. You make the dough and form a long flat tube, then wrap that and put it in the icebox." She explained the shape with her hands too. "Then slice and bake them the next day. Or later if you want. They are supposed to keep well."

Inga took a bite and chewed, a thoughtful look on her face. "I like crunchy cookies like this." She took another bite. "But they aren't real sweet. Maybe sprinkle sugar on them like we do the sugar cookies."

Ingeborg and Freda exchanged raised eyebrow looks.

"Or maybe raisins." Inga reached for another one. "I like gingerbread men better."

"You don't have to roll these out. I think that is why somebody came up with this idea." Freda dunked her cookie in her coffee and took a bite. "Now, that is perfect."

Ingeborg drained her coffee cup. "I'm going over to Kaaren's for a session with our nursing students, so you stay here and help Tante Freda with the beans. I'll be gone about an hour."

"Back for dinner?" Inga reached for another cookie.

"Ja. And then we'll pick raspberries. This will probably be the last picking."

"Shortcake?" Inga's eyes lit up, but then her smile dimmed. "Grandpa won't be here for shortcake."

"We'll make shortcake out of the canned berries when he comes back." Ingeborg took off her apron and hung it on a hook. "I'll hurry." She picked up her black leather bag and strode down the walk to the front fence gate.

Walking along the lane now that the short pasture was fenced off for the heifers, Ingeborg hummed a tune to herself. When the meadowlark flying above loosed a trill of notes down on her, she smiled, watching him settle on a goldenrod, bending the top over. "So you sing better than I do. Show off."

When she arrived at Kaaren's, she entered the two-story building through the school door rather than the family door. "Where are you?"

"In here," Kaaren called from the first classroom.

Ingeborg joined the small group of ladies and sat down, setting her medical bag on the floor beside her.

"We have been studying different types of wounds and how to recognize them. Do you want to talk about burns?"

How do I talk about burns when they don't know the language? "Ah, how are you communicating?"

"Signs and wonders. Pictures help. Here in the medical book is the section on burns, but since we don't agree with the common treatment, I would use the pictures."

Ingeborg nodded. She stood and moved to the front of the room, picking up the book. "There are three levels of burns." She held up three fingers. "First-degree burns make the skin red." She showed the picture. "Sunburn, steam, touching a hot kettle. The surface skin is burned." They nodded at the pictures.

Deborah looked up. "But this burn can still leave a mark?"

Ingeborg nodded. "Sunburns peel, and the skin can bubble after a few days. Cold water helps relieve the pain. I'm thinking that powdered willow bark worked into a salve might be effective too. After all, we make willow bark tea to reduce pain and fever." This was something to think on. What if it could help bites and stings too?

Gray Smoke, the shorter of the two Indians, spoke up. She patted her skin. "No sunburn."

"Really?" Ingeborg remembered Astrid saying that the women understood more English than they could speak. "Darker skin doesn't burn?" She patted her skin, then Gray Smoke's arm.

"Maybe we should ask Mrs. Sam," Deborah volunteered.

"Good idea." Ingeborg smiled at her students. By the time she had explained the other levels of burns and treatments, noon was near. Today Ellie was feeding the few men left at home to do the chores, so when Kaaren suggested they eat at her house, Ingeborg telephoned home and asked Freda and Inga to walk over.

When Inga greeted the two ladies in the Sioux language, the two smiled and responded with a stream of words. Inga stared at them, obviously trying to listen hard. When they saw she didn't understand, they laughed and patted her shoulder.

"You good," Gray Smoke said while Shy Fawn nodded.

Inga looked up at her grandmother. "Emmy only taught me some words. I don't know very much."

"What do you know?"

"How to say hello, good-bye, hungry . . ." She wrinkled her face, trying to remember. "Horse, food, friend." She gave the Sioux words along with the English. "I wish I had learned more."

"I wish you had too, and I wish I had learned more from Metiz. But hers was a mixture of Sioux and French, and I have forgotten much of what I did learn."

They all sat down at the table, and after Kaaren said the grace, they passed the bread, meat, and cheese around the table, along with sliced pickles and lettuce. Kaaren demonstrated how to make a sandwich, and everyone laughed when her pickle fell out as she took a bite.

"You have to cut them in half or hang on tighter." She demonstrated as she spoke, and the others made their own sandwiches. Everyone enjoyed the glasses of cold milk, but as usual, the cookies were the biggest hit.

"Emmy would really like this," Inga said, dunking her cookie in the milk.

The two Indian women copied her, and the delight on their faces made everyone smile and chuckle.

"What will you do this afternoon?" Ingeborg asked.

"Practice making beds, changing beds with people in them, and rolling bandages. We have started a box for the reservation and will fill it as we go. Sterilizing things will be tomorrow, including boiling laundry. Astrid said she taught them some of that down on the reservation."

"Do you need my help?"

"No, but I want to get to bandaging and dressing wounds the day after."

"I'll be here."

Ingeborg walked home with Freda and Inga, Inga swinging between them. Her laughter was indeed contagious, even making sober Freda chuckle. The three of them picked the remaining raspberries, and while Freda made a batch of raspberry jam, Inga and Ingeborg finished snapping the beans and packing them in the jars for canning.

"Since we only have one potful, we'll set them to boiling once the sun goes down so the kitchen won't get so hot. We'll dry the rest."

"Do I get to spend the night again?" Inga asked, red juice from the berries dripping down her chin.

"What did your mother say?"

"I didn't ask. You ask better'n me."

"I see. I take it you want to spend the night?"

"And go fishing with Carl in the morning?"

"And if we catch lots of fish?"

"Then everyone can come here for supper. A fish fry again." Inga clapped her hands.

Ingeborg glanced up to see Freda rolling her eyes. Knowing that Freda thought she spoiled her granddaughter, she tried to be more firm but never could keep from laughing, at least inside, at Inga's antics.

"But what if we don't catch a lot of fish?"

Inga sighed. "Then I guess they have to cook their own supper."

Even Freda smiled.

————

BUT THEY DID CATCH a lot of fish, and the next evening when everyone gathered at Ingeborg's, one of the guests was Daniel Jeffers, thanks to Thorliff's invitation.

"Why didn't you bring your mother with you?" Ingeborg asked when he entered the house.

"She's busy teaching English to the immigrants and said she hated to miss even one evening. They are trying hard, and she is excited about their progress. Even Boris is doing well, although he had some catching up to do."

"Is he back to work full time now?"

"Yes, and the second man is half time. He had a much lighter case. Thanks to the Bjorklund doctors, these men are nearly finished digging cellars, and we will start pouring concrete next week on the first two."

"One of those being your house?"

"Yes. Although now I'm thinking Mother is doing better at the boardinghouse. I thought a home of her own would be the best for her, to help her get through the mourning."

"Your mother has a mission now. We all do better with a mission or two." Ingeborg glanced down when she felt a hand on her skirt. "Excuse me. Yes, Carl? What is it?"

"Inga push me down."

"I did not. I touched him and he fell. He doesn't want to be it."

Andrew stopped behind his niece. "Let's go outside and talk about this. Grandma is busy right now." He lifted Carl in one arm and took Inga's hand. "Sorry," he said over his shoulder.

Ingeborg turned back to her guest. "Why don't you come out on the back porch, where it is cooler. I think the others are gathering there."

"Thank you. I mean, you didn't know you were having extra company."

"Mr. Jeffers, you need to understand something about this family. We welcome everyone to our homes. When you moved to Blessing, you became part of our family. Especially when you partnered with my son. Our town is too small to not be all family."

"Thank you. Someday I'd like to tell you how much I appreciate the way Thorliff has stepped in and helped me realize my father's dream. You are an amazing family."

"No. Just a much blessed family that wants to share what God has given to us." She motioned for him to follow her to the porch, where Thorliff, Elizabeth, and Astrid were having a discussion, one that appeared from the tone of their voices to be getting warmer and warmer.

Then again, maybe you don't want to get in the middle of this. But Ingeborg kept her thoughts to herself. "Perhaps we can continue this discussion after supper?"

"But it has been more than a week with nothing further done on the hospital." Astrid leaned forward. "The deadline is drawing close, far more quickly than I think you realize."

"We said we would meet the November first dedication date,

and we will do that. You just take care of your part and stop fussing about the construction."

"Thorliff." Elizabeth laid a hand on her husband's arm. When he ignored her, she spoke louder. "Thorliff. Astrid. Your mother is speaking."

"We're doing the best we can. Who could have planned for a typhoid scare?" Thorliff glared at his sister and sent his wife a look too. He turned his attention to his mother. "Sorry. What was that you were saying?"

"I'm saying that we have company, and Freda is about done frying the fish."

"I know we have company. I brought him. Actually, he should be helping defend me from this unprovoked attack."

Astrid rolled her eyes. "All I did was ask when the hospital would be ready for occupancy."

"By occupancy," Daniel Jeffers started, keeping his voice calm and his attention focused on Astrid, "do you mean ready for patients or finishing the interior enough to be ready to move equipment in?"

"Not the patients. We won't be ready for patients until December at the very earliest. But setting up the operating rooms will take more time than we originally thought."

"As I said, everyone, we are ready to sit down to eat," Ingeborg said firmly. "Make sure the children are washed up. Andrew, will you say the grace tonight?" Ingeborg turned and opened the screen door, motioning the others to go ahead of her.

What was happening that Astrid and Thorliff should get into a heated discussion like that? *Haakan, come home. I need you here.*

22

Astrid couldn't remember ever being put out with her brother like this.

"All right, you two," Elizabeth said firmly the next evening. "This has to stop. You both have been so polite that I am about to scream. What in the world is going on?"

Astrid stared at her fingernails, knowing Elizabeth was right. Why did everything Thorliff said or did set her teeth on edge? She understood why they had taken the crew off the hospital to work on the houses to get them started. She knew better than to blame the typhoid scare on him, and she knew she really didn't, but that was one thing that came up—from him. She glanced up to see Thorliff staring at her, stone-faced and cold.

The nerve of him, acting as if this was all her fault. She clamped her jaw on the words of apology she'd been about to utter, then locked her arms across her chest. Were all men like these two? First Joshua messing up his life and now Thorliff. Men! Why in heaven's name did she think she wanted one in her life? Elizabeth was already married to this stubborn, bull-headed man, so she had to remain in this house with him, but Astrid was his sister, and she could leave—anytime.

"You two are acting like children. This isn't like either one of you. What is the matter?" Elizabeth stood, shaking her head.

Astrid was glad Inga had stayed out at her grandmother's place again.

"Thank you for your wise observations. I have work to do." Thorliff turned, and while his shoulders said he was stomping the floor as he left, his shoes didn't make a sound.

"You know what, Elizabeth? I'm going out to stay with Mor for a while. Maybe he can work his temper off. I'll see you in the morning."

"Astrid, don't be silly."

"Now I'm silly, along with childish? The way I feel, I'll end up picking a fight with you too. Much better that I hoe the garden or something like that. Hard physical work is a good antidote." She fetched her medical bag. "Once I figure out what is going on, you'll be the first to know."

She tried to pray, but even that didn't work. Striding along the road, which was barely more than a lane, she kicked a clod of dirt and flinched at the pain in her toes. Red River black dirt dried harder than concrete. And as heavy. Why had she ever snapped back at Thorliff like that? Why did what he said bother her anyway? What was it he said? Something about . . . She felt like yelling. But then surely someone would see her, and in a flash the news would be all over town. Dr. Astrid Bjorklund is losing her mind, screaming at something all by herself out in the country.

If she couldn't even remember what he said, why was she so steamed?

She couldn't talk with Far because he was off somewhere threshing wheat. She could go talk with Pastor Solberg, but what could she say? "Thorliff and I are having a bad time?" A fight? An argument? Was that it? He would say, "Over what?" And she would say, "I have no idea." And he would say, "Then what is the problem?" She would answer, "We are acting like children, according to Elizabeth."

Lord, are you listening? You probably are, but what am I saying? I am saying that I am concerned, no . . . worried, that the hospital is not going to be finished in time. And since Thorliff was the one with the idea to pull the work crew off that building, I guess I blame him. But to spend over a week away from the building, that was a lot of time.

She turned into the lane leading to her mother's home. Her own home really, because she did not have a home of her own. And the way things went with Joshua, she might never have a home of her own, or at least a family of her own. She could have a house built for her if she wanted one. But who wanted a house all to oneself?

Inga saw her first. "Tante Astrid!"

Surely Andrew and Ellie could hear the greeting clear over at their house. The little girl threw open the gate and came pelting down the path to throw her arms around Astrid's neck as she bent over to hug her niece.

"I didn't know you was coming. You stay all night?"

"Yes, that's the plan."

"You be here in the morning?"

Astrid took her hand, and they swung hands together all the way up the walk, the porch, and into the kitchen.

"Grandma, look who is here." While the walls caged Inga's shout, they shuddered in the doing.

"Astrid, is something wrong?"

The half shrug, half nod said more than words could.

"Oh dear." Ingeborg pushed her reading glasses back up on her nose. "Come in here. I was just reading my verses for the evening." She hooked her arm through Astrid's and drew her along. "Sit here."

How good it felt to be mothered. Astrid spent so many hours of her days taking care of other people that these simple commands seeped into her aching heart and nestled. "Guess I'm like a little bird coming back to the nest."

Inga looked up at her, then squinted and shook her head slowly. "You no baby bird. You Dr. Bjorklund, like Ma."

"Thank you, Inga. You say the best things." Astrid hugged Inga to her side and dropped a kiss on the part in her hair.

"Inga, I think it is time you got ready for bed." Ingeborg's voice came gentle in the dusking room.

"I will." She stared at her grandma. "No bath."

"All right, but wash good, including your feet."

Inga stared down at her bare feet. "Dirty, huh?"

"'Fraid so."

Inga liked a bath about as much as a cat did. She slid down from the sofa by Astrid. "Will you sleep in my bed?"

"If you want."

Inga nodded. "Or I sleep with Grandma?" She watched for a reaction, then smiled. "You pick."

Perhaps having a little body in bed with her would be a good thing. "Do you promise not to kick?" Astrid asked.

Inga rolled her eyes and shook her head, but as she headed for the bathroom, she threw a giggle over her shoulder.

"So you need to talk?"

"I guess so. I'm acting in ways that aren't like me."

"The argument with Thorliff?"

"Ja, and it didn't quit. I mean, he didn't yell at me, not really, but as Elizabeth said, 'Stop acting like children.' Only I don't remember ever arguing with him like this."

"What started it?"

"I commented on whether the hospital would be ready by the deadline. He got all angry."

"I imagine he is feeling a lot of pressure with all the building going on, the typhoid slowing things down, fears for the men, and getting the other buildings up too. He's taken on a lot of responsibility."

"Don't forget the newspaper."

"I think that has become almost a hobby, albeit one with deadlines always looming. Your far and I have been praying extra for him. You might do that too."

"I might. Mor, I really don't like feeling like this."

"I can understand that. You like things out in the open, where you can see them and deal with them."

"I do?" Astrid thought a moment. "I guess I do. I thought that was how I was being with Joshua, er, Mr. Landsverk too, but he went stomping off, and I heard he tried to resign but Thorliff wouldn't let him. Why would he feel he has to leave town? I'm not mad at him or anything."

Inga wandered into the room in her nightdress, yawning. "You say my prayers?"

"Which of us?"

"Grandma."

"I'm coming. You go on up and get into bed."

"You coming now?"

Ingeborg put her glasses on top of her Bible on the whatnot table beside her rocking chair. When she stood up, Inga headed up the stairs. "I'll be right back. Don't go away or lose those thoughts."

Astrid heard the two of them upstairs, seeing herself in Inga. All those years her mother tucked her in and said prayers with her. If only all her fears and worries could be wiped away as easily now as then. She leaned her head against the back of the sofa. *Lord, how come I can feel you closer here than on the road out from town? Prince of Peace, you fill this room, this house. No wonder I wanted, no, needed to come home.* She stared at her mother's Bible lying open in the pool of lamplight. Her own lay closed by her bed. Seldom did she leave it open. Why was that? She remembered her mother saying one time that she left her Bible open so that when she passed by, she could stop and see what God was trying to tell her at that moment. She said that sometimes words seemed to leap off the page and yell, "Here, here, listen to me."

Astrid sat and listened. The whisper seemed to come from the corner. *Be still and know that I am God.* Be still. "I haven't been still much lately, have I?" She waited for an answer, but all she heard was the sigh of the curtains on the evening breeze. *Be still. Be still.*

The cricket chorus tuned up outside the window. She heard her mother's soft steps on a creaky stair, the curtain fluttering at the window. *Be still.*

"Where is Freda?" she asked in the dimness after her mother settled back in her rocker.

"Over at Kaaren's. She wanted to spend some time with Anna now that Solem is off with the threshing crew. We need to find housing for them once the deaf school starts again. Between Anna helping Kaaren and Solem farming with Haakan and Lars, they have been such a help."

"So tonight it is just you and me?"

"Ja, it is."

"What are you reading?"

"Matthew. I decided to read the gospels through again. I finished Isaiah a couple of nights ago."

"I've not been in the Word much lately."

"Why?"

"I get busy. I know that's no excuse, but maybe that is what this thing is all about. For me to take time to listen more. I needed to listen, not let Thorliff's pressure become my pressure. When he flared, I should have spoken softly like Proverbs says about words of gold. 'A soft answer turneth away wrath.' And 'slow to speak, slow to wrath.' "

"You heard all that while I went upstairs?"

"No, mostly I heard 'Be still, be still.' And then the others had a chance to come slipping into my mind."

"So what are you going to do about it?"

"Be still. And make sure I am still more often. Isn't it strange that the faster you go, the less you hear the Spirit and the Word?"

"Ah, but it is so true. I let myself get really sad when Emmy was taken away. Inga said my eyes didn't smile anymore. So I've spent more time reading my Bible again, listening to what God wants to tell me."

"And He said don't be sad?"

"Pretty much. He said to sing praises, to rejoice, to know that He loves each of us. He loves Emmy more than I can, and I pray that He brings her back here. But I have to trust Him with those I love." A gentle pause lasted on the cricket song. "Like you on Rosebud Reservation. Your far there too. Now him on the threshing crew. Emmy with her uncle. Carl and Inga. All of you. I cannot keep you safe, but God can. And does."

"No worry, nor fear."

"Fear not. Two such simple words, but sometimes not easy. Not easy at all."

Astrid stood and crossed to her mother, kneeling beside her to put her head in her mother's lap. Ingeborg stroked her daughter's hair, like she had so many times through the years. They stayed that way a long while before Astrid stood. "Thank you, Mor. Mange tusen takk. I'll sleep here, but in the morning, if I'm not back by the time Inga wakes up, tell her I'll be back soon."

"You'll go see Thorliff?"

"Ja." She kissed her mother's soft cheek. "'Night. I love you, Mor."

Up in bed Inga was breathing softly. Astrid blew out the kerosene lamp and knelt by the window, the billowing curtains kissing her cheeks. "Thank you, heavenly Father." A line of pale gold marked the western horizon, and above that the evening star twinkled at her. "Amen."

———

THE ROOSTER'S CROWING woke her up, reminding her of the years that the chickens were her responsibility. As she dressed, memories of the evening before brought her peace again. Carrying her shoes down the stairs, she sat on the top step of the porch, put her shoes on, then took off for town. Andrew waved at her on his way to the barn to start the milking. She waved back but kept on going. When she got to town, Thorliff wasn't at the office yet, so she headed for the house and met him coming out the back door.

"I was coming to see you."

"Good. Then I got here first." She smiled up at her brother. "I'm sorry. I did indeed act like a child, and I don't want to be like that. Please forgive me."

He laid a finger on her lips. "I say the same. Please forgive me."

She wrapped her arms around his waist and, laying her cheek against his chest, hugged him hard. His arms around her were doing the same.

"We'll make it, Astrid. God willing, we will make it."

"Those are the best words, *God willing*. I was sure I heard Him speaking in the parlor at home last night."

"That's not surprising, you know. Not with all the prayer and talk and Bible reading that has gone on in that room."

"I know. I need to get back before Inga wakes up, but I had to tell you this."

"I was on my way out there, so how about we go together and have breakfast at Mor's with Inga."

"Good." The two locked arms and strode out the road she had just traveled.

"I think I know what this was all about," she said after a bit.

"What?"

"To make me realize how much I need to be like Mor. To read the Word for pleasure, not just because I should."

Thorliff nodded. "How to find time. I know I have to make time, because I will never find it. But the knowing and the doing are two different things. By the way, I got Joshua to give me another month before we talk about his leaving again. Are you all right with that?"

"I don't want him to leave Blessing. He belongs here. And now his brother is here too. This is his home. I don't bear him any ill will, and I hope he can come to that with me. We are just not suited for each other. God revealed that very clearly. I pray he will come to see that too and find the woman that God wants for him."

"That sounds really good, but if it is someone from Blessing, will you be jealous?"

"Please, Lord, I hope not. I wish Joshua Landsverk all the happiness he can have." She heaved a breath.

"What was that for?"

"I do want a husband some day, a fine man like you and Far. I want a home and children. What if I missed out?"

"Astrid, you have plenty of time to find a man. Or have a fine man find you."

"I hope you are right." She hugged his arm close. "Oh, I forgot to tell you. I found out Mr. Sidorov has a wife and son in New York City. One of the Norwegian immigrants figured out what he was trying to say, using a combination of motions and drawing pictures."

"They were all supposed to be single men," Thorliff said.

"Desperation causes one to do something he normally wouldn't, like lie to get a job. Maybe I would too."

Thorliff heaved a sigh. "We need to ask each of them directly if they came from the old country with a wife and children. It doesn't matter if they left their family in their homeland. They can bring them over later themselves."

"So what are you going to do?"

"Find the families, of course."

She smiled up at him. "As I said, I want an honorable man like my brother." *But no matter what you say, Thorliff Bjorklund, I might indeed have missed my chance.*

23

I'll be leaving, then, in a couple hours."

"All right, Daniel. Thanks for putting off this trip until we got through the onslaught. We'll handle things here." Thorliff straightened a stack of papers on his desk. "Hjelmer will be back in a couple weeks, and that will help."

"You might suggest he is needed more here now than off selling wells and windmills. The real money is in these buildings." Daniel motioned to the drawings of the hospital and the seeder plant that they had tacked to the walls. "You're doing all you can with the hospital and housing construction, along with the newspaper."

"Ja. Well, Hjelmer has always marched to his own drum. He is a born salesman."

"Then perhaps we should send him out to these meetings. I'd much rather stay here. Do you think he'd go?"

Thorliff nodded. "I think you just came up with the best idea of the day, maybe the week. When you get back, we'll talk about it. Hope you can find us some new employees at the same time. Someone who can set type and run a printer part time would be good."

"My list keeps growing. I need to go pack." Daniel stopped at the door. "Do you think your sister would be offended if I wrote to her?"

"Not at all." Thorliff raised an eyebrow. "Do you want her to write back?"

"That would be hard. I'll be moving around so much. Thanks." He shut the door behind himself. Why had it been so hard to ask such a simple question? Leave it to Thorliff to raise one more question.

He stopped to knock on the door to his mother's room.

"Come in."

He found her studying manuals for teaching English to her students. "How are you coming with this?"

"I'm glad I didn't try to teach the women and the men together. They would have been terribly uncomfortable."

"The women or the men?"

"Both." She reached up and patted his cheek. "I suppose you are getting ready to leave?"

"I am. Will you be all right here?"

"What do you mean? Of course I'll be all right. For a woman in mourning, I am having the time of my life. There are people who need something that I can do. Bless you for suggesting this for me. I teach the women in the morning and the men in the evening. Now they come here rather than my going to the schoolhouse—the men I mean. Young Johnny takes me in the buggy out to the Knutsons' and picks me up again. How could I ask for anything more?"

Her wide smile told him she meant every word.

He leaned down to kiss her cheek. "It is wonderful to see you so alive again. I must tell you, I was worried about you after Father disappeared."

"I was too. It was all the uncertainty. Once I knew for sure he'd gone to his heavenly home, I could grieve and trust that God was taking care of both him and us. Thank you for talking me into coming to Blessing. I believe we will both have new lives here."

"Me too. I'll write."

"Thank you, but you won't be gone that long—or will you?"

"Probably two weeks, anyway. I need to be free to follow some leads, if I find any. Thorliff and I just discussed having Hjelmer be the salesman for the company. If he would do that, I would be really pleased. He loves travel, and I would rather stay right here and get the parts into production. We will have a real celebration when those first orders ship."

"Your father is so proud of you."

"I hope he would be."

"No, he is."

"Good." He squeezed her hand and turned to the door.

"Go with God."

"I will and do. You always said that to Father too. Thank you." He closed the door behind him before the tear that was trickling down his mother's cheek could slow him down. They didn't talk much about his father, and he just hated to see his mother cry. She had shed rivers of tears, enough that she had seemed to be melting away before his eyes. Now, even though she wore gowns of gray instead of the hateful black, she looked her more beautiful self. His father had always been so proud of his wife and so in love with her. He hoped to find someone to love like his father had loved his mother. So far none of the young women he had met interested him. Until Dr. Bjorklund. At first he thought she was spoken for. But apparently she'd turned Landsverk down, because he'd talked of leaving.

While he felt sorry for the man, he rejoiced on his part. Whistling, he packed a deep carpetbag with his clothes and another with the brochures Thorliff had printed for him. Increased grain yields and ease of adaptation were the hallmarks of their new product.

Packed and downstairs, he set his bags by the door and entered the dining room, where Miss Christopherson was inspecting the dinner seating and preparations.

"Good morning, Mr. Jeffers. You are early for dinner."

"I know. I'm catching the noon train and wondered if I could have a sandwich to take with me."

"Of course. You sit right down there, and I'll bring it out to you. Would you like some coffee while you wait?"

"No, thank you. I'm fine." He watched as she hurried back to the kitchen. Mrs. Wiste was certainly blessed to have a woman like Miss Christopherson in charge of the dining room. She made everyone feel right at home. He'd watched the immigrant workmen last night. They always sat together at the tables over in the corner. How long would it take for them to begin to feel like they were part of the community? He pulled a small pad of paper from his chest pocket and jotted a note for Thorliff. Finished, he folded it and wrote *Thorliff* on the outside. Surely someone would deliver it for him.

Later, on the train heading east, he pulled his journal out of his bag to write some reminders to himself. While he didn't keep a formal journal like his father had, this book was never far from reach. Of course his mother had told him not to bother to write—he remembered her saying that to her husband too—but Daniel also remembered her great joy in receiving letters. When traveling, his father had made it a habit to write to his wife twice a week and always include notes for the children.

He added a typesetter to the list of needed employees and made a note to price a more up-to-date printer for Thorliff. The purchase was long overdue. Norwegians were famous for making do rather than investing in something new. He'd seen it in action with his partner. But the Bjorklunds farmed with the latest machinery, so they were forward-thinking business men too. He wrote himself some more notes before putting the journal away and bringing out his latest novel, *Tom Sawyer, Detective*, by Mark Twain.

A desire to read was one thing his mother had instilled in him. While he read a great deal and a great variety, fiction was his favorite. And as of right now, Mark Twain was his favorite American author.

When the train pulled into the Minneapolis station, he got off and made his way to the hotel his father had always stayed at. He had appointments at several farm machinery sales lots.

———

BY THE TIME he left for Chicago two days later, he had enough orders to make him pleased. Selling to the sellers was the best way to do business. Let them sell to the farmers.

Settled in his next hotel, he took some hotel stationery and sat down to write.

Dear Dr. Bjorklund,

I asked Thorliff if you would mind if I wrote to you, and he said he didn't think you would, so that is what I am doing. I am in Chicago, Illinois, and have a list of appointments for this area. So far, the Twin Cities were remarkably open to our modification for seeders. My father was right when he said the product he invented would make a difference for not only wheat crops but other grains as well.

I enjoy seeing the country from a railroad car. The trip is so much faster than any other way, as you well know. I stopped by an automobile dealership and looked at some of the new designs. As Hjelmer has said so often, automobiles will be the next big addition to travel. One man boasted that his Oldsmobile would cover ten miles in one hour. While I wanted to drive one, I did not have the time or the training.

I wonder why Hjelmer sold his. He always likes the latest thing, and these certainly are. The salesman said that one day there would be roads all over America for automobile travel. There were plenty of cars on the streets of Minneapolis. I saw a team of horses panic when the automobile near them backfired, which seems to be a common occurrence. Needless to say, I will not be bringing one to Blessing, at least not yet.

I hope the progress being made on the hospital building meets your approval.

Sincerely,
Daniel Jeffers

He read through it again, folded it, and placed it in one of the hotel envelopes, addressing it to Dr. Astrid Bjorklund, Blessing, North Dakota. Then he wrote a letter to his mother, this time describing the flowers and houses he had seen, as well as a hat that he thought she might like, and assuring her that all was well and the trip profitable—so far, at least.

———

ON SUNDAY HE WALKED to the nearest Lutheran church and attended the worship service. The pipe organ alone was worth the walk. Singing along with an instrument like that made him wonder if heaven would have music to top it.

"Thank you for such an uplifting service," he said to the pastor greeting people at the door. "Your organ is wonderful and the organist a maestro."

"We are very fortunate in having them both. I hope you come again."

"I'm just traveling through on business. If I am in Chicago again, I will be back."

He responded to greetings from several other folks and made his way back to his hotel. Would Blessing ever have a church large enough for a pipe organ? Even a pump organ could add to the music they already had. Did Dr. Elizabeth Bjorklund play the organ? She sure knew how to make the piano sing.

The organ music remained one of the highlights of his trip, which was seeming longer than the days he was actually gone. When he decided to write to Astrid again, he realized he would be home before the letter got there, so he read his book instead. He was homesick for Blessing. It wasn't as if he'd lived there for years, and he'd never really been homesick for the place he grew up.

Was it Astrid who was drawing him back?

24

Grace is coming home today!" Sophie called from the doorway of the surgery.

Astrid excused herself and stepped into the hallway, closing the door behind her. She strode out to the waiting room, which at that moment was empty, thank goodness.

"Sophie, this is a doctor's office. You must be polite here."

"Not when Grace is coming home, this time to stay. I had to tell someone, and you were the closest." Sophie clapped her hands and would have spun in place like she did as a little girl had Astrid not been trying to look stern.

Astrid hugged her cousin. "I have a patient, but if you will sit outside on the porch swing, I'll be out as soon as I can. It shouldn't be long."

"Where's Elizabeth?"

"Over at the hospital, talking over some changes with Thorliff."

"All right, I'll wait. But you hurry. The train could be here pretty quick."

Astrid glanced at the watch face she wore pinned to her apron. "It's at least an hour before the train comes."

"Maybe Thelma has something good to drink in the icebox. See you on the porch."

Astrid assured the little girl sitting on her examining table that the hair her brother had shaved off her scalp would come back and the cut would heal quickly. She turned to the mother. "Head wounds bleed severely, but this was just a surface cut. If you come back in three or four days, I'll remove the stitches. Or if you have a slender scissors, you can do that at home. Just slide the tip of the blade under the stitch and snip. Pull it out with a tweezers or your fingernails. Don't worry if a drop of blood appears. It will scab over."

"Thank you, Dr. Bjorklund. I can't believe he did this to his sister."

"We were just playing barber, Ma. He didn't mean to hurt me."

Astrid rolled her lips to keep from grinning. This was a first. "Maybe you should play school or store instead. It would be a lot safer." She accepted the payment and ushered them out the door.

Thelma was already in the room cleaning up. Even she snorted when Astrid told her the story. "Children nowadays, *tsk, tsk.* Too much time for playing." She shook her head and bundled up the bloody cloths. "Mrs. Wiste is out on the back porch. She has your glass out there too."

"Thank you, Thelma. You do such a good job of caring for all of us."

Astrid wasn't sure what Thelma's mutter said, but she left the examining room with a light heart. One needed a good laugh now and then. Well, really more now than then.

She had another laugh when she told Sophie, who laughed and asked for the barber tale again.

"Playing barber. I never."

"Good thing he didn't try to pull her teeth."

That brought on another spate of giggles.

"You should tell that story to all the others at our girl party. Don't forget, it's tomorrow night."

"I won't forget."

As they sipped their glasses down to the tiny ice chunks, they shared the town news, being careful not to gossip.

"How do we know when it is gossiping and when it is just sharing the news?"

"I guess it depends on what our motive is and what the news is."

"I suppose so." Sophie laid her glass against her cheek. "Every bit of coolness counts on days like today."

"Put your feet up, Sophie. Your ankles are swelling." After the advice, Astrid continued with her thought. "I'm thinking we'll be having a thunderstorm." She nodded toward the west, where dark clouds were massing. "Feels like one too."

"I know. We need the rain, and it should help clear the air."

"Remember when we used to go puddling with Mor and Tante Ingeborg? Washing our hair in the rain and then sitting on the porch to brush it out and dry once the sun came out?"

"Even though we have running water, I'd rather wash my hair in the water from the rain barrel to this day."

"Me too. And with a lemon rinse. Mor was livid one time when we took the precious lemon and rinsed our hair with it. But it sure felt good and smelled wonderful."

"What about when you cut your hair in a fringe?"

Sophie rolled her eyes. "Anything for excitement and something different. I think going to Seattle killed that adventurous spirit I had."

"I'm glad it didn't kill more than that. You could have been in so much trouble after Hamre died. I cried for you for days and was so happy when you came back."

"I heard a line that I like. 'Home is where they always have to take you in.' I was afraid Mor and Far wouldn't let me come back."

"Really afraid?"

"Terrified. I knew I had hurt them badly. I was most certainly selfish and headstrong. And now I'm as happy as anyone can be. Mor has always said that God works in mysterious ways, and I am living proof of that."

"We all are." Astrid checked her watch just as they heard the far-off whistle blow. "Let's go meet Grace."

Jonathan and Kaaren were there before the girls arrived. The three females hung back while the young man paced the platform, as if his stomping could bring the train more quickly.

"And here I always thought he was the model of patience." Astrid smiled at her aunt and cousin.

"He is a young man in love. That's for sure." Sophie clasped her mother's hand and held the parasol over them both. "I wish they didn't have to wait so long to get married."

"Less than a year now." Kaaren flinched as the screech of wheels and the shriek of steam announced the arrival of the monstrous black engine. By the time it stopped, the engine was in place for the water to refill the boiler, and the passenger cars lined the station platform.

The conductor put the stool at the bottom of the stairs, and Grace stepped gracefully down to them, only to be swung around in a hug and dance step by the tall young man who let out a whoop of joy. She clapped her hand on her straw hat and tried to look dignified but failed miserably.

Astrid enjoyed the sight. Grace was more lovely than ever, aided by the beauty of love as she saw her Jonathan again. The two turned as one and smiled at the waiting family members. Sophie and Astrid stepped back so Kaaren could greet her longed-for daughter.

"And you are really home to stay?" Kaaren asked.

"I really am." Grace spoke, but it was easy to tell that she'd been communicating in sign more than speech back in New York these last two years. She stumbled over some words, her pronunciation harsh on others. But with all the new people that had arrived in Blessing, not everyone signed any longer, so her speaking the words was all the more important.

"Except when we visit my family," Jonathan added, even though he stood behind Grace. "Or when she teaches at training centers."

Kaaren looked at her daughter. "Are things happening we don't know about yet?"

"I have much to tell you. We will need a wagon for my trunks, but I see you brought the buggy." She turned to Astrid and held her arms wide. "Well, Dr. Bjorklund, you don't look a whole lot different, but you have a wonderful title. I know you earned every letter of it."

"I did and I'm doing what I like best. And the best part is I am home in Blessing and not in Africa."

"I wondered for a while, but one day when I was praying, it was like God was speaking right to me. He said, 'Fear not.' That's something He has said to me too many times. 'Fear not.' I always feel like He's waiting to catch me if I trip, or waiting to make sure I am where He wants me."

Astrid could only nod. For Grace to make such a long speech took plenty of effort on her part. So she tapped the cousins' secret code into Grace's hand. And they both smiled, Astrid with one eyebrow slightly raised. Grace nodded. "We will."

Sophie dabbed at her eyes.

"What's wrong?" Astrid, ever watchful, asked.

"I'm just so happy. My other half is back in this part of the world, where she belongs."

Grace gave Sophie another hug. Then at Jonathan's nudge, they walked over to the buggy.

"Now remember, Grace, like I told you in my letter, we are having a girl party tomorrow night in your honor. Well, in everyone's honor, because the daughters of Blessing are all together again." Sophie threw her arms wide as if to encompass the entire town. "And, Mr. Gould, you'll be able to live without her for at least one evening."

"As if I have any choice in the matter." His woeful look made them all laugh again. This was a good day for laughter.

The whistle blew and the train eased forward, steam billowing again, the conductor waving from the bottom step of the passenger car. "All aboard!" His call lingered behind on the wind as the train picked up speed.

Jonathan helped Kaaren into the buggy first and then Grace, before taking the front seat to drive.

Astrid and Sophie waved good-bye, laughing at the stack of luggage that belonged to Grace, and strolled off the platform.

"I think we need a soda."

"I think you are right." Astrid and Sophie turned left instead of right to the boardinghouse. They pushed open the door to Rebecca's Blessing Soda Shoppe to find it empty.

"Rebecca?" Sophie called.

"Back here. Just a minute."

"Where's Benny?"

"Knute and Dorothy took him out to the farm for a couple of days," she said as she emerged from the back. "He is having a wonderful time." Rebecca finished tying her apron in place.

"She's going to have her hands full when her baby arrives in November," Sophie commented.

"She'll handle it with ease, I'm sure," Rebecca said. "Now, what can I get for you ladies?"

256

"Ladies?" Astrid and Sophie turned to look at each other. "Ladies?"

"Sophie might be but not me, at least not yet."

"Dr. Bjorklund is not a lady? Now, that sounds strange."

"Dr. Bjorklund is Elizabeth. Isn't it funny that I still feel that way?" Astrid paused and made a huff in her throat. "When I was at Rosebud, I felt like Dr. Bjorklund. I forgot how young I really am and did what had to be done. Then I come back here and sometimes I feel like I'm playing at being a doctor. That I really was never away, and—"

"Astrid, sometimes I wonder about you," Sophie said, shaking her head. "Give her your latest kind of soda and wake her up a bit. Stitching heads and setting broken bones and birthing babies is *not* playing at doctor."

"I agree." Rebecca turned to fetch a glass, and Astrid could see the mound growing under her friend's apron.

"Are you feeling all right?" Astrid asked.

"Sometimes I get a bit tired, so I do what you told me and go sit on the porch in the shade with my feet up. That's what I was doing when you came. After all, I am not due until January."

"Good for you." Astrid turned to Sophie. "Guess I can't be playing at it when even my friends do what I tell them."

"Don't get too smug. Not all your friends and not all the time."

"Right. Some things will never change. You are the one that needs your feet up, Sophie. Your time will be here before we know it."

"It couldn't come soon enough for me. Being so close to term in the summer is not the best of situations. Winter is much better." Sophie took a quick look at the menu. "Make three sodas, Rebecca, whatever kind you recommend, and we'll all sit on your back porch. If we sit in front, half the town will decide they need to come and visit."

But when Sophie put down the money for the three sodas, Rebecca argued.

"I can too buy you a soda, if I want," Sophie insisted.

"Sophie!"

"Just hush. Let's go hide on the back porch."

———

THE NEXT EVENING the daughters of Blessing gathered at Sophie's house as ordered.

"Where are the children?" Deborah asked.

"Next door at Helga's. She will take May too, Ellie, so you can forget about anything else but having a good time."

Ellie went next door and handed her baby into Helga's waiting arms. "Are you sure you want to take her? I didn't expect this. She's been fed and is sleepy, ready for bed. I can just put her down here. Carl is home with his pa."

"That's all right. I'll take her." Helga smiled down at the sleepy little girl. "So precious she is." Helga Larson and her family moved from Minneapolis to Blessing to be close to her brother Garth, Sophie's husband. Helga's husband, Dan, worked at the flour mill.

Back at Sophie's, Astrid led a frustrated Sophie into the parlor, where a wing chair and ottoman sat in front of the tall windows overlooking the backyard. "Why don't you sit here? With the fan going, this will give you some real relaxation."

"Oh, Astrid, I don't have time for this." But she sank into the chair with a sigh. "I know putting my feet up will indeed feel good, but I'm the hostess." Sophie tucked her full skirt around her legs while Astrid removed her shoes.

"As if we don't know where things are." Astrid probed Sophie's ankles. "When did this puffiness start?"

"Just the last couple of days. It's been so hot, and I've been canning string beans—oh, and making jam too. It goes away at night."

"How about if Freda comes to finish your canning and you knit sweaters or something instead?"

"Astrid, I have four children to take care of and—"

"And Freda or Helga don't know how to do that?" Astrid beckoned to Deborah. "See how her ankles are swelling? As a nurse, that is something to look for in pregnant patients. While in the summer the heat and humidity might contribute to the swelling, it can be a sign of possible problems. I think nurses will play a larger part in caring for pregnant patients. At least at our hospital they will."

Sophie and Grace clapped their hands. "Bravo, Dr. Bjorklund."

Astrid shook her head. "I get no respect here, and you wonder why I feel as if I am playing doctor?" She looked over at Rebecca, who was reclining on the sofa. "Go over and check her out. Tell me what you find."

Deborah did as she was told, making a joke about free medical care. "Your ankles are swelling a bit too. Is this an epidemic, or what?"

"No, the typhoid was, or could have been, an epidemic. This is pregnancies and hot, humid weather. Well, not as hot as before the rainstorm yesterday, but it's still a steam bath today." Astrid brushed a hank of hair off her cheek.

After Deborah gave her report, Sophie clapped her hands. "Enough medical stuff. Let's eat and drink and be merry."

"I think that refers to another kind of drinking," Grace said and signed.

"You know what I mean." Sophie stood and bowed. "Supper is served, my friends. Help yourselves and then bring your plates back in here."

Deborah interrupted her. "You sit. We will fill plates for our pregnant people, and if you don't like what we bring, oh well." The face she made brought laughter from all.

Once their plates were full and they were gathered in the parlor again, Sophie started the discussion. "We have three married women, one engaged, and two who are still not attached. I think we need to talk about this to figure out how we can help the two not yet attached."

"You can help best by not helping at all," Astrid offered.

"Okay, then let's begin with you." Sophie pointed to a chair she had moved into the center of the somewhat circle. "Sit."

"I'm not going to sit in the middle like that so you can all stare at me."

"Sit. Sit. Sit." The chorus made her roll her eyes, but she sat, taking a forkful of salad at the same time.

"Now, I thought there was a budding romance going on here between you and Joshua Landsverk. When he sings, my heart goes pitty-pat." Sophie patted her chest. "Well?"

Astrid's smile disappeared. "There was. I broke it off."

"My land, why? He's handsome, charming, building a house for his wife—"

"And he cannot deal with his wife being a doctor who puts her patients before her family."

"Oh, Astrid, I'm so sorry." Grace came and knelt at Astrid's knees, taking her cousin's hand. "But it is better to see that now than to live a miserable life together."

"I came to understand that. But he was not happy when I told him again."

"Again?"

Astrid nodded, swallowing against the lump growing in her throat. "I pray that God has the perfect woman for him and they will be as happy as can be."

"We have to find a husband for Astrid. That is all there is to it." Sophie arranged her bulk and settled down on the floor next to Grace.

"It worked for me," Maydell said, sitting next to Grace. "Gus still blushes when I remind him."

A chuckle grew contagious.

"There are not many marriageable men in town," Rebecca said, moving to the edge of the seat. "Either you bring the party over here to me or we move this thing closer to the party."

They rearranged the room so they could be closer together. "This is more like it used to be when we put our pallets in a circle and brushed each other's hair."

"Back to Astrid."

"What about Deborah?" Astrid asked, hoping to take the attention off her.

"She's next."

"Oh, wonderful." Deborah drew her knees up under her skirt and wrapped her arms around her knees. "We can solve that in one sentence. I am going to be an old maid nurse who takes care of all the women in the family way at our hospital."

"I thought you kind of liked Toby," Grace said.

"He's a friend, is all." Deborah's cheeks pinked.

Sophie leaned forward. "Is that red on your face? Deborah, you have never in all our lives been able to tell a lie. You *are* interested in Toby Valders."

"Sophie, for—"

"Look at her. Am I right or am I right?"

Deborah covered her telltale cheeks with her hands and ducked her head. "But he isn't interested in me." The last word turned into a small wail.

Astrid chuckled as she saw her cousin switch into full-out matchmaking mode.

"Then it is time he comes to reality. He for you and you for he." She waved her hands. "See, tonight I am even a poet. Did you catch that?"

Groans spoke admissions.

"You better watch out, Deborah, Astrid. When our Sophie goes on the attack, you have not a chance. Or rather, the man in question has no chance."

"Speaking from true experience, Rebecca?"

"That's for sure. Although, perhaps Gerald would have come around in time." She blushed. "But I'm glad you speeded things up."

"Good." Sophie propped her hands on her knees. "So how do we do this, ladies?" She looked over her shoulder. "And don't you think you are off the hook either, cousin. The night is just beginning."

"I think Daniel Jeffers is an interesting man," Rebecca said. "Don't you, Astrid?"

"He's a very nice man."

"He takes such good care of his mother, and yet he is not a mama's boy." Sophie contemplated Astrid. "That's an interesting thought."

Astrid rolled her eyes. "Sorry, Soph. I am just not interested in any man right now. I need time to get over the debacle of before."

"We shall see."

25

"Why is Haakan's being gone bothering me so much this year?" Ingeborg asked, gazing out on Saturday from her seat on the porch.

Kaaren shook her head. "Perhaps because we are getting older. I feel the same with Lars, and he didn't spend weeks down on the reservation."

"He went down earlier."

"I know, but for you these two things are closer together. Haakan wasn't home that long before he left again." Kaaren picked up the nursing manual they had been studying. "We need to pick and choose what is most important for our Indian women to learn. After all, if Dr. Red Hawk is to be here for the dedication, we don't have much time."

Ingeborg shook her head. How could it be nearly the end of August already? She felt more behind every day, and yet it wasn't that she wasn't busy. With the corn ripening, she'd been canning that, as well as drying corn that she'd cut off the cob and spread on screens. And that really had to be dry. One year she'd tried to hurry the drying process and ended up with mold, losing the entire batch. Now she stored it in smaller tins. It was safer that way.

"They've learned to apply dressings, recognize some illnesses, listen to the heart and lungs." Kaaren smiled at Ingeborg. "The day they were listening to each other's chests—it was all I could do not to burst out laughing."

"Me too. When Gray Smoke did me, she couldn't even look me in the eye. As if she were invading me or something." Ingeborg chuckled. "We need to find some non-healthy hearts and lungs for them to listen to, so they can learn the difference. I also think Deborah should be sent to Grand Forks for schooling. She has a real affinity for nursing."

"Let's face it, Deborah can do whatever she sets her mind to. People don't realize what a bright young woman she is, because she is always just doing whatever is asked. She did great on the switchboard, she's worked at the boardinghouse, she's taken care of mothers and newly birthed babies . . . she's helped out wherever she was needed. I can just see her running that hospital."

Ingeborg stared at her dearest friend, whom she still considered her sister, even though both of their first husbands—brothers—had died. "I never thought of that. Of course. We need to mention that to Elizabeth and Astrid. I know they are starting to think of staffing."

"You and I just never get much time to talk anymore. I'll be glad when quilting starts, so we can visit on the way over and back." She flipped through some more pages. "I taught the women how to treat croup, and you did burns. Do you want to do a day on stitching wounds closed?"

"The doctors would do that, rather than the nurses."

"But in an emergency?"

"True. I'll do that one this week, then." Ingeborg thought for a moment. "What are we going to do when your deaf students start returning next week?"

"I was thinking our nurses in training could have the room that Ilse and George used to have. Now that they have a house, I've used their room for storage or for overflow students." She heaved a sigh. "I cannot tell you how happy I am to have Grace home again. Getting the new students up to signing well enough to enter the regular school will make things easier."

"How many new ones do you have coming?"

"Ten. It is a shame how many people are hidden away because they can't hear and families don't know what to do, other than treat them as animals. I have three boys coming in who have never had any kind of training, so we will start from the very basics. George is such a help with children like that." George McBride had come to the school as a student in the early days and, after marrying Ilse, Kaaren's assistant, stayed on to teach woodworking and other necessary farming skills that did not demand that the worker needed to talk well.

"Grace will take the others?"

"We all will, but we should be able to give more one-on-one help now. And Grace has new techniques to teach us, things they have studied and learned at the larger schools."

"All right. This week we will go over bed care again, dressings, and sepsis. And I'll ask Astrid if she will come to help us teach a class on birthing. We could invite Sophie and maybe Rebecca to join us too. That way they'll be able to listen to the baby's heart and see the progress." Ingeborg wrote some notes on her paper. "I'm sure both of our Indian women have helped birth babies in the past, so only Deborah will be completely new with it."

"Marvelous. Here we are teaching birthing to an unmarried

young woman who isn't supposed to know anything about birthing or what leads up to it."

"What do nursing schools do in this situation?" Ingeborg wondered aloud.

"I don't know."

"I don't know either. I got all my training during the action. I remember Mor leaving home in the middle of the night after a man came pounding on the door. I guess I got my love of things medical from her. We became midwives and nurses out of sheer necessity."

"Oh—tomorrow Mrs. Jeffers is coming out with Deborah," Kaaren said, "so she will be teaching English during our review."

"Good. Do you want a cup of coffee as bad as I do?" At the nod Ingeborg rose and went inside to the kitchen, bringing back coffee, cups, and a plate of cookies. "Try these icebox cookies, a new recipe Freda found and tried. Inga says they need to be sweeter, but then again, Inga wants absolutely everything sweeter."

ON MONDAY MORNING, Ingeborg pulled Deborah aside. "Something has been bothering me, and I decided I'd better let you make your own decision. You know that today we are starting on birthing." Deborah nodded. "Since you are not married, this is not really proper for you to hear and learn." Ingeborg finished in a rush. "We could be seriously criticized for allowing you to continue."

"I understand," Deborah said but then shook her head. "But remember, I grew up on a farm, and I know a lot about reproduction and birthing. After Zeb left, I helped with calves and lambs, puppies and kittens. One day when Manda was raising and training horses, she made me help with one of the mares when she was having trouble with the stallion. Granted, I'm not married, but I'm serious about wanting to be a nurse. I say we proceed as we planned and ignore anyone who thinks they are the last word on what is proper."

Ingeborg rolled her eyes. They both knew whom they were talking about but kept from naming her. Besides, this could offend some of the other women too. And the men, for that matter. While strictures regarding proper behavior were much weaker there in Blessing, still, some things were going beyond the permissible. And this would be one of them.

Later in the morning, when Gray Smoke put a stethoscope on Rebecca's expanding middle, her eyes sparkled, and she listened again. First to the baby's heart, then to Rebecca's.

"Fast. Beat fast." Gray Smoke patted Rebecca's shoulder. "You hear?"

Rebecca smiled and nodded. "Astrid has let me listen. I really do have a baby in there."

Next they listened to Sophie's heart and her baby's. Their eyes widened.

"Big baby."

"A rapidly growing baby. When is your baby due?" Kaaren asked.

"Early September." Sophie sat up when Kaaren offered her a hand. "I seem to be awfully big, but then, compared to the twins . . ." She shook her head. "I shouldn't compare."

"You aren't unduly large. You should have seen Kaaren when she was carrying the twins. She was even bigger than you were, Sophie." Ingeborg chuckled at the memory.

"I needed a wheelbarrow to carry my front. I didn't walk, I wad-dled, and as little of that as possible. At least that wasn't my first, so I had some idea of what to expect."

"The girls were the first twins I ever helped with. One baby is always so exciting, but two! Sophie was born first, squalling like we'd beat her. Grace was so still, I was concerned for her at first. But she nursed and grew well. She just couldn't hear." Ingeborg helped

Sophie back into her dress. "Good thing we made this gown with lots of room. There's not much more to let out."

With the students grouped around her, Ingeborg held up the drawings they had found in one of Astrid's medical books. They talked about how a baby grew and what happened during the birthing. Gray Smoke and Shy Fawn had both assisted women in their tribe, but they didn't have the English skills to describe their experiences. Still, they nodded often.

When Mrs. Jeffers arrived, she taught the Indian women the words they needed to learn, and they repeated them after her. When she asked what the Sioux words were and repeated what they said, the women giggled but encouraged her. Both Kaaren and Ingeborg joined in, and while Deborah knew some Sioux words, thanks to her brother-in-law, Baptiste, they certainly weren't medical terms.

"I am making a Sioux-English dictionary as we go along," Mrs. Jeffers said. "Perhaps, Astrid, you could ask Dr. Red Hawk to provide the necessary words."

"That's a very good idea. Why didn't I think of it earlier?"

"I'd guess because your mind has been on a few other things. I'm sure there must be a dictionary like this somewhere, but probably not a medical one. Maybe he would know where we could get that too."

"I should have asked Mr. Moore, the Indian agent down on the reservation." Astrid often wished she'd pushed harder for Mrs. Moore to come to Blessing to have her baby. Working with these two delightful women might have helped her overcome her aversion to Indians. She resolved to get a letter off that evening—two, in fact. One to Dr. Red Hawk and one to the Moores.

After dinner when Ingeborg and the others went home, Ingeborg headed out to the garden to pick and shuck corn again. She shucked it as she picked, leaving the husks on the soil to help keep the weeds down. Metiz had taught her to bury the fish heads and innards along the garden rows and return everything back into the garden to enrich the soil. Much went to the pigs and chickens too, and then their manure was dug into the ground, making the garden soil rich and friable, not tending to solid chunks like much of the fields. Good farmers that they were, Lars and Haakan took all the cow manure and bedding from the winter in the barn and spread it back on the soil too.

The only thing they burned was the thistles everyone pulled as soon as they saw them. Thistles left to go to seed could take over the land in no time.

With a bucket of golden cobs of corn, she returned to the porch and, after using a brush to remove all the silk, started cutting off the kernels. Corn milk spattered her apron, her face, her arms, and half the porch, but at least not the kitchen.

"Yoo-hoo. I brought out your mail."

"Back here on the porch." Surely it couldn't be Mrs. Valders, but that voice could belong to none other. Ingeborg brushed off her hands. "Mrs. Valders, how good of you to bring it out."

"I haven't seen you for too long, and I really needed a walk." The woman's face glowed red in spite of her wide-brimmed straw hat. "I didn't realize how warm it was today." She handed Ingeborg a packet of mail. "I thought you'd want the letter right away."

"It's from Haakan. Oh, my dear Hildegunn, thank you so much. Can you sit down for a bit? I have cold drinks in the icebox, or the coffee could be hot in a jiffy."

"Oh, cold drinks for certain. You are cutting corn, eh?"

"Yes, I'm canning some, but corn takes so long that I dry a lot too." She set the precious letter down and fetched the pitcher. "You know what I found in a magazine? A receipt for a drink that goes way back to Colonial times. It's called a shrub, and it is so like our swizzles that I had to laugh. I went ahead and made it. See if you can tell the difference."

She poured the glasses. "Out on the porch is much cooler, since

"I didn't plant as big a garden this year." Hildegunn settled herself in the rocker. "Oh, this feels so good."

"Take off your hat and let the breeze make you more comfortable." Ingeborg wiped the perspiration away from her neck with the hem of her apron. "I don't even have cookies to offer. Inga took the last ones home with her."

"You go ahead and read your letter. I'm just going to sit here and catch my breath." She took a drink of the shrub. "This is very good. Has a little less vinegar, doesn't it?"

"I used the last of my vinegar making pickles. I might have to buy some to finish."

"Oh, I have plenty. Come get some from me."

Ingeborg slit the envelope open with a knife and pulled out the precious letter. Haakan did not write often, so this treat was doubly rich.

My dear Ingeborg,

I wanted to telephone you so that I could hear your voice, but none of the farmers out here have telephones yet. They say Blessing is taking on airs, trying to become a city with all the fancy innovations we have. And they are right on one hand—as soon as we can get electricity in, we will do so.

Threshing is going well, but there are some spotty areas that didn't get enough rain, so the harvest is lean. I feel sorry for the farmers caught in that situation.

Everyone is well on our crew. I must admit I am homesick. I was not home long enough between the reservation and threshing. I heard you wondering where the time has gone, and I must agree. Am I slowing down, so it seems to take longer to do things I used to do quickly? Some of the younger men are easing me into the less strenuous jobs, not that there are many of those on a threshing crew. Lars is saying the same as me. Maybe it is time to turn this over to the younger men, but who would that be? Everyone back in town is so busy with the new construction.

If I had my way, I would turn and head back to Blessing tomorrow instead of moving north and west. We are committed for at least another week, possibly more. Another threshing crew has moved into the area, so they might take some of our farms. That is a good thing. Railroad cars are lined up to haul the wheat to the flour mill in Blessing.

Good night and God bless and keep you.

Your Haakan

Ingeborg caught herself blinking at his signature. She sniffed and looked up at Hildegunn. "Sorry for sniffing like this. Reading his letter makes me miss him even more."

"They are all right? No accidents?"

"He says they are fine. Hard as it is to admit, we aren't getting any younger."

"Ingeborg Bjorklund, don't be silly. You still work rings around the younger women."

They rocked in silence for a moment.

"This morning I was sewing new shirts for Benny for school," Hildegunn said, "and I remembered when Penny started carrying the sewing machines in her store and we all had to have one. Mr. Valders always reminds me of that when I am sewing in the evening. He laughs every time."

Ingeborg folded her letter and put it in the envelope. Mr. Valders laughed? Hildegunn was sitting on the Bjorklund porch, chatting as if they were the best of friends. What kind of miracle had God worked this time?

"They sure put that house up fast for Mr. Landsverk. He and his brother are sleeping there now. So much building going on in Blessing. Don't you feel like we are a balloon about to burst?"

"I sure hope not. We need to make room for more people to come here. Think back to all those years ago. Who would have dreamed we would grow like this?"

"I said that one day, and Mr. Valders said he saw it coming. Our bank is sound and our people have made wise decisions. That's what he said."

"Haakan said that people from as far away as Devil's Lake are shipping their wheat to our flour mill instead of to Minneapolis. We will need to build more storage."

"Those words again—'need to build more.' Uff da. I am thinking that those of us who have extra rooms might think about taking in boarders until more housing is finished. We have Gerald's room. I thought I would bring this up at quilting. I have so missed our meetings this summer. I'm looking forward to next week. When the children go back to school, the ladies go back to quilting." She pushed herself to her feet. "Takk for taking time for a visit. I'll see you either at the post office or in church on Sunday. God bless."

"God bless." Ingeborg almost hugged her and then thought the better of it. Hildegunn had never been one for hugging. "Thank you for coming out here. I really needed this. Isn't God amazing to provide us with friends and family?"

"There are some letters in there for Kaaren too." She waved and sailed on down the lane.

Miracles indeed. *Thank you, Lord. Only a week until school starts. Lord, please bring Emmy back to me.*

26

There's a letter on the table for you," Elizabeth told Astrid as she joined her sister-in-law on the porch.

"Thanks. Elizabeth, are you feeling all right?"

"Other than being tired at times, yes. If you ask if I've regained all my strength, I would have to say no." Elizabeth sagged into a chair. "And if you suggest I take it any easier, I will be forced to be firm with you. Using muscles builds more muscles. Lying around makes one weaker. There is a fine line between the two, I know. So I am eating the best I can, even though I don't feel like it at times, and resting when I am weary, and I can tell you that sitting with all those catalogs and pamphlets is wearing me out."

"So we switch. You take care of more of our patients, and I will work on the hospital planning."

"Fine. Now go read your letter."

When Astrid turned to leave, Elizabeth added, "And stop worrying. Worry is a sin. The Bible says so."

Astrid chuckled as she left the back porch, which had become their second office. The first was upstairs and fine for winter, but not for summer. By this time next year their offices would be in the new hospital. She sat down in another rocker in the parlor and slit open the letter. From Mr. Jeffers. What a nice surprise. She read it through, smiled, and read it again. So Thorliff told him she wouldn't mind a letter from him. Putting the letter back in the envelope, she thought a bit, tapping the edge of the envelope on the back of her other hand.

"I wonder where that brother of mine is," she said to the two kittens that lay entwined in the basket by the chair. One cat opened an eye and yawned, showing needle-shaped white teeth and a curled pink tongue, and nestled back to sleep. "You're no help."

She got to her feet and headed for the newspaper/construction office behind the stable behind the house. Thorliff sat at his newspaper desk, writing and editing, but looked up when she tapped on the screen door.

"Come on in. You needn't knock."

"Well, I hate to bother you. I know how tight your schedule is."

"Never too tight for family. What's on your mind?"

"This." She laid the envelope in front of him.

"Well, I'll be switched. Daniel did get up the nerve to write." He grinned up at her. "You didn't mind, did you?"

"No, of course not. He's a nice man, and anyone who can put up with you as a partner must be a candidate for sainthood."

"Thanks for the vote of confidence."

"When will he be back?"

"Could be as early as today. He's been doing well with the orders.

Sounds like our adapter will be real popular, and the orders for the new seeders are coming in too."

"The building will be finished soon enough to produce the new seeders?"

"It's going to be tight, but yes."

"And the hospital?"

"We'll get the first stage done for the dedication and then work on the rest of the building through the winter. We will have houses in the same condition, weathered in to be finished this winter."

"I'll tell him thank you when he returns."

"Good, and if he asks you to walk with him, you'll do that too?"

"Thorliff, are you in league with Sophie?"

"How so?"

"Matchmaking?"

"Nope. I don't have time for shenanigans like that. Now, I need to finish this up so I can spend the evening with my wife and daughter."

"For a change. You do know that Inga is out at Mor's?"

"I do. I'm going out to get her as soon as I'm done here. You want to come along?"

"I do. I'll be in the surgery."

"Patients?"

"No. Checking on supplies." She waved good-bye and returned to the house to begin inventorying supplies in all their cabinets and drawers, making a list of the things that were low as she counted. She could have assigned the job to Thelma, but with all the canning, Thelma hardly took time to sleep as it was. "I should have the nursing students here for this," she said to herself.

"What did you say?" Elizabeth asked as she came into the room.

"Our students need to learn how to take inventory."

"You are so right. We'll invite them tomorrow."

"Can our Indian ladies count?"

Elizabeth stared at her. "I don't know, but I will ask Tante Kaaren.

I'll be right back." When she returned from the telephone, she said, "One can count to ten, but the other can't."

"So we invite them and let them work as a team with Deborah overseeing?"

"Before or after patients?"

"We close at noon."

———

LATER THAT AFTERNOON, Astrid saw Mr. Jeffers climbing the steps to the boardinghouse. She'd heard the train whistle but not paid any attention until now. He was back. So all she had to do was thank him for the letter—when she saw him. *Do you want to see him?* she asked herself. *After all, you said no more men after that fiasco with Mr. Landsverk. You are married to your medical practice.*

It wasn't long before the telephone rang the requisite long and a short. Thelma came to the door. "It is for you."

"A patient?"

"I don't think so. Mrs. Jeffers."

"Oh, thank you." When Astrid put the earpiece to her ear and said hello, a warm chuckle answered her.

"This is Amelia Jeffers, and I was wondering if you would like to join my son and me for supper in the dining room this evening. Had we our own home, it might be more personal, but this will have to do."

"Of course. I'd be delighted. What time?"

"Say, six o'clock?"

"Very good. I will see you then." As she returned the earpiece to the prongs, she shook her head. This was a bit strange, but oh well. Perhaps they had invited others too.

"What should I wear?" she asked Elizabeth.

"How about that blue dimity? You hardly ever wear it, and it looks so nice on you."

"All right, I guess. I wonder why I never wear it."

"All you ever wear are plain skirts with a light waist, all covered with our aprons. That's all either of us wears. Even for supper out at your mother's I neglected to change into something nicer. We need to remedy this."

"But dressing up takes so much time. Good enough for Sunday church or a party, but that's about all."

"If we don't keep to the fashions for this town, who will?"

"Who cares about fashion anyway?"

But Astrid did freshen up and change her clothes, and she even twisted her long hair into a figure eight at the back of her head, leaving trailing wisps on her forehead. She pinched her cheeks to give them some color and added the necklace with a blue stone that Elizabeth insisted she wear.

"Astrid?" Thorliff stopped and stared at her coming down the stairs.

"Oh, stop that. You know it's me."

"You look lovely."

Elizabeth tucked her arm into his. "She does, doesn't she?" She nodded. "I was right. We need to make more of an effort around here. Set a good example like Sophie does."

"Sophie has always enjoyed lovely clothes, even when we were little."

"Have a good time." Elizabeth waved.

"It's not like I'm going to Grand Forks or something. Just down the street." But Astrid waved back and continued on her way. Both of the Jefferses were sitting in rocking chairs on the front porch of the boardinghouse. They waved as she crossed the street, being careful to keep her skirt hem out of the dust.

"Thank you, dear, for coming on such short notice and an invitation by telephone, no less. My but we are getting lax in the social graces."

"Funny you should say that. Elizabeth and I were just discussing the same thing. She had to remind me to put a hat on." Astrid climbed the three steps. "Aren't porches one of the better inventions?" She turned to Mr. Jeffers. "Welcome home. It sounds like you had a very successful trip."

He stood and motioned for her to take his chair. "Thank you. No, you sit here, and I'll pull up another one."

Mrs. Jeffers leaned across and patted her hand on the arm of the chair. "This is such a pleasure. I don't know why I haven't done this before."

"Perhaps because you believed the edicts regarding proper decorum for grieving widows." Mr. Jeffers set another chair down and settled into it. "I think that is one of the things I love about Blessing. There is more freedom here. Not so many people trying to tell you what to do because that is the way we have always done it," he said, mimicking a whiny voice on the last.

Astrid chuckled. "I've heard about that, especially when I attended the missionary school in Georgia. Many of the people there could not abide the idea of a young unmarried female doctor going off to Africa as a missionary. Fortunately there were some who felt that God will use anyone He wants as He wants."

"But you didn't go to Africa?"

"No. Dr. Elizabeth nearly died with her last baby, and I understood God to say I could come home. I didn't really want to go to Africa, but if He was calling me there, I would go."

"You are an adventuresome young woman."

Astrid leaned forward. "I just want to do what God wants me to do. Sometimes I seem to lean on the hard-of-listening side."

"Listening?" Mr. Jeffers raised an eyebrow.

Astrid looked at him with a slight smile. "I know I have good hearing, so it must be listening that is the problem."

"Hearing the voice of God takes one deeper. When my husband disappeared, I felt like God had left also. But I made myself listen harder, read the Word, search for what He said He will do. And the comfort came. Not in a rush like I wanted, but it came trickling in, surprising me in small ways and helping me to sleep better. I was certain my Daniel was safe in God's hands. Learning he was gone and not suffering somewhere was a relief. And then I came here."

"And I'm so glad you did. Thank you." Astrid pushed with her foot to set the chair to rocking. "I so appreciate your teaching my nurses how to speak English. It seems to have lightened their fears, so they smile and laugh more. At first I was afraid I had made a mistake in bringing them here, but now I know it was right."

"Our construction crew is the same way. The men can laugh at their mistakes in speaking, fall back into their native tongue, and try again. Thorliff is so good because he can speak Norwegian to some of them. And Mr. Geddick takes care of the others. Poor Boris Sidorov. He struggles on alone, but I give him credit. He is a good carpenter and uses what new words he has."

"I think we should go in to eat now," Mrs. Jeffers said. "They've most likely served the majority of the people."

Mr. Jeffers held the door for them both and escorted them into the dining room to a table set apart with a small vase of flowers in the middle.

"Isn't this lovely?" Mrs. Jeffers turned to Astrid. "I asked for flowers. I miss my garden so. That is one thing I am looking forward to once I'm in my own house again."

"If you wanted to go out and putter in the garden behind the boardinghouse, I know that Sophie would be delighted. She wants her guests to feel at home, and if that will help you, so be it."

"She wouldn't be offended? Not Mrs. Sam either?"

"No. Most people in Blessing are not easily offended. I think it goes back to that freedom we were talking about. You could come over to the yard around the surgery too or go out to my mor's. We all love to share both the bounty and the beauty." She smiled up at Mr. Jeffers as he helped seat her. "Thank you."

"Thank *you*." His emphasis on the *you* made her heart trip.

Her slight laugh covered a bit of discomfort. What was going on? Surely she wasn't attracted to this man.

"Good evening," Miss Christopherson said as she stopped at their table. "I hope you've had a pleasant day. Welcome back, Mr. Jeffers."

"It's good to be back," Mr. Jeffers said.

"Good evening, Miss Christopherson. I would like something cold to drink to start with."

"We have milk, buttermilk, raspberry swizzle, and lemonade."

As they all placed their orders, Astrid kept herself from looking across the table at Daniel Jeffers. "I received your letter today," she told him when Miss Christopherson left.

"I'm sorry it didn't arrive sooner. I carried it in my pocket for two days before finding a post office."

"That's quite all right. I really wasn't expecting to receive it."

Mrs. Jeffers picked up the vase and smelled the flowers. Daisies, delphinium, and baby's breath. "Isn't this lovely," she commented as she replaced the flowers in the middle of the table. "At home I had flowers in every room through the summer months. In winter I used pine boughs and fir with dried birch branches and sometimes holly berries. I always watched for the pussy willows to announce that spring was on its way. One year I saw an ad for a curly willow. From then on I had willow branches with plenty of personality. I wonder if that will grow here."

"Wild willow does. We use the dried bark for several different medications. Mor gathers the bark during the summer, then once it dries, pulverizes it for her collection. It tastes bitter, so we add honey for our patients."

"I've heard many good things about your mother and her medical knowledge. I think you inherited that from her." Mrs. Jeffers glanced from Astrid to her son. "I wonder what you inherited from me."

"Pure stubborn tenacity, I think."

"Are you saying I am stubborn?" Her eyes twinkled.

"Not exactly, but tenacity is what kept me looking for my father. Without that I would have stopped before we learned the truth."

"So are you saying you are still searching for information?" Astrid asked.

"Yes. I feel there is more to the story. You have to admit there are many strange things that happened. Someone, somewhere, knows more of the answers."

"Thorliff is like that. Says he has a nose for news. That's why he runs a newspaper."

"His newspaper should get awards for quality for a town this small. In fact, for towns far larger. Few local papers have a women's page like his does or opinion columns of this quality." Mrs. Jeffers smiled her thanks when Lily Mae set their cold drinks in front of them.

Astrid enjoyed hearing them discuss Thorliff's newspaper. She'd always thought it was good, but then, she'd not had much to compare it to. The conversation through dinner ranged from the growth of Blessing to garden flowers and on to indoor plumbing and the advent of electricity.

Astrid enjoyed every minute. When they were finished with dessert and coffee, she thanked her hostess.

"I'll walk you home," Daniel said.

Astrid started to object but decided that would be rude, even though her home was less than two blocks away. They made a detour past his house, which had the cellar dug and the concrete set. In the morning the men would be laying the floor joists and beginning to frame the walls. They had purchased the quarter-acre lot north of the surgery, or Thorliff's house.

"This won't be as large as our house in Iowa, but the yard will be near the same size. I think I will eventually put up a garage for when I buy an automobile, but not now."

"No horse and buggy?"

"No. I'll continue to rent those from the livery whenever the need arises. Would you be interested in a ride one of these Sundays?"

"I don't know why not." They ambled back to the surgery and sat down on the swing on the front porch, talking all the while. He asked her about her time training to become a doctor and then told her what going to college had been like. She asked about his sister, and he told her stories of when he was young.

"I always knew I wanted to produce my father's inventions. He had such good ideas, and I believe he was on the brink of something really big. I have a trunk full of his notes and drawings and plans. Once we get the seeder in production, I want to look at his papers more critically and decide what to work on next."

"I wish I had met him."

"You would have liked him. He would have fit in so well here in Blessing."

"Have you talked any of these things over with Mr. Sam? He runs the livery and the blacksmith shop."

"No, but Thorliff mentioned that one day. He says the man is a genius at duplicating a broken part."

"He is. I'm sure if he'd had any schooling, he'd be an engineer for sure."

"Sometimes schooling isn't the only answer. Experience counts for more in the long run. I'll make a point of befriending the man."

"I better go in before Thorliff sends a posse out looking for me."

She rose and he with her. "Good night, Mr. Jeffers. I had a delightful evening."

"So did I. We will do this again." He touched her hand and strolled down the steps to whistle his way up the street.

She covered the spot with her other hand. *Hmm.*

27

"Look at this." Thorliff laid the letter in front of Daniel the next morning.

"Who is it from?" Daniel glanced down to the signature, then back to Thorliff. "A sheriff in Kansas?"

"Yes, and I think he has our man. There aren't too many going by the name of Harlan Jeffers. And the description fits him to a tee. His actions are indicative of the man who left here."

Daniel scanned the letter and then read it again more slowly. "He's in jail in Wichita, Kansas, for bilking the local citizenry, and Sheriff Connally thinks he is our man." He blew out a breath. "I've dreamed of this minute. I can be ready to leave in half an hour. Will you come with me?"

Thorliff thought for a moment. "I would go, but I think taking

Pastor Solberg might be better. They won't argue with a man of the cloth, and he knows all that went on here too. Let me give him a call."

Daniel read the letter again. Could this really be the man who last saw his father alive? The sheriff in the town where he'd located the body had said they thought his father died of natural causes, but this might be one more page in the story. His thought that he should tell his mother was tempered with *What if this isn't the right man?* He hated to see her disappointed again.

Thorliff returned. "He said he'd meet you at the train."

"I guess that locks this in. I'll wire the sheriff to let him know we are coming." Daniel quickly finished up some paper work in the office, met his mother in the dining room, and made the eastbound train by waving and hollering to the conductor when he called "All aboard."

"I didn't think you were going to make it," Pastor Solberg said when Daniel dropped into the seat beside him.

"I think this time I cut it almost too close. I've not had to run for a train before." He puffed out a breath and stashed his carpetbag under the seat. "Thank you for joining me. I sure wouldn't recognize the man."

"I can still hear his voice. It had a perpetual whine to it, whether he was smiling or not. I didn't trust him from the first time I met him, but you can't turn a town against a man over a feeling." Solberg shook his head. "I can't believe the amount of traveling I've been doing lately. All these years I never left Blessing for more than Grand Forks, and here I am on my way to Kansas."

"Via Nebraska."

"And it was South Dakota before that."

"Where were you from, before you came to Blessing?"

"I grew up in Minnesota, so I haven't traveled too far. Attended

Augsburg Seminary in Minneapolis. Back in the really early days. I never dreamed I'd still be in Blessing all these years later."

"Between teaching school and pastoring your church, you keep very busy."

"After this summer, teaching will seem like a vacation."

———

BY THE TIME the train pulled into Wichita the next day, the two men had become fast friends. Daniel spent part of the time on paper work for the business while Pastor Solberg read a book. Then Daniel started two letters that he planned to add to each day. If he mailed them before heading home, so be it, but if he didn't, his mother and Astrid would both have a journal, each from a slightly different point of view, of his journey. Why he was doing this for Dr. Bjorklund, he wasn't sure, but it seemed a good thing to do.

They made their way to the sheriff's office and pushed open the door.

"Good afternoon, gentlemen," the man said after the men from Blessing gave him their names. "You are the witnesses from—" he glanced down at a paper on his desk—"Blessing, North Dakota?"

"Yes, sir. And yes, that is the real name of the town. I am Daniel Jeffers, and this is Pastor John Solberg of the Blessing Lutheran Church. Since I have never met this Harlan Jeffers, it seemed a good idea to bring someone who had."

"Very wise. Sit down, please." He indicated the two chairs at the corners of his desk. "Can I get you anything? Coffee? Something stronger?"

"No, thanks. Can we see the man?"

"In a moment. I need to write some notes here. Pastor Solberg, you knew a man named Harlan Jeffers in Blessing?"

287

"Yes, he came to town and bought the general store from Mrs. Hjelmer Bjorklund, who was moving. He had sufficient money to place a sizable amount down and signed a contract that said he would make regular monthly payments until the balance of the account was paid off."

"And did he live up to his word?"

"For a time, but bit by bit he managed to offend the people of Blessing to the extent that they quit shopping there, so he had no money to restock. Then he started selling liquor from under the counter. We have a dry town in Blessing, and that further angered the townsfolk. But when he made unwelcome advances on one of our town daughters and then attacked her, he signed his time away in Blessing. People were ready to run him out of town on a rail, including tar and feathering. Mrs. Bjorklund agreed to take back her store, and we hustled him out before he was attacked, with a signed agreement that he would never return to Blessing."

"He sounds like a real winner." The sheriff turned to Daniel Jeffers. "Now tell me your side of this convoluted tale."

"My father set out to find investors to help him produce a piece of equipment he had invented to improve the quality of seeding machines. All of a sudden, we, my mother and I, quit hearing from him. I journeyed out to see if he was injured or dead or to find whatever news I could. I kept hitting blank walls until I heard of a man in Blessing, North Dakota, by the name of Harlan Jeffers who had purchased a store there. Thinking that might be a clue, I went to Blessing, only to find that the man Harlan Jeffers, who had left by then, bore no resemblance to my father. But in an accidental way, the people of Blessing found something of my father's taped to the bottom of the store's cash register drawer.

"The man seemed to have disappeared, but I backtracked to a town in southern Minnesota, where they had found a man lying dead by the road with no identification. He seemed to have died of natural causes, so they buried him. I identified him as my father by a couple of scars and his unusual right thumb, which was missing half of it. But that is all we knew. The money and papers he'd had with him were never found, other than that piece under the cash register drawer.

"My friend and now business partner, Thorliff Bjorklund, who owns the newspaper in Blessing, sent out the information to see if anything would ever happen."

"I see." The sheriff looked up from his notes. "Let me take you back to talk with this man." He unlocked the door to the row of cells and led them to the third cell, where a man lay sleeping on the cot chained to the wall. He banged on the bars. "Jeffers, you have company."

The man turned his head, and his eyes widened. "Pastor Solberg, you gotta believe me. I didn't kill nobody. I never killed no one." He sat up, scratching and shaking his head.

"Guess that answers one question," the sheriff said. "He's your man all right."

"Not my man, but he is the one we ran out of Blessing." Solberg turned back to face the prisoner. "I think you would do well to tell the whole story, the true story, or you might be facing a hanging."

"I didn't kill him. He was dead when I found him."

"So, you—"

"Took all his clothes and his money and satchel and thought I was the luckiest man alive." He shook his head. "Stupidest thing I ever done. Oh, and I took his name too. Found it on the papers."

"But my father's name was Daniel Jeffers."

"Harlan is my first name. Thought I would do better if I had something of my own." He stared down at his hands. "But I didn't kill him. He were already dead but not too long. He was laying there by the road, all crumpled, is all I know."

Daniel heaved a sigh. "Then that is the end of that. I could sue you for the money you stole from my family, but that would indeed be a waste of time. I'm sure you've broken some laws, but I am finished with you. Thank you for pasting my father's plans under that drawer."

Harlan screwed up his face, then snorted. "So that's where it went to. Forgot all about that."

Solberg looked at the sheriff. "Do you need us for anything more?"

"Nope. Thank you for putting some more pieces in the puzzle. He'll probably do some time for swindling the good folks of Wichita, but since his story pretty much agrees with your story, he won't be indicted for murder. At least not that one."

"I never killed nobody. Never."

Daniel turned back to the bars. "What is your entire real name?"

"Harlan D. Jones."

"Please stop going by Jeffers. I hate that smudge on our family name, Mr. Jones."

The thief nodded. "All right."

"Do you have the law after you by your real name?" Sheriff Connally asked.

Harlan shrugged. "Don't rightly know. That was a long time ago."

The three men sighed as one and stalked down the hall.

That night on the train bound for Kansas City and the Twin Cities after that, Daniel wrote the entire tale up for his mother and a briefer version for Astrid, sealing them in separate envelopes. For his mother, this would mean an end to her speculation. For Astrid? He wasn't sure if he would give the pages to her when he returned to Blessing or somewhere down the road. It would depend on which road they took. At least he still had his father's trunk and all the wealth of his ideas.

Was it time to seriously pursue something he'd only dreamed of—a wife? For the first time in his life, he thought he'd found one he wanted. Now all he had to do was convince her of the idea.

28

"I guess Emmy not coming back, huh, Grandma?"

"Don't give up yet. School isn't quite here," Ingeborg consoled her morose little granddaughter.

"But her kitten is near grown, and she doesn't even know her. And school starts next week." She glanced down at her new pinafore. "I get to go to school too."

"Only in the mornings."

"I know."

"Emmy goes all day. Carl's too little." Inga nibbled on the edge of a ginger cookie that she had decorated with three raisins. "I miss Emmy."

"Me too." Every day she kept watch for a man walking across the land with a little girl following him. How would he know when it was time for school? Had he really nodded or had she been living a pipe dream all summer? *Lord, I have to trust you on this. Not only because there is nothing I can do, but because I want to. I want to trust you in all things.*

Of course she was trusting Him with Haakan too. How easy it would be to come up with all the bad things that could happen to the men on the threshing crew. *Why is that so hard at times like this?* She thought for a moment. *Well, any hard time for that matter. Lord, I will trust you. Lord, I am trusting you. I am.*

"Grandma, you look sad."

"I know, Inga. But I am asking God to help me look happier."

"Will He do that?"

"He says He will."

Inga swung her legs, knocking her bare feet against the leg of the chair, the look on her face one of pondering also. "Will He make me happier too?"

"If you ask."

"I asked Him to bring Emmy home, and she is not here."

"Yet."

"Ja, yet." She picked off a raisin and ate that alone, then nibbled on her cookie again, going all around it, one little bite at a time.

Most children, Carl for example, just gobbled a cookie down and asked for another. But not Inga. She had always had her own ways of doing things. *Lord God, what do you have in mind for this child I love so dearly?*

"Do you want some coffee with your cookie?"

Inga's face brightened. "You too?"

"Me too, and if that is who I think it is coming up the lane, we will have someone else for coffee."

Inga bailed off her chair and ran to the door. "Tante Astrid is coming." She slammed open the screen door and charged down the steps and the walk to meet her aunt at the gate and throw her arms around her.

Ingeborg watched from the doorway, not sure which of the two was happier. Astrid swung Inga around in a circle, and the two walked up to the house with locked hands swinging and smiles that dimmed the sun. *Lord God, what gifts you bring to me. You made me happier in an instant. And look at Inga. She's radiant.*

"What are you doing out here on a workday?"

"Elizabeth is taking care of patients, and I had to get away from that stack of catalogs and books and pictures and . . ." She shook her head, tipping her wide-brimmed straw hat slightly to the side. Reaching up, she pulled out the hatpin and removed the hat to lay it on the table on the porch. "There. Now it can't slip any further."

"Coffee?"

"And cookies," Inga added. "I helped bake them."

"We had a telephone call from Pastor Solberg and Mr. Jeffers. They identified the man in jail as Harlan Jeffers, but his real last name is Jones. He did not kill Mr. Jeffers, the father. He found him lying crumpled beside the road. So now the Jefferses can know that all is finished. I'm sure he called his mother too. He and Pastor are on their way back." Astrid set the cups on the tray, and Inga added a plate of cookies.

"That will be a huge relief for Amelia, although she knew her husband had not been killed, or at least it didn't appear that way. She says that moving here was the best thing to happen to her in a long while. There were just too many memories in their house. Her daughter and her family moved into it when Mrs. Jeffers came here. So the house stays in the family." Ingeborg poured the coffee and set the pot back. "Let's go outside. You know, I've been thinking that we should screen in the porch, since we live out there so much. Get rid of the flies and hornets. Cut down on the mosquitoes too."

Astrid picked up the tray. "Open the door, Inga. We're coming out."

"I am. Hurry. The bee is trying to come in." She slammed the screen door shut, then opened it again. "Ha!"

"Did you get him?"

"No, but he didn't get in." She held the door for Astrid and Ingeborg, then went inside to fetch the flyswatter.

Astrid and her mother sat down in the rocking chairs after setting the tray on the low table. "I am happy for them," Astrid continued.

"Me too. Amelia is so enjoying her teaching, and the students enjoy her. I hear them laughing, the women anyway."

"Mor, when are Far and the rest of the crew coming home?"

"Probably another week. Why?"

"You just don't seem yourself. Are you feeling ill or anything?"

"No, Dr. Bjorklund, my health is fine. I would ask you to check me over if I thought there was something wrong." She paused. "I just miss Haakan more than I ever have."

"And Emmy too." Inga was obviously listening, even though she kept watching the hornet. When it landed on the table, she slapped the flyswatter down right on it. "I got it. I killed him." She started to reach for the still critter.

"No!" Ingeborg grabbed her hand. "It can still sting you."

"But he's not moving, not even his wings."

"I know, but if you touch that stinger, you'll get stung." Ingeborg used the swatter to flip the hornet over the porch wall.

"I killed him. I did."

"Have another cookie."

"To dunk in your coffee? Mine is all gone."

Ingeborg held out her cup. "I just love cookie crumbs in my coffee."

"You do?"

Astrid snickered. "She's teasing you."

"We need to plan a party for when the men come home." Ingeborg set her rocker to singing. "We didn't have a Fourth of July celebration, so we need a harvest one for sure."

"We always have a harvest celebration."

"I know. What if we have a box dinner auction? We need some new textbooks for the school. And we'll need new desks if Blessing keeps growing."

"Mor, did you know Mr. Sidorov has a family in New York City? We telephoned Mr. Gould, and he said he would look into it, but so far we've not heard a thing. Any ideas?"

"Do you have people praying about this?"

Astrid shrugged. "Pastor Solberg knows, so I assume so. What if they are wandering the streets of New York with no place to stay and no money?"

"Why didn't he just be honest and tell them he had a family?"

"I'm sure because he wanted the work so terribly. No one can talk to him and find out if there are relatives or anything."

"Walhalla. There is a group of Russians settled up there. I don't know any of them, but Haakan has threshed for some of them. Maybe we could get someone from there to come here to talk with him, or we could take him up there."

"How do we contact someone?"

"Maybe Mary Martha knows if Pastor Solberg knows someone. The ministers of this area have gotten together a few times." Ingeborg rose. "Some days, like right now, I am wonderfully thankful for the telephone."

When Mary Martha picked up the receiver and said hello, Ingeborg chuckled.

"Ingeborg, how are you?"

"Good. Astrid is here, and she just told me that Mr. Boris Sidorov has a family that he left in New York when he got this job."

"How did they find that out?"

"One of our Norwegian immigrants was able to understand him with a combination of motions and pictures. I was wondering if Pastor Solberg has mentioned knowing anyone up in the Walhalla area."

"Ja, he knows a pastor up there."

"But no telephones."

"No, I don't think so. Let me think a minute. We could write a letter and send it."

"I know, but like Astrid says, what if his family is penniless and with no help?"

"And Mr. Gould?"

"We've heard nothing back."

"A man could ride to Walhalla in one day and come back the next. If we send Mr. Sidorov up with him . . ."

"Does the train go up there?"

"Not the main line, but there are tracks. They send their wheat down here to be milled."

"So who could we ask to go?"

"Samuel?"

"I was thinking Johnny, but he's too young for that. But Samuel came back from the reservation more a man than ever. He is wise enough to ask directions. If only John were here. He would know what to do." Ingeborg thought for a moment. "I'll talk with Thorliff. I think Samuel is our man. Thank you."

"Any news on Emmy?"

"No, none. Inga and I are trying to cheer each other up."

As soon as they hung up, Ingeborg rang for Thorliff and told him the situation.

"So what do you think?"

"I think that is a very good idea. If Gould finds anything, he will let us know. I'll talk with Samuel. He's working on the Jeffers house. They could leave in the morning."

She'd just hung up when the telephone jangled. "Hello?"

"Tante Ingeborg, this is Sophie."

"I know. Is everything all right?"

"Of course. Why?"

"There's just a lot going on. How can I help you?"

"I want to invite you to supper the day after tomorrow, Saturday."

"Well, that is very nice of you. I would love to come."

"Oh good. Elizabeth said Astrid is with you."

"She is. Do you want to speak to her?"

"No. Just tell her she is invited too. Six o'clock."

"Can I bring anything?"

"No. I have the menu all planned. Thank you."

After hanging up, Ingeborg stared at the oak box on her kitchen wall. Something was up with Sophie, of that she was certain, but what could it be? Shaking her head, she returned to the porch, where Astrid and Inga were playing rock, scissors, paper and giggling like two little girls instead of one grown.

"I'm ahead, Grandma. You want to play?"

"I think not. Mary Martha knows the name of a pastor up in Walhalla, and we agreed that Samuel would be a good man to send with Mr. Sidorov, to leave tomorrow morning."

"That is fast work. What about a telegram?"

"To say they are coming?" Ingeborg nodded. "Good idea. Why didn't I think of that? Mary Martha will telephone me with the pastor's name. She has to find it. Thorliff is going to talk with Samuel and Mr. Sidorov."

"All will be well?" Astrid quirked an eyebrow and made the scissors motion. Inga groaned because she did the paper motion.

"Ja, that is so. All is already well." Ingeborg watched the two play another round. "Oh, I almost forgot. Sophie has invited you and me to supper at her house on Friday at six o'clock. She asked me to tell you."

"Oh really? That sounds like fun. Did she mention anyone else?"

"No, just us, I guess. But when I asked if I could bring something, she said no. But I can't go there for supper without taking something."

"School starts on Tuesday, and this is Thursday, so I have . . ." Inga counted the days out on her fingers. "Friday, Saturday, Sunday, Monday, Tuesday. Five days until I go to school. Grandma made me a new dress and two new pinafores." She turned to her grandma. "What is Emmy going to wear?"

"I made her two dresses too."

"And pinafores?"

"Ja."

"Good. I sure hope her uncle brings her back soon. She hates to miss any school days."

"I hope so too, Inga. Me too." *Lord, please?*

29

"If Sophie doesn't have that baby pretty soon, it'll be born walking."

Elizabeth chuckled. "She has a baby due, and you are walking the floor."

"It helps me think better," Astrid responded.

"Well, it's not helping *me* think any better. With Inga over at Sophie's, I thought I'd get a lot done."

"You should have left her out with Mor."

"Mor's feeding the men today. Did Samuel and Mr. Sidorov get off?"

"At daybreak. That man had never been on a horse before. Samuel is leading his and teaching Sidorov how to ride. I sure hope we get some solid information to go on. I feel sorry for the man, he's alone so much."

"Thorliff says he is a hard worker. Astrid."

"What?"

"You are still pacing. What is bothering you?"

Astrid stopped at the south-facing upstairs window. "Someone's coming."

"To the surgery?"

"No, to town. Trygve and the windmill crew are back. Hjelmer is back too. I wonder where they met up. You know how shiny black that wagon was? It's not anymore." She could see the smoke from the train stack. "The train's coming too."

"Good. Go meet the train."

"This is a good window for keeping track of things going on in Blessing." Astrid turned. "We have a patient." She left the room in a flurry of skirts. Perhaps Mr. Jeffers and Pastor Solberg would be on the train. Their stories would most assuredly be interesting. She opened the door to the waiting room. "Mrs. Geddick, come right in." She showed the woman into an examining room and to a chair while she sat on the stool. "How can I help you today?"

"I think something is wrong." Mrs. Geddick never had lost her heavy German accent.

"Tell me what you feel."

"Tired, weak. I keep bleeding and bleeding."

As the conversation progressed, all Astrid could think was that this sounded just like her mother's symptoms a few years earlier. She'd finally gone to the Women's Hospital in Chicago for a hysterectomy and came home feeling one hundred percent better.

Astrid quizzed the woman about her monthlies and the bleeding. She listened to heart, lungs, belly. Palpitating the lower abdomen, she could feel a growth of some kind. Ovarian cysts could be causing this too. "Do you have a lot of pain?"

"I do. I use Dr. Benjamin's elixir. It helps."

It should, Astrid thought. *There's opium in that mixture.* While she had a good idea what was going on, she'd never done a surgery like this condition required, and she didn't think Elizabeth had either. It just wasn't common enough, or else most women just suffered through until it passed or they died. Dr. Morganstein had said that surgery was the only option for Mor. What would she say here? Maybe this was something their hospital could become known for like the Chicago one—treating female diseases. She brought herself back to the situation at hand. Further study and research would come later.

"I need to consult with another doctor on this. Would you please come in as soon as you've gone three days without bleeding so I can examine you again?"

Mrs. Geddick nodded. "Danke, Dr. Bjorklund."

"Taking a nap in the afternoon would be a good idea too. And eat plenty of liver and spinach. Those contain iron, which you need."

"I wonder where I would get liver."

"I'll ask around and see if anyone is butchering. Chicken livers could help."

"I have chickens."

As soon as Mrs. Geddick went out the front door, Astrid headed for the library and the medical books, making a detour through the kitchen. She brought a pitcher of lemonade mixed with raspberry juice to the counter, poured two glasses, and after putting the pitcher back, headed upstairs. She thrust one glass into Elizabeth's hand and half drained her own. "Mrs. Geddick looks to be in the same shape as Mor was. Have you ever done any female surgeries?"

"No. I hope you have."

"No. That might have been one of the advantages of my staying longer. I'm going to call Dr. Morganstein and see what she suggests. Is there anything you want to talk to her about?"

"No, but Mr. Jeffers and Pastor Solberg are back. I heard Thorliff talking with them."

Astrid paused. What had just happened? Elizabeth said the name Jeffers, and her heart had skipped? Surely not.

"What is it?"

"Nothing." She drank some more. "I'm going to make that telephone call now so she can get back to me soon if she is not available." She knew she was chattering, and the look on Elizabeth's face said she knew it too. Sometimes the best offense was a good defense, or exit, in this case.

Since Dr. Morganstein was not available, she left a detailed message with Mrs. Hancock, who was still managing the front desk and the office, and promised to not let so much time elapse between visits.

After deciding that talking with her mother might yield more assistance than digging in books, Astrid strode out to the farm, her feet pounding the dirt, raising dust swirls because it was so dry. They really needed a good soaking rain both for the moisture and to relieve the heat.

Why all this interest in Daniel Jeffers? *God, I thought you wanted me to remain single, not become interested in another man. But then, this isn't just any man. Now, where did that idea come from? Haven't we been through this before, where I am trying to find out your will for me, and things change faster than I can assimilate them? Now my biggest concern is Mrs. Geddick. You have said that you have all the answers and that the Holy Spirit will show them to me. So . . .* She heaved a sigh. The thought that ripped through her mind was not one she wanted to hear. *Wait.* She almost laughed but shook her head and kept on walking. *All right. I will praise you. I will seek wisdom. I will wait. I will be silent before you.*

A huge black and yellow butterfly flitted across the road in front of her. It stopped for a sip on a goldenrod, fluttered on, and then stopped on a daisy. "Oh, so beautiful," she breathed. "Thank you for butterflies, for daisies, and goldenrod. All these things you have made so beautifully. Mrs. Geddick. Such a hardworking, uncomplaining woman, who loves you and loves her family. Thank you for her, for her life, for the opportunity to make her feel better. Healing is your job. O God, I am your hands, so I know you will guide my hands and my mind. I know that. Thank you."

She set the thank-yous to a flittering little tune and sang them the rest of the way to her mother's porch.

"Astrid, is that you?"

"Ja, where are you?"

"Back here, where it is cooler."

Astrid walked around the porch to find her mother scrubbing cucumbers. "What are you making?"

"Pickles. Probably the last batch. I'm going to set these in the last crock. I filled one with cabbage this morning for sauerkraut. I ran out of horseradish leaves to put on top. Have a seat."

"Do you want something to drink?" Astrid asked.

"There's a pitcher of water in the icebox. That would be good. Was that you I heard singing?"

Astrid paused at the door. "Yes, I guess it was. I thought I was humming, but then I found myself singing, and I guess I got carried away." She brought the pitcher and two glasses back to the porch. "Mor, I need your advice." Pouring a glass, she handed it to her mother and then poured her own.

"On what?"

"Several things. Number one, sources of iron for an anemic patient. What did Dr. Morganstein tell you to do when you were suffering from the bleeding?"

"Liver is always first."

"I know, but where do we get it at this time of year?"

"Chicken liver, I guess. If we lived in a city, we could buy it at a local butcher. Shame the grocery store doesn't have a meat market."

She drank and set the glass down. "You could telephone a store in Grand Forks and have it sent out on the train."

"What else?"

"I have put nails in a glass of water to rust, then boiled the water to purify it, and added the rusty water to juice or honey to make it palatable to drink. Do you want me to look this up for you?"

"If you would. Second thing. How severe were your symptoms when they decided surgery was the best way to go?"

"I was severely anemic, the pains were ferocious, and I fainted a couple of times. That frightened Haakan beyond description. He would hardly leave me by myself. He went to Elizabeth and told her she had to do something, but he was against the surgery right up until they put me under. I know it was because he was afraid I was going to die."

"Were you afraid?"

"Not afraid, just concerned for him. I mean, I couldn't lose. Either home in heaven or home here. And the Father left me here and healthy again."

"A woman came to see me today with the same kind of situation. I need to know how best to help her."

"Do you want me to talk with her?"

"Would you mind?"

"Not a bit."

"I'll check with her and see if she minds if I share her medical information with you."

"That would be fine. If she agrees, tell her I could go see her tomorrow. And I'll look up some simples too. Oh, I know one. Beets and beet greens are good. Root vegetables pull iron from the soil and feed it into our bodies. Which reminds me, I need to pull more of the beets. Don't buttered beets sound wonderful for supper?"

"Do you want me to go pull some?" Astrid asked.

"If you don't mind. Then I can finish these cucumbers. Was there anything else on your list?"

"One more thing, but I'll go pull the beets first. How many?"

"Enough for eating, not for canning. Can you stay for supper?"

"Yes, I guess so. Where is Freda?"

"Out at the cheese house. She'll be here for supper too. I think Jonathan will eat over to Kaaren's."

Astrid grabbed a basket and took it out to the garden to fill with beets. She pulled a carrot and scrubbed the dirt off of it with the feathery tops to eat while she picked. Rows of pole beans had drying pods, bush beans the same. Much of the corn was already harvested, but she found half a dozen ears to shuck and add to her basket. Back on the porch, she scrubbed the beets in a bucket of water and broke off the tops an inch or so above the beet.

"Your garden is starting to look forlorn."

"I know. So much is already canned and dried. Did you notice the pumpkins? We used a nail to write Inga, Emmy, and Carl on three of them. Remember how we used to do that for you and the boys?"

"Inga was explaining to me about missing Emmy." She picked up her clean beets and took them into the kitchen. The fire needed feeding, so Astrid did that too and covered the beets with water before she set the kettle on the hot part of the stove. Jars of canned corn lined one counter, and pints of corn relish too waited to be carried to the cellar. A washed four-gallon crock waited for the cucumbers, and stalks of dill stood in water to stay fresh for the same.

Back out on the porch, Astrid picked up a brush and joined her mother in scrubbing the spines off the cucumbers.

"What else is on your mind?"

"I'm not sure." She sucked in a breath of courage. "I am finding myself attracted to Daniel Jeffers."

"And what is wrong with that?"

"I thought I was to remain single to be a better doctor."

"What made you think that?"

"That last discussion with Mr. Landsverk." Astrid sighed. "If I were to get married, I would need a man like Far or Thorliff, who are happy their wives are doctors or midwives or—"

"There are not a lot of men like your far. Or Thorliff either. But being married to a person who always puts patients first is not easy on either a man or a woman."

"But men put their jobs before their wives and families."

"That is true. But things are different for a woman. God has called you to be a doctor, and you are a good one who will only get better. So whomever you marry has to deal with that. The real question is this: Is Mr. Jeffers that kind of man?"

"So what am I supposed to do? Ask him that right out front and make an absolute fool of myself?" Astrid threw a cucumber into the clean water with enough force to make it splash on both of them. "Sorry."

"Is he showing interest in you?"

"He asked Thorliff if I would mind if he wrote to me, and he did write."

"And did you mind?"

"Not at all. I enjoyed it. I had supper with him and his mother at the boardinghouse and he walked me home afterward. I really enjoy talking with him. He has a good mind and plenty of dreams. He loves it here in Blessing, and he is so very good to his mother."

"Is he a man of faith? That is supremely important."

"He attends church. He believes in God. He was raised like we were, only in town, in Iowa or Ohio, I forget which. His family cares about one another."

"Sounds to me like you've given this a lot of thought."

Astrid stared at her mother. "I guess I have, haven't I?"

The three women were just sitting down to supper when a voice came from some distance. "Grandma, I'm coming."

Astrid looked at her mother. "Did you just hear someone call your name?"

"I did." Ingeborg rose and hurried to the door. With a cry she pushed it open and flew down the stairs.

Astrid and Freda jumped up and followed her.

Emmy burst through the gate and threw herself into Ingeborg's waiting arms. "I came back, Grandma. Uncle said I could. See? He brought me."

Astrid looked up to see an Indian man, his graying hair pulled back in a club. The wrinkles on his face spoke of many years in the weather. "Will you join us for supper, sir?"

He nodded. Another Indian girl stood beside him. "This Two Shells."

"Can my cousin come too, Grandma?" asked Emmy. "She needs to go to school too."

Ingeborg stood and nodded to both the girl and the old man. "Thank you for bringing her back to me."

"It is good," he said.

"Would you like to spend the night?"

"Go back."

"But you will eat with us?"

He nodded.

"Come in, then. We were just sitting down to supper."

Emmy took Ingeborg's hand. "Uncle eats on the porch."

"I see." Ingeborg turned to the other girl. "Welcome to my home, to Emmy's other home, Two Shells. Come in, all of you."

Astrid fixed a plate and took it out to the uncle. "May I ask your name?"

He took the plate. "Wolf Runs. Uncle to Little Sky and Two Shells."

"Thank you for bringing her back. My mother loves her dearly."

"True." He sat down on the step and began to eat.

When Ingeborg came out a few minutes later, he was gone, the empty plate sitting on the porch railing. She shaded her eyes with her hand to peer out across the fields. He was heading north. "Go with God," she whispered. "And thank you."

Astrid stood at the door and watched her mother. When Far came home, her world would again be complete. Another reason to praise, which she sang on the way back to town. The buttered beets had indeed been delicious. Somehow, she also knew she had her mother's blessing, no matter what she decided.

30

Welcome, Dr. Bjorklund. I was afraid I'd have to send a scout out to find you." Sophie held the door wide and invited Astrid and Ingeborg to come in. "And you too, Tante Ingeborg. I'm glad you could come."

Astrid paused as she heard laughter from the parlor—male laughter. "Are we not the only ones here?"

"No, we are having a dinner party. I told you that."

"No, Sophie, you didn't." The laughter sounded a lot like Daniel Jeffers. She'd been set up. Did he know of the situation? Astrid glared at her cousin, who shrugged with a grin. "I told you not to meddle."

"I'm not. I just invited a few friends over for supper. I thought Mrs. Jeffers and Tante Ingeborg would enjoy each other's company, and Garth said he wanted to get to know Mr. Jeffers better. So I thought of you to fill out our party."

How Sophie could look so innocent and be such a conniver never ceased to amaze Astrid. At least she had dressed up a bit for the occasion. Sophie slipped her arms around her relatives and guided them into the parlor, where the others were sipping from chilled glasses and laughing at a funny story Mr. Wiste, Garth, was telling.

Sophie waited for the laughter to die down, then announced, "Now that we are all here, Anna has supper ready. Let's adjourn to the dining room."

Before Astrid could do more than smile and nod to Mr. Jeffers, she was herded to a place right next to him, which was not a surprise at all. He held her chair and whispered in her ear, "I did not know of this either."

Somehow that made her feel better. One of these days she would figure out a way to get even with Sophie. Mrs. Jeffers and Ingeborg were seated across the table from them and the Wistes at either end.

As soon as they were all seated, Sophie said sweetly, "Garth, would you please say the grace?" They all bowed their heads as Garth took in a deep breath and spoke softly.

"Heavenly Father, we thank you for our friends and families who make our lives so much richer. We thank you for the food prepared for our supper and for the time we can be together. Amen."

"Thank you, Garth, that was lovely," Ingeborg said. "Where have you sent all the children?"

"My sister Helga has them next door. It isn't often we do something like this, so we enjoy the special time too." He turned to Mrs. Jeffers. "I hear you are doing a marvelous job teaching English to the immigrant workers. Toby said he can now give simple instructions in English, and they understand."

"Thank you. I'm doing something different than I did in the past. This time I am teaching construction and building terms first.

They can learn daily life things like *fork* and *hot* and *no* and *thank you* later."

Astrid spoke up. "She has done the same thing with our Indian women in the nursing program. They are learning quickly, and then Deborah reinforces what they learned throughout the day."

Anna entered the room with a serving tray and began setting small plates of pickled beets and cheese and tiny cuts of bread at each place.

"Cousin Anna, you help out wherever, don't you?"

"Ja, Sophie is teaching me the proper way to serve." She glanced at Ingeborg and rolled her eyes, which made Astrid hide a grin.

"And Helga is teaching her some of the fancier cooking. We all know what a marvelous cook she is already."

Anna blushed and shook her head as she left the room.

As Astrid set aside her disgust with Sophie and joined in the conversation, she realized how delightful an elegant supper could be. She and Mr. Jeffers could talk as easily as they had that evening before with his mother, and tonight Ingeborg added comments and questions as if they had all been meeting like this for ages. Sophie and Garth teased each other and the guests, and when they moved back into the parlor, the conversations continued.

Mr. Jeffers had them laughing at his tales of growing up with a father who was an inventor. Many of his inventions didn't amount to anything, but others did, like the adaptation to seeders that he was selling now.

As the hour grew late, Garth took Ingeborg home in the buggy, and Mr. Jeffers walked Astrid and his mother home. They dropped Mrs. Jeffers off at the boardinghouse and continued walking toward the surgery. "I brought you something," he said, removing a paper from the pocket inside his suit jacket. He handed it to her with a shrug. "I don't know if you want this or not, but I kept a journal of this journey, and I thought you might like to read it."

"Why, thank you." Astrid fingered the envelope that must have held several sheets of paper, thick as it was.

"I can't always say what I am thinking. I do better on paper."

"I am the same way. Sometimes I keep a journal. I did when I was in Georgia, but lately I've let that slide. Which is a shame, because it helps sometimes to be able to go back and read about an earlier event in case you begin to forget it."

"I agree. My mother has always kept what she called her prayer book, writing down what she prays for and then going back and dating when and how God answered. I used to love to read that, I guess because so many of the prayers were for me."

"My mor has done the same. I haven't looked at it for a long while, mostly because I no longer live at home. But I know how faithful she is about it. That's something I want—to be faithful in prayer and Bible reading. I get busy and let it slide, and then I feel guilty. It's a vicious circle."

"Coming to Blessing and listening to Pastor Solberg has brought me back to thinking about God's things more. He is such a good teacher."

They'd reached the gate in the picket fence to the surgery when they heard a low chuckle. There sat Thorliff and Elizabeth on the porch swing, enjoying the evening breeze.

"Welcome home." Elizabeth covered her mouth in a yawn. "Pardon me. I hope you had a good time."

"We really did." Astrid looked to Mr. Jeffers, who nodded. "Even though I got tricked into going."

"No, Sophie wouldn't do such a thing." Elizabeth's laugh made Astrid smile.

"Welcome to the machinations of my cousin Sophie. We never knew what she would do next, and I guess that hasn't changed," Astrid added with a chuckle.

"You have to admit, she has a good heart," Thorliff reminded her.

"Here, Astrid, you sit on the swing, and Daniel and I can use the porch railing." The four of them talked about the news of Blessing, Teddy Roosevelt's running for president, and the outcome of Daniel's trip.

"I think my mother feels the greater sense of relief for finally knowing this much. I'll tell you, when that man made a remark about my father's body, I wanted to go through those bars and choke the life out of him. He cares for nothing but himself and acts as if everyone is out to get him."

"Mostly they are, because he infuriates people wherever he goes." Thorliff shook his head. "That last meeting Mr. Valders and I had with him . . . Huh. We should have let the townspeople tar and feather him as they threatened."

"You know the most interesting thing," Astrid said softly. "Rebecca and I talked about his attack on her, and she told me that she forgave him before he left. She is far more gracious than I."

"She is wise beyond her years." Thorliff swatted a mosquito. "The breeze is dying, so here come the bloodsuckers." He stood and reached for Elizabeth's hand. "We are saying good-night, but let's do this again sometime."

"I agree." Astrid stood as well. "Thank you, Mr. Jeffers, for walking me home again. I'll see you soon, I trust."

"Yes, you will." He turned to leave. "Good night, all." And, like before, he strolled whistling down the walk.

"That is one very nice gentleman," Elizabeth said.

"I agree." Astrid felt the crinkle of paper in her pocket. An interesting man too. *Thank you, Lord, for an exceptional evening.* As she climbed the stairs to her room, she reminded herself to write Sophie a thank-you note—with perhaps a hint of accusation in it. It was a shame she hadn't invited Grace and Jonathan.

The telephone rang in the middle of the night. Astrid thought she heard something, and when Thelma appeared at her door, she knew there was an emergency. She was out of bed before Thelma said, "Sophie is having her baby."

"Oh good. It's about time." Astrid threw on her clothes and then bundled her hair into a snood as she made her way down the stairs.

"I told Mr. Wiste what he needed to do, but he said they were all ready. They've done this enough to know."

Astrid tried to stifle a yawn but failed. "At least it won't be twins this time." She checked her bag and let herself out of the house. Stars patterned the indigo sky like holes letting the light of heaven shine through. *Lord, I thank you for a night such as this. I know any time is a good time for a baby to enter this world, but surely it is your spirit sending the breeze that will make Sophie more comfortable. Thank you for a healthy baby and for allowing me to help with the miracle of birth. Oh, Lord, I rejoice. And again I say rejoice.*

Garth met her at the door.

"We've been walking and walking."

"Good. How is she doing?"

"She says it is going to be soon."

"Some different than last time, eh?"

"Oh yes. We moved a bed into the parlor so we didn't have to contend with the stairs."

Just then an extended groan came from that direction.

Astrid stepped into the room and smiled at Sophie, who glared back at her.

"You almost missed this."

"I think not. How far apart are the contractions?"

"Two minutes or so?" Garth tucked his watch back into his vest pocket.

"Good. Let's have a look."

Garth sat beside Sophie so she could squeeze his hands.

Astrid checked the progress. "Well, what do we have here?" She smiled at Sophie over the tented raised knees. "We have a bit of head showing. I think you can push any time you feel like it."

"You think—" Sophie groaned again, the tone rising as she scrunched her face. When she relaxed, she was panting. "This is hard work, you know."

"I know, and you are doing wonderfully well. I'd say you were made for having babies."

"Aren't all women?" She let Garth wipe the perspiration from her face and neck. "Thank you."

"No. I'm sad to say that not all women are made to give birth." Astrid heaved a sigh, thinking of Mrs. Moore down on the Rosebud Reservation. Even if the woman returned to her mother's, she was going to have a hard time.

"Here . . ."

"Garth, get behind her so she can push against you."

He scrambled to do so while Sophie's groan turned to a wail.

"All right, cousin mine, let's get this over with. On this next contraction, give it all you've got. Right now, we have a dark-haired baby, more like his pa. Or *her* pa."

Sophie pushed so hard she nearly squished her husband against the headboard.

"We have a whole head now. Good work, Sophie. Easy . . . let me turn these shoulders. Okay now, push."

Sophie bit off the scream and collapsed back against Garth as the baby girl slid into Astrid's waiting hands.

"Oh, Sophie, she is beautiful." Astrid wiped the mucus from the baby's face and laid her on her mother's chest. Using the corner of her apron, Astrid wiped her eyes and sniffed again. "Thank you, heavenly Father, for this gift from heaven, for the easy birth and—"

The baby let out a yell that sounded more like an angry two-month old than a newborn.

The three of them burst into laughter. Then Astrid saw the

cord go slack and moved beside Sophie to begin kneading her lower abdomen.

"Ow! What are you doing?"

"Getting the uterus to contract and expel the afterbirth."

"I'm not bread dough, you know." She ran a finger over her daughter's head. "Aren't you lovely, little one? Ow!"

"That's it." Astrid folded the cloth over the afterbirth and, after tying off the cord, took the scissors from the disinfectant bath and cut the cord. "Here, let me have her for a few minutes."

Taking the baby, she cleaned her up, wound a bandage around her middle, diapered her, and wrapped her in a soft flannel baby blanket. Handing the baby to Garth, she smiled. "You get to know her while I get Sophie cleaned up. Then, if you'll make us some tea, I'll leave the three of you to get some rest."

A few minutes later with the bed changed, Sophie washed and in a clean nightdress, Astrid laid the baby against her mother's breast and watched as she began rooting around for the nipple.

"She's awfully strong, isn't she?"

"She didn't spend a whole lot of time being born—that's why. Good for baby and good for mother."

Garth entered the room with the tea tray. "Here you go." He set the tray down and packed some pillows behind his wife before handing her a cup of tea.

"Ow, you little piglet, you." Sophie grimaced as the baby sucked.

"What are you going to call her?"

"I think Marie, after Garth's favorite aunt. We're not sure of a middle name yet."

"That is a beautiful name. Marie Wiste." Astrid watched as the baby nursed. "You'd think she was much older."

"Well, she should have been born a week or two ago. Maybe that's the difference. The twins were born early and so much smaller." Sophie stroked her baby's cheek and forehead with feather love touches.

"Should I telephone your mother?" Garth asked.

"No. Let her sleep. We can do that in the morning." Sophie sipped from her tea. "I think I am ready to call it a night. With your approval, Dr. Bjorklund?"

"I'll leave all the linens bundled in the kitchen." Astrid stood and kissed the tops of both mother's and baby's head. "God bless. Now if you start really bleeding, you call me instantly."

"I will."

Garth walked her to the door. "You want me to walk you home?"

"No. You go be with them. See you in the morning. I feel like I could fly anyway." She swung her bag as she walked down the street. What a wonder-filled way to spend such a small part of the night.

She left a note for Thorliff and Elizabeth and made her way up the stairs. *Thank you, Lord,* sang in her heart as she washed up and slid a nightdress over her head. Morning would come mighty soon.

The entire town seemed to be celebrating the new life the next morning and throughout the day.

"Tante Sophie's baby is named Marie?" Inga asked, or stated, for the third or fourth time.

Astrid nodded. "And no, you cannot go see her today."

"Tomorrow?"

"Maybe."

———

"SO WHY THE LONG FACE?" Astrid asked Inga at the breakfast table a few mornings later.

"She thought school started today." Thorliff flipped his newspaper open.

"But it does."

"Not for kindergarten."

"Emmy and Two Shells went to school but not me." Inga crossed her arms over her chest and stuck out her lower lip.

"How long till she starts?"

"Two more days." He looked over the top of the paper. "If you're not careful, a bird might sit on your pouting lip."

"Birds don't come in the house."

"At least we hope not." Thelma set a bowl of oatmeal with raisins on it in front of Astrid. "Brown sugar is in the bowl."

"Thank you. This looks perfect." She tapped her brother's arm. "Where's Elizabeth?"

"I told her to sleep in. She had a bad night."

"Any particular reason?"

"Not sure. I keep telling her not to worry about the hospital. It will all work out."

Astrid winked at Inga, but the frown deepened. "Did you take Emmy her kitten?"

Inga nodded. "She named it Smokey 'cause it's so gray. Grandma said the big orange cat might not like the new one."

"She is kind of old. She might not be patient with a kitten around."

"Will she hurt it?"

"Probably not bad, but she might take a swat at it and hiss." Astrid sipped her coffee. "I have a couple of appointments this morning, but then I am going out to Mor's. May Inga go with me?"

Thorliff looked at his daughter. "Pouty girls don't get special treats."

Inga smiled sweetly. "I'm not pouting no more."

"*Any*more."

She took a spoonful of oatmeal. "Anymore what?"

Thorliff started to explain but instead shook his head. "I'm printing tonight, Thelma, so don't plan on me for supper."

"We'll bring you a plate."

Astrid hid her smile behind her coffee cup. They had the same conversation every print day. Was it a game, or did they not even realize they did it?

A knock at the door sounded and Thorliff called, "Come in."

Mr. Jeffers opened the door and stepped in. "Good morning."

Astrid caught a quick breath. She hadn't planned on seeing him today, but even this bit made her smile. She caught Thorliff's eye as he put the newspaper down, and his knowing look made the heat rise in her neck. Mr. Jeffers had a most pleasant voice.

"Joshua stopped me at breakfast and said he has some things to talk over this morning. I just saw him pass by on his way to the office and wondered how long until you'd be out there."

"Coming right now." Thorliff pushed back his chair. He leaned toward his daughter. "Yes, you may go with Tante Astrid, but you must wait patiently until she is ready. No questions, you understand?"

"Yes, Pa."

"Good morning, Dr. Bjorklund. Fine day."

"It is that. A tinge of fall, don't you think?"

"Do you want a cup of coffee, Mr. Jeffers?" Thelma asked.

"No, thanks. I need to get out there," he said, speaking to Thelma, but somehow his gaze caught Astrid's.

"Did he say what he wanted?" Thorliff asked, as he ushered the other man out the door first.

"No."

Astrid listened as their shoes clunked on the porch stairs. Seeing Mr. Jeffers was a surprise, a nice surprise. Good thing she'd fixed her hair and dressed for the day before coming downstairs. No more nightdress with a robe over it. Not that she did that very often, especially on days when she was the one in the office. She took in a deep breath and blew it out before realizing Inga was studying her. Astrid smiled, wondering what was going through the child's mind.

"Thank you for breakfast, Thelma. I heard the doorbell, so someone is waiting."

The next two hours passed swiftly as Astrid examined Dorothy again for her monthly prenatal checkup. "You are doing wonderfully well. Do you have any questions?"

"No. I guess I've been through this enough by now that I know the procedures. Hard to believe, but Sarah went off to school today. She was so excited. Swen went by and pulled Benny's wagon over to the school with him. Those two have become the best of friends."

"Cousins should be best friends. When I think of those years with Sophie and Grace and me—we had wonderful times together. You should have seen us when we were all learning to sign."

When Dorothy left, Mary Martha was waiting.

"What can I do for you today?"

Mary Martha shook her head. "This is so embarrassing."

"This is Astrid you are talking to. How many years have we known each other?"

"A lot. But how many times do you treat boils?"

"Not often, but it's easy. I lance it and dress it, and you apply this black ointment I'll give you to draw it out, and it goes away. Where is it?"

"On my lower back, my way lower back."

Astrid rolled her lips together. "Good thing you have a female doctor then, isn't it?"

"Since I have never been to a male doctor, I have been spared that embarrassment. So what do you want me to do?"

"You can remove your clothes, put on one of these gowns with the ties to the back, and lie down on your stomach on the table while I get things ready. If you want, I can leave the room."

"Just turn your back."

Astrid turned to the cabinet and removed a lancet from the jar of alcohol, some gauze pads, and the jar of ointment, and laid them all on a sterile tray. "My mother used to do all these things, but most people just soaked the boil until it erupted or lanced it with a hot needle. But in your case, it would be difficult for you to do. Although I'm sure Pastor Solberg would have helped you."

"Yes, but he would tease me too, and I'm not in the mood to be teased. This thing hurts."

"Are you ready?"

"Yes."

Astrid swabbed the area with alcohol and sliced into the raised and angry-looking boil. Mopping up the pus, she waited until it ran clean blood and then packed the gauze on it. When it stopped bleeding, she spread ointment on and bandaged it. "Do you have any more?"

"Not that I know of. What causes such a thing?"

"Could have been a pimple or an ingrown hair that got infected. Hot compresses will help, and use this ointment." She handed Mary Martha the little jar. "You can buy the whole thing or bring it back when you are done."

"I'll bring it back."

As Astrid cleaned up the supplies, Mary Martha dressed again. "You know, it feels better already."

"That ointment is very soothing. Works on things like sunburn and insect bites too. When we set up our pharmacopoeia at the hospital, we will carry things like this." She walked Mary Martha to the door to find a construction worker there, with Toby at his side. The worker was supporting his injured hand, wrapped in a handkerchief but still dripping blood, with the other.

"Come right this way." Astrid led the way to the other examining room and pointed to the chair. "Sit."

Toby followed them. "He cut himself pretty bad. Do you need me to help?"

"What language does he speak?"

"German. I could get Mr. Geddick off the seeder plant."

"We'll see." She laid a towel on the table by the chair and motioned the man to lay his hand down. Unwrapping the handkerchief, she nodded. "Wait here."

"I'll stay," Toby assured her.

She left the room and asked Thelma to heat up some water to scrub the wound. "Keep your finger on that artery," she said to Toby when she returned, pointing to the middle of the inner wrist. He pressed the spot, and in a few moments the bleeding slowed and then stopped. Thelma brought in a basin with steaming water and a pitcher with more.

"I'll need to stitch this." She smiled and spoke Norwegian slowly to the man. After cleansing the wound across the palm of his hand and scrubbing the hand too, she picked up the needle and quickly took four tight stitches in the hand. After coating the wound with more of the black salve, she bandaged it, tying the ends of the dressing on the back of his hand. "You have to keep this clean."

The man made a face indicating he wasn't sure what she meant.

She turned to Toby. "Make sure he wears gloves and comes here after work every day to have the dressing changed. I don't want this to get infected, and with all that debris it could."

"I will tell Mr. Geddick to make it clear. Thank you for seeing him so quickly."

"What else could I do? Have him bleed all over the porch?"

Toby shook his head. "Leave it to Astrid, er, Dr. Bjorklund. Send us the bill."

"I will." She indicated to the man that they could leave.

He nodded. "Danke. Danke."

"You are welcome."

After they left, Thelma entered the room and started cleaning. "How bad was it?"

"Four stitches. Could have been a lot worse. It didn't look terribly deep, but it sure bled."

"I can tell."

Astrid checked, and since there were no more patients, she went upstairs to see Elizabeth. Mother and daughter were sitting on the settee by the window, with Elizabeth reading and Inga leaning against her. "Now, this is a lovely picture."

"You going to Grandma's?" Inga asked.

"That I am." Hearing a steam whistle, Astrid went to the window. "The threshing crew is home."

"Grandpa?"

"Maybe we can ride out on one of the wagons. Come on."

"Have fun. I'll take care of the office this afternoon," Elizabeth assured her.

"All right." Astrid and Inga hustled down the stairs, grabbed their straw hats, and headed out the door. "We'll catch them at the corner."

Half of the town lined Main Street, waving and laughing, welcoming the entourage home. The steam engine snorted and hissed in the front of the parade, pulling the threshing machine. The cook shack followed, and the wagons and teams came behind.

Astrid waved to Gilbert. "Can we ride?"

He stopped and they hopped onto the back of the wagon, their feet over the tailgate.

As they passed the school, all the students came out to wave and shout too.

"The party will be Saturday night," Pastor Solberg called. "We'll celebrate!"

Haakan and Lars waved that they understood.

"I like parties," Inga shouted.

"Me too." *And this time I might have even more fun. I wonder if Daniel is a good dancer.*

31

"How does one get clues as to which girl made which box?" Daniel asked Thorliff late in the afternoon on Saturday. Daniel hoped that if he looked pathetic enough, his partner would give him some bit of information.

"Those are closely guarded secrets. I remember when I was young and single, the girl I loved would not give me even a hint."

"Not Dr. Bjorklund, I take it?"

"No, this was before I went to St. Olaf for college. I thought I had all the answers back then, and now I wonder sometimes if I even know the questions."

"So did you bid on the right box?"

"No. I thought hers was a different one. Everyone laughed at the joke, but I had supper with a little girl who still wore her hair in braids." He paused and a twinkle lit his eyes. "She grew up into a mighty pretty young lady."

Daniel heaved a sigh. "Hopefully the one I want will be one of the last to be bid upon, and that way I might get lucky."

"I take it you want my sister's box?"

"I do."

"If I get a hint, I'll pass it on. But I know she is out at the farm, and Mor will not be any help."

"What about Inga?"

"You might be able to bribe her. She loves peppermint sticks."

Daniel shook his head. "I can't remember when I last took part in something like this. My mother tried to tell me that since she is still in mourning she will stay home, but Mrs. Wiste came and asked her to help with something. I think that young woman knows more of what is going on around here than do all the others put together."

"Sophie has always loved to boss people around. Talk about head-strong. It would take hours to tell you all the escapades she's led, and she'd tar and feather me if I did. Life in Blessing has never been boring. That's for sure."

"We moved two times when I was in school, so I didn't have that close kind of relationship with anyone. I seldom saw my cousins, and distance makes friendships fade." Daniel studied the plans taped to his desk, then shook his head. "We have three applications now for machinists. Mr. Holt, the man I enticed away from John Deere, will be here in two to three weeks. And Mother says she knows of someone to work in the office. She is getting me an address to write to him. So the machine shop is pretty close to staffed."

"When are the drill presses due to arrive?"

"About the same time as Holt. He has a family of five children, only one too young for school. I told him we'd get him housing as soon as possible. I figured that the largest of the single houses could be his."

"Dr. Deming, the dentist, plans on being here before Christmas or as soon as we have his office finished, whichever comes first. He and his wife will live at the boardinghouse until their house is ready."

"We better put in another order."

"I know. And get the cellars dug now." Thorliff scratched his chin. "How do we manage to keep ahead of all this?"

"Not only with the business side but think about the party tonight. With all our single men in town, the women here better plan on dancing till their feet give out."

"Did you have Joshua and Toby tell them that there will be no liquor at the party?"

"Ja, after all, where would they get it?"

"Good question." Thorliff pushed back his chair. "We're done for the day. The bidding starts at the schoolhouse at six thirty, and knowing Pastor Solberg, it will start on time."

When Daniel and his mother arrived at the schoolhouse, boxes of all colors and shapes covered a table. The benches had been pushed back to line the walls, and people were milling around visiting and laughing. The construction crews waited around outside, as if unsure of their welcome. Ingeborg and Haakan together personally invited them in to join the festivities.

At six thirty Pastor Solberg held up the first box, one decorated with red-and-white-polka-dotted cloth. "How much am I bid for this sumptuous supper?"

One by one the boxes were bid on, and males and females met and found a place to sit. Four boxes remained. Joshua bid the highest on one, and with a grin as big as his face escorted Miss Christopherson to a bench. Three boxes left.

"Jonathan, aren't you going to bid?" Thorliff called.

"I have, but I get outbid every time."

Grace, Astrid, and Deborah still had no partners, and three boxes remained.

"Folks, I know you've been real generous tonight, but we have three boxes left and three lovely ladies to share the meal. What'll you give for this one?" Solberg held up a white box with a plaid bow.

Daniel bid a dollar. Jonathan bid a dollar and a quarter. Toby upped it another quarter. One of the immigrants yelled, "Two dollar."

The bid quickly went up to six dollars, and Jonathan managed to get it by bidding ten. It turned out to be Grace's box.

Toby grinned at Daniel and whispered, "If we don't get the one we want, we could switch after the bidding."

Daniel nodded. "But what about those other men?"

"Outbid them, like Jonathan did."

The bidding grew wild on the next box, one wrapped in green plaid fabric. Deborah and Astrid flinched at each of the increases in bidding. Past six, on to eight. Toby yelled "Twelve dollars," and the box and Deborah were his. He poked Daniel in the ribs. "You better make it good."

Daniel and four men were bidding on the final box. The bids came in quarters and fifty cents, but after eight dollars, Astrid leaned over to her mother. "They all know it is me. I feel like I'm on the auction block."

"It's all for the good of the school," Haakan said, joining their conversation.

"I know, but my word." The bidding reached thirteen dollars. "Those men can't afford this. Far, put a stop to it."

"Not me." He backed away.

"Fifteen dollars," Daniel Jeffers called.

"Going, going, gone!" Solberg slammed the gavel down. "Dr. Bjorklund, Mr. Jeffers, enjoy your supper, and thank you all for helping to provide new textbooks for this year. With so many new students, we will need them all."

Daniel picked up the box and came over to Astrid. "I was afraid I was going to go hungry tonight."

"There's plenty of food for those who didn't bid on boxes."

"But, you see, I wanted your box."

Astrid could feel the heat rising, and she knew it wasn't the school-room warmth that was causing it. The way he'd said *your box* made her swallow. "Thank you. Where would you like to eat?"

"How about outside, where it is cooler?"

"All right."

They found a bench and sat to eat the fried chicken, pickled green tomatoes, fresh rolls, and potato salad. Astrid poured glasses of rhubarb and strawberry shrub, and they finished off the chocolate cake last. Before they were done, the musicians had started tuning up by the piano that sat outside on a low deck to keep it out of the dirt. Besides Joshua and Johnny Solberg on the guitars, Joshua's brother on a banjo, and Lars with his fiddle, one of the construction work-ers brought out a mouth organ and another a banjo. Daniel knew Jonathan and Elizabeth would be trading off on the piano.

"We really have a big group tonight," Astrid said, wiping her fingers with a napkin.

"This will be fun."

As predicted, there were more men than women, and everyone wanted to dance. Mrs. Jeffers tried to demur, but her son waltzed her off, and from then on others cut in. Astrid was dancing with Thorliff when Daniel cut in.

"I can't seem to get a full dance with you."

"I know. This is the wildest dance we've ever had." She smiled up at him and caught her breath. The moonlight gilded his hair, and his smile melted right into her bones. She stumbled, but his firm hand at her waist steadied her. The smile he gave her made her heart flutter.

At the end of the dance she headed for the punch bowl. What had happened out there? She joined her mother and Mrs. Jeffers, who were dispensing the cold liquid.

"You look to be having a good time," Mrs. Jeffers said.

"I am." Astrid reached for the cup, but a male hand took it from his mother and handed it to her. Then waited for his own.

Daniel and Astrid stood watching the Texas Star square dance, with Mr. Valders calling.

The moon was so bright that the lanterns weren't even needed, and the fire was allowed to sink into coals.

When the musicians took a break, she watched Joshua as he took some punch over to Miss Christopherson. Astrid looked to see if her mother was noticing and received a nod in return. And there were Deborah and Toby, and if she wasn't mistaken, they were sharing a cup.

After the break she danced the polka with the man whose hand she had stitched, and he thanked her again.

When they called for the last dance of the evening, she found herself in Daniel's arms again, a slow waltz that made it easy for him to draw her closer. Romance under a harvest moon was the way she described it to Grace later.

Grace agreed. "Jonathan leaves tomorrow."

"I'm sorry."

"Me too, but this is our last year to wait. And I am home to stay."

Jonathan and Daniel came up at the same time.

"May I walk you home?" Daniel asked.

"If you'd like." Astrid turned to smile at him. There it was again. Surely it was the moonlight. "What about your mother?"

"Mrs. Wiste had a buggy brought out for those who wanted a ride back. I don't think my mother has ever had an evening like this."

"I hope she isn't too tired." As they walked along, his hand brushed hers, sending tingles clear up to her shoulder. What would it be like to hold hands with this man? Thorliff and Elizabeth had left a bit earlier to take Inga home, but they were sitting on the porch swing when Astrid and Daniel arrived.

"I'm too keyed up to go to bed yet," Elizabeth said with a chuckle.

"I had no idea you could play the piano like that." Daniel took his place on the railing and was joined by Thorliff.

"Elizabeth played for all our dances before Jonathan arrived. For dances and church and sing-a-longs. We've been so fortunate to have musicians. And after tonight we have even more." Astrid leaned against the swing back. "What fun that was."

"Did you see Mr. Landsverk and Maisie Christopherson? That just tickles me. She is such a lady."

"I know." Astrid nodded. "And if I'm not mistaken, Deborah might be getting her wish."

"What's that?" Thorliff asked.

"At the girl party, she finally admitted she's been wishing Toby would notice her, you know, as more than just a longtime friend."

"I think he got the idea." Thorliff shook his head. "The girl party?"

"Well, we all grew up together and—"

"I know, but you aren't exactly girls any longer."

"Ah, so you've noticed." His wife gave him a teasing look.

"You know what I mean."

"Come on, Thorliff, before you put your foot in your mouth and can't walk. Good night, you two." Elizabeth took her husband's hand and pulled him to his feet.

"'Night."

"May I walk you to church in the morning?"

"I . . . I guess."

"Good. Then I'll say good-night too." He touched her hand and bowed slightly before heading up the street, whistling as usual. This was getting to be a habit—a rather nice habit, she thought as she closed the door behind her.

———

CHURCH IN THE MORNING was bittersweet when Pastor Solberg thanked Jonathan for his musical contributions and asked that everyone would pray along with him for this young man to finish his schooling and return to become a permanent part of Blessing. There was more than one handkerchief touching eyes as the prayer time ended.

Astrid stood between Daniel Jeffers and her mother, with Daniel's mother on his other side and her father on her mother's other side with his hand on Emmy's shoulder. How could this feel like a family so easily?

When Daniel and his mother accepted Ingeborg's invitation to come for Sunday dinner, Astrid smiled up at him. "You don't know what you are in for."

"What do you mean?"

"Just wait and see. Oh, and I'm sure there will be a baseball game, so you might want to change clothes."

After dinner at the farm, Jonathan came downstairs with his suitcases packed, and after telling everyone good-bye, he and Grace took the buggy to the train station.

While Astrid helped clean up in the kitchen, Daniel asked if he could talk with Haakan.

"Of course. How about out on the front porch." Haakan led the way. "Now, what can I do for you?"

"I . . . I would like your permission to court your daughter."

"I see." Haakan puffed on his pipe, nodding. "I have a question for you."

"What is that?"

"My daughter is a doctor, first and foremost. The man she marries has to understand that. It is not easy. I can attest to that, since her mother was the only doctor in these parts for years. Babies and illness and accidents rarely happen during office hours. Can you live with that? Without her duties causing you or her hard feelings toward each other?"

Daniel nodded. "I've always known she is a doctor. That is a part of who she is. Like my mother is a teacher. I see that Thorliff and Dr. Bjorklund manage. It can be done if two people agree and are willing to work together."

"That is a very good answer. One more thing. This will take prayer, a lot of prayer for her health and her safety. I believe you are a man of God, and if this is God's plan for your lives, He will reveal it to you both."

"Yes, sir. And thank you." Daniel extended his hand to shake Haakan's. "I am honored that you give me this permission."

"Does Astrid know how you feel?"

"I've never mentioned anything, because I had to speak with you first."

"Then we will all pray for God's perfect will. Agreed?"

Daniel nodded. Now if only God and Astrid would agree.

32

O CTOBER 1 9 0 4

I can't believe it is really here." Astrid stood at the door to the operating room in the soon-to-be-dedicated Blessing Hospital.

"Me either." Elizabeth stood beside her.

"So, what do you think?" Thorliff asked them both.

"I am overwhelmed." Elizabeth leaned back against her husband's strong chest. "I believe you and your men are miracle workers to have managed to get this ready for the dedication."

"And on time," Astrid added.

"I was hoping for completion on a few more rooms, but that will come soon." Thorliff shook his head.

"All of our guests from Chicago will be here tomorrow." Astrid heaved a sigh. All this planning and working and reworking, but—

There could be no more *buts*. "You even got the construction mess all cleaned up."

"Thanks to Mrs. Sidorov and her sister. When we found that family, we found a treasure." Daniel joined them.

After Samuel had taken Boris Sidorov to Walhalla to find someone who spoke Russian, they gleaned enough information for the elder Mr. Gould to locate the missing family in New York. He put them on the train and by mid-September, the man was reunited with his wife, their two children, and his wife's sister. Mrs. Jeffers took on the new students, and they too were learning to speak English. One of Mr. Sidorov's sons was old enough for school, so he was learning English there too.

"There is nothing more to be done here, so let's go home. Thelma has supper waiting." Thorliff took his wife's arm.

Daniel smiled at Astrid. "Tomorrow will be a big day for the whole town."

"Not as big as the next." Astrid glanced down at the sheaf of papers in her hand. She'd been going over the schedule for the dedication to make sure everything would happen as planned. There would be speeches by Dr. Morganstein and Mrs. Josephson's nephew, Jason, on behalf of his deceased aunt, along with several local people. Then would come a thank-you speech from Thorliff and the blessing by Pastor Solberg. Then lastly, the ribbon would be cut and the hospital would be open for tours.

"Are you coming?" Daniel asked.

"Oh yes, of course." Astrid tried to smile, but all of a sudden she felt like a balloon with all her air escaping, zipping around and then going flat. "I think I am too tired to eat."

"We'll make sure this is short, then." He touched the middle of her back with a gentle hand, guiding her toward the door.

Why did she all of a sudden feel like weeping? She blinked and swallowed. This was silly. She should be dancing and whooping for joy, yet all she wanted to do was collapse in the corner and bawl. *I want my mother.* That thought caught her by surprise. Ingeborg would be at the station in the morning as part of the official greeters for the visitors. They had buggies to take them to the hospital to see it before heading to the boardinghouse, where they would all be staying.

The four walked back to the Bjorklund house, which would soon lose its designation as the surgery.

———

THE NEXT MORNING arrived almost before Astrid fell asleep, or at least it seemed that way. A rooster crowing woke her before the full light of day. She sat up and pushed the pillows behind her, taking a few minutes to stare out the window and focus on her heavenly Father.

"All this you have prepared and accomplished for these next days. The hospital could not be ready without your intervention and without your blessing. Thank you for guiding those working on it, both here and in Chicago. In places where there could have been dissension, you poured out peace. You prevented any major accidents and brought swift and clean healing to those injured. You kept me calm when I wanted to scream. Lord God, I praise your name, for this hospital is rising in your name and for the sake of your people." She blew out a breath of night and sucked in a deep breath of fresh morning. "And to think I even went to sleep right away and slept all through the night. Thank you. I hope Elizabeth did too. Amen, Lord God, amen."

Throwing back the sheet and blanket, she went behind her screen to wash and dress. The train would be in around eleven. With the cooling weather, she pulled on a navy serge skirt with a kick pleat in back for walking. She would add the jacket later. After buttoning the front of a new high-necked blouse with straight sleeves to fit under the jacket, she sat down at the dressing table and brushed out her night braid. Brushing her hair was always calming. She twisted the mass and formed a bun at the base of her skull so her new hat with a curved feather would sit properly on her head. On the way out the door, she snagged one of the coverall aprons that they wore when treating patients. It should keep her clothes clean until she needed to go to the station.

Downstairs, Thelma had the coffee started. "You're up early."

"I know. On one hand I think I have a million things to do, and on the other . . ." She shrugged and let her raised hands fall. "I think we got it all done. If that is really possible."

"I've checked all the lists, and I think we're done."

Astrid fetched a pitcher of milk from the icebox. "I think I'll just have bread and milk for breakfast."

"You want it toasted?"

"That would be good."

While the bread toasted over an open burner, she set the butter, jam, and sugar on the table. She could hear Thorliff tromping around upstairs, but he always came down before Elizabeth. Not a peep from Inga's room. As soon as she woke up, she would run across her room and into her mother's to say good morning, then run down the stairs and into the kitchen. She could make a whirlwind blush from ineptitude.

Astrid took her toasted bread and sat down to break it into pieces into her bowl. She poured in milk and sprinkled sugar, thinking what a good idea this was. After buttering and spreading jam on half a piece of toast, she dug in, enjoying the snap of the fire in the cookstove and the birds awakening outside. Many had already left for the south, but the chickadees would stay through the winter, along with the juncos.

Thorliff entered the room, settling his tie into his vest. "You were mighty quiet this morning."

Astrid nodded, having just taken a bite of milk and toast.

"Do you have anything to do besides nervous pacing until the train arrives?"

She shook her head. "Not unless a patient is desperate. I put up the *Emergencies Only* sign."

When they met the train, both Astrid and Elizabeth, along with the others, waited on the platform as the train screeched to a stop. When Mr. Josephson assisted Dr. Morganstein down, the two doctors Bjorklund exchanged looks of sadness before assuming their welcoming smiles. Dr. Morganstein had aged in the last year to the point of weakness.

Dear doctor Morganstein, are you ill, or what is happening that you are so weak? But she knew not to ask, at least not at this point. "Thank you for coming all this way."

"I wouldn't miss this for the world—our first distance hospital." Dr. Morganstein's smile had not lost its force but her voice quivered— just a bit, but noticeable to her two protégés. She took Astrid's arm and smiled her thanks when Elizabeth took her parasol and her other arm. "Now I am set. What an adventure this has been."

"If you stand right here at the edge of the platform," Astrid told her, "you can see the hospital. Not much but a slice."

They paused a moment while she took a look.

"We have the buggies here so that we can drive all of you by the hospital before taking you to the boardinghouse," Elizabeth said.

Dr. Morganstein turned to Mr. Josephson. "Where is Dr. Red Hawk?"

The younger man turned. "I thought he was right behind me."

Astrid knew instantly where he was. She scanned the crowd for her two nurses in training. Sure enough, there in the shade of the station, a dark-haired man in a gray suit stood talking with the two women. The look of awe on their faces was a sight to behold. "He'll be along in a minute. I'm sure our two Indian nurses are thrilled to hear their own tongue for a change."

Dr. Morganstein squeezed her protégés' arms. "You have gone beyond what I dreamed for here already. Are they ready to return to the reservation with him?"

"Not what I'd call ready, but they are a far distance from when they came here. They both learned quickly and seemed to enjoy their schooling. Learning to speak English was harder than learning nursing." Elizabeth motioned for the doctor to climb up in the buggy. Thorliff assisted her on one side and Astrid the other. Ingeborg waited in the buggy.

"Ah, Mrs. Bjorklund, what a delight to see you again." Dr. Morganstein took the arm Ingeborg offered to steady her and help her to sit.

"We are so glad to have you here in Blessing. I can't thank you enough for all that you have already done."

"And this is just the beginning." Dr. Morganstein leaned against the buggy seat. "My, I forget how wearing these trips can be. I was just so excited to come."

"The men are taking the luggage to the boardinghouse, so your things will be there waiting for you. We thought you might want to rest awhile before the meeting at four o'clock, followed by supper in the dining room."

"Do we have an itinerary?"

"Right here." Astrid handed her a copy. "I gave one to Mr. Josephson too, and there will be one for Dr. Red Hawk. How many people are there in your party?"

"Four. I brought one of the nurses along to assist me. These old joints have trouble sometimes with buttons and pins."

"Good. Are you still running the hospital?"

"Officially yes, but Mrs. Hancock oversees all the business matters, and Dr. Whitaker is in charge of all things medical. We have a new man in charge of the training programs. Dr. Hammond came to us from Johns Hopkins. He wanted to come along, but some people needed to stay in Chicago to keep things running. He is as excited about our distance facility as I am, or rather, as we all are."

Thorliff made sure Astrid and Elizabeth were settled in the rear-facing seat and clucked the team forward.

"What is that new building?" Dr. Morganstein asked.

"That is the factory building—just now ready to move the machinery in—in which a seeder adapter as well as a new seeder will be produced and sold to farmers."

"And all these new houses."

"People who come here to work need places to live." He turned the corner so she could see the hospital. "Most of the exterior is finished, but much of it is just the shell. We'll be working on it all winter, or at least much of it, most likely."

"Stop, please."

Thorliff did so and waited while the doctor stared across the empty block to see the entire building.

"As many times as I have studied the plans, seeing it for the first time like this takes my breath away," Dr. Morganstein said.

"We built it with the knowledge that we will add on later, which will probably be soon in actuality. So far, we will have six rooms with two beds each and two wards that will hold six to ten beds each. I think this will be sufficient for a few years." Astrid stopped. "Of course, you know all that from the plans."

"We get a bit more excited every time we come out here," Elizabeth said with a smile at Astrid. "This makes our present surgery seem antiquated."

"Antiquated or not, you have saved lives with what you have, and that is all that counts. I think I will wait to see the inside until tomorrow, if that is all right with you."

"Of course. Whatever you need, please tell us so we can provide it."

"Right now I need a washup and a rest. This body gets tired, and it tells me so in no uncertain terms. So irritating."

Ingeborg patted the doctor's arm. "I will bring you some tea, if you'd like. That is a bit of a restorative. I often drink it in the afternoon now."

Astrid stared at her mother. She did? And never mentioned it? *Hmm.* Maybe there was something there that needed looking into. Ingeborg caught her look and raised her eyebrows, not so easy to see behind the slip of veiling that brushed across her forehead. Back at the boardinghouse the women walked Dr. Morganstein to her room, where her middle-aged nurse was waiting. She greeted both of the younger doctors and smiled when introduced to Ingeborg.

"Thank you for your care and the view of the hospital. I'll see you at supper." Dr. Morganstein turned and slowly sat down in the chair by the window.

"Please let us know if there is anything else that we can provide," Elizabeth said.

"I will."

The three from Blessing left their guest and stepped into the parlor that was once a bedroom and selected one of the gathered chairs. Sophie had it all set up for the evening social, with chairs grouped around the room and a table for the coffee and tea service.

"Do you think she is all right?" Elizabeth asked.

"A bit of rest will do wonders, and when she wakes, the tea will be there for her. Riding the train like that is wearing to a younger person, let alone one who is aging." Ingeborg spoke with the authority of experience.

"I always felt like she would never get old," Astrid added. "When I was in Chicago, she could still stride those halls quickly. Keeping up with her was not easy. I think something has happened in these last months that she is not telling us."

"Do you know how old she is?" Ingeborg asked.

Both doctors shook their heads. "It's not polite to ask, you know."

———

THAT NIGHT AT THE SOCIAL after supper, Astrid made her way to Dr. Morganstein's side, where she sat in a wing chair. "Thank you for coming."

"I couldn't miss this part of the celebration. The people of this town have worked so hard, I wanted to be able to thank them." She turned to Astrid. "Now, who is that young man over there who never takes his eyes off you?"

Astrid looked in the direction indicated. "That's Daniel Jeffers. You met his mother at supper, the teacher of English." She could feel the heat climbing her throat. Surely he didn't watch her like that. "He is partners with my brother and has become a good friend."

"I should say so, and if one were to ask, I am sure he would like to be more than a friend."

"Dr. Morganstein!"

"Oh, don't be silly. He's a handsome young man, and you are a beautiful young woman. He is the mind behind the seeder company?"

"It was his father's dream. A long story there, but he and Thorliff run the construction company that is doing all the building around here. They have been stretched nearly to the breaking point."

"Well, you make sure to continue that friendship. I have a feeling . . ." She turned to greet Dr. Red Hawk. "So you have toured the hospital?"

"Inside and out. Knowing what I do about the plans and financing, I think they have done well." He looked to Astrid. "I see where you come from. No wonder you are who you are." He nodded. "This is all good. And my nurses speak highly of you and all the training they have received. Also, how they were received."

His look reminded her of some of their discussions while in Chicago. "You are ready now to return to Rosebud?"

"I am. And they with me."

"They can stay longer if you'd like."

"No. They are ready to go home. You have given them a good basis. I hope to send others here for training."

Dr. Morganstein smiled at Astrid. "This is just the beginning, you know."

"I know. And thanks to you and my mor, I know how to dream big too."

"You and Elizabeth are a good team. She is still recovering?"

"Yes." Astrid nodded to Miss Christopherson. "I need to see to something." She rose, and as she left, Dr. Red Hawk took her chair. Were they all protecting their protector?

———

IT LOOKED AS IF the entire town and half the surrounding countryside were gathered in front of the hospital, where a stand had been erected for the dignitaries so they could be seen and heard. By nine thirty the light frost had burned off, and the sun shone a benediction down on the crowd. Right at ten, the dignitaries filed onto the stage and sat in chairs on both sides of the lectern. Thorliff thanked the people for coming and motioned for Pastor Solberg to give the opening prayer.

When everyone joined in the amen, Thorliff motioned to his mother.

Ingeborg rose and stepped behind the lectern. "Today, God is answering prayers that started many years ago when we prayed for healing for the sick, health for mothers and babies, and for God to use

His powers of healing far beyond what we could assist Him with. He taught us all and helped us turn these prairies into the rich farmland we have today. We are indeed blessed, and as always, it is 'blessed to be a blessing.' " She smiled and sat down. The applause crescendoed and fell away as she nodded and smiled at all the people gathered.

From her seat by her mother, Astrid gazed over the crowd. She saw Joshua standing beside Maisie Christopherson. Closer than he needed to, and when Maisie turned to say something to him, she leaned even closer to him. It was all Astrid could do to keep from smiling. Those two would be perfect for each other. *Thank you, God, for working that out.*

Thorliff said a few words before introducing Elizabeth, who then stood and moved to the front. She looked across the crowd.

"I didn't start life in Blessing like some others, but once I married Thorliff and came here, Blessing became my home. I thank you for the privilege of becoming your physician. I know that a woman doctor was hard for some of you to accept, but I thank you for allowing me to be the doctor I dreamed of. And I, like Ingeborg, dreamed of more ways to provide medical services for all of you. When we built our home with the surgery as part of it, you came. When Astrid grew up wanting to know more about medical things, she continued this family tradition of caring for those around us. We dreamed of more. More rooms, more equipment, and more knowledge. Thank you for making those dreams possible."

Thorliff rose again as Elizabeth sat down, and then nodded to Astrid. "If it seems like I am introducing all my family, that's not quite true. My baby sister, Dr. Astrid Bjorklund."

Astrid strode to the podium, her heart threatening to leap out of her chest. Never had she spoken to so many people at once. She saw Red Hawk off to the side, his face sober, his eyes daring her. Daniel sat beside his mother, his smile and slight nod encouraging her.

"When we dreamed of a hospital for Blessing and distance clinics for outlying communities, we hoped it would happen in our lifetime. So I stand before you, young in years but older in medical knowledge. Knowledge that began when I trailed behind my mother as she roamed the prairies collecting her *simples*, as she called them, medicines that have benefited us all at various times. I trained with Dr. Bjorklund here and with Dr. Morganstein at her hospital in Chicago. We talked of a hospital, the need for one in this area, yet how expensive such a property would be. We talked here in Blessing, and some discussions got a bit heated, but God sent us other dreamers who wanted to invest in our small town in North Dakota. A small town with big dreams. A town that is growing for all of us."

When she sat down, Thorliff waited for the applause to fade off, and then he began. "It is my privilege to introduce the doctor who trained both of the Bjorklund doctors. Dr. Morganstein fulfilled her own dream of having a hospital for women and children in Chicago, the Alfred Morganstein Hospital for Women and Children. Today, I present Dr. Althea Morganstein." He stepped to the side and offered her his arm. She rose and stood behind the lectern, but he stayed with her, offering her support.

"I am here because of dreams. I cannot begin to tell you the thrill this is for me. I love my Chicago hospital, but there was nowhere else for it to grow, unless we moved it out of the center of Chicago, where it is most needed. So when I met the doctors Bjorklund and listened to their dreams, an idea hatched that could assist us all. I talked with the people on my board of directors, and one woman in particular, Mrs. Issy Josephson, got excited about the prospects. While she has gone on to her heavenly home, her nephew, Jason Josephson, is here in her stead, ready to administer the estate she bequeathed to our two hospitals. It is thanks to her that we had the finances to assist with constructing this hospital in Blessing, North Dakota. I thank you for your dreams, and I thank God for my friend for giving her wealth to bless us all." She clung to Thorliff's arm as he helped her sit back down.

"And now Mr. Josephson will say a few words."

Mr. Josephson stood before the crowd, every inch the wealthy businessman. "Thank you, people of Blessing, for being the kind of town that my aunt wanted to help. She saw your caring, your generosity, your faith, and your need. All the pieces of the puzzle came together here in Blessing, North Dakota. May this hospital always be known not only for its excellent medical care but also for the depth of caring given to those who need more than medical attention. Thank you for allowing us to be a part of your dream." He sat down to ongoing applause.

Astrid could not look at her mother, for she knew if she did, they would both be crying. When she glanced to the side, she saw Mrs. Jeffers nodding and smiling and beside her, Daniel, who caught her eye whenever she allowed her gaze to rove the gathering. Did he watch her all the time, as Dr. Morganstein said? The thought made her want to smile back. Maybe there was indeed something good happening between them. Was that possible? Did she dare look into her heart and see how she was feeling?

When the clapping stopped, Thorliff stood again. "Pastor Solberg, will you do the honor of blessing our hospital?"

John Solberg stood at the edge of the platform facing the audience. "Let us pray. Heavenly Father, you have given us great gifts all these years, blessings beyond what we deserve but always through your grace and mercy. Let this hospital be known for grace and mercy, for the love you have so poured out upon us. We will have a chapel for those in need to worship you, but more than that, we ask that you permeate this building with your presence, that all who enter here will feel your love, your mercy, your grace. Thank you for giving us big dreams so that we can work with you, but more so, watch you in action. Lord God, we praise your mighty name. Amen."

A mighty amen rolled back to him.

"And now we will cut the ribbon and declare the Blessing Hospital open for visitors." He turned and, along with Thorliff, helped Dr. Morganstein down the stairs and over to the entrance. The others followed and moved around the podium to stand behind them.

Dr. Morganstein took the scissors, large ones made by Mr. Sam for this very event, and, using a hand on each loop, cut the ribbon through on the first slice. A great cheer went up, and those closest to the front were not the only ones wiping their eyes.

Astrid realized Daniel was right beside her when he handed her his handkerchief. "Thank you."

"Congratulations, Dr. Bjorklund."

"Thank you for helping build this whole thing."

"Thorliff ran this one. I ran the seeder plant."

"Right." She knew it had all been a team effort. So many people were part of the team. The entire town had a part.

"Hey, My Doc. Dr. B."

Astrid turned to see Benny on his father's shoulders. "Hi there, Benny. Did we do all right?"

"You did real good." He leaned forward. "That old lady doctor. I remember her."

"Dr. Morganstein gave us permission for you to come here."

"I know. I liked her too. Tell her thank you for me."

"You tell her. She's right over here." Astrid turned and led the way to where Dr. Morganstein was sitting in a chair, shaking hands with people.

"Dr. Morganstein, do you remember Benny?"

"Of course I do. Oh my, you have grown so much. Look at you. I hear you are doing well in school too."

"I like school." Benny leaned forward, and Gerald bent down so his son could shake the doctor's hand. "Thank you."

"Thank you, Benny. I knew you would become a real man someday."

"Not yet."

"No, but here you have the chance to do that."

"I do. My pa and ma, they take good care of me. And My Doc."

Astrid had to swallow hard as she saw the sheen of tears in her mentor's eyes. This had indeed been an amazing day.

As the crowd shifted, Dr. Morganstein reached for Astrid's hand. "Do you have a moment?"

"Of course." Astrid glanced around for a chair, and as soon as he realized what she wanted, Daniel brought one over for her.

"Thank you. Are you a mind reader?"

"Not that I know of. Can I get you anything else?"

"Not that I know of." Her smile brought one in return. He leaned forward. "Perhaps we can talk later?"

"Of course." Astrid sat in the chair and leaned closer to Dr. Morganstein. "I cannot thank you enough for all you have done here."

"It is I who am thankful. Isn't it wonderful what all has been accomplished? All the work you are doing here has made this old woman delighted beyond measure. I know my husband is dancing on clouds up there to see us all together, building another hospital to add to the one he started to make my dreams come true." She laid her gloved hand over Astrid's on the arm of the chair. "The two Bjorklund doctors will accomplish much."

"Along with all the others who come here for treatment or for training. I have a feeling we are just seeing the beginning."

"I have a confession to make."

"Really?"

"I am so glad and grateful you didn't go to Africa. I just didn't feel that was where you were to go, but I knew you had to find your calling."

"Red Hawk said to me one day, 'What if helping my people is your Africa?' "

"Very wise. I know it was hard for you, but I'm glad you have learned to listen well."

"I don't know about well, but I am trying to listen."

"Listening is something doctors must learn to do. Listening to patients, listening to their bodies, to their families, to doctors wiser, and to new ideas that come."

"My mor said that God gave us two ears and only one mouth for a reason."

"Leave it to your mother. I know how glad she is to have you home in Blessing."

Home in Blessing. The words stayed with her. She knew she'd always had a heart for her home, this town of Blessing. Feeling someone's eyes on her, she glanced up to see Daniel Jeffers smiling at her. That same little quiver started in her middle, swooped around her heart, and flew out to the tips of her fingers. He was indeed a gentle man and a real gentleman. Her far had told her that Daniel asked if he could court her. She would not say no, for every time they were together, she realized even more what a special man he was. A solid man like her far, a businessman like Thorliff, a dreamer like his father, and a son to make his mother proud. While he'd not yet captured her heart completely, she was willing to follow along to see if this was indeed the next step where God was leading her. Like Dr. Morganstein said, listening was definitely in order.

EPILOGUE

....

MAY 1905

No, you can't see her today. You know what they say, 'It is bad luck to see your bride before the wedding.' " Sophie barred the door of the meeting room at the boardinghouse.

Daniel Jeffers heaved a sigh. "Then will you give her this? It is from my mother for her 'something blue.' " He handed her a wide satin ribbon with a verse embroidered on it. "Mother had this in her Bible on her wedding day."

"All right. That I can do." Sophie waited for him to walk away, then eased herself back into the room where the daughters of Blessing were gathered around Astrid, helping her dress.

"Here, this is from Mrs. Jeffers to put in your Bible. The 'something blue.' "

Astrid smiled at her cousin, then read the verse. " 'And they shall be one flesh.' " She read it again and blinked quickly a couple of times. Why were the tears so close to the surface today? She wasn't sad. Excited, joyful, a bit of trepidation, and peaceful too. This was so right, and the last months had proven that over and over again. There was no doubt in her mind that Daniel Jeffers understood her commitment to being a doctor and was proud of her accomplishments. Which made it so easy to trust him. *And they shall be one flesh.*

Sophie snapped her fingers. "Astrid Bjorklund, come back. Hello . . . You need to put your dress on."

Astrid came back to the present and tucked the blue ribbon into her Bible. She raised her arms for her friends to ease her dress over her arms and down to swirl around her. It was made of ice-blue washed silk, with a heart-shaped neckline and a fitted waist that flowed into a skirt and fell straight down to the tops of her toes. A two-layered pleat in the back would make walking easier. Not a train but a hint of one.

"You look positively regal," Grace said, her eyes shining.

"Just think, two more weeks and you will be the one getting dressed in this room."

Sophie settled an ice-blue hat with a half veil onto Astrid's head, securing it with a hatpin into the figure eight of golden hair. Wisps of hair framed Astrid's face, the blue of the dress making her eyes look even more like bits of a North Dakota summer sky.

Haakan tapped on the door and then opened it a crack. "The buggy is here."

Astrid looked once more in the full-length mirror. The white leather Bible now held a blue ribbon marker; the golden daffodils lay like a sheaf on the cover.

"Are we all ready?"

Ingeborg kissed her cheek. "You are so beautiful, both inside and out."

Astrid blinked again. "I love you, Mor."

Sophie and Grace wore matching yellow dresses and carried three golden trumpet daffodils each.

Haakan crossed the room and held out his arm to his daughter, his eyes glistening with unshed tears. "Are you ready?"

"I am."

He helped her into the buggy, and then the two cousins, Ingeborg, and himself. The drive to the church took only minutes. They could hear the organ from the hitching rail. He helped each one down, and they lifted their skirts to keep them out of the dust, then mounted the stairs and stepped into the vestibule.

Elizabeth had been practicing ever since the organ was installed a month earlier, so the music surrounded them, rich and glorious.

"They are ready." Lars smiled at Astrid, and she nodded. He opened the door and Sophie stepped in the doorway. The music swelled and first Sophie, then Grace walked down the aisle to the front, where Pastor Solberg waited with Daniel, Thorliff, and Trygve.

Astrid and Haakan paused in the doorway. The church was full with extra chairs set up in the back and along the sides. The music changed again, and they began the walk. Astrid kept her gaze on the man waiting for her. *If you cry, I will cry, so please . . .* His smile bore his love toward her like the fragrance of roses on a summer breeze. It wrapped around her and made her quivering lips settle into a smile that never dimmed throughout the ceremony.

They spoke their vows without hesitation, their eyes looking deep into each other's, pledging more than words could utter. Then Pastor Solberg said, "I now pronounce you man and wife. What God hath joined together, let not man put asunder." He raised his hands and spoke the benediction as though it had been written just for them. "The Lord bless thee and keep thee. . . ."

Thank you, Lord. She missed a few words, caught in her own thoughts and the look in Daniel's eyes. "And give thee His peace. Amen. You may kiss your bride."

When his lips claimed hers, Astrid lost herself in pure sensation. His smile at the end promised a lifetime.

They walked down the aisle, arm in arm, greeting friends and family.

"Hey, My Doc." Benny reached for her from his father's arms. He held her hand to his cheek and stared right at Daniel. "You take good care of My Doc."

"Oh, Benny, you needn't worry. I will."

The organ burst into music that followed them out the door and into the welcome arms of a May day of golden sun and greening fields, all promises of life renewing and rejoicing in the growing town of Blessing, North Dakota.

Valley *of* Dreams

WILD WEST WIND #1

....

AVAILABLE NOVEMBER 2011

1

FALL 1906
DICKINSON, NORTH DAKOTA

Something was wrong—but what?

Sensing something ominous in the wind, Cassie Lockwood studied the performers of the Lockwood and Talbot Wild West Show as they lined up for the opening parade around the arena. The United States flag snapped in the breeze above the uniformed riders waiting for the big wooden gates to be swung open. The snorts of horses, the jingle of harnesses, the laughter from another performer, and the musicians tuning their instruments were all normal sounds. She glanced down at the scruffy dog sitting placidly by her pinto, Wind Dancer. If Othello wasn't picking up on it, then surely the feeling was only in her head.

Ignore it, her mind commanded. *Concentrate on the parade and getting through this performance.*

The drums crashed, the trumpets blared, the gates swung open, and the Saturday afternoon performers of the internationally known company burst into the arena, led by horse-mounted flag bearers. Jason Talbot, owner of the traveling show, decked out in cutaway frock coat and wide-brimmed hat, enthusiastically welcomed the crowd that filled not only the wooden bleachers but overflowed to line the far fences. This final performance in Dickinson, North Dakota, was off to a sparkling start, the crisp fall breeze finally breaking the heat spell that had locked the area in cloying humidity.

As the mounted Indians nudged their horses into a gallop, Wind Dancer waited for Cassie's signal to join the parade. Behind them were the chuck wagons, the horses tugging at their bits, the excitement as contagious to the animals as to the human performers.

The applause swelled when Cassie passed through the gates. She was called the Shooting Princess and the greatest sharpshooter since Annie Oakley, and people flocked to watch her perform. Between trick riding and sharpshooting, she always managed to fulfill their high expectations. She circled the arena now, waved to the crowds, and then exited the arena behind the Indians. It wasn't her time to perform. The western scenes of Indians, marching soldiers, and pioneers were on first.

Knowing it would be about an hour before her turn in the ring, Cassie dismounted in front of her tent and tied her horse to the hitching post. A good brushing would soothe both of them, so she pulled off Wind Dancer's saddle and chest collar, setting them on the other end of the rail, and went for a brush and currycomb. Othello flopped down in the shade of the tent after scratching one ear with a long hind leg. He was not the most handsome dog around, but he more than made up for his looks in the brain department. He often knew what Cassie was going to do before she did. Between Wind Dancer and Othello, she knew she had the most stalwart and faithful friends anyone could ask for.

After the brushing and a wipe-down with a cloth, she checked her guns and ammunition. When she heard the applause after the attack on the settlers' cabin, she replaced her tack and mounted to head back to the arena.

"You have everything?" Micah, who'd never given his last name, asked as he picked up the leather satchels that contained her guns. Micah spent most of his time caring for the animals, but he made it a point to check Cassie's gear and make sure it was where it was supposed to be at showtime.

"Thanks, Micah. I don't know what I'd do without you."

He nodded, never one to waste words. He'd come to the Wild West Show as a gangling moon-faced young man with the thick-tongued speech and less-than-normal coordination of one born with Mongolism. Cassie saw behind these differences, taking on anyone she caught making fun of him, even threatening to maim a pair of now former members of the troupe when they had teased him and called him Cassie's trained pet. Word got around after that, and no one had harassed him for a long time.

As a matter of habit, she let her gaze rove over the performers and backstage hands as they went about their assigned duties. Everything seemed perfectly normal, but something didn't feel right. If only her father were there to talk this over with, but he had died five years earlier after an attack of pneumonia in England, almost to the day her mother had died four years earlier. He'd often said he didn't see how he could live without the woman who made his life complete, so his passing hadn't really been a surprise after he took sick. Cassie had stayed with the Lockwood and Talbot Show because she knew no other life, and "Uncle" Jason had pleaded with her to continue and promised he would always watch out for her, just as he'd promised her father.

The exit gate swung open, and the performers poured out.

"Easy, boy." Cassie tightened the reins as she and Wind Dancer waited for their signal. Never sure who was more impatient, she or her mount, she swallowed again, counting the beats of the fife and drum so they would enter at exactly the right moment. "Six, five, four, three, two, one. Go!"

Wind Dancer leaped forward and hit his stride as they breezed through their mounted shooting act. She drew her revolvers and nailed the targets as they galloped by. Coming around the far side of the arena, she swung down to the side and shot from under the pinto's neck to set a line of bells ringing. They slid to a stop in the center of the ring and, sliding her pistols back into the holsters, she waved to the crowd, turned, and did the same again. As the horse kept his hindquarters in one spot and spun around with his front legs, she pulled the shotgun from the scabbard at her left knee and downed each of the clay pigeons shot into the air, nudged Wind Dancer into a lope, and blew the heads off three puppets as they popped up from behind a wooden wall. Had her hidden assistant been off even a whisker, she'd have failed. Cassie hated failure worse than anything, and would've been fighting anger if she'd missed a shot.

Known officially as the Shooting Princess—her mother had been a member of the Norwegian royal family, thus the *princess* tag—Cassie absolutely forbade any trickery in her act. There was no one ringing the bells if she missed or breaking the glass balls if her shots were off. She had a reputation to uphold, much like her hero, Annie Oakley.

Cassie had started trick riding at age six on the back of her pony, with her trick-riding father and mother as her coaches. The three of them had been billed as the Fancy Riding Lockwoods since they introduced her into their act when she was seven. By then she'd been riding for four years. Growing up in the world-renowned Wild West Show gave Cassie a different kind of education from most young people.

Wind Dancer again slid to a stop in the center of the arena, both of them bowing after she dismounted. She gave him a pat on the shoulder and waved him toward the exit, through which he galloped with applause following. Cassie continued her act by using her rifle to shoot an apple off her dog's head—an act used often by Annie Oakley—wowing the crowds. Othello had learned to sit perfectly still as her shot split the apple. The audience always laughed when he ate half and brought the other half to her.

She then shot the ashes off a cigarette smoked by her current assistant, Joe Bingham. After reloading her six-shooters, she split plates and performed a variety of other shooting stunts before her black-and-white pinto tore back into the arena. Catching the saddle horn and swinging aboard, she executed several more riding tricks while galloping around the arena and waving her hat. Then she stopped in the center, bowed from her horse, and rode out to thunderous applause.

"And that, ladies and gentlemen, is our final act for today."

Three chuck wagons burst into the arena.

"Pardon me. Those cowboys insist on a chuck-wagon race, so hang on to your hats, folks."

Cassie barely heard the announcer's voice, but she well knew what he was saying. She dismounted by her tent and let Wind Dancer rub his forehead against her shoulder, all the while telling him what a good horse he was.

"Wonderful, as always." Joe slapped his hat against his thigh. "Working with you has made me a real believer in not smoking."

"I saw you flinch—not much but enough to see."

"Just can't get used to a bullet flying by that close to my nose. The urge to duck and run . . . it's all I can do to stand there."

"No one else would know that." After unbuckling the chest collar, she uncinched her saddle and pulled it from the horse's back. Joe took it and carried it into her tent to set it on the stand built for it. Cassie removed the silver-studded bridle and buckled a halter in place instead. Brushing Wind Dancer helped her relax after the high tension of her act. Her father had always told her to take care of her own horse and equipment, not to give the job to someone whose life did not depend on top performance of everything associated with her act.

She'd never gone a day without thinking about him, now more than most other times, as she replayed her act in her mind to see if there was anything that needed tightening or if there was something new she could add. While she enjoyed the competition of shooting matches in the States and in Europe, the show took another kind of preparation and practice. When she was shooting in a match, it was just her and her guns. And her competitor, of course. But a successful show took into consideration everything and everyone around her.

Father, if you could give me an inkling of what I'm sensing, I'd sure appreciate it. Moments like this she wasn't sure if she was speaking to her dead pa or to her living heavenly Father, whom she'd met early on at her mother's knee.

"You going to the meeting?" Joe asked.

"What meeting?"

"In the food tent. A sign was posted at breakfast."

"What's the meeting for?"

"I have no idea. Didn't you read the sign?"

"Didn't go to breakfast. Who called the meeting?"

"Jason, I'm sure. Who else?"

The little worm of concern popped its head up again. "Receipts were good, weren't they?"

"A crowd like we had should help make up for the last couple of shows." People hadn't come out as much in the rain like they had in Bismarck the week before.

Why did the idea of a called meeting bother her? Perhaps because so often Uncle Jason used a meeting as a place to announce bad news. Jason Talbot wasn't really her uncle, but since he and her parents had been good friends, as well as business partners, she'd always called him that. Besides, he was the one who promised to see to her welfare after her father passed on.

Prescient, her mother had often called her. Days like today pre-science was not a comfortable trait to have.

"You need some help, or should I go check on the others?"

She knew Joe had a sweet spot for April, one of the women who played in several of the western scenes. Joe played the part of the wagon master on the trail and was a soldier in another scene. Most of the actors played various parts. The more parts they played, the better their chances of staying on with the show for more than one season.

"You go on. I'm going to clean my guns before supper."

"Okay."

She watched him walk away, the slight limp he'd earned from being stomped by a bucking bronco more obvious when he was tired or upset. As they'd added more rodeo-type events to the program, several of the men bore the scars of a flying fall. Calf roping and steer dogging weren't quite as dangerous.

After Micah had taken Wind Dancer back to the rope strung between several trees where the horses were tied and fed, she brought out her cleaning supplies and, using the top of her trunk for a table, set to cleaning her guns, starting with the pistols and finishing with the twenty-gauge shotgun. Her favorite was her Marlin lever-action rifle, with the etching of a valley on the brass plate on the stock. Her father's valley of dreams had become her own. Someday she would find that valley and make his dreams of breeding horses, particularly the Indian Appaloosas, and raising cattle come true.

When the gunpowder and lead residue were cleaned out and her guns lubricated, she wrapped them in soft cotton and laid them in the leather satchels, ready for the next performance. The ringing of the supper bell brought Othello to his feet. He stretched and glanced over his shoulder to make sure she got the point.

"I'm coming." She set the satchels inside the tent and, making sure nothing was out of place, set off for the dull gray tent that had once been white. As she walked to the meal tent, she glanced at the painted wagon her father and mother used to live in. Uncle Jason had appropriated it after the funeral, sending Cassie to live with an aging pair of performers who had since left the show. The gilt was in need of polishing, and some of the paint could use freshening up too, but everyone still referred to it as the Gypsy Wagon, the name her father had christened it many years ago. The words that arched over a charging buffalo, *Lockwood and Talbot Wild West Show*, still stood for quality and fair treatment for all the members of the troupe.

Lately, however, she'd heard some grumbling, especially from the show Indians who were hired on a seasonal basis. The exceptions were those who had become permanent members, like Chief, who drove the boss's wagon in the opening parade.

Why did these thoughts keep plaguing her? "Come on, Othello. Let's get our food and go eat." She broke into a dogtrot and laughed when he gamboled beside her. "We need to go hunting one of these days. You think Micah would like to go along?"

"Go along where?" Joe fell into step beside her.

"Hunting. Othello said he wants to go hunting. For birds, most likely."

Joe rolled his eyes and shook his head. "How come no one understands that dog but you?"

"Friends are like that. He doesn't flinch when I shoot the apple off his head."

"I told you—"

She raised a hand to stop him. "I was just teasing."

"Oh." Joe glanced down to see Othello staring up at him. "I didn't yell at her, so don't go glaring at me." He muttered more under his breath but stopped when Othello bumped his leg with a sturdy nose.

"You know his hearing is far stronger than ours."

"And his nose and—"

"What set you off?" A grin broke across her face. "April didn't want any help—is that it?"

He stepped back and motioned for her to enter the tent before him.

She tossed a grin over her shoulder. "Sorry."

"You are not." He stepped back when Othello paused and his tail stopped wagging. "All right."

After the last person was served and before the early diners got up to leave, Jason Talbot stood up from the table off to the north corner that had become his. "Folks," he called. When the din continued, he raised his voice and clapped his hands. "I have an announcement to make." He paused and waited. Slowly the people quieted and focused on him, waiting.

"Much to my sorrow, I have to tell you that this has been the final performance of the Lockwood and Talbot Wild West Show. Pick up your pay envelopes. We are just not making enough money to cover expenses, and there is nothing else I can do but close it down."

Cassie stared at him, her stomach in a knot. Surely he couldn't be serious.